HELLO, SUMMER

HELLO, SUMMER

Mary Kay Andrews

St. Martin's Press
New York

First published in the United States by St. Martin's Press,
an imprint of St. Martin's Publishing Group

HELLO, SUMMER. Copyright © 2020 by Whodunnit, Inc. All rights reserved.
Printed in the United States of America. For information, address
St. Martin's Publishing Group, 120 Broadway, New York, NY 10271.

www.stmartins.com

Library of Congress Cataloging-in-Publication Data

Names: Andrews, Mary Kay, 1954– author.
Title: Hello, summer / Mary Kay Andrews.
Description: First U.S. edition. | New York : St. Martin's Press, 2020. |
Identifiers: LCCN 2020006746 | ISBN 9781250256928 (hardcover) |
    ISBN 9781250272195 (international, sold outside the U.S., subject to rights
    availability) | ISBN 9781250273642 (signed) | ISBN 9781250256898 (ebook)
Classification: LCC PS3570.R587 H45 2020 | DDC 813/.54—dc23
LC record available at https://lccn.loc.gov/2020006746

Our books may be purchased in bulk for promotional, educational, or business use.
Please contact your local bookseller or the Macmillan Corporate and
Premium Sales Department at 1-800-221-7945, extension 5442, or by email
at MacmillanSpecialMarkets@macmillan.com.

First U.S. Edition: May 2020
First International Edition: May 2020

10 9 8 7 6 5 4 3 2 1

Dedicated with sincere admiration and deep gratitude to all the journalists—especially print journalists—past and present. Keep asking the difficult questions. May you persist, nevertheless.

HELLO, SUMMER

1

"I hate these things," Conley Hawkins said, gazing toward the newsroom's glass-encased conference room, where the rest of the staff was gathering. "Stale sheet cake, lukewarm champagne, and tepid farewells. It's such a farce. At least a third of the people in that room don't even like me. I've said goodbye to the people I care about. Can't we just leave it at that?"

She'd almost succeeded in making a clean break, only feet away from the elevator, when Butch caught her trying to sneak out. "You can't skip your own going-away party," he'd said. "Everybody's waiting. You'll look like an ingrate if you try to duck out."

Before she could argue, he'd deftly taken the cardboard box she'd just finished packing and placed it on her desktop.

Her *former* desk in the fourth-floor newsroom at *The Atlanta Journal-Constitution,* her home away from home for the past four years.

"It's actually more like two-thirds of the people in the room who detest you," Butch pointed out, steering her toward the conference room. "Nothing personal. Call it professional jealousy. Well, except for Rattigan. Nothing professional about his feelings, right?"

Butch Culpepper wasn't just some dude who'd sat at the desk right next to hers for the past three years. He was her social conscience and self-appointed office husband and, therefore, privy to most of her secrets.

She winced at the mention of Kevin Rattigan. "Don't."

He raised an eyebrow. "Too soon?"

"I really didn't think he'd take it so personally," she protested. "We weren't even all that serious."

"You were living together," Butch pointed out. "Most women I know would call that serious."

"It was only for six weeks, and I only let him move in because he couldn't afford a two-bedroom after his roommate got transferred to Miami."

By now, they were standing right outside the open doorway of the conference room, and Roger Sistrunk, her assignment editor, was waving her inside.

"Hawkins! Get your ass in here! You might not have anything better to do, but some of us still have a paper to get out today."

"Oh God," she mumbled.

And then the champagne corks were popping, and she was being presented with the signed caricature from the paper's political cartoonist, and Roger was making a well-meaning speech about how much she'd be missed, using a rolled-up copy of the Metro section as a makeshift megaphone.

"Attention! Attention, please," he called. "Okay, well, somehow, our esteemed colleague Conley Hawkins managed to scam these pinheads in D.C. into offering her a job making twice as much money for half as much work," Sistrunk began. His bald head gleamed under the fluorescent lights.

Light laughter and a few catcalls. She smiled weakly, and despite herself, her eyes sought out Kevin, who was standing, stony-faced, in a far corner of the room. His wheat-colored bangs flopped over his glasses, and her fingers itched to push the hair back, clean the smudges from the glasses, and whisper a smutty joke in his ear, just to watch the bright pink flush spread over his pale freckled face. He caught her staring and quickly looked away.

Butch pressed a paper cup into her hand, and she drained the champagne in two gulps.

She didn't catch the rest of what Roger was saying. Tiana Baggett approached and flung an arm over her shoulder and leaned her head against Conley's. "Gonna miss you, girlfriend," she said, sniffling loudly. "I can't believe you're really gonna go and leave me behind. Who's gonna watch scary slasher movies with me now? Who's gonna rewrite my ledes?"

Aside from Butch, Tiana, the Metro section's police beat reporter, was her best friend on staff.

"Come on, Tia. Don't do this to me," Conley begged. "Look, you know as soon as I hear about an opening up there, I'll put your name in the hat."

Tiana sniffed again, extended her arm, and attempted to take a selfie with her smartphone. "Aw, damn," she said, shaking it. "I've got no juice. Gimme your phone."

Conley pulled her phone from her pocket, extended her arm, and clicked off three quick frames. As she was shoving it back in the pocket of her jeans, she heard the distinctive bicycle bell ringtone alerting her to an incoming text message.

Tiana looked down. "Who's the text from? Kevin?" She looked hopefully across the room. She was the one who'd set them up and who'd accused Conley, more than once, of being heartless since the breakup.

"No." Conley shook her head. "He won't even look me in the eye. It's actually from my sister."

"Grayson? The one you think can't stand you?"

"I don't think it, I know it. Wonder where she got my phone number?" The text had a link to a Bloomberg wire story. She tapped the link and read the first paragraph.

Intelligentsia, *the trailblazing digital investigative news service, announced today that it will suspend publication immediately, citing the failure of a recent round of venture capital financing.*

Conley stared down at the sentence, her brain and tongue temporarily frozen. Beads of sweat popped out on her forehead.

"What's wrong? Did somebody die?"

Conley handed her the phone.

"Jesus Hopscotching Christ," Tiana muttered. "Is this your sister's idea of a joke?"

"Grayson is incapable of joking," Conley said. "She lacks a humor chromosome."

"You think it's true?" Tiana asked. "About *Intelligentsia*? I mean, if it were true, you would have heard something, right? Maybe it's just a rumor."

"Maybe."

"You should call that guy, the editor, what's his name?"

"Fred Ward." She pulled up the list of recent callers, but there was nothing from Fred Ward, nor were there any calls with a D.C. prefix.

"Conley! You need to cut the damn cake!" called one of the sports-writers.

"Yeah," another voice chimed in. "Let's get this party started. I got a story to file."

She looked up. So many faces watching hers. She swallowed hard, fighting back against a wave of nausea swelling up from her gut, the champagne sour in her mouth.

"Just do it," Tia whispered.

Roger was holding out the pica pole, which was tied with a faded red ribbon. The pica pole was a quaint relic from another era, from the Marietta Street days, back when newspapers were physically laid out on drafting tables in the downtown composing room, instead of digitally designed in this gleaming smoked-glass box in a suburban office park.

Conley took the stiff aluminum ruler and made a horizontal slash through the gooey white frosting, then another vertical slash, dividing the cake into quadrants. She handed the pole back to her editor. "You do the rest," she said, forcing a smile. "I can't eat cake. I'm gluten-free."

His dark eyes studied her. "Since when?"

"Give me a break," she said quietly. "Something's come up. Please?"

"Okay, but see me before you take off. And I mean it."

While the staff clustered around the table, helping themselves to slices of cake and more champagne, she walked down to the ladies' room on the third floor. She locked herself into a stall and reread the story. *Suspended publication*. What did that mean?

She found Fred Ward's name in her list of contacts and tapped his number.

The phone rang once before clicking over to his voice mail. His deep, sonorous voice oozed from the phone like an amber stream of cane syrup. "This is Fred Ward, managing editor at *Intelligentsia*. I can't come to the phone right now cuz I'm fixin' to put the paper to bed. Leave me a message, and I'll eventually get back to you."

"Fred?" She tried not to sound too panicky. "Hey. It's Conley Hawkins down in Atlanta." She gave a shaky laugh. "I just saw the craziest item on the Bloomberg wire, saying you guys are shutting down. Call me, okay?"

She disconnected and waited five minutes. She walked slowly up the stairs to her now-stripped cubicle. The space, in the back row of the newsroom, facing a bank of windows looking out on the continually under-construction interstate, had been home for the past four and a half years. Now, though, her stuff—the books, clip files, the stained coffee mug, even the dozens of lanyards with laminated press credentials from events she'd covered over the years . . . in short, the detritus of a career—was all packed in cardboard cartons stacked in the back seat of her Subaru.

This day, the one she'd been anticipating since the thrilling email from Fred Ward—subject line: "When can you start?"—had finally arrived. Sarah Conley Hawkins was ready to leave the *AJC* and Atlanta in the rearview mirror. The question was, where would she be going?

"Hawkins?"

Roger sat down in Butch's vacant chair. He frowned, his rubbery face arranged in jowly folds, speckled with the gray of his five-o'clock shadow. "What's up?"

"Nothing." She shrugged. "I suck at goodbyes. Guess I'm gonna miss all you assholes after all."

"Try again."

She sighed and showed him the text message from her sister.

He looked up, his wire-rimmed bifocals sliding to the end of his nose. "I take it this is the first you've heard?"

Conley nodded.

He reread the text message. "This is your sister who runs your family's newspaper? Back in Florida? I take it the two of you have some issues?"

"We've got more issues than *The New Yorker*," she said, sighing. "This is Grayson's way of saying, 'Nonny nonny boo boo.'"

"And you've called that character who hired you away? Fred Ward?"

"The call went directly to voice mail."

He swiveled around and typed his password into Butch's computer. He found the Web browser, typed in "Intelligentsia," and a moment later, he was shaking his head.

"According to *The Wall Street Journal,* it's a done deal. Their lead investor was some hedge fund genius who decided new media was too risky." He grimaced. "The publisher pulled the plug last night. Sixty-five people showed up for work in Bethesda this morning and found the place shuttered."

Conley stared out the window, past the construction cranes and high-rises. Traffic was already backed up on I-285. It was four o'clock. She'd planned to be on the road by now. Headed for D.C.

"Hawkins?" Sistrunk's hand, surprisingly small and delicate for such a burly, bearlike man, rested gently on her forearm. "I'm sorry." He pushed the glasses back up his nose. "You know I'd do anything for you. I fought like hell to try to match their offer, but the money's just not there. You know what our budget's like."

She nodded. "And you've already hired my replacement. I know that, Roger."

"I could make some phone calls. Since you won the Polk Award, your name's a commodity. Epstein's at the *LA Times* now. He's not a bad guy, and he owes me big-time. Charlene's kicking ass in Miami, and she always liked you. I bet she could put in a good word."

"Yeah," Conley said, pushing herself up from the desk. She grabbed the last cardboard box. "That would be great, thanks."

They both knew the reality. The world of print journalism was shrinking. Every newspaper in the country was cutting back, laying off reporters, tightening belts. Once-thriving major metro papers were either shutting down or going to digital only. Epstein was lucky to have a job in LA, and Charlene had gone from assistant managing editor at the *AJC* to beat reporter in Miami with zero say in new hires.

"What are your plans?" Roger asked. "You got a place to land while you figure things out?"

"Oh yeah," she lied. "My lease isn't up until the end of the month."

"Good," he said, relieved. "That's good. I'll walk you out, okay?"

"Not necessary. But could you do me a favor?"

"Anything."

"Just, uh, keep the *Intelligentsia* thing to yourself, for now. I mean, people are gonna find out, but I'd just as soon not be the object of pity until I'm actually out of the building."

"You got it."

She was standing in front of the elevator when he hurried over.

"Hey, uh, I almost forgot. HR sent me a memo reminding me that you're supposed to turn in your ID badge."

The lie rolled easily off her tongue. "I don't have it, Roger. I think I packed it yesterday."

"How'd you get in the building this morning?"

"Butch and I met for breakfast before work. He badged me in. I'll mail it back to you. Okay?"

"Whatever."

It looked as though he was going to hug her. Mercifully, the elevator doors slid open, and she hopped inside, punched the down button, and nodded goodbye.

She'd just merged onto I-85 southbound when her phone rang. She could see the caller ID screen. Butch. He'd keep calling until she answered.

"Sneaky bitch," he said. "I thought we had a dinner date."

"Roger found *The Wall Street Journal* story online. It's all true. Sorry. I had to get out of there before word started to spread."

"Where are you now?"

"Headed home."

"I thought Kevin took over the Seventh Street lease. Isn't that going to be awkward?"

"Not home to Midtown. Home, home."

"You mean, like, Lickskillet, Florida?"

"It's Silver Bay. Sweet Home, Florida."

"Seriously? Is that really necessary?"

"Afraid so," she said. "Where else could I go? Tiana's place is the size of a shoebox, and anyway, I'm allergic to her cats."

"I have a perfectly nice sofa, no cats, and premium cable," he said.

"You also have a brand-new boyfriend," Conley said.

"So that's it? You're disappearing, just like that?"

"Strictly temporary. Roger promised to make some calls for me, and in the meantime, I'll start sending out my résumé and clips. I'll be fine, I promise."

"I guess Florida is better than camping out in a van down by the river," he said, sounding unconvinced.

"Lots better. I'll stay with my grandmother. Her house is a God-honest mansion. She's been begging me to come home for months now."

"You'd better call me as soon as you get there," he said. "What's the name of that town again?"

"Silver Bay."

He sniffed. "Never heard of it."

2

Conley's phone rang just as she was merging onto I-185 near Columbus.

Fred Ward. She punched the Connect button.

"Uh, hi, Conley." His voice, amplified on the phone's speaker, filled the car's box-filled interior. "Sorry it took me so long to get back to you. Things have been crazy."

"So *The Wall Street Journal* had it right? You're shutting down *Intelligentsia*?"

"Shit. *The Journal* has the story?"

"My sister, who runs a crappy weekly in Florida, had the story three hours ago." She knew she sounded shrill and unhinged, but she didn't care.

"Yeah, I'm sorry you had to hear about it like that," he said. "It's been a pretty wild couple of days."

"You couldn't have let me know the company was about to tank six weeks ago? When you extended the job offer?"

"Six weeks ago, we all thought we were getting a ten-million-dollar infusion of new capital," Ward said, immediately on the defensive. "The publisher didn't let anybody know how dire things were until this latest round of financing failed. If it makes you feel any better, I'm out of a job too. We all are."

Her voice shook with fury. "It doesn't make me feel any better. I quit my job, broke up with my boyfriend, gave up my apartment in Atlanta. I'm out like $5,000 on the deposits for what was supposed to be my new place in D.C."

"Sorry," he said. "You'll be hearing from HR. They're working on outplacement."

"Awesome," Conley said, her voice dripping sarcasm. "Good luck, Fred."

She tapped the disconnect button and turned her eyes back to the road. Two hours later, she spotted the familiar billboard.

WELCOME TO FLORIDA. THE SUNSHINE STATE.

"More like welcome to hell," she muttered.

She waited until seven o'clock, central time, to call. Cocktail hour was sacred to Lorraine DuBignon Conley, and woe be to anyone who interrupted.

"Hello?"

"G'mama? It's Conley."

"Who did you say?"

"It's me, G'mama. Sarah Conley."

"Oh my goodness. Sarah, what a nice surprise! Are you still in Atlanta, or did you already move to Washington? I did get your Mother's Day card with your new address, but I guess I've lost track of the date."

Conley took a deep breath. "I'm actually on the way to see you. I'm probably still an hour and a half away, though."

"You're not in Washington? I thought you were moving. Now I'm confused."

"You're not confused. It's a long, sad story. I'll explain everything when I get to town. Is it okay if I stay with you for a few days?"

"Well, I guess that would be all right." G'mama hesitated a beat. "Yes, I think there are clean linens in your old room."

Lorraine sounded flustered. Conley frowned. Her grandmother was the most unflappable woman she'd ever met. "You're out at the beach, right?"

Her grandmother opened the Dunes, the family's rambling 1920s home on Silver Bay, every year on the dot on May 1. And every year, on Columbus Day weekend in October, she closed the house down and moved back to the tidy Victorian cottage on Felicity Street, where she'd been born.

"Welllll," the word stretched out. "No, darlin'. I'm still in town."

"Really? It's the middle of May. Are you feeling okay?"

"I'm fine," Lorraine said. "Your sister thought perhaps this year I should wait a few weeks before opening up. It's a lot of work for Winnie, and she's not getting any younger."

"G'mama, Winnie isn't that much younger than you."

"Don't be impertinent," Lorraine said. "You know I don't discuss my age. Anyway, I'll probably open the house up in a week or so. It's been so rainy here, the damp has been playing the devil with her arthritis. Now let's talk about you. What time shall I expect you? And will you have eaten? Winnie's gone home, but I can probably heat up a can of soup or something."

"Don't worry about feeding me. I'll stop and get something. And don't wait up. Just leave the porch light burning. Do you have any bourbon in the house?"

Lorraine's throaty laugh erupted in a hoarse cough. "Foolish child. When have you ever known me to run out of bourbon? Now drive safe, and don't talk to strange men."

The familiar phrase gave Conley the first moment of comfort she'd had that very long, very bad day. She replied automatically, "But the strange men are always the most fun."

Eventually, she exited the interstate and followed the two-lane blacktop west as it meandered through soybean and cotton fields and endless stands of longleaf pines. Occasionally, she saw lights glowing from within an old farmhouse or a knot of double-wide trailers. She slowed the Subaru as she passed through scattered tiny communities with shuttered downtown storefronts and the ubiquitous gas stations and dollar stores.

So much of this area had never recovered from Hurricane Matthew. Sure, the downed power lines had been fixed, and the mountains of splintered trees and ruined roofs, furniture, and construction debris had finally been hauled off, but the lasting cost of the devastation was still mounting.

She passed the abandoned Verner Brothers textile plant, with a faded INDUSTRIAL PROPERTY AVAILABLE sign posted on a high, barbed wire–topped fence. The redbrick mill building's roof had caved in, and sapling trees now poked through what was left. The plant, which had once produced denim for blue jeans, was shuttered in the '80s, like so many other textile mills in this part of the country.

Conley's mood lightened as she approached the outskirts of Silver Bay. Even from here, she could see the jaunty red-and-white-striped tower atop the *Silver Bay Beacon* building, its searchlight bathing the downtown in an eerie yellow glow.

Her great-grandfather, Arthur DuBignon, had bought what was then a steeple from a financially ailing church in Pensacola in the middle of the Depression, and the family legend was that he'd hired two men to load it onto a mule-drawn wagon for the trip to Silver Bay. Great-Granddaddy Dub, as he was called, then had the steeple hoisted onto the roof of the yellow-brick *Beacon* building and proceeded to install a light in the place of the old church bell.

"It's a beacon of hope for the people of this community," he'd told his wife, Mattie Lou, when she'd protested this foolhardy expense. "The Depression won't last forever, and when it's over, people will know that *The Silver Bay Beacon* was a source of truth and enlightenment for this county."

"They'll know Arthur DuBignon had more dollars than sense," Mattie told her closest friends, but she knew better than to try to dampen her husband's grand schemes.

A blue-and-gray sheriff's car sat idling in front of the magnolia-shaded redbrick Griffin County Courthouse. The granite plinth with the statue of a defiant Confederate general still stood, up-lit and oblivious to political correctness, in the middle of the grassy court-house square, circled with neat beds of red geraniums, white petunias, and blue salvias.

As she rounded the square, she noted Holy Redeemer, the Episcopal church, on one corner and First Baptist directly across the street. On the opposite side of the square stood the Silver Bay Presbyterian Church where her own family worshipped.

As always when she was in her hometown, Conley marveled at the number of churches. Who filled all these pews on Sunday mornings?

Halfway around the square, she made a right turn and drove two more blocks. When she pulled up to the house at 38 Felicity Street, she felt herself slowly exhaling. The porch light was on, and the polished brass coach lanterns that flanked the lipstick-red front door flickered a welcome. Before she could get out of the Subaru, Lorraine was standing in the doorway in her pink satin quilted bathrobe, impatiently waving her inside.

Conley perched on the edge of the sofa in the den, careful not to drip tomato soup onto the pale aqua silk damask upholstery.

"This is great," she said, gesturing at her now-empty bowl. "When did you start cooking?"

"I haven't," Lorraine said. "Winnie made it Saturday. Used up the rest of the canned tomatoes from last summer's garden. Now can we please talk about what's going on with your new job?"

"There is no new job," Conley said. "I was about to cut the cake at my going-away party today when my darling sister texted me a link to a *Wall Street Journal* story telling me that *Intelligentsia* had ceased publication."

"Just like that? And you weren't notified?" Lorraine looked aghast.

"Exactly. I finally managed to get Fred Ward—he's the managing editor—to return my calls. He said the news caught everybody unawares. Something about a venture capitalist who decided not to invest."

"Assholes." Lorraine took another sip from the cut-glass tumbler of Knob Creek.

Conley smiled despite herself. Her grandmother delighted in trying to shock the world by peppering sentences with the salty words she claimed she'd learned at Agnes Scott, the "girls' college" she'd attended in Atlanta.

"My editor at the *AJC* offered to put out some feelers. He's got pretty good connections."

Her grandmother tilted her head and studied Conley's face. "You don't look very hopeful."

"I'll go through the motions, but the thing is, there really aren't any jobs. Papers aren't hiring these days—they're laying people off, buying out any reporter over the age of twelve. You of all people should know that, G'mama."

"Print is dead? Is that what you're saying?" Lorraine clinked the ice cubes in her mostly empty glass.

"I sure as hell hope it's not completely dead," Conley said wearily. "What does Grayson say about things at the *Beacon*?"

"You know your sister. She's a total pessimist. With her, the glass isn't just half-empty, it's cracked and ready for the trash heap." Lorraine stared down into her glass. "She thinks we should sell the *Beacon*. There's a chain out of Kansas City, they've been sniffing around for the past year or so."

"Not the Massey Group, I hope," Conley said, suddenly alarmed. "Tell me she isn't thinking of selling to those bottom-feeders."

"They flew here in their private jet," Lorraine said. "Wined and dined us at the nicest restaurant in Pensacola. Grayson seems very smitten with them."

"Grayson is easily impressed," Conley said. "Show her a Mercedes and a Rolex watch and she'll follow you anywhere."

"That's not very nice," Lorraine said mildly.

"But it's true. And you know it. She can't sell the paper unless you agree, right?"

"I'm still majority stockholder, yes. And you have a say in the matter too, you know."

"Not as much say as Grayson," Conley pointed out.

Lorraine patted her hand over her mouth, stifling a yawn. "It's too late to think about things like this. I know you must be exhausted. And it's way past my bedtime."

Conley smiled. "Who are you kidding? It's not even midnight. We both know you're part werewolf." She stood up and reached out a hand to help her grandmother up. But Lorraine shook off the offer, grasped the carved wooden arms of the chair, and slowly rose without assistance.

"Oh, I don't stay up like I did when I was younger," Lorraine said. "You go on upstairs now. I need to straighten up the kitchen. Winnie will have a cat fit if everything isn't put back just so."

Conley dragged her suitcase up the stairs past the gold-framed oil paintings, family portraits, and a group of landscapes done by a long-forgotten relative, that threatened to blot out the familiar green-and-white-flowered wallpaper. At the end of the long, narrow hallway, the door to her old bedroom was slightly ajar. She nudged it open with her foot and reached for the light switch.

The familiar sights and scents of her childhood flooded back. There was the bulletin board, with magazine photos of the Backstreet Boys and Britney Spears. The mahogany dressing table held a bowl of dusty potpourri and a long-forgotten assortment of ill-advised cosmetics and an almost-full bottle of Chanel No. 5 given her by an old flame from her college days.

The room was spotlessly clean. Winnie had seen to that. But it was musty from disuse.

How long had it been since she'd slept here? Most of her visits home in recent years had come during the summer, when she'd stayed at the Dunes.

The air-conditioning was on, but she went to the bank of windows that overlooked Felicity Street and tugged at the middle sash, flinging it upward, then leaning close, inhaling the humid, jasmine-scented air.

She was home, whether she liked it or not.

Sometime past midnight, she heard the soft ding of an incoming text. She reached for her phone and tapped the message icon.

I heard about Intelligentsia. *Sucks, big-time. Where are u? Call if you want to talk.*

"Oh, Kev," she breathed his name out loud and after a moment's hesitation started typing.

I'm in Silver Bay. Guzzling bourbon and licking my wounds. Can't talk yet. Maybe later. Thanks. C.

3

In the morning, Conley followed the smell of frying bacon down the stairs and through the dining room.

For a moment, she paused outside the kitchen door, taking in all the familiar sensations. The scent of coffee and biscuits, the drone of the local radio station punctuated with the pops and sizzles of frying bacon. There was a jelly jar of pink, orange, and yellow zinnias on the windowsill, and Winnie's ever-present turquoise transistor radio stood beside it. The green linoleum floor appeared to have been freshly mopped. The time could have been now or five or ten or twenty years ago.

Nothing had changed. Nothing ever did, she thought.

Winnie stood at the massive six-burner range, tending a cast-iron skillet. She glanced over her shoulder and nodded, unsurprised at Conley's presence. "Hey, shug. Coffee's on. I got biscuits coming out of the oven in another five minutes. Sit yourself down."

Conley greeted her grandmother's housekeeper with a light pat on the arm. Winnie was not a hugger or a toucher. G'mama said maybe that was because Winnie had been in prison.

Winnie had come to work for the family years earlier, when Conley was a young child.

In all the years Conley had known her, Winnie's appearance had changed little. She still dyed her hair the same shade of pinky red, still wore it in a plait that hung down nearly to her waist. Her eyebrows were an iron gray now, but her pale face was surprisingly unlined. As always, she wore a white, button-down man's shirt, tucked into elastic-waisted, black double-knit slacks she must have stocked up on in the seventies. Her black, lace-up shoes were polished, and she peered down at the frying pan through thick-lensed glasses.

"Hey," Conley said. "How're you, Winnie?"

"Can't complain. You want juice, there's some in the fridge."

Conley took a mug from the row of cups hanging by hooks beneath the cabinet by the sink and lifted the battered aluminum percolator from the stove top.

"Well, look who's here."

Conley turned, coffeepot still in hand. She hadn't seen her there, tucked away in the built-in banquette overlooking the backyard. Grayson raised her own mug in a mock salute.

"Oh, hey, Gray," she said. "What brings you over here?"

"Bacon and biscuits brings her here. She shows up every morning on the regular, just like that damn stray cat I keep telling your grandmother to stop feeding," Winnie said. "And just like that cat, she never gains an ounce."

Conley took her coffee and sat down on the bench opposite her older sister. Gray was dressed for the office. Unlike the casual blue jeans and tennis shoes Conley's coworkers at the Atlanta paper favored, Grayson Hawkins was dressed like the small-town Rotarian she was—a navy pantsuit, pale pink cotton blouse, single strand of pearls.

"You don't eat breakfast with your husband?" Conley asked.

"Not if I can help it. Tony's idea of breakfast is a bowl of açai berries and hemp hearts, washed down with that kombucha crap."

"They sell kombucha at the Piggly Wiggly? I'm impressed."

"Piggly Wiggly closed last summer," Winnie reported. "All we got now is the IGA."

"Tony orders a lot of stuff online," Grayson said. "Anyway, G'mama called me last night after she heard you were on your way. I wanted to come over this morning to welcome my little sister home."

Conley regarded her warily over the rim of her mug. With her straight, dark hair and olive skin, every year Grayson looked more like their mother, or at least what she could remember about her mother.

"Get real," she said. "You're here to gloat."

"Not at all," Grayson protested. "I was shocked when I read that *Wall Street Journal* story. I mean, *Intelligentsia* was big league. I assume you'd already heard?"

"No." She let that hang in the air between them.

Grayson sipped her coffee. "What are your plans now?"

"I thought I'd lie low out at the beach for a while, work on my tan, and send out my résumé and clips. I've already got a couple of irons in the fire."

This was a lie, and she was pretty sure her sister knew it.

"That's a relief," was all Grayson said.

Conley sipped her coffee. "What's up with G'mama still being in town? She told me last night you didn't want her to open up the Dunes because it's too much work for her and Winnie."

"What's that you say?" Winnie asked, her long-handled fork poised over the skillet.

"It's actually G'mama I'm worried about," her sister said, her voice low. "But don't say anything to her about that. She's fallen a couple of times. So far, the only injury is to one of Granddaddy's highball glasses, but I don't like the idea of them way out at the beach, fifteen miles away from town and her doctor, if something should happen."

Winnie slapped the heavy ironstone platter of bacon and scrambled eggs down on the tabletop, followed by the basket of biscuits. "For your information, we can take care of ourselves," she said. "Been doing just fine for a long time now."

"Says the woman who needs a hip replacement," Grayson retorted.

"Says who?" Winnie ferried the plates and silverware to the table, then sat down on the old, green, metal step stool that was her familiar perch in the kitchen.

"Says Jack Holloway, your doctor. He also happens to agree that G'mama needs—"

The door swung open, and Lorraine entered the kitchen. "G'mama needs what?" she demanded, glowering at her granddaughter. "According to who? Grayson, you know I despise you talking about me behind my back."

"Somebody has to," she said, shaking her head. "Jack says G'mama is prediabetic. He's given her a prescription, but she refuses to get it filled, and she refuses to listen to her doctor." She looked across the table at her sister. "But maybe she'll listen to you."

"Scoot over," Lorraine told Conley.

Conley did as she was told. "G'mama, is that true? This is the first I'm hearing about any of this stuff. Sis says you've had a couple of falls. And what's this about diabetes?"

Winnie brought the percolator to the table and handed a mug to her employer. Lorraine scowled at both her grandchildren.

"I tripped on the coffee table, which *somebody* moved without consulting me." This time, Winnie was on the receiving end of Lorraine's ire. "It was dark, and it was absolutely nothing. I scraped my shin a little, that's all."

"She had a knot the size of a turnip on her forehead for a week," Grayson said. "I had to physically force her into my car to take her to see Jack."

"She lied and told me we were going to the liquor store," Lorraine said. She placed a slice of bacon and a spoonful of eggs on the plate Winnie had provided and was about to serve herself a biscuit when Winnie deftly slid it out of her reach.

"Did you check your sugar this morning?"

"Not you too," Lorraine said. "My blood sugar is perfectly fine. My diet is fine. Jack gave me a food plan to keep things in check, and I've been sticking to it." She pointed first at Grayson, then Conley, then Winnie. "This topic of discussion is officially closed."

Grayson rolled her eyes. "Hardheaded old mule."

"Out!" Lorraine said. "Out of my kitchen. This minute." Grayson grinned, grabbed for the basket, and helped herself to a biscuit, which she sliced open and mounded with butter and homemade fig preserves before topping her creation with bacon.

"I'm deeply wounded," Grayson said, glancing at her watch. "Oops, I've got a phone call in fifteen minutes. Later, haters."

After breakfast, Conley set her laptop up on the dining room table. She dreaded having to job hunt, but with the state of the industry, she knew she had to get her résumé out immediately.

"G'mama," she said when Lorraine passed through on her way to the den. "What's the Wi-Fi password?"

"Oh," Lorraine said. She wrinkled her forehead. "Grayson set it up. Now let me think. It's something easy. Something obvious."

"It's the address here," Winnie said, dragging the vacuum cleaner into the room. "Thirty-eight Felicity."

"That's right." Lorraine brightened. "It's been so long since she set everything up, I'd forgotten. Am I being nosy if I ask what you're working on?"

"Not at all. I thought I'd send out some emails to my contacts in the business. One of my former editors is now at the *Miami Herald,* another is in LA. And one of my college classmates is actually a bureau chief for Reuters, in London."

"London!" Her grandmother sounded alarmed. "Surely you wouldn't consider leaving the country. Or even taking a job all the way out on the West Coast."

"Why not?"

"It's too far away," Lorraine said. "I mean, Washington, D.C., is one thing. Winnie and I were looking forward to visiting, once you got yourself settled in. I haven't been to D.C. since Jimmy Carter's inauguration."

"I'll consider any job I'm offered," Conley said. "As long as the salary's in the right range."

"Why not stay here? Work at the *Beacon*?"

Conley laughed, but she stopped mid-chuckle when she noticed Lorraine's serious demeanor. "You're kidding, right?"

"Not at all. The *Beacon* is a family enterprise; it always has been. It's not just a business. It's your heritage, Sarah Conley. I know you've always been ambitious for a career, but you've already done marvelous things, first over there in Greenville, then in Charlotte, and now at the Atlanta paper. You've more than proven yourself. Why not take all those skills, all that experience, and put it to work here, where you could really make a difference?"

Conley swallowed hard and thought about the best way to couch all the objections that immediately flooded her mind.

"G'mama, it's not that easy. I need a job. A real job with a real paycheck. It's sweet that you want me to work at the *Beacon,* but it would mean a huge pay cut. And I've got bills to pay."

"I realize that," Lorraine said quietly. "But think how much cheaper it is to live here in Silver Bay. And how much nicer. I wouldn't expect you to live here, with me. You could get your own place quite cheaply. Or live at the Dunes. You've always loved the beach. Despite what your sister thinks, fifteen miles is not on the next continent."

"No," Conley said. "Even if I wanted to stay here and work at the *Beacon*, which I don't, you're overlooking the obvious."

"Which is?"

"Grayson is the publisher and the managing editor of the *Beacon.* I love her, and I have a sneaking suspicion she loves me, at least a little, but I guarantee you, she does *not* want me as an employee."

Lorraine patted her carefully coiffed head and smiled. She was still a strikingly beautiful woman, Conley thought. Her wavy silver hair was arranged in a simple, flattering style. As always, she wore her signature shade of Dior lipstick, and her posture was, as always, perfect. She really didn't look much different from the glamorous portrait that hung in the hallway portrait gallery, the one her grandfather had commissioned for Lorraine's Mobile debut.

"Grayson has the title of publisher, it's true. But as I mentioned last night, I'm the majority stockholder, and I'm still chairman of the board of Beacon Enterprises. So I assure you, Sarah, that if I want you to stay here and work at my paper, that *will* happen."

She snapped her long, tapered fingers. "And it will happen just like that."

4

Hi, Sloane. Hope all is well with you and Michele. Not sure if you heard the news, but Intelligentsia *closed up shop yesterday, which means I'm officially out of a job I hadn't even started. I know things are tight everywhere, but if you happen to have an opening at the* Trib *for a hard-charging, pushy investigative reporter, I'm your girl. Obviously, relocation isn't an issue. I'm attaching my updated résumé. Love to catch up and talk jobs at your convenience. All best, Conley.*

She typed out variations on the same theme and shipped them out, to Sloane at the *Chicago Tribune,* Epstein at the *Los Angeles Times,* Martin at *The Dallas Morning News,* and Trudy at the *Seattle Post-Intelligencer,* checking each off her list of job possibilities.

Last on her list of queries was *The New York Times.* She wrote, revised, and re-revised the note, searching in vain for the right tone. It wasn't that she didn't have the clips or the street cred to apply for a job at the *Times.*

The problem was with her connection there. His name was Pete Kazmaryk. They'd been coworkers at the *AJC* for two years and an item for less than a year when he'd landed a job with the *Times.* Pete wanted her to make the move with him, suggesting she apply for a job with the *Times* or any of half a dozen media outlets in New York. But the timing had been off. She was in the middle of an investigation into a corrupt Atlanta city councilman and wanted to see the project through to completion. Pete had accused her of putting her career ahead of their relationship.

When she'd pointed out that he was doing the exact same thing, he'd gotten angry and defensive. So Pete had moved to Brooklyn, the Atlanta councilman was indicted, tried, and convicted of bribery, mail fraud, and embezzlement, and Conley had been named a finalist for a Pulitzer.

In the end, she'd lost a man she cared about, and somebody else—a reporter in Wyoming, for God's sake—had won for a series on education inequity.

After a futile third attempt at writing a lighthearted note to her old lover, Conley closed her laptop and wandered into the kitchen.

Winnie sat at the dinette, a pencil poised over her crossword puzzle book. The radio was still on, the announcer talking in a hurried, high-pitched voice about a train derailment in Varnedoe, which was in Bronson County, the next county over from Griffin.

"There's an ambulance on the scene, and the police have the perimeter roped off, because one of the railcars contained chemicals," the announcer said excitedly. "Stay tuned to WSVR, and we'll get you all the breaking news as it unfolds."

"Who's that?" Conley asked, pouring herself a mug of coffee and gesturing toward the radio.

"Buddy Bright," Winnie said. "You don't remember him? He's been at that radio station a good while now."

Conley shrugged and looked around the kitchen. "Where's G'mama?"

"Out in the garden."

Lorraine stood in a rectangular patch of deep green grass, using her left hand to splash the hose in the direction of the long floral border that ran alongside the garage. She clutched a walking stick in her right hand, leaning heavily on it. The flowers were a seamless riot of impressionistic colors, soft pinks, blues, lilacs, white, chartreuse, with a few dots of red, orange, and pale yellow. Conley knew the names of only a few—zinnias, hollyhocks, daisies, and always, the deep blue mophead hydrangeas that were her grandmother's favorites.

Opie, her grandmother's Jack Russell terrier, was crouched in the grass nearby. As Conley approached, he raised his graying snout and sniffed hopefully, and when no doggie treats were forthcoming, he snuffled loudly, twitched an ear, then settled back into his previous pose.

"Everything looks amazing, G'mama," Conley said, walking around the fenced yard. "I don't know how you do it. I can't keep a cactus alive."

Lorraine's face was shaded by a wide-brimmed, floppy straw hat. "Joe does most of the hard work," she said, referring to her yardman. She shook her head. "I really thought we'd be out at the Dunes by now. That's why I haven't bothered planting much this spring."

"What else could you plant?" Conley asked, amused. "There's not a square foot of ground here that's not in bloom."

G'mama shook her head impatiently. "Not here. At the Dunes. I need to get my tomatoes and peppers put in the ground out at the beach this week, or it'll get too hot." She pointed at the brick-paved patio shaded by a sprawling live oak, where a line of plastic pots held foot-high vegetable plants. "I can't get that hardheaded sister of yours to understand why any of this is so important to me."

Conley made a snap decision. "Come on," she said, taking the hose from her grandmother. "We need to get your tomatoes going. I'm itching to get out to the beach too. It won't be that much work. You go on upstairs and start packing what you need to take. Winnie can go on home and get her stuff together, and if we hurry, we should be able to get on the road by two. Right?"

"Maybe we should wait until tomorrow," Lorraine said, tilting her head to look up at the sky. "The news said we might get a big storm moving through this afternoon."

"A little rain won't hurt anything," Conley said, but her grandmother's blue eyes looked troubled. "Unless you really don't feel like moving in out at the Dunes just yet. I mean, it's totally up to you."

"Oh no, it's not that. For weeks now, I've been champing at the bit to get out there. You can ask Winnie. It's just that Grayson's been so sweet. So worried about me. I don't want her to think I'm ungrateful or anything."

Conley had to bite back her impatience. She'd been in her hometown less than twenty-four hours and was already feeling claustrophobic. "I guess it won't hurt to wait another day. But you could still start packing whatever you want to take. And then we could leave in the morning. Right?"

"That's a wonderful idea," Lorraine said, looking relieved. "I'll go inside and light a fire under Winnie. You know how poky she is. I'll tell her we're absolutely leaving here at nine in the morning, and she'd better be ready or we'll leave without her."

"Oh, God no," Conley said, acting horrified. "If we leave her here, who'll do the cooking?"

Lorraine laughed and adjusted the string of pearls she was never seen without. "That's an excellent point." She leaned over and kissed her granddaughter's cheek. "I'll let you break the news to your sister about our new plan."

Conley went back to the makeshift office she'd set up in the dining room. She fiddled with her query letters for another thirty minutes, but it was no good. She clicked around the internet, looking at job postings on various journalism websites, but the prospects were depressing and the truth even more so.

She was an award-winning reporter, at mid-career, in a shrinking industry that no longer seemed to value experience, tenacity, talent, and nerve.

"I'm screwed," she mumbled, closing the laptop.

She was also bored, unused to any kind of idleness or inaction.

She went out to the kitchen in search of something to do. Winnie was at the kitchen table, with the previous week's *Beacon* spread out and heaped with an intimidating mountain of sterling silver flatware on top of it.

"Are we having a party I don't know about?" Conley asked, picking up a teaspoon and examining her reflection in the gleaming silver bowl.

"Nope." Winnie looked up. "Your grandmother says we're leaving for the Dunes in the morning."

"That's right."

"Which means I need to get this silver polished before I head home."

"Why's that?"

The older woman shrugged. "That's just what we do. Whenever Lorraine goes on a long trip or moves out to the beach, we get the house redded up. Joe's coming tomorrow to wash all the windows. I've already cleaned the oven and cleared out the fridge."

She held up a long-handled implement with a curiously flat-shaped, triangular pierced head, rubbed at an invisible speck of tarnish with her rag, then set it aside.

"What exactly is that thing for?"

"That's a tomato server," Winnie said.

"I get why you clean out the fridge, but why polish silver that no-body's going to be around to use?" Conley said, holding up another piece. "What's this one?"

"Asparagus tongs." Winnie took the piece, inspected, and nodded her approval.

"We've never really discussed the *why* part," the housekeeper admitted. "But your grandmama isn't getting any younger. She don't allow anybody to know her age, but I think it's because every time she leaves this house now, she thinks, 'This could be the last time. Next time I come back here, it might be in a coffin.' So she wants everything nice. Just in case her next cocktail party ends up being her own wake."

"Speaking of cocktail parties," Conley said, holding up an inside page of the *Beacon*. "Rowena Meigs? I can't believe we're still running that ridiculous column of hers."

Winnie glanced at the newspaper. "I never pay any attention to it, but your grandmama says lots of folks only get the paper so they can read Hello, Summer."

"Listen to this," Conley said, reading aloud in her most exaggerated Southern accent.

Wedding Bells were ringing last Saturday at Silver Bay First United Methodist when Miss Katherine Ann Cruikshank and Mr. Frederick Mark Eppington Jr. pledged their troth in front of a multitude of some of the finest members of local society. Katherine, known to all as Kitsy, is the daughter of Tinkie and Raymond Cruikshank. Ray Cruikshank is the owner of the Silver Bay IGA, and Tinkie is a fearsome adversary at the bridge table. The bride was radiant in a strapless dress of blush duchesse satin with a hand-sewn pearl bodice made from her own design.

"What the hell is *duchesse satin*?" Conley asked, pausing her read-aloud.

"Beats me, but it sounds pretty fancy," Winnie said.

Conley read on.

Her veil, of Alençon lace attached to a pearl-and-rhinestone-studded tiara, was a family heirloom handed down from her great-grandmother. The wedding bouquet consisted of exquisite freesias, white orchids, white sweetheart roses, and baby's breath. Katherine was attended by a bevy of beauties arrayed in striking ombré-pink satin sheath dresses. "Rick," who is the son of Dr. and Mrs. Frederick M. Eppington of Bonita Springs, wore a black Hugo Boss tuxedo, as did his groomsmen. The ballroom at the Silver Bay Country Club was arrayed in dazzling ropes of tiny white lights, ferns, and a multitude of white princess roses. Guests dined on steamship round of roast beef, crab imperial, and—in a novel twist—a mashed potato martini bar. The wedding cake was a scale model of White Columns, the bride's maternal grandparents' antebellum home in Thomasville, Georgia.

"Oh my God! A mashed potato martini bar and a wedding cake shaped like Scarlett O'Hara's plantation house!" Conley howled with laughter. "But wait, here's the best part yet."

*Young and old frolicked the night away to the tunes of Mickey Man-
nington and the Moderntones. Kitsy and Rick will honeymoon in
Aruba, then return home to their apartment in Panama City,
where they are both employed by Pirate's Alley Mini-Golf.*

"The Moderntones!" Conley said, giggling. "I think they played at
our junior high cotillion."

"I don't think Rowena means for her column to be funny," Winnie
said.

"Which makes it even more tragic—that we still print it," Conley said,
balling up the newspaper page and tossing it in the trash.

She reached over to the stack of silver and held up a large serving
spoon, admiring the elaborate whorls and flourishes of the engraved
monogram. "Just how long have you been working here, Winnie?"

"Well, let's see. I believe you were maybe two, and Grayson was
probably four. So how many years is that?"

"I'm thirty-four, She's thirty-six. So you've been here thirty-two
years. And how old do you think G'mama was back then?"

"Don't know," Winnie said. "Older than me, for sure, and I'll be
seventy-four in September. If I had to guess, I'd say she's mideighties.
And still sharp as a tack too."

"You knew my mom, right? From before?"

Winnie shifted uncomfortably in her chair. "We weren't friends, if
that's what you mean. My folks, they didn't have nothing. I came up on
the wrong side of the wrong side of the tracks over in Plattesville, and
well, Melinda grew up here."

"Was she always crazy, or did that come later?"

"*High-spirited* was what your granddaddy called her."

"Which is a Southern euphemism for *crazy as a bedbug.*"

"I'm not a psychiatrist," Winnie said. "She was always different.
So funny! You never knew what she was gonna say or do next. I think
you get your sense of humor from her. And of course, it didn't hurt
that she was drop-dead gorgeous. Had those light green eyes and all
that dark hair, same color as Grayson's. Everybody said she looked
exactly like a young Natalie Wood. I guess that's what made your

daddy fall for her and then stay married to her all those years when she was acting out."

"'Acting out,'" Conley said bitterly. "Another quaint Southern euphemism for *having a flaming affair with a guy you meet at the Jiffy Lube*. Or *dropping off your kids at your parents' house, then skipping off to a 'weekend yoga retreat' and forgetting to check in for another six years*."

Winnie piled the polished silver into a plastic dishpan and dumped it into a sink of soapy water. She wiped her hands on a dish towel and turned around to face Conley.

"You ever hear from Melinda?"

"Not in a long, long time. Last I heard, she was living out west someplace. Oregon, maybe. She'd read a piece I'd written when I was working at *The Charlotte Observer*, and it went out on the Associated Press wire. She saw it in a paper out west and sent me a postcard, care of the paper. A postcard, for God's sake!"

"She's broken your grandmama's heart so many times, I can't believe it's still beating," Winnie said sadly. "She still believes Melinda might come home any day now."

She pointed at the ancient black rotary phone that had been hanging on the wall by the pantry for as long as Conley could remember. "Every time that phone rings, she jumps up, hoping and praying it's your mama on the other end," Winnie said. "Ain't nobody calling on that landline except rip-off artists and people selling time-shares in Mexico, but you can't tell Lorraine that."

Conley nodded. "That sounds right."

She'd initiated the conversation about her mother, but suddenly she couldn't stand to be in this kitchen, with that phone and her grandmother's heartbreak, for one more minute. She looked around the room and spotted Opie snoozing on his bed near the air-conditioning vent.

She found his leash hanging on a nail by the back door. "Come on, Opie," she said, kneeling beside him. "Let's go for a walk."

Opie opened one bloodshot eye, snuffled, then returned to slumbering.

"A walk?" Winnie said with a hoot. "Only thing that spoiled mutt wants is a nap and a treat."

"He's had way too many treats," Conley said, poking the dog's generous flank. "Jack Russells aren't supposed to be this fat." She clipped the leash to his collar and gave a gentle tug. "Come on, boy, let's go."

The dog struggled to his feet and gave her an expectant look. She gave the leash another tug, and he plopped down on his haunches.

"He won't move a muscle without a treat," Winnie advised. She went to the Donald Duck cookie jar on the counter, reached in, and pulled out a dog biscuit, then handed it to Conley. "Carrot and stick," she said, nodding. "Wave it under his nose and start walking. Works every time with old men, mules, and dogs."

5

She started off at a slow, even jog but hadn't made it to the end of the block before Opie went out on strike, plopping down onto his belly, his legs splayed out beneath him.

"Come on, boy." She yanked at the leash, and in response, he lowered his head to the sidewalk.

She gave the leash another tug. "Come on, Opie! Let's get moving."

In desperation, she waved a dog treat under his nose. He looked up, his dark eyes showing a glimmer of interest. She moved the treat at arm's length from his snout.

"Carrot and stick, buddy," she said as he clambered to his feet. "Carrot and stick."

In the end, they reached a compromise. Opie agreed to walk at an agonizingly slow pace, and she agreed to reward his progress with a snack every so often.

She twitched the leash impatiently as the old dog trailed along in her wake. Conley had been a woman in motion her whole life, always speeding toward her next deadline, next job, next relationship. She was unused to walking anywhere.

It wasn't even noon yet, but already the oppressive coastal Florida heat and humidity settled over her shoulders like a suffocating cloak.

The rubber soles of her running shoes slapped on the hot concrete, and the slow pace forced her to look up and down the street where she'd spent so much of her childhood.

Woodlawn had always been a wealthy neighborhood that lived up to the name, with live oaks and crape myrtles lining the streets, thickly carpeted lawns, hedges of blooming hibiscus, and poisonous but pretty pink and white oleanders. The air was perfumed with the confederate jasmine that clambered up brick foundations and wrapped tendrils around lacy wrought iron columns and trim.

Two blocks down from G'mama's house, the sprinklers were on in the front yard of the handsome two-story colonial that had once belonged to the Snyders. Kristin Snyder had been her best friend until the start of eighth grade, when Conley had been packed off to the same Virginia boarding school her grandmother and mother had attended.

Who lives here now? Conley wondered idly, prodding Opie with the toe of her sneaker to get him moving again.

As her walk took her farther from home and closer to the center of town, a distance of less than a mile, the tree-shaded blocks of Woodlawn transitioned to a slightly shabbier neighborhood, with one-story concrete block homes on smaller lots. Lacking the shade of the tree canopy, she could feel the heat of the asphalt street beneath her shoes.

She guided Opie off the street and onto the grassy verge, where he stopped and took a long time to pee on a telephone pole. While she waited, thunder rumbled overhead, where an ominous tower of pillow-shaped dark clouds were gathering. Fat, warm droplets of rain began to pelt her bare shoulders, and steam rose up from the sunbaked asphalt.

Should she try to run for home? Or keep moving? Opie looked up at her expectantly. She realized that they were only a block from the *Beacon* building. Maybe she'd drop in on her sister and tell her, face-to-face, about the change in plans. She scooped the dog into her arms and began to run through the rain toward the newspaper offices.

Grayson glowered at her from across her cluttered desktop. "That's the worst idea I've ever heard. Did you not hear a word I said this morning?"

"Hmm?" Conley was staring out the open door of her sister's office and into the newsroom of her family legacy—*The Silver Bay Beacon*.

Or what passed as a newsroom. It still held eight hulking metal tanker desks that had been in the office for as long as Conley could remember, but only two of the desks seemed occupied. The rest were piled high with what looked like decades' worth of broken or outdated equipment—ancient manual Underwood typewriters, bulky beige IBM Selectrics, office chairs missing backs or casters, stacks of phone books, and dusty black rotary telephones.

Conley dropped Opie's leash, and the dog immediately sought shelter beneath her chair. "You thinking of opening a museum out there, Gray?"

"Cute," Grayson said. "You're really cute, little sister. But don't try changing the subject on me." She slumped down into her chair. "I told you this morning, it's not a good idea having G'mama and Winnie out at the beach just now. Winnie won't say anything, but I know for a fact that she's in constant pain with her hip. Her nephew flat out told me he wants her to quit working, but Winnie won't listen. As for G'mama—you do realize she's in her eighties now, right? She's started falling. So far, she hasn't broken anything, but it's just a matter of time."

"Fifteen miles just isn't that far, Gray. And I'll be right there. If either of them needs to come into town to see a doctor or whatever, I can do that. And besides, G'mama wants to be out at the beach. You should have seen her face today when I told her I'd help her pack and get the house opened up. She was like a kid, skipping around, making plans. Winnie too. This is what they want. It's what they've been doing their whole lives. You can't take that away from them just because they're getting older."

Grayson braced both hands on the desktop. "You think you can just parachute in here and fix things, right? You get to be the golden girl who gives G'mama what she wants, and I get to be the bitchy sister, the killjoy who always says no. But what happens to them when you get bored out at the beach? What happens when you get a new job? You'll be out of here like a shot, and I'll be the one making the midnight runs out to the beach—or God forbid, to the emergency room."

Her smooth olive skin was flushed with anger. "What? No answers? I thought you always had all the answers."

"You never told me G'mama has been sick," Conley said, her voice low. "You didn't tell me she'd fallen until this morning. Or that you were worried about her health. Or Winnie's."

"What would you have done if you'd known?" Grayson demanded. "Would you have dropped everything and come running? Give me a break! You didn't even come home for Christmas this year."

"I was working," Conley said. It sounded feeble, even to her.

"Working at what? Proving to the world how awesome you are? Proving you don't need anybody? Can you even remember the last time you came home to see your family for more than a day or two?"

"Dad's funeral," Conley said, without hesitation. "I was home for a week when Dad died. It was all the time the paper would give me."

"Six years ago," Grayson said. "Dad's been gone six years, and since that time, you haven't spent more than a weekend here."

Conley opened her mouth to protest, but her sister was right. She hadn't been home, and it wasn't because she couldn't get away.

The hurt and shock of her father's death, not just the loss of his steady, reassuring presence in their lives but the how and the why of it that she'd never shared with anyone, had filled her with dread every time she'd returned home.

Grayson was watching, waiting for Conley to make yet another lame excuse. Then she glanced at her watch, stood abruptly, opened the office door, and poked her head out. "Lillian!" she called. "Michael?" Her words echoed around the high-ceilinged room. "Where the hell is everybody?"

"Quit your hollerin'," the answer came. A petite, compact-bodied black woman emerged from the newsroom's outer office. Her short hair was salt and pepper gray, and she wore a flowing, tentlike yellow-and-black-striped dress.

"Lillian, do you happen to know where Michael is?" Grayson demanded, pointing up at the clock on the wall. "Don't we have a staff meeting scheduled for right now?"

"We do," the receptionist replied calmly. "But there's a big freight train derailed over in Varnedoe. Chemical spill, according to Buddy Bright. I heard it on the radio and called up Michael, told him to get on over there."

"Hello?" A woman's voice called from the outer office. "Hellooooo! Where is everybody?"

"Jesus, take the wheel," Lillian whispered.

"Yoo-hoo, Grayson, honey. I'm here." A spritely woman with a cottony puff of snow-white hair made her way into the editor's office, her walking stick cocked at an insouciant angle. She wore a pale pink polyester suit that had seen better days, a pearl choker, suntan stockings in a shade Conley hadn't seen since the early nineties, and sensible, lace-up shoes. Her oversize straw pocketbook held a small dog with a matching hairdo.

"Oh, hi, Rowena," Grayson said, forcing a smile.

"Hello, dear. And here's this week's column, right on time, as always," she said, flourishing a stack of paper before sliding it onto the editor's desk. She looked around the office. "Where is everybody else?"

"Seems like we've got a breaking news story," Grayson said. "We'll, uh, have to postpone this week's meeting."

"Breaking news? How exciting! What's happened?"

"Train derailment," Lillian answered. "You know, Rowena, columnists really aren't obligated to come to staffer meetings."

Grayson cleared her throat and shot Lillian a meaningful look.

"But of course, we love it when you drop in," Lillian said hastily. She picked up the stack of paper and began to retreat from the office. "I'll start typing this into the system." She glanced over at her boss. "What do you want to do about the train thing?"

Grayson let out a long sigh. "Damn it. Buddy Bright knew about it before we did? Again? Why do we have police scanners? Why do we bother to call ourselves reporters? All right. Call Michael and tell him to make sure to find out what kind of chemicals we're talking about. Has the area been evacuated? Do we know if there are any injuries?"

"Buddy said there are ambulances at the scene," Lillian said. "That's all I know."

"Does Michael have the good camera with him?"

Lillian pointed at a black camera bag slung over the back of a nearby chair. "You mean that one right there? No, he thought he was going to the hospital meeting, so there wasn't any need to take it."

"Damn it," Grayson muttered under her breath. "Sorry, Rowena."

The columnist smiled. "Well, I guess if there's no meeting, Tuffy and I will head on to our next appointment. The Viburnum Garden Club has a guest speaker all the way from Orlando today."

She turned to leave. "Give your grandmother my love, Grayson. I guess I'll see her at the women's circle next week."

"I'll do that," Grayson said.

Rowena pointed her walking stick at Conley. "And who is this, dear? A new reporter?"

"Guess you don't remember me," Conley spoke up. "I'm Conley Hawkins."

"Conley?" The old woman wrinkled her forehead. "I'm sorry, dear, I don't recognize that name. Are your people from around here?"

"Yes, ma'am," Conley said, amused. "I'm Lorraine's granddaughter. And Grayson's sister."

"She was *Sarah* when she was growing up here, Rowena," Grayson explained. "Then she went off and got a job at the paper in Atlanta and started calling herself *Conley*."

"Of course!" the columnist said. "Of course you're a Hawkins." She leaned in closer, peering up at Conley through glasses with tinted lenses. "Oh my. You even have your grandfather's distinctive nose."

"Lucky me," Conley said.

"So nice to see you again, Sarah," Rowena said, patting her hand. "Tell your grandmother to bring you to the women's circle, why don't you?"

Conley watched the columnist make her way slowly through the newsroom. "Seriously, Grayson? Rowena Meigs is still writing that sappy column of hers? Isn't she like a hundred and two years old?"

Lillian, who was standing directly behind the boss, rolled her eyes dramatically and nodded in agreement.

"It just so happens that our readers love that sappy stuff. They love

Rowena, and they love Hello, Summer," Grayson said, instantly defensive. "They eat up the church picnics and the sip-and-see teas and all that crap. They eat up the gossipy stuff. But mostly they love seeing their names in the paper."

Conley picked up Rowena's column and started reading the pages aloud, in a singsongy, cartoonish Southern accent.

"Hello, Summer!" she trilled, in a dead-on Rowena imitation.

Mrs. Myra Womble feted her delightful niece Cheyenne on Saturday with a bridal shower at her charming beach house, SAY LA VIE. Mrs. Womble's sister Sonya (Mrs. G. W.) Roland was delighted to have daughter Cheyenne Roland back home in the family "nest" for the weekend, and the younger set who "flocked" to the affair enjoyed a yummy repast, including Crab Puffs a la Myra, congealed 7UP salad, and shrimp "mocktail." Cheyenne and fiancé, Jerrod Corley, will pledge their troth in June at Silver Bay First United Methodist Church . . . Speaking of our feathered friends, a little bird tells your correspondent that City Clerk Morton Pfansteel will be honored at a retirement ceremony at City Hall next week at 7:00 p.m. A light repast will be served afterward. Morton tells us he and Anita plan to drive their RV all the way to Maine, stopping in Sumter, SC, to visit with grandchildren . . . Eagle-eyed locals may be seeing much less of a prominent local jurist who shall remain nameless. Our spies tell us said jurist's wife put her hubby on a strict diet of salads and unsweetened tea, and they've even been spotted jogging at Civitan Park on recent mornings! . . . The Sojourners Sunday School Class at Silver Bay First Baptistt sponsored a fun-filled summer potluck after services this past Sunday. Entertainment was provided by the Praisesayers Gospel Quartet, who visited from Panama City. And now a personal note: your correspondent has noticed, of late, a shocking tendency for young ladies to be "out and about" in attire better suited for bedtime than public. I refer, of course, to the distasteful trend of "pajama pants." Mothers, you should be monitoring your children's wardrobes closer than this. And while I'm on this topic—

young men need to be told to wear their trousers securely fastened at the waist with a suitable belt. The world does not need to see your underpants!

"It's worse than I remembered," Conley said, chortling. "It's like a parody. 'Pledging troth'? When was the last time anybody ever used that phrase?"

Grayson snatched the papers from her hand. "Like it or not, Rowena Meigs is a community fixture. She also happens to be one of G'mama's oldest buddies."

"Oldest biddies is more like it," Lillian put in. "Of course, Miss Grayson, you're the managing editor, so let's not forget, you're not the one who has to retype that mess into something readable. That old lady can't spell, can't punctuate, and can't get her facts straight half the time. Thinks she's better than everybody else and her shit don't stink."

Grayson sighed heavily. "I realize Rowena's not exactly a crackerjack reporter, but so what? She's from a different generation."

Lillian looked from one sister to the other. "This is like beating a dead horse. Look here, Grayson, what do you want to do about that train derailment? I already slotted the hospital board story for the front page, even though they never actually do anything. You want me to bump it to the bottom of the page and hold to see what Michael comes back with?"

Grayson gazed out the window for a moment. "Remind me what else we've got on the front?"

"My feature story on Naleeni Coombs. She's the girl from Plattesville that got the full ride to MIT. First in her family to finish high school, let alone go to college. She's a real sweet kid. Goes to my church."

"Leave the feel-good story on the front, below the fold. I'm thinking a twenty-inch hole for the train thing; we jump it if we can get decent photos on the front," Gray said. "Bump the hospital story inside. Unless we've got dead bodies, then we tear up the whole page."

Grayson picked up the camera bag and looped the strap over her shoulder, then grabbed her pocketbook from the back of her desk chair.

"I've got to get over to Varnedoe," she said, pausing in the doorway.

"I guess I can't stop you from going on out to the beach tomorrow, Conley. I sure as hell can't stop G'mama, now that she's got you on her side. Just make sure she takes it easy, okay? She still thinks she's a thirty-year-old. She overdoes it, then gets sick and there's hell to pay."

"Got it," Conley said. "I'll give you a call tomorrow, once we get out to the house."

"Make sure she packs all her meds," Grayson said. "Winnie knows what all she needs. And keep a lid on her drinking. Two drinks, then you have to take the bottle and hide it."

"I've got it, Gray," Conley repeated. "Just go cover your train crash, will ya? Nothing's gonna happen to G'mama or Winnie. Nothing ever happens in Silver Bay."

6

G'mama was dragging an ancient green aluminum Coleman cooler into the entry hall just as Conley returned to the house.

"What's all this?" Conley asked. Three suitcases stood at the foot of the stairs, along with a huge wicker picnic hamper, a flowered hatbox, a bulky-looking television, a bulging hot-pink zippered garment bag, a lumpy dog bed, and a pair of enormous potted ferns.

"Just a few things we'll need at the beach," Lorraine said, reaching down to scratch Opie's ears. "Were you a good boy?"

The dog flopped down onto the floor and rolled over onto his back.

"G'mama, this won't fit in my car. Are you even sure you need all this stuff?" She nudged the cooler with the toe of her sneaker. "I thought we'd buy groceries on the way out to the beach in the morning."

"This is just the basics. The corn and green beans and field peas Winnie froze from the garden last year and a few other essentials." Lorraine gave her granddaughter a sunny smile. "Don't worry. There are several quarts of Winnie's vegetable soup and Brunswick stew in here too, along with a peach pie and a chocolate pound cake."

"That's great, but where will we put Winnie? And Opie? And the ferns?" She gestured helplessly at the stack of luggage. "And the rest of this stuff?"

"We'll take the Wagoneer," Lorraine said. "I had Winnie drive it home so it'll be all gassed up and ready in the morning."

"You still have Pops's old car?"

"Of course," Lorraine said. "And it runs like a Swiss watch. I do just like your grandfather always did—oil change every three thousand miles, tires rotated twice a year. Lamar at the Pure Station says he's never seen such a well-maintained vehicle. He keeps making noises about buying it, but I can't let go of Pops's car, can I?"

"You're not still driving it, I hope."

"Why wouldn't I be? I'm not *that* old, Sarah Conley."

"Grayson says your eyesight is deplorable."

"Your sister needs to mind her own beeswax," Lorraine said. "I drive when I want to. Now. Do you want your supper? I already had some cottage cheese and tomatoes, but Winnie left you a plate out in the kitchen."

"Supper?" Conley glanced at her watch. "It's not even six yet."

"Dining late doesn't agree with my digestive tract," G'mama said. She turned toward the stairs. "I've got to finish my packing, and then my show comes on at seven."

"Right." Conley grinned. "You're still watching *Wheel of Fortune*?"

"Of course. It keeps my brain agile. And just between us girls, that Pat Sajak is mighty easy on the eyes, isn't he?"

"Very," Conley agreed.

When Conley went into the den shortly after nine, she found her grandmother slumped into the side arm on the sofa, her head resting on her shoulder, mouth ajar, snoring softly in perfect rhythm with Opie's loud, shuddering snorts. Lorraine held the remote control tightly between her be-ringed fingers.

The room, which had once been her grandfather's office, was pine-paneled and lined with overstuffed bookshelves, and at the moment, it was bathed in the blue light of the television, which was tuned to Lorraine's other favorite channel, Turner Classic Movies.

Conley was trying to slip the remote control from Lorraine's grasp when her hand was swatted away.

"I'm watching this," G'mama said, struggling to sit upright.

"You were sound asleep. Come on, let me walk you upstairs to bed."

"I'm fine right here," Lorraine replied. "Opie will wake me up when he wants to go out for his potty break, then we'll both go upstairs."

"Suit yourself," Conley said. "I think I might go out for a ride."

"So late?" Lorraine frowned. "Where do you think you'll go this hour of night?"

Conley shrugged. "I'm going stir-crazy just sitting around the house. My stuff is all packed. Don't worry about me. I'm a big girl."

Lorraine adjusted her eyeglasses and gazed up at her granddaughter. "You've been telling me that since you were five years old."

"And you've been worrying and fussing at me since then too," Conley said.

"This isn't Atlanta, you know. Nothing respectable is open this late at night."

"Who says I want respectable?" Conley winked, and when she went to kiss her grandmother's papery cheek, she was surprised when Lorraine pressed her hand to the side of Conley's face, caressing it briefly.

"Headstrong," she said. "Keep your car doors locked, will you? And promise me you won't do anything foolish."

"Me? Foolish? Never."

Conley drove aimlessly through what was left of her hometown's business district, growing more depressed by the moment. Silver Bay, it seemed, hadn't yet fully recovered from the last hurricane to blow through town. The sidewalks were rolled up tight.

What she needed was a drink. But the only half-decent restaurant in town, the Lamplighter, which had a small bar, closed at nine. She drove toward the Bowl-A-Rama, which was where she'd first experienced the thrill of being served an underaged beer when she was home from her senior year of boarding school. The bartender at the time was one of Grayson's many former admirers, and he'd slid the icy can of Natty Light across the polished bar top with a knowing smile and the equally magical phrase *on the house*. The guy—his name was Jeb—called her the next night to ask her to the Christmas formal, and she'd turned him down flat, explaining that she had a firm policy about dating her big sister's exes.

He'd been shocked into silence for a moment, then disconnected without another word.

Conley slowed the car when she reached the shopping center where the Bowl-A-Rama had been a fixture for as long as she could remember, and now it was her turn to be shocked. The shopping center was still there, but the Publix had been replaced with something called Pawn World, and on the spot where the bowling alley had once stood, nothing remained but a weedy patch of cracked asphalt.

"Damn it," she muttered, racking her brain to come up with a viable alternative. "Not the Bowl-A-Rama."

She racked her brain for another late night option. There was always the bar at the country club, where her great-grandfather had been a founding member, but her tank top and jeans would hardly meet the dress code. Anyway, there was a distinct possibility she might run into Grayson and some of her country club pals, and she really didn't feel like knocking back a cold one with her sister after their testy exchange earlier in the day.

As far as Conley could recall, there was only one other actual bar within the fifteen-minute drive she was willing to make for a drink and some company.

"The Legion it is," she muttered, pulling back onto the highway.

7

The Silver Bay American Legion Post 42 was ten miles outside the city limits. The parking lot outside the boxy redbrick building was half full, most of the vehicles pickup trucks or late-model sedans, heavy on American-made, light on Hondas and Kias.

The bar at the Legion looked like something out of a seventies movie, with knotty pine paneling, neon beer signs, a variety of taxidermied bass and bucks, wall-mounted televisions, and nicotine-stained everything, although Conley was relieved to spot the large NO SMOKING signs posted near the door. She was also relieved to note that she wasn't the only female on the premises. The bartender was a woman, and she spotted six or seven other women in the room too.

There was a jukebox, and it was playing Patsy Cline. She was fairly sure "I Fall to Pieces" had been playing the last time she'd been to the Legion. One wall of the room was lined with booths, and there were a dozen small four-tops scattered between the booths and the long bar.

Conley found a vacant stool in the middle of the bar. She didn't recognize anybody, but this was not a surprise, since she hadn't darkened the door of the Legion in at least fifteen years.

"What are you drinking?" The bartender gave her an appraising look. She looked to be in her early twenties, with a burgundy-tinted pixie haircut, pale skin, and tattoo sleeves on both her well-muscled arms. Sort of like a punk version of Audrey Hepburn.

"Um, what kind of bourbon do you have?"

"You're probably not gonna like any of the rotgut shit we sell. Best I can offer is Four Roses."

Conley laughed. "What makes you think I don't like rotgut?"

"I'm a bartender. I read people. Those shredded jeans you're wearing cost hundred-eighty a pair, and you didn't get that cut and color anywhere around here. At home, you probably drink Knob. Or maybe one of those boutique brands. Pappy Van Winkle? Right?"

"Guess I should be flattered," Conley said. "I couldn't afford Pappy even when I was working. Now? I'm just an out-of-work newspaper reporter."

"So Four Roses?"

She nodded. "On the rocks, with water."

As the bartender moved away, Conley felt a hand clap her shoulder and a grizzled cheek rubbing against her own.

"Well, look what the cat drug in! Sarah Conley Hawkins, what in the hell are you doing here?"

She pulled away from the stranger. But it wasn't a stranger after all.

"Skelly?" Conley whooped and threw her arms around the slender man's shoulders. "Skelly! Oh my God!"

He hugged her back and rubbed his graying beard against her face until she laughed and pushed him away.

Sean Kelly's family lived two doors down from G'mama's house. He was a year younger than Grayson, a year older than Conley. His father was a doctor and his mother was a pharmacist, but Skelly, as he'd been called since their childhood, didn't fit in that mold.

Tall and thin, with spaghetti-like arms and legs, he was the neighborhood prankster, with an outsize personality and an underwhelming academic record in school. He'd flunked second grade—in a small-town elementary school where virtually every kid got what was charitably called *a social promotion,* and had been delighted to land in Conley's second-grade class the next year.

They'd been running mates and best friends until puberty hit Skelly upside the head at the age of thirteen and he no longer had time for skateboarding, crank-calling the cool kids, and shoplifting cigarettes and Cokes from the 7-Eleven.

Now he parked himself on the stool beside Conley's. A self-described late bloomer, Skelly had gone off to college and surprised everyone, including himself, by graduating with honors and then going on to pharmacy school. He'd filled out some over the years, but he was still tall and lanky, with a streak of silver in his straight brown hair. His graying beard looked untamed, and he'd started wearing glasses since the last time she'd seen him. "Trish! Beer me!"

The bartender finished pouring Conley's drink, then reached into a cooler and pulled out a longneck.

"You know this troublemaker?" the bartender asked her, setting their drinks on the bar.

"Know me? I gave this girl her first kiss." Skelly took a long pull from his beer.

"And then I gave him his first black eye," Conley shot back.

"But all is forgiven," Skelly said. "Trish, meet my oldest friend on the planet, Sarah Conley Hawkins."

Trish stuck out her hand. "Nice to meet you, Sarah."

"Just Conley, if you don't mind."

"Conley here is a big-deal, award-winning reporter in Atlanta," Skelly said, a little too loudly. "But she's homegrown talent all the way. Her family owns the *Beacon*."

"Cool," Trish said, unimpressed.

"Hey," called a blonde two stools down. "Are we playing or what?"

Trish reached for a deck of cards and held them up to Skelly and Conley. "You guys in?"

"In for what?" Conley asked.

"Screw your neighbor," Trish said.

"Don't mind if I do," Skelly said, reaching into his hip pocket for his billfold.

Conley rolled her eyes.

"Put up or shut up," Trish said, tapping the bar with the flat of her hand. The two patrons sitting on either side of Skelly and Conley each tossed a dollar bill onto the counter, and the bartender shuffled the cards, then dealt one to each of the players.

Skelly tapped Conley's forearm. "You remember how to play, right?"

"Duh," she said, fishing bills from the pocket of her jeans and putting a single on the bar top. "Kings high, aces low." She picked up her card. It was the eight of hearts. She placed it facedown on the bar and took a sip of her bourbon.

Skelly looked at his card. "Pass." He handed it off to a fresh-faced preppie guy sitting the next stool over and picked up a new card from the top of the deck. The prepster peeked at his own card, hesitated, then accepted Skelly's card, and passed his own to the blonde.

"So?" he asked, looking over at Conley. "What's up?"

"Not much." She shrugged. "I had some time off from work, so I decided to come home and check in with G'mama. Grayson's kinda worried about her health. What's up with you? How's Danielle?"

He tilted his bottle to his lips and drained it. "Danielle moved back to Memphis eighteen months ago."

"Oh. Sorry. I hadn't heard. So you guys are officially split up again?"

He flashed his left hand, displaying a pale band of untanned skin. "She says it's for good this time."

"She always says that."

He ran a finger over the spot where his wedding band had been, then looked up at Conley. His lips were smiling, but she could see the pain in his dark eyes. "She's getting remarried, Sarah. I was refilling Jodi Pilgreen's acid reflux medicine, and Danielle just called me up at the store today and blurted it out. Said she didn't want me to hear it from somebody else."

"That was quick," Conley said.

"They work together at the university."

"Sucks," Conley said.

"Majorly," he agreed.

The bartender was standing in front of them, looking expectant.

"Check it out," Trish said, turning her card faceup on the bar. It was the jack of spades. The preppie turned over the card Skelly had given him. The nine of diamonds. The blonde went next. She had the queen of clubs. Skelly had the nine of hearts. He looked over at Conley. She turned over her eight with a sigh.

"All mine," Trish said, raking in the small stack of bills. She reached for the bourbon bottle and poured a hefty shot into Conley's half-empty glass.

"Drink up," Skelly ordered.

Conley tossed the drink back. It burned as it went down, but not in a good way.

Trish dealt another hand of cards.

"How long you home for?" Skelly asked.

"To be determined." Conley hesitated. "I'm sorta kind of between jobs."

"You?" He pretended to look shocked.

"I was supposed to start work at a digital investigative outlet next week, but things changed. I'd already quit my job at the *AJC* and given up my apartment, so now here I am."

"You'll find another job," he said.

"That's the plan. Until then, I'm gonna move G'mama out to the Dunes tomorrow and hang out at the beach."

"When's the last time you were home?" Skelly asked. "Been a while, right?"

"According to my dear sister, it's been too long," Conley said. She was struck with a sudden pang of guilt. She clutched his arm. "Oh God, Skelly. I just remembered about your dad. I really am a horrible person. I meant to send a card or flowers or something."

He shrugged. "It's okay. Grayson put a real nice write-up in the *Beacon*." He laughed ruefully. "We had to let people into the funeral home in shifts."

"I know Doc could be tough on you, but he was always so sweet to me. He delivered me, did you know that?"

"You and half the population of Griffin County," Skelly said.

"Are you two playing or chatting?" Trish demanded, waving cards in front of their faces.

"Hit me," Skelly said.

"I'm in," Conley agreed.

They played six more rounds, and Conley lost two more times. The drinks got stronger, and she laughed harder and talked louder than she had in a long, long time.

"I'm done," Conley said after she'd downed her third shot of whiskey. "Any more and they'll have to send me home in an ambulance."

Skelly pointed toward the handkerchief-size dance floor, where a lone couple shuffled back and forth to a mournful country song she didn't recognize. "C'mon, kid. Let's dance."

"Skelly, no. I'm about drunk, and so are you."

He pulled her from her barstool. "Best reason in the world."

He went over to the jukebox and studied the playlist, finally nodding and mashing the correct buttons.

"C'mon," he said, leading her to the dance floor. The last notes of the country song were still fading when Skelly's selection started to play. Conley recognized it immediately.

"Not this," she moaned. "Not Shania." But she put her arms around his neck, and he draped his loosely around her waist.

She'd forgotten what a good dancer Skelly was. He was surprisingly light on his feet, and she was just buzzed enough to forget her usual inhibitions, lean in, and let him lead. He skimmed her gracefully across the dance floor, humming softly in her ear. "From this moment . . ."

"No, no, no," she mumbled.

"Remember the last time we danced to this song?" he asked.

"You mean that time your mom made you take me to the country club dance because your real girlfriend was such a skank?"

"Steffi? She wasn't a skank," he protested.

"Oh, please. She put out like a gas station Coke box."

"Wonder whatever happened to her?" He looked down at Conley. "My mom didn't *make* me take you, you know."

"You took me straight home after the dance, when everybody else was going out to Cady Alexander's beach house for the after-party. The next day, I heard you hooked up with Steffi there."

He winced. "High school guys are pigs. I didn't know you knew."

"I knew," Conley said. "Steffi made sure."

"But you were dating that dude from the fancy Virginia prep school, so what difference did it make anyway?" Skelly asked. "We were just friends, right? Besides, your big sister would have called the cops on me if I'd tried anything funny with you."

She waved away his protests. "Water under the bridge." She yawned widely and just then spotted the neon clock mounted over the bar. "Oh, man. It's nearly three!"

"So?"

She stopped dancing and shook her head. "I promised G'mama we'd leave for the beach at nine! It'll take me forever to load up all the crap she and Winnie are taking."

He grabbed for her arm and missed. "Hey, slow down."

"Can't. I gotta go." She dug in her pocket for her car keys, and Skelly snatched them away.

"No way," he said firmly. "You're wasted. Those were double shots Trish was pouring you tonight."

She grabbed for his arm but missed, stumbled, and nearly tripped over her own feet.

"Whoa. Yeah. Maybe you're right."

She gave him a weak smile. "Gimme a ride home?"

He tucked his arm through hers. "I think I can remember the way."

8

The man in black leaned into the mic and let out a long, exaggerated yawn that had become his signature. "Okay, night stalkers. It's the witching hour, so I'm passing the baton to my friend Mara. This is WSVR, the voice of Silver Bay, and you've been listening to *Up All Night with Buddy Bright.*" He flipped a switch and cued his sign-off music, Wilson Pickett's "In the Midnight Hour."

Mara, who'd been standing just inside the carpeted walls of the broadcast booth, nodded, then slid into the still-warm chair he'd just vacated, adjusting her dark hair before donning the headset.

He gathered his stuff—his keys, smokes, and lighter—and walked outside. It had cooled some, and for that, he was grateful. He lit a cigarette, inhaling deeply to draw the smoke into his lungs. After he'd smoked exactly half the cigarette, he dropped the butt to the sidewalk and crushed it with the heel of his black, lizard-skin boot.

The Corvette was parked around back of the studio. It would have been more convenient to park in the spot out front, the one the station had painted with a sign that said RESERVED FOR THE MAN IN BLACK, but there was too much traffic out front. Too many passersby and careless drivers. He unlocked and then circled the car, flicking bits of leaves and dead bugs from the body, looking for any dings or dents. Nothing.

Good. The white 1986 Vette was the only vestige of his old life, the only thing of value that he'd salvaged from the ruins of his past.

His knees cracked as he lowered himself into the driver's seat. He was getting too old for this shit. He told himself that every night. Every morning. He started the car and let the engine idle, listening appreciatively to the low rumble of the powerful motor.

He pulled into the alley behind the station, then onto the street. He drove slowly around the square. It was deserted. When he passed the courthouse and the sheriff's office, with the patrol car parked out front, he felt the inevitable ping of anxiety as he always did, but then he brushed it aside as he had earlier with the desiccated bug on the Corvette's right rear bumper.

All the local cops knew him, joked with him at the ball games, gave him the inside scoop when there was a bad wreck or some actual news around town worth reporting. He'd stop by the sheriff's office when he worked the afternoon shift, check out the incident reports, see if there was any news. He drank coffee with these guys, shot the shit with them. But he never let up his guard. Never.

Wariness wasn't just a habit for him, it was a way of life. So he was watchful as he drove, as he passed the old abandoned mill and then the high school. God, he was glad school and, with it, baseball season were over. He hated sweating his balls off in the wooden press box, doing the play-by-play for a miserable hundred bucks a game. Still, that was money he'd miss until football season started up again in the fall. It was gas money, cigarette money, rent money. He'd need to line up some gigs for the summer, a prospect he dreaded. In the meantime, he'd keep working extra shifts at the station. Sleep? Who needed it?

Soon he was on the county road and clear of the Silver Bay city limits. Moonlight painted the pavement silver. He lowered the Vette's windows and pressed down on the accelerator.

He was doing eighty now, and his carefully moussed and combed hair whipped about his narrow, angular face, but he didn't care. He was Buddy Bright, Up All Night, a thing of his own creation.

He punched a button on the dashboard, and music poured from the speakers. He'd found a new station out of Tallahassee, run by college kids at the university. It didn't suck as much as the corporate-owned radio factories that had taken over the airwaves in the past decade. These little smart-asses played good music—some alt-rock, yeah, but their overnight deejay, a guy who called himself Cosmic, played the kind of headbanging heavy metal stuff he himself had played back in the day.

"Here's a good-time tune for my man Buddy over on the Panhandle," Cosmic said after a long, depressing set of Nirvana.

He cranked up the volume and thumped the steering wheel as Van Halen's "Dance the Night Away" blasted out of the speakers.

Before he knew it, he'd driven all the way out the causeway to the beach, slowing when he approached the bridge, because he knew the cops liked to lurk behind the now-darkened surf shop to ambush speeding teenagers.

The Vette cruised down to the end of the narrow island, to the tiny marina, and then he turned around, finally parking in the driveway of a house under construction. He got out, locked the car, and picked his way carefully through the construction debris and down to the edge of the dunes.

He stared out at the huge moon reflected in the calm waters of the Gulf, mesmerized as always, after all those years he'd spent in the Midwest, by the mere existence of such a seemingly endless body of water. For a minute, he thought about walking down onto the beach, but the idea was instantly rejected when he glanced down and remembered these were his favorite boots. Instead, he inhaled a lungful of salt air, releasing it slowly. This, he realized, was the only time he liked being at the beach. At night.

Back in the car, he cruised aimlessly, one arm resting on the windowsill, over the bridge, then out onto the county road, passing vast green farm fields, stands of timber, rows and rows of pine trees planted in military precision. He passed a sign alerting him that he'd crossed into Bronson County. The land was hillier here, the tree line thicker. This was quail country, he knew from countless nights traveling this same territory. He slowed, glimpsing moss-draped oak and pecan trees lining driveways half-hidden behind elaborate wrought iron gates set in brick walls.

The names of the plantations were all familiar now: Whileaway,

Pinehaven, Folley, Buie's Creek. He was startled at the presence of another car, pausing briefly at the gates of the plantation up ahead.

Oak Springs Farm, that was the one. As he watched, the gates
swung open, and a gleaming black SUV bounced onto the highway,
tires squealing as the car accelerated after hitting the pavement.

What the hell? He instantly recognized the car and the driver, an
older man he sometimes encountered on his nocturnal ramblings.

The last time had been only a few weeks earlier. He'd walked into the
Waffle House near the bypass and slumped onto a stool at the counter.
It was past two, and he'd worked a double that day. A moment later, the
door opened, and the man paused, then sat next to him. Not really a
stranger. It had only taken a moment for Buddy to recognize the man,
but he kept his cool.

The waitress knew Buddy, knew the older man too. She poured his
coffee, then poised the pot over the empty mug on the counter.

"Y'all want some food?"

"Just coffee for me," Buddy'd said.

But the stranger asked for grits. No bacon, no eggs, no toast, he'd
said. "Just grits."

Then he turned and gazed at his new companion. "Say that again?"

"What? Just coffee?"

The older man gave it some thought. "I know that voice from somewhere. From the radio, right?"

He'd nodded, stuck out his hand. "Buddy."

The old guy snapped his fingers. *"Up All Night with Buddy Bright."*
He shook hands. "I'm, uh, Symmes. I've seen you in here a time or two
before, right?"

"Now that you say it, yeah, I've seen you in here, but I've seen you
someplace else too."

"Maybe the WANTED—DEAD OR ALIVE posters at the post office?"
The old dude chuckled at his own joke.

The waitress slid a steaming plate of grits with a melting pat of butter
in the middle onto the counter. He lifted his fork, tasted, then sprinkled
the grits liberally with salt and pepper.

"I got it," Buddy said, laying it on thick. "You're the politician. Senator Robinette. Am I right?"

"Representative Robinette," Symmes said. "But let's keep that just between us."

Buddy gave a lame laugh. They were the only customers in the place. "You live around here? Or in Washington?" he asked.

"Both. We have a house in Georgetown and, of course, a place back here in my district."

"Whereabouts?"

Symmes took a bite of grits, closing his eyes in reverence. "Hmm? Oh, uh, we have a place over at Sugar Key."

Buddy rubbed his thumb and forefinger together, and Symmes's face flushed. "We, uh, got a good deal because the developer's an old friend."

"Must be nice to have friends that rich," Buddy commented, and Symmes shifted uncomfortably on the stool.

Buddy sipped his coffee and stared out the window at the SUV, which was a new Escalade. He'd worked drive time at a station in Detroit, back in the '80s, and he knew his cars. This one was top-of-the-line. American too. He liked that.

"Gotta say, I'm kind of surprised to see a VIP driving himself around this time of night," he said. "Me, I got insomnia, a product of all those years working the overnight shift. But what about you?"

"Same thing," Symmes said. "I'm not sleeping well these days."

"Guilty conscience, huh?" Buddy gave a broad wink to say he was kidding, but Symmes looked stricken.

"Something like that," he muttered, going back to his grits. He took two more bites, paused, then took another before pushing the plate away.

The waitress pounced. "Something wrong with your grits?"

"No, they were fine. Delicious as always," Symmes said.

"Okay." She cleared away his plate.

When the waitress was gone, Symmes said, "I don't have much of an appetite these days." He patted his abdomen.

"You sick?" Buddy was just making conversation, killing time, but Symmes seized the moment.

"Off the record?"

"Sure," Buddy said.

"Actually, I *am* sick. I don't like to talk about it because it upsets my wife."

"Gut problems?" Buddy made sympathetic noises. "Me too, man. Ulcers. The doctors told me I gotta stop drinking coffee, but what the hell?"

"It's cancer," Symmes said quietly. He leaned in. "Non-Hodgkin's lymphoma."

"Shit, man. That's bad, right?"

"So they tell me," Symmes said. He used his napkin to pat his lips. "It's not public knowledge, so I'd appreciate it if you'd keep that in strictest confidence."

Buddy was already regretting his promise. This was news, that Silver Bay's silver fox congressman was suffering from cancer.

"Can they operate? Give you chemo? Like that?"

Symmes looked around to make sure he couldn't be overheard, but the waitress was nodding off in a booth by the door, and the grill cook was texting on his phone.

"No surgery. I've been doing chemo, but now the doctors say there's nothing else they can do. And again, this is off the record."

"Shit," Buddy repeated. "I'm sorry, man. No wonder you're not sleeping."

Symmes stared down at his coffee. "It makes you think about things, you know? Makes you take a hard look at your past."

When Symmes looked up, his face pale, his eyes bleak, Buddy recognized that it wasn't just cancer eating away at the old man's gut and keeping him awake at night. He'd seen the same expression in the mirror for years and years now.

"You're saying you've got regrets?"

The congressman gave him a long, sorrowful look. "You don't even know."

"Everybody's got shit in their past," Buddy said, shrugging.

"Not like this," Symmes said. He raised the mug to his mouth to drink, but his hands shook badly and coffee sloshed onto the countertop.

He plucked a napkin from a metal dispenser on the counter and mopped up the spill. "I did things. In my personal life, my professional life. I hurt people." He looked directly at Buddy. "People died. Because of things I did. Or didn't do."

"You're saying you killed people?"

"Indirectly."

"Any way you can make things right? Like they tell you in AA? What's it called? Making amends?"

"I'm trying," Robinette said. "But it's not that easy. My own family . . ." He let the sentence trail off and then die. He shrugged. "I know it's probably too late, but I have to try, don't I?"

Buddy gave that some thought. "I think once you've come to terms with what you've done, you have to figure out how to forgive yourself. And that's easier said than done."

Symmes glanced down at his watch. "I'd better go. If Vanessa wakes up and finds me gone again, there'll be hell to pay. She doesn't think I should be driving with my, uh, condition. She worries, you know?"

He stood, cleared his throat, and the waitress rushed over. "Anything else?"

"No, thanks." He put a twenty-dollar bill on the counter between the two coffee cups. "That should take care of things for my friend and me."

He clapped Buddy on the shoulder. "I've enjoyed our talk tonight, Buddy. But that's not your real name, right?"

Buddy's face froze, and his gut pinged. "What's that supposed to mean?"

"Deejays always have made-up names, right? Like Wolfman Jack? I mean, who's really named Buddy Bright? I was just wondering what your real name is. No offense."

"Off the record?"

Robinette nodded.

"It's Richard," he said. "Take care of yourself, okay?"

Buddy had been back to the Waffle House half a dozen times since that night, but he hadn't run into Robinette again. Until tonight. The Escalade was speeding and weaving back and forth, crossing the centerline of the two-lane road.

Buddy hung back, wondering if the old man was drunk or sick or both. He glanced down at his cell phone. Should he call somebody, let them know an impaired driver was on the road? What if somebody had done that for him three decades earlier? No, it was no good wondering about that stuff. The past was the past. And anyway, he'd learned the hard way that you can't really save people from themselves.

9

"We'll take your car," Skelly announced when they were in the parking lot. "I'll get somebody at the store to ride me out here in the morning to pick up my truck."

"You sure?"

"Positive."

She smiled. "I don't care what Danielle thinks. You're a good guy, Sean Kelly."

He started the car, they turned onto the county road, and she leaned back against the headrest and closed her eyes.

"What about you?" he said suddenly. "Still unattached?"

Conley sighed heavily. "I was actually living with a guy. Another reporter at the paper. Dumb move on my part, getting involved with a colleague."

"And?"

"And nothing. I was supposed to be moving to D.C. this week. He thought I cared more about my career than I did about our relationship."

"Did you?"

"He felt threatened by my success," Conley said. "Like it was some kind of a crime that I wanted to pursue success instead of staying in Atlanta with him."

Skelly shook his head but said nothing.

"What? You think I should have turned down a fabulous career opportunity because of a guy? Typical."

He shot her a look. "I didn't say that."

"He could have found a job in D.C. if he was really committed to the relationship. But he wouldn't even try," Conley insisted.

"But you ended up not moving to Washington after all," Skelly pointed out. "So the whole thing is a moot point, right?"

"No."

She couldn't explain to him how it was with Kevin, because she couldn't really explain it to herself.

Instead, she pressed her forehead against the window and looked out at the passing scenery. There were no streetlights in this part of the county, just a nearly full moon overhead, lending a ghostly silver iridescence to the green cotton and soybean fields interspersed with acres of scrub pine and palmetto.

"What's done is done," she said softly. She saw a doe standing in the middle of a cornfield, calmly munching on the tender green stalks, and nearby, she spotted two fawns half-hidden in a clump of trees.

She glanced over at him. "Ever kill a deer?"

"Who, me? No. I'm a lousy shot."

"I did."

"For real?"

"One of my boy cousins bagged an eight-point buck one year right before Thanksgiving. My granddad put his picture on the front page of the *Beacon*. You would've thought he'd won a Nobel Prize. So I started practicing in secret—"

"Holy shit!" Skelly yelped.

She turned in time to glimpse something in the road just as Skelly slammed on the brakes, veering sharply to the right to avoid a collision.

It was an overturned vehicle, a gleaming black SUV.

The Subaru jounced onto the shoulder of the road, coming to rest against a barbed wire fence.

"Call 911," Skelly said, fumbling around for his cell phone.

But Conley was already out of the Subaru and running. Oily black smoke poured from beneath the hood of the wrecked vehicle. She squatted on the pavement beside the driver's window and peered inside.

"There's somebody in here!" she called to Skelly as he sprinted to her side.

He flattened himself against the pavement, trying to get a look, then began tugging at the handle of the door, grunting with exertion. "It's locked."

Conley ran around to the other side of the SUV and yanked at the door handle to no avail. She could see the shape of a person inside, slumped forward against the shattered windshield, see the back of a balding head and a trickle of blood on a white collar. His arm was flung sideways, and she saw the gleam of a heavy gold wristwatch. She tugged again, harder this time.

"Hey!" she called loudly, rapping on the window. "Sir? Are you okay?"

No answer. She banged again on the window. "Wake up! You gotta get out of the vehicle!"

"Get away!" Skelly yelled, running around the end of the SUV.

"We gotta do something." Conley protested.

"I already called 911."

"That'll take forever. The fire station's at least fifteen minutes away," Conley called.

"Have you got a tire iron in your trunk?" Skelly asked.

"Yeah. Under the carpet in the cargo area."

A moment later, he was back with a tire iron. "Get back," he cautioned.

He aimed the tool squarely at the driver's-side window and swung. The glass stayed intact. "Damn it," he muttered. He took a step backward, poised to swing again, then stopped. Flames were licking from beneath the hood of the vehicle. "It's on fire!" he yelled.

Conley stood rooted to the spot.

"Get away!" Skelly grabbed her arm and pulled her toward the shoulder of the road.

She stumbled, corrected, then slowly backed away from the SUV, watching helplessly as the flames rose higher, sending sparks shooting into the thick night air. The intense heat drove them backward, and they were both coughing and choking from the oily fumes.

She gave Skelly a pleading look. He shrugged and started back toward the SUV, but within seconds, it was engulfed in rolling waves of black smoke.

"Come on," he urged, tugging her toward the Subaru. "These SUVs have huge gas tanks. This thing could explode."

Choking and coughing from the noxious fumes, they backed farther away. Finally, in the distance, they heard the wail of a siren. Probably too late for the injured driver.

"Do you recognize the car?" Conley asked. "Anybody from around here?"

"It's got a Griffin County license tag," he said, pointing.

"There was some kind of parking decal on the front windshield, but upside down like that, I couldn't make out what it said," Conley added. "It was like a green sort of crest."

"SBCC," he said. "Silver Bay Country Club. I've got the same one on my truck."

"Right. G'mama and Grayson have the same decal."

Without thinking, she grabbed her cell phone and, standing beside the Subaru, began clicking the camera's shutter. She was scrolling through the contacts on her phone, getting ready to call the *AJC*'s city desk to let them know she'd just witnessed a wreck with a possible fatality.

"What the hell are you doing?" Skelly asked.

Conley sighed and stopped scrolling. "I was trying to do my job. But it just occurred to me: I don't have a job anymore."

But she raised the phone anyway and began shooting video of the inferno, of the fire truck as it roared up as the first responders clambered down and began what would surely be a doomed rescue attempt.

She decided it didn't matter that she didn't actually have a job in Atlanta. Whoever was in that SUV tonight was surely dead. Pretty soon, somebody would get a phone call, and their lives would be changed forever. There was a story to tell here, and that's what she did. It was who she was. She'd figure out the rest later.

"He's dead, right?" Conley asked as the firefighters trained their hoses on the blazing Escalade. She stopped shooting and wearily leaned her head on Skelly's shoulder.

"Oh yeah," Skelly said, absentmindedly rubbing her arm. "Jesus, what a way to die."

Conley looked up the road and pointed at the approaching vehicle, blue lights flashing. "Police. Better late than never, I guess."

The Bronson County sheriff's vehicle pulled behind the Subaru. Conley watched warily as the deputy approached. He was huge, with a thick neck and shoulders and a blocklike body. His right hand rested on his holstered gun, and he held a flashlight in his left, which he played over Conley.

"Ma'am? Are you the one that called this in?"

"That was me." Skelly spoke up.

The cop stared at him. "Do I know you?"

"Don't think so," Skelly said.

The cop shone his flashlight on Skelly's face. "I need some ID."

Skelly brought out his billfold and handed over his driver's license.

"Son of a bitch!" the cop exclaimed. "I knew it. Sean Kelly! You skinny son of a bitch." He clamped a thick mitt on Skelly's shoulder. "It's me, Walter Poppell!"

The deputy held the flashlight under his own chin, illuminating a fleshy head the approximate size of a garbage can lid.

"Popps?" Skelly did a double take. "Holy shit! You're a cop?"

Poppell shrugged. "Right? Y'all used to take bets on who'd be the first guy on the team to end up in jail. Guess what? It's me—only I'm the one locking up all y'all's sorry asses." The cop gestured toward Conley. "This your lady?"

"No!" Conley exclaimed.

The deputy flicked the beam of the flashlight up and down her body. "Too bad."

"Cool it, Popps. We're old friends. Neighbors, actually," Skelly said.

"We bumped into each other earlier tonight at the Legion, and we were headed home when we ran up on this." He pointed at the Escalade.

"Y'all been drinking?" The cop's voice was stern. "Which one of you was driving?"

"I was driving, and I stopped after two beers," Skelly said. "Way before midnight."

"Screw it, then," Poppell said. "Dispatch said there was just the driver, that right? No passengers?"

"Not as far as we could tell," Skelly said. "It must have happened right before we drove up. Sarah—I mean, Conley—ran up to try to open the door while I called 911."

"I saw the driver. He was slumped sideways, and I could see some blood on his collar," Conley said. "I called to him, but he didn't respond. I guess he was unconscious."

"Well, if the dude wasn't dead before, he's toast now. Literally." Poppell chuckled.

Conley winced and looked past the cop, letting her eyes focus on anything other than him or the blaze that the firefighters had almost extinguished.

"The door was jammed shut," Skelly said. "I tried to break the window in with a tire iron, but I only got one swing in before the vehicle caught fire. The blaze was so hot, there was nothing we could do. I was afraid it would explode."

"Y'all didn't recognize the driver?" Poppell asked.

"No."

"All right," Poppell said. "Guess there's nothing to do now but wait for the ambulance."

"Can we go?" Conley asked abruptly. She had no desire to watch the rest of this inevitable scene unfold.

"Don't see why not," Poppell said. He unbuttoned a flap on his breast pocket and brought out a small notebook. "Here. Y'all write down your phone numbers and contact info. We'll be in touch if we need anything else."

Conley scribbled her cell phone number and handed the pad to her friend, who did the same.

"What are you up to these days, Skelly?" the deputy asked.

"Same old, same old. Running the drugstore, trying to stay out of trouble."

Skelly held the passenger door open, and Conley climbed onto the seat.

"See ya around, Popps," Skelly said, turning to go.

"Hey, we should get the guys together sometime," Poppell said. "Grab a beer or something." He reached back into his pocket and brought out a card. "Gimme a call, okay?"

"For sure," Skelly said. He started the Subaru and steered carefully around the blackened, smoldering wreck. The firefighters were packing up their gear to go too, and in the distance, they heard the wail of an approaching ambulance.

Conley leaned her head back and closed her eyes. "How do you know that creep?"

"Popps? We played jayvee football together. He was six two, weighed two-forty in eighth grade. Started shaving in seventh grade. He played left tackle. And when I tell you he was dumber than a box of rocks, that's being charitable."

"I didn't know you'd played football."

"There's a lot you don't know about me," Skelly said.

"So when do you think you'll be getting together with good ol' Popps to throw back some brewskis?" she asked.

"Hmmm. I'd say never-ish."

10

"Sarah! Sarah Conley. Sarah. Conley. Hawkins." The voice in her ear was soft but persistent. "Come on now. Wake up."

She rolled onto her stomach, but now someone was tapping her shoulder. Tap. "Sarah." Tap. "Wake up." Tap. "I'm not going away, so you'd best just get up so we can all get going."

Conley groaned and sat up. Winnie stood by her bed with a steaming mug of coffee in her outstretched hand.

"That's better. If you don't get dressed and get downstairs right this minute, I swear your grandmother is going to finish loading the car and drive herself out to the beach, and ain't nobody wants that," Winnie said.

"What time is it?"

"It's quarter 'til nine. Lorraine called me at seven, told me to get myself over here no later than eight."

Conley took a sip of coffee and yawned.

"Late night?" Winnie raised an eyebrow.

"Too late," Conley said as she headed toward the bathroom. "You can tell G'mama I said to hold her horses. I'm already packed. I'll be downstairs in fifteen minutes, and then we can get started."

. . .

Winnie was dragging the potted fern out the front door just as Conley reached the hallway.

"For Pete's sake, Winnie. I'll get that." She sat her suitcase near the bottom step. "Where's G'mama?"

"Been setting out in the car for ten minutes. You didn't hear her honking the horn?"

"I was in the shower," Conley said. She picked up the fern and steered her rolling suitcase out onto the front step and was greeted by a long blast from the Wagoneer's horn.

Lorraine sat in the front seat, arms crossed over her chest, Opie draped across her lap.

Conley raised the Wagoneer's hatch. Suitcases, coolers, garment bags, the television, and Opie's dog bed took up the entire cargo area. She managed to shove the fern inside the dog bed, but there was not another spare inch in the car as far as she could see.

She sighed and shook her head, then turned back toward the house.

G'mama rolled down the window and stuck her head out. "Where do you think you're going? It's blazing hot in this car, and I'm not getting any younger, you know."

Conley didn't bother to answer. When she got back to the car, she used a pair of bungee cords to strap her own suitcase to the Wagoneer's roof.

Lorraine sulked in silence for the first ten minutes of the drive.

Conley decided to ignore her grandmother and instead engaged in a friendly conversation with the housekeeper.

"How're your nephews doing, Winnie?"

"Real good. Jesse, the youngest, got out of the army, and he's back working at the auto body shop and driving their tow truck, says he's fixing to buy the shop from old man Widener. Jason's down in Tampa, working as a longshoreman at the port authority. And Jerry just got promoted to head teller at the bank. Everybody says he'll be the next branch manager."

"That's amazing," Conley said. "I know Nedra would be so proud of them, and grateful to you, for raising them into such successful young men."

"Those boys gave me a run for my money, that's for sure," Winnie said.

"Not to mention a lot of gray hair," Lorraine put in. "Same as you did me, staying out all hours of the night last night."

Conley rolled her eyes but kept quiet.

"I almost called the sheriff's office last night to ask them to put out an APB on you," Lorraine said. "But then I finally fell asleep. What time did you actually come dragging home?"

"It was after three," Conley admitted.

"Three o'clock in the morning? No wonder you're a mess. Like I always used to tell your mother, nothing good happens after midnight. What kind of foolishness were you up to?"

"I went to the American Legion. You'll never guess who I ran into there."

"Nobody decent, I bet."

"Skelly was there," Conley said. "It's all his fault. We got to talking and catching up."

Lorraine's face softened at the mention of Sean Kelly's name. "I always did like that boy. Such a shame about Doc, and of course, now June."

"What's wrong with Skelly's mother?" Conley said, alarmed. "Don't tell me she died too. G'mama, you never said anything about Miss June dying."

"Be better if she had passed," Winnie put in. "Poor woman has dementia. I heard she thinks young Sean is her husband. You know he moved back home after that wife took off and left. He's got a lady comes in and stays with Miss June, but still, that's a boy loves his mama."

"He didn't mention anything about his mom," Conley said sadly.

"Did he tell you he's single again?" Lorraine asked eagerly.

"He mentioned it."

"I never liked that girl," Lorraine said. "She put Sean through hell

and back, and then she up and leaves him again. He deserves better."
She gave her granddaughter a meaningful sidelong glance.

"Forget it, G'mama," Conley said flatly. "Skelly's like a brother to
me. And I am definitely not interested in romance."

"We'll see about that," Lorraine said. "But you still haven't said what
kept you out so late. I didn't know there were any bars in town that
stayed open 'til three."

Conley exhaled slowly. They were approaching the turn onto the
beach road. The memory of the previous night's inferno came rushing
back, and her stomach churned.

"There was a terrible one-car wreck on the county road, about fifteen miles out of town," she said. "It must have happened right before
we got there. An SUV had flipped completely upside down. As soon as
we saw it, Skelly called 911, and we ran over and tried to get the driver
out, but . . ." She shuddered at the memory. "We were too late. The engine was already smoking and the doors were locked, so we were trying
to break one of the windows, but then flames were coming from under
the hood, and the heat and smoke were so intense we had to back away."

"Oh my Lord," G'mama said. "How awful."

"It really was," Conley agreed. "There was nothing anybody could
do. The firefighters got there as quickly as they could, but really, we
knew it was too late."

"Any idea who it was?" Lorraine asked. "Nobody we know, I hope."

"Not sure. The car did have Griffin County tags, and there was also
a country club parking decal on the windshield."

Lorraine looked shocked. "What kind of car did you say it was?"

"A black Escalade. It looked pretty new."

"I don't really know one car from another these days," G'mama admitted.

"An Escalade is a kind of Cadillac," Winnie said.

"Did you call Grayson and let her know about the wreck?" G'mama
asked.

"I didn't get a moment's peace this morning, because *somebody* was
in such a hurry to leave for the beach, it was all I could do to swallow

some coffee and strap my suitcase to the roof of the car," Conley said. "Besides, I'm not sure Grayson wants to hear anything from me. We kinda had words yesterday when I went by the paper to tell her I was moving you out here today."

"I'll call her myself when we get to the Dunes."

"Be my guest," Conley said, adding as an afterthought, "I guess you could tell her I took some photos and some video of the wreck with my phone. Just in case she's interested."

"Oh!" G'mama said abruptly as they were passing through the island's tiny business district. "Pull in here, Sarah." She pointed at the island's IGA. "Winnie and I need to get our groceries."

"G'mama, we can't fit as much as a stick of gum in this car right now. We'll make a grocery run after we get unpacked."

Five minutes later, she steered the Wagoneer onto Gulfview Lane, and a minute after that, she turned into the sandy driveway at the Dunes.

G'mama exhaled deeply and turned around in her seat to face Winnie. "The old girl's still standing."

"No thanks to that last hurricane," Winnie said.

Conley was surprised to find herself blinking back tears as she surveyed the rambling old wood-frame house that had been the family's summer home for the past sixty years.

The house had been built in the 1920s by a wealthy Birmingham department store owner who'd been one of Conley's great-grandfather's golf buddies. In the 1930s, after the man died suddenly, her great-grandfather agreed to buy the house, sight unseen, from the widow.

Hurricanes had buffeted this part of the Florida Panhandle for decades, but because the house was built on a section of beach that resembled a bite out of the curving coastline, it had somehow escaped the fate of other nearby Gulf-front homes.

The Dunes's cedar-shingle exterior was painted a dark spruce green. The trim was white, and the front door was dark red. Mindful of hurricane-force winds and the threat of flooding at high tide, in the early sixties her grandfather had the house jacked up and placed on concrete pilings. Four cars could pull underneath the house now, and a wide screened-in staircase led to the porch that wrapped all the way around the house.

Lorraine pulled a huge brass ring from the depths of her pocketbook. She looked at the stairs and sighed. "You know, when Pops insisted on putting in that doggone elevator fifteen years ago, I told him he was crazy to spend that kind of money. Wasn't a reason in the world why able-bodied people like us couldn't use the stairs. Told him it would keep us young."

Conley recoiled in mock surprise. "Are you saying you were actually wrong about something? Stop the presses!"

"Smart aleck," Lorraine said. "Go ahead and take Opie for a potty break. Winnie and I will take up the first load and get the house unlocked."

"Leave the heavy stuff for me," Conley said.

The front porch floorboards creaked with each step she took. G'mama had left the front door ajar. With a suitcase in each hand and a wriggling Opie tucked under her arm, Conley bumped the door with her hip and stepped inside.

She set Opie down on the floor, closed her eyes, and inhaled deeply, letting the old beach house scents settle into her bones. It was a peculiar bouquet unique to this shabby but beloved home of her heart; of old wood and lemon oil, salt air, and maybe a hint of mildew.

Winnie and Lorraine were already busy, tugging at the heat-swollen sashes of the dozen windows that ran across the front of the house, separating the porch from the main house. Tattered cotton curtains fluttered limply in the faint breeze.

"Bring up the cooler next," G'mama instructed. "I want one of those cold sodas we brought from the house."

An hour later, Conley was drenched in perspiration, and her legs felt like rubber after making dozens of trips from the car to the tiny two-person elevator and into the house.

She sank down onto a wicker armchair near the fireplace, and a fine dusting of paint chips fluttered onto the hooked rug beneath her feet. There must have been two dozen pieces of wicker just in this room alone—a combination of living room, dining room, and library, united by the age-darkened, heart pine shiplap walls and the worn wooden floors. None of the sofas, chairs, rockers, and tables were an exact match, but all wore the same shade of pale aqua G'mama had been painting them for decades.

The lumpy cushions were in a faded deep green bark cloth pattern featuring ferns and caladiums, and Conley knew that when this generation of cushions got too threadbare, her grandmother would have Jacky, her seamstress in town, run up another set from the huge bolt of the same fabric that she'd purchased decades ago, long before Conley was born.

Her grandmother approached with a broom in her hand. She'd already changed out of her "town" clothes and into a neatly pressed flowered cotton top and pastel cotton pants. She had a silk scarf fastened over her hair and wore a pair of white Keds without shoelaces. This was G'mama's cleaning uniform.

"I'm putting you upstairs in the big room," Lorraine announced. "Winnie and I will stay down here."

"In the girls' bunk rooms?"

"It's cooler down here," Lorraine said matter-of-factly. "And Winnie doesn't need to be climbing all those stairs, what with her bad hip and all." She raised the broom and began batting at the long strands of cobwebs that crisscrossed the mantel and whitewashed brick fireplace surround.

Conley set her suitcase on a luggage rack she found in the cedar-lined closet of the "big room" on the second floor, trying not to feel guilty about occupying what was indisputably the best room in the house.

This had been her grandparents' bedroom for as long as she could remember. Unlike any of the other five bedrooms in the house, including the two others on this floor, this one had a small, attached bathroom, featuring a claw-foot bathtub, a commode with the original pull-chain flush, and a minuscule corner-mounted sink.

The heavy brass bed was dressed with a white chenille bedspread with a pattern of blue-and-green peacocks that Conley had always loved as a child. As G'mama had pointed out, there was no air-conditioning up here, only a ceiling fan whose blades whirred ineffectively overhead.

The room was stifling in the late-afternoon heat, the wooden floor littered with the dried corpses of long-dead bugs.

She wrenched open the heavy french doors at the foot of the bed and stepped onto the porch.

The shimmering turquoise waters of the Gulf of Mexico beckoned beyond the dune line. The water was calm, but she could hear waves lapping at the sand. She needed to unpack and find sheets to make up her bed. She needed to sweep the floor and find a putty knife to pry open the heavy wooden window sashes that were nearly impossible to open. Then she needed to go downstairs and take her grandmother to the grocery store.

But Conley did none of these things. Instead, she kicked off her flip-flops, peeled off her sweaty clothes, and climbed into her bathing suit. Then she hurried down the back stairs, through the path across the dunes. She waded into the warm Gulf water and dove headlong into the first medium-size wave she could find.

11

When Conley returned from the IGA, she saw her sister's aging silver BMW parked under the house. She considered making up another errand for herself, but shrugged and pulled in alongside Grayson's car. No use delaying the inevitable.

She found the three of them—G'mama, Winnie, and Grayson—seated on the back porch, their chairs pulled into a companionable semicircle, highball glasses in hand, gazing out at the sky, which was blazing coral and orange and pink as the sun sank toward the horizon.

The frosty glasses were beaded with condensation, and Conley knew they were drinking what G'mama called her *sunsetters*—pink grapefruit juice, vodka, club soda, and a slice of lime.

"Oh, hey, Gray. Did you drive all the way out here to make sure I'm taking good care of G'mama?"

Her grandmother shot her a reproving glance and tapped the folded copy of the *Beacon* resting on the wicker table beside her. "Grayson always delivers my copy of the paper in person. Every week." She gave her oldest grandchild an indulgent smile. "It's an excellent issue. I think that new reporter of yours did a nice job on the train derailment piece. What's his name again?"

"Michael Torpy," Grayson said. "He's a good kid. Young, but definitely a hard worker. And he's willing to learn, which a lot of these millennials aren't."

Lorraine picked up the paper and ran her finger across the front page, bringing it to rest on the column running down the left-hand well of the page.

"And then there's this." She jabbed at Rowena Meigs's outdated photo topping the Hello, Summer column and sighed deeply. "I hate to say it, but I really believe it might be time for Rowena to retire."

"I'll second that motion," Conley said eagerly. "I know she's a friend of yours, G'mama, but the truth is, Rowena is a dinosaur. Her writing stinks, she's out of touch, and she can't even spell. According to Lillian, half the time, she doesn't even get the names right. She's an embarrassment."

"I'd love to fire Rowena," Grayson said. "Or retire her or whatever. But it's not that simple. She's as beloved and unmovable a community fixture as that damn Confederate statue on the courthouse square. Plus she basically works for free."

"Goes to show you get what you pay for," Winnie commented.

Grayson gulped a slug of her cocktail. "Have you two forgotten what happened the last time we tried to get rid of Hello, Summer?"

Lorraine rocked backward in her chair, shaking her head. "Actually, I had forgotten. Never mind. We don't need to go through all *that* again."

"All what?" Conley asked.

"It was years ago. I can't remember the specifics, just that it was so awful, so libelous, that Pops *did* fire her."

"I remember," Winnie said suddenly. "It was Rowena's usual crap column, rich-lady tea parties and such, but then she wrote something about the new youth minister at the Baptist church, how he'd been seen 'gadding about town' in a shiny new convertible with the pastor's wife."

Lorraine shuddered. "Oh dear Lord. It's all coming back now. Rowena as much as inferred that the youth minister and the pastor's wife were having some sort of torrid affair. She wrote some catty comment questioning how he could afford an expensive car on his salary. She all but accused him of embezzling money from the church."

It was Winnie's turn again. "Turns out the convertible belonged to the pastor's father-in-law, or maybe it was the youth minister's father . . ."

"Doesn't matter," Lorraine said. "It was a deeply unfortunate incident. Pops made Rowena write a retraction, and he ran it on the front page of the *Beacon,* and then he fired her."

"And yet she's still writing Hello, Summer, with the same airbrushed photo sig that she must have had done at Glamour Shots thirty years ago."

"The day after she was fired, calls started coming into the office. Rowena's friends from church. Her friends from the women's circle, bridge club, garden club, the United Daughters of the Confederacy, *and* the DAR." Lorraine ticked off the list one by one. "They all threatened to cancel their subscription to the paper if Rowena's column was dropped."

"Pops folded to public pressure?" Conley asked, disappointed. "Rowena couldn't have had that many friends. I mean, back in the day, the *Beacon* was the only paper around. Every family in town had a subscription. I know, because I used to ride my bike to deliver the copies on our block."

"It wasn't the loss of subscriptions," Lorraine said. "We could have withstood that. Two weeks after the firing, Sam Greenbaum came into the office and had a confidential talk with Pops. And the week after that, what do you know? Hello, Summer was back."

"Sam Greenbaum?" Conley looked from Lorraine to Grayson.

"He owned Green's Department Store," Grayson explained. "They were the *Beacon*'s biggest advertiser. Back in the day, they'd run four, sometimes six full-page display ads. Every week. And in September, we'd publish a full-color back-to-school fashions preprint section. Eight pages. Same thing at Christmas."

"I remember Green's Department Store," Conley said. "That's where we'd go see Santa Claus every year. So this Mr. Greenbaum was a friend of Rowena's too?"

"Oh Lord, no!" Lorraine said, chuckling. "Sam—may he rest in peace—definitely was not a fan of hers. But say what you want about Rowena—she may be crazy—but she's not stupid. No, Rowena got all her friends, those DAR and UDC and garden club ladies, all of them, to march themselves down to Green's and threaten to cut up their credit cards unless Sam Greenbaum persuaded your grandfather to put Rowena back in the *Beacon*."

"Oh." Conley shook her head.

"Conley thinks it's terrible that Pops caved in to pressure from our biggest advertiser," Grayson told their grandmother, her voice mocking. "She probably never realized that ad revenue paid for her expensive boarding school and out-of-state college tuition."

"That's enough, Grayson," G'mama said, her voice sharp. "Sarah is part of this family and part of the *Beacon* ownership. She has a right to question our editorial decisions. Just as you have a right to explain our rationale."

"Okay," Conley said slowly. "But Green's Department Store has been out of business since, what, the nineties? So you actually could fire Rowena now, right?"

"We could," Grayson agreed. "If we wanted to lose our status as the county's legal organ, and if revenue from our legal ads wasn't the only thing keeping us from financial ruin."

"I don't understand," Conley admitted. "I mean, I know the *Beacon* is the official legal organ for Griffin County, which means we run all the bankruptcy, liquor license applications, and death and divorce notices. But what's Rowena got to do with that?"

"It's not Rowena," Grayson said, scowling. "It's her grandson, Rusty."

"Wait. I didn't know Rowena was ever married," Conley said. "And she had a kid too?"

"Lawton Meigs was a darling man," Lorraine said. "Everyone adored him."

"Smartest thing he ever did was have the good sense to drop dead of a heart attack before that woman could make his life a living hell," Winnie said.

"Rowena had a daughter, Rebecca," Lorraine said, "who ran off at seventeen when she got pregnant. A few years later, she married an older man, who adopted Rebecca's son, Rusty."

"And Rusty Cummings is the Griffin County clerk of court," Grayson concluded. "Who, coincidentally, holds the power to appoint any publication as the county's legal organ of record."

"Oh." Conley picked up the newspaper and fanned herself with it. "Thus, it's either Hello, Summer or goodbye, legal ads."

"Exactly," Grayson said.

"There's another reason I came out here today," Grayson said. "G'mama asked me to pick up her prescription." She held up a small white paper bag and shook it. "She was *supposed* to have you pick up her prescription before y'all headed out here this morning."

"I forgot, all right?" Lorraine snapped. "Sometimes things slip my mind. It doesn't mean I'm senile."

"No, it means her hair was about on fire to get out here to the beach," Winnie said.

Lorraine glared at her housekeeper. "I called Grayson to ask her something, and she very sweetly volunteered to bring my medicine out to me. And to stop at the liquor store on the way."

Grayson wagged a finger in G'mama's direction. "One sunsetter a day, agreed?"

Lorraine shrugged and looked away.

"There's something else on my mind," Grayson said, sitting back in her chair. "Skelly and I were chatting, and he told me about that wreck you guys came across last night. He said you took some pictures?"

Conley nodded, waiting.

"Do they know who was in the car?" G'mama asked.

"I called Michael in and had him make some phone calls. I just heard from him as I was driving out here. Nothing official yet, but it looks like it was Symmes Robinette."

"What?" G'mama's drink slipped from her hand, the glass shattering on the wooden floor.

"Oh my God," Winnie said, her face turning pale. She jumped up from her chair. "Don't move, y'all. I'll get the broom."

"Symmes Robinette? For real?" Conley asked, just as shocked as her grandmother.

Symmes Robinette was actually Congressman Charles Symmes

Robinette, a longtime member of the U.S. House of Representatives, from Florida's Thirty-fifth District, which included Griffin County.

Conley hadn't kept up much with local politics over the years. She'd been sent off to Virginia to boarding school as a teenager and hadn't really lived in Silver Bay since graduating from college, but she knew the Robinette family, particularly the congressman's son, C. Symmes Robinette Jr.—or Charlie, as he liked to be called—on a personal—and painful—level.

"I can't believe it," Lorraine said.

Grayson went to the bar cart and deftly assembled another cocktail, handing one to Conley, and then, after a moment's hesitation, fixing a replacement drink for their grandmother.

"They're sure it was Symmes?" Lorraine asked.

Grayson nodded.

Winnie returned with the broom and a metal dustpan and attacked the shards of glass and ice cubes with a vengeance.

"The accident was actually just over the county line in Bronson," Grayson said. "The sheriff's office there told Michael it won't be official until their coroner makes a ruling. I gather the body was pretty badly burned."

Conley dug her cell phone from her pocketbook and opened the photo library. She tapped the video of the car engulfed in flames and felt another twinge of queasiness before handing the phone to her sister.

"Oh my Lord." Grayson pushed the phone away. "No way anybody walked away from that."

"No," Conley agreed. "They got there as fast as they could, I'm sure, but it took the firefighters a while to put out the flames. Skelly and I didn't have the stomach to hang around and watch the recovery effort."

"Poor Vanessa," Lorraine said. "What a tragedy." She sighed heavily. "I suppose the women's circle will do the reception after the funeral. I should call Bunny and the other girls."

"No!" Grayson put a hand on G'mama's arm. "I mean, please don't do that. Michael had to swear he'd hold on to the story until the coroner's report comes in. It hasn't been made public yet."

"But Vanessa knows, right?" Lorraine asked, her eyebrow raised.

"According to the police, she's been notified," Grayson said. "But again, it's not for public consumption yet."

"I guess you've got your front-page story for next week," Conley said. "Big news, right?"

"That's what I wanted to talk to you about. You were there. You could write a hell of a first-person story to go along with those photos."

"Me?" Conley was taken aback by the request.

"Why not? It's not like you've got anything else going on."

"Grayson Hawkins!" G'mama's unspoken rebuke was sharp.

"Thanks," Conley said bitterly. "Way to go, Grayson! Reminding me that I'm out of work is a surefire way to get me to do you a favor."

Grayson had the grace to blush. "Okay. I'm sorry. Really. But like you said, this is a big story. Symmes Robinette wasn't just a big deal in Silver Bay. This is national news, sis. I mean, eighteen-term congressman, senior member of the Florida delegation. You could do a great piece about what a Cinderella story his was—a mill kid from Varnedoe, raised by a widowed mother. Joined the Marines and went to Vietnam, law school on the GI Bill, the whole thing." Grayson's normally placid face became animated as she continued her pitch. "This is a guy who literally never made a wrong move. He gets out of law school and makes the right kinds of friends in local politics. The local Dems anoint Symmes to run for and win a seat in the statehouse."

"I remember that," Lorraine said. "The paper endorsed him. Your grandfather had reservations, because Symmes was so young, but Pops said he was a young man with a future."

"I checked," Grayson said. "The only time the *Beacon* didn't endorse Symmes Robinette for office was when he switched parties, back in the eighties."

"It caused quite an uproar when he joined the GOP," Lorraine said. "Hard to believe the Democrats once held such a death grip on politics in this state."

"From the state legislature, he goes to Congress. I'm telling you, this is a great story, Sarah."

"No." Conley shook her head vigorously. "I'll download the video and photos, you can use them with your story, but no, thanks. Not interested."

"Sarah!" G'mama said. "Why on earth not?"

Grayson was leaning forward, her hands clamped on her tanned knees. "If it's about money, I'll pay you. We don't run a lot of freelance, but obviously, this is a whole different set of circumstances. What do you say to five hundred?"

"No, thanks. It's not about the money."

Grayson raised one delicately plucked eyebrow. "Oh. Oh yeah," she said softly. "I forgot about your history with Charlie Robinette. I wouldn't worry about that. Most people never even knew you two were a *thing*."

"Fuck you, Gray," Conley said from behind her gritted teeth.

"Sarah Conley!" G'mama's voice sounded a warning note.

Grayson's lips tightened, and her eyes narrowed. "You don't want your byline in a shitty, hometown weekly, do you? Big-deal Conley Hawkins is just too good for *The Silver Bay Beacon*. Too good for Silver Bay, right?"

"No," Conley said, trying to keep her cool. "I don't know anything about local politics. You've got a reporter; let him write the story. How is this kid Michael going to feel if you hand the biggest story of the year off to your sister, who just shows up—what's that word you used yesterday? Somebody who parachutes in from out of town and assumes she knows best?"

"You let me worry about my staff," Grayson said heatedly. "You don't give a shit about this paper or this town. Or this family. You never have."

"That's enough," Lorraine said suddenly. "It's quite enough."

She grabbed each sibling by the hand, the way she'd done when they were young children, bickering over whose turn it was to ride in the front seat or battling over the remote control.

"I won't have this fighting," she said, her voice steely. "We are family, and I, by God, will not have the two of you at each other's throats like this." Lorraine released their hands. "Now. Sarah? Grayson was absolutely out of line with some of her remarks. Especially that dig about Charlie Robinette. I feel certain that what your sister meant to say was that she couldn't imagine anyone who could do a finer job of writing up a story about this tragic accident. I'm sure she feels that it would be an honor to have a Hawkins byline in our family newspaper again. Isn't that right, Grayson?"

Grayson picked at the cuticle on her right thumb until it started to bleed. "Yeah," she muttered. "Something like that."

"Good," G'mama said. "So that's settled. "Sarah will write a first-person piece about Symmes Robinette's death for next week's paper."

"What?" Conley started to object, but her grandmother quickly shushed her.

"You've been bored and restless practically since the minute you got back home. This will give you something constructive to do with your time."

"But I've never covered Florida politics—"

"Then you'd better get started doing your research," G'mama said. She picked a slice of lime from her drink and nibbled at the rind.

Conley knew she'd been beaten. So much for her plan to loll on the beach and sip fruity umbrella drinks. "Okay," she said, putting her drink down. "If you need me, I'll be upstairs in my room, looking up Symmes Robinette in the *Congressional Record*."

"And, Grayson?" Lorraine said, turning to her other grandchild.

"Yes, ma'am?"

"You'll pay Sarah $1,000. But that includes the main story and whatever sidebars you two decide are necessary."

"A thousand!" Grayson exclaimed. "That's a full week's payroll for me. What if my other reporters find out I'm paying my sister that kind of money?"

"They won't," Lorraine said serenely. "Your sister knows how to be discreet."

"Okay, but she's gotta do the police blotter too," Grayson said, as she headed for the door.

"One last tiny detail," Lorraine called after her. "From now on, I want Sarah to do rewrites on Rowena's column. We may not be able to fire her, but at the very least, we can make Hello, Summer literate and accurate."

Conley was standing by the wide french doors that separated the porch from the living room. "What? No, absolutely not. I can't be baby-sitting that old lady."

"Rowena won't stand for that," Grayson said. "You know what she's like."

"I'm sure you'll figure out a way to make it sound like a great opportunity," Lorraine said. She held out her glass and jiggled the half-melted ice cubes. "But before you go, dear, fix me another sunsetter, would you? That last one tasted awfully light on the vodka."

12

Winnie stood at the huge, old, cast-iron kitchen sink peeling shrimp, with Opie directly underfoot while Lorraine sat at the kitchen table working a crossword puzzle. The turquoise transistor radio was perched on the windowsill, and they were listening to the news on NPR.

"Hey, shug," G'mama said when Conley walked into the kitchen with her laptop. She pointed at the radio. "Buddy Bright just announced that Symmes Robinette was killed in an accident in his home district. But 'no further details are available.'"

"That was fast," Conley said. "Hey, do we not have Wi-Fi here? I've been upstairs trying to get online."

"No Wi-Fi, no cable television, no dishwasher," Winnie grumbled. She pointed at the rust-tinged water trickling from the kitchen faucet. "Might as well be living in a covered wagon out here."

"I meant to ask you what's going on with the water after I showered this morning," Conley said. "There's hardly any water pressure upstairs, and what water there is looks kinda weird."

"It's an old house with old pipes," Lorraine said. "You've gotten spoiled living in Atlanta."

"You want some supper?" Winnie asked, ignoring her employer. "I was just fixing to holler up at you." She placed a plate with sliced hard-boiled eggs, shredded iceberg lettuce, and a mound of shrimp in the center of the table, then spooned pale coral remoulade sauce over the salad.

"I guess." Conley took a seat across from her grandmother and poured a glass of iced tea from the pitcher in the center of the table.

Lorraine set aside her puzzle book and watched as Conley spooned salad onto her plate and began eating.

"Are you mad at me for making you work for your sister?"

Conley edged some of the shrimp salad onto a saltine cracker and chewed before answering. "A little bit. Yeah. Grayson resents me. She resents my success. I really think working for her is a terrible idea."

"I know," Lorraine said calmly.

"You do?"

"Yes. Your sister also resents the fact that she's been stuck here in Silver Bay all these years, doing a job she never wanted, trying to keep a family business afloat and having to look after a cantankerous grandmother instead of having power lunches—whatever those are—and working for a white-shoe law firm anyplace but here."

"Cantankerous? That's putting it mildly," Winnie remarked, joining them at the table.

"Hush," Lorraine said. "Look," she went on. "I didn't want to burden you with this, but now that you're here and between jobs, as it were, you might as well know. This is make-or-break time for the *Beacon*. For all of us in this business. We—that is, Grayson and I—could really use your help."

"How bad is it?" Conley asked, shocked to hear her grandmother asking for help.

Lorraine nibbled at a bit of shrimp. "Our circulation has never been this low before. Ever. Grayson's done everything she knows to do, but she tells me this new generation doesn't read newspapers. That's not how they get their news."

"I know," Conley said sadly. "Print journalism seems to be a dying form. Digital is the future. Or at least, it was supposed to be."

"Advertising is the one thing that keeps us going," Lorraine said. "Of course, it's nowhere near what it used to be. Green's is long gone, and we don't have the used-car advertising we used to get, thanks to that damn Craigslist, but we do have a few loyal longtime advertisers. The IGA, the hardware store, and there's the new Dollar Holler, and they buy the occasional preprint ad inserts, so that helps." She pointed a finger at her granddaughter. "Anyway, since you're here, what's the harm in writing a few stories for the *Beacon*?"

"You really think Grayson is going to like anything I write?" Conley asked, scowling.

"Yes. She may resent you, but your sister is a pragmatist. She'll never admit it to your face, but she knows how good you are. She read every word of that series you did for the Atlanta paper."

"She did?"

"We both did. We have an online subscription to the *AJC*. Or we did. Sarah, we were both so proud of the work you did, and winning that Polk Award, well, I kept wishing Pops were still alive."

"Think he would have put it on the front page of the *Beacon*?"

Winnie scoffed. "That old man? You were always his little pet. He woulda put out a whole special edition."

"Okay," Conley said, resigned to her fate. "Enough with the flattery. I don't really have a choice here. Since we don't have Wi-Fi, and the word's out about the congressman's death, I guess I'd better get busy. I'm gonna run into town and use the Wi-Fi at the house. Okay?"

"That's fine," G'mama said. "Just promise you won't stay out until three again."

On the way into town, Conley made a detour to the Bronson County Sheriff's Office.

Varnedoe, the county seat, was an even smaller town than Silver Bay, with two stoplights and a business district that consisted of a single block of stores and office buildings that clustered around a courthouse square dominated by a Civil War–era cannon and a marble plinth serving as a memorial to the county's soldiers killed in the two world wars. The streetlights were on, bathing the empty landscape in a melancholy yellow glow.

The sheriff's office was a single-story, tan-brick building on the east side of the courthouse square, dwarfed by a magnolia tree that seemed to have swallowed up half the building.

A lone police cruiser was parked on the street out front. Conley found the deputy on duty sitting behind a counter separated from the lobby entrance by a sheet of bulletproof glass.

He looked up from the computer monitor he'd been staring at. "Can I help you?"

He was in his early forties, with blond hair fading to gray. The name-plate fastened to his khaki uniform shirt said he was J. DuPuy.

"Yes," she said, her manner crisply professional. "I'm Conley Hawkins, from the *Beacon*, and I'd like to see the incident report for Symmes Robinette's accident yesterday."

He tilted his head and frowned. "The *Beacon*? What's that?"

"*The Silver Bay Beacon*."

"Y'all still got a paper over there?" He chuckled at his own joke.

"Just the oldest weekly newspaper in the state," Conley said. "And I'd like to see that incident report. Please."

"I'd have to ask the sheriff if that kind of thing is authorized," DuPuy said. "You can check back tomorrow."

"Police reports are a matter of public record in Florida," Conley said. "The sheriff's office is required by law to make them available— and in a timely manner."

"That so?" He raised one eyebrow.

She was doing a slow burn, trying not to let him bait her. "Look, we both know the law here. Why do you want to hassle me? I'm like you. I'm doing my job."

"How'd you hear about the congressman?" he asked.

"It was on the radio. And as it happens, my friend and I were the first ones on the scene. We called 911 and tried to get him out of the car, but it was already smoking when we got there."

That piqued his interest. "What'd you say your name was?"

"Conley Hawkins," she repeated. "From the *Beacon*."

He began typing on the computer's keyboard. After a moment, he nodded and silently read the document on the screen.

"Okay. I see here that the patrol officer interviewed you and your friend. Kelly?"

"Yes. Sean Kelly."

"Three fifteen in the morning? What were y'all doing out running around that time of night?"

She chewed the inside of her cheek. "What was the congressman doing out running around at that time of night? He's what, in his seventies?"

"The sheriff's looking into that," DuPuy said. "Now what about you?"

"What's that got to do with anything? I'm a member of the media, and I've requested that report. Which you are obliged to hand over to me."

"You got any ID? I mean, how do I know you're who you say you are?" Deputy DuPuy was really enjoying himself now.

Conley passed her driver's license through the small slot in the window.

He studied it like it was a blood-spattered knife instead of a laminated driver's license. "This says you live in Atlanta."

"I did. Until this week. Now I live in Silver Bay. Can I get that incident report, please? I'm on a deadline."

He gave her a stern look. "You'll need to get yourself a Florida driver's license, you know. Now that you've moved here."

Haven't had a Florida license since I was twenty-one, and I ain't getting one anytime soon again, she thought.

"I won't be here that long, but thanks," she said impatiently. "This is sort of a . . . temporary arrangement. I really need to get back to work now. Okay?"

"Says here your name is Sarah," DuPuy passed the driver's license back to her.

"It's my first name, but I go by my middle name." She looked over at him. "How about you, Deputy DuPuy? What's the *J* stand for?"

Jerk? Jerkwater? Jerk-off? she wondered.

"James. Not Jim or Jimmy. Just James."

"Okay, James. I really need that report."

"It's *Deputy DuPuy* to you, *Sarah.*"

He tapped some keys, and she heard the whir of a printer coming from beneath the counter. He stapled four sheets of paper together. "There's a fee for copying. A dollar a sheet. Think your paper can afford it?"

Probably not.

She handed over the bills, and he handed her the incident report. There was a wooden bench bolted to the wall opposite the counter window. Conley sat on the bench and skimmed through the report.

Not much here she didn't already know. The Escalade, or what was left of it after the body was removed and the fire was extinguished, had been towed to Wiley's Garage. Symmes Robinette's body had been transported to Gulf Regional Hospital, and then to Apalachicola, to the regional medical examiner's lab.

Her own name and contact information—and Skelly's—were part of the report's narrative, which was signed by good old W. R. Poppell.

Conley went back to the front counter. "I'm going to need to speak to your sheriff. When will he be available?"

DuPuy didn't look up from the computer. "The sheriff doesn't like to talk to reporters as a rule."

"Well, he's gonna have to make an exception this time," she said. "This is a national story. Symmes Robinette was a public figure."

DuPuy shook his head. "Sheriff Goggins will be in tomorrow at eight. You can leave your number, and I'll pass it along. That's the best I can do."

Conley hadn't covered the police beat since her early days working for a crappy weekly in Belvedere, Louisiana, but things hadn't changed much in the intervening years. Cops were still notoriously close-mouthed, even antagonistic to members of the press. She had no doubt that she'd be calling the sheriff, repeatedly, starting first thing in the morning.

She stopped at the Silver Bay Police Department on her way back from Varndoe to skim through the week's incident reports, before driving back to G'mama's house on Felicity Street. When she unlocked the door and stepped inside, the only sound was the loud ticking of the antique grandfather clock in the dimly lit front hallway.

As soon as she'd set up the laptop, she anxiously skimmed her email entries, hoping to find responses to her job queries. Nothing.

Too soon, she told herself. *Don't be so pathetic. Don't be so needy. Don't be so desperate.*

She opened her browser and began to immerse herself in the life and times of Charles Symmes Robinette, which, up until two nights ago, had seemingly been made up of a remarkable combination of good fortune, good timing, and shrewd friendships. Some details she already knew; others were a revelation.

As Grayson had pointed out, Symmes's story had the makings of a small-town fairy tale. According to his official congressional biography, he'd been born in 1943 and grew up in Griffin County. His father was a World War II vet who'd worked as a long-haul trucker.

Conley did some quick math. Symmes Robinette had been seventy-seven. She scrolled back and scrutinized his most recent campaign photo with a now-jaundiced eye. He'd obviously started dyeing his hair sometime in the last couple of decades and, in the portrait anyway, augmented it with an artfully arranged toupee. Maybe, she thought, he'd also had some work done? Plastic surgery, she knew, wasn't just for fading movie stars.

Young Symmes was only ten when his father died of heart disease. His mother, Marva Robinette, went to work as a secretary in a local textile plant, and when Symmes was sixteen, she got remarried to the much-older manager of the plant.

Symmes played high school football and baseball and graduated at age eighteen. He worked in a textile mill and at other menial jobs and took some classes at a junior college before enlisting in the Marines in 1964. He'd served two tours in Vietnam, then returned to Florida in 1968. He went to college and eventually law school, both at Florida State University in Tallahassee, on the GI Bill.

He'd won a Florida senate seat in 1978. According to what she'd read in the *Tallahassee Democrat,* he was already being touted as a potential gubernatorial candidate when, conveniently, the U.S. representative for the Thirty-fifth District dropped dead shortly into his fourth term in office—which was how Symmes earned the unfortunate statehouse nickname "the Symmes Reaper."

She found an old feature story from *The Washington Post*'s Lifestyles section, showing photos of the Robinette family at a White House Easter Egg Roll during the Reagan administration.

Symmes had to have been nearly forty-five in the photo, and Conley noted, not for the first time, how much younger Vanessa Robinette appeared to be—maybe half her husband's age?

Conley scowled down at the image of the adorable, towheaded Charlie Robinette in his mama's arms.

"Behold, the Little Prince," she muttered.

She read on for another hour, making notes of Robinette's career in the U.S. House—he'd served on the Appropriations, Agriculture, and Veteran's Affairs committees and, she discovered, his name had been briefly mentioned as a possible vice presidential candidate for George H. W. Bush.

Symmes had excelled at bringing home the bacon for his district, managing to snag tens of millions of dollars of federal funding for military bases, interstate improvements, and even an agriculture research station at his alma mater, which had been named in his honor.

A sterling citizen, she thought, yawning. It was nearly midnight, and the lack of sleep was starting to wreak havoc with her concentration.

She was powering down her laptop when she heard a light knock at the front door. Peeping out from behind the dining room curtains, she recognized the man standing on the doorstep, holding a bottle of beer in each hand.

"Is this the Silver Bay version of Uber Eats?" she asked, opening the door.

"I was taking out the trash at my mom's house when I saw the light on over here," Skelly said, looking slightly embarrassed. "You said y'all were moving out to the beach today, so I thought I'd just check up, make sure Miss Lorraine's house wasn't being burgled."

"Do you always serve beer to the burglars on this block?"

"Just the cute ones." He handed her one of the bottles. It was icy to the touch.

"Wanna come in?"

Skelly stepped back toward the edge of the porch and looked out at the deserted street. "Maybe we could sit out here?" he asked, gesturing at the rocking chairs. "If Mom wakes up and I'm not there, she's liable to get confused and wander outside looking for me."

They sat on the rockers and uncapped the beers, clinking the bottles together in a silent toast.

"She's that bad, huh?" Conley asked.

"Oh yeah," Skelly said. "It's weird. Some days, she's fine. Insists on going to the store with me, putting on her lab coat. She greets old customers, even talks about their prescriptions. She still thinks she's running the store. Other days, she doesn't recognize me, can't figure out how to put on her own shoes. Some days, she thinks I'm my dad. Other times, she thinks I'm her own father."

"I don't know what to say," Conley said.

"Nothing to say." He tipped his bottle to his lips and drank.

"Hey, did you hear about Symmes Robinette?" he asked. "He was the guy. In the wreck."

"I did. In fact, Grayson and G'mama ganged up and browbeat me into doing a story for the *Beacon*. That's why I'm here tonight. We don't have Wi-Fi at the Dunes, and I needed to start doing research for the obit."

Skelly rocked backward, crossing one leg over the other. "Too bad you can't talk to my mom. She went to high school with Toddie, you know."

"Who's Toddie?"

"Toddie Robinette. Symmes's first wife."

"For real?" Conley sat up straight. "I've been in there doing research on Symmes for a couple of hours. I never saw anything about a first wife."

He shrugged. "I think they kept the split real quiet when it happened. I don't know much about her, just that Mom used to cuss every time anybody mentioned Symmes's name. She was never interested in politics, but after the divorce, she by God made sure she went to the polls and voted against him every time he ran for reelection."

"Verrrry interesting," Conley said. "Fascinating."

"See?" Skelly said. "Silver Bay's got all kinds of shit going on, if you just know where to look."

13

Skelly sat with his back against the white-painted columns on Lorraine's front porch, gazing up at the sky. An owl hooted from the top of an ancient pecan tree that shaded the far end of the house. "It's sure a pretty night. Clear as a bell. I bet you don't see this kind of night in Atlanta, with all the lights of the city around."

Conley stole a glance at her old friend's profile. There were fine lines etched around his eyes, and she could see flecks of silver in Skelly's beard.

"No," she agreed, inhaling the scent of the night-blooming jasmine that wound around the wrought iron porch railing. "To tell you the truth, I can't remember the last time I even looked up to see the night sky in Atlanta."

"Everything all right out at the beach when you finally got there?" he asked.

"Yeah. Well, actually, it was kind of sad. The Dunes seems so run-down, and G'mama has me kind of worried. I didn't want to believe Gray, but G'mama really has started to slow down. This year, she said she and Winnie want to stay downstairs in the bunk rooms. She made out like it was because of Winnie's bad hip, but I think she really doesn't want to have to go up and down those stairs all the time. She insisted that I take her old room on the top floor."

"How old is Miss Lorraine?"

"It's a state secret. Eighty something?"

"Count yourself lucky that she's in as good a shape as she is," Skelly said. "My mom is only sixty-eight, and some days, she can't figure out how to button her own shirt or fasten a bra."

"Oh, Skelly." Conley touched his knee. "Don't tell me you have to—"

"Not yet, thank God," he said, smiling ruefully. "I hired an aide who comes in every day to help her bathe and get dressed. I bought her a bunch of ladies' undershirts, the kind we always used to call *wifebeaters*? She's awful skinny now, so it's not like she really needs a bra. And then I finally just gave away all her blouses and tops with buttons, and now she wears T-shirts that she can just pull on. And pants with elastic."

"Pretty resourceful," Conley said.

"She cried when she saw I'd cleaned out her closet," Skelly said. "She keeps asking me what happened to all her pretty church dresses and high-heel shoes."

"Your mama was always the most stylish woman in town," Conley said. "I always used to love her clothes."

"I've got three big trash bags at home if you need some church dresses," he said. "I still don't have the heart to just throw 'em out."

"Your mama was like a size 4," Conley said. "I couldn't get in one of her dresses if my life depended on it."

"I doubt that."

"Hey," she said, deciding it was time to switch up the topic of discussion. "I detoured by the Bronson County Sheriff's Office on the way into town earlier to pick up the police report on Symmes Robinette's accident."

"Oh yeah? Anything interesting?"

"Not really. I'm hoping to talk to the sheriff in the morning. Merle Goggins. You know him?"

Skelly shook his head.

"I need to find out if the cops have any idea of what caused that wreck. We sure didn't see any cars coming or going, right?"

"Right."

"And then, the obvious question is, what was a seventy-seven-year-old man doing cruising around way out in the boonies at that hour? The police report said Robinette's house is someplace called Sugar Key. Where's that? I've never heard of it before."

"It's a new *gated community* some developer built out at the end of Pelican Point," Skelly said. "Very ritzy. Very exclusive. There's an eighteen-hole golf course and a swim and tennis facility under construction, but only about nine or ten houses have been sold so far. From what I've heard, the cheapest house starts at around two mil."

"Huh. From what I remember, Pelican Point has to be at least thirty miles from where we found that wreck," Conley said. "And that's mighty rich real estate for a Podunk place like Silver Bay. I wouldn't have guessed there were that many folks with that kind of money living in this part of the state."

"Believe it," Skelly said. "They keep it low-key, but they're around. I hear the CEO of GulfBanc has a second home out there, and a venture capital guy from Birmingham lives there full-time now. And of course Miles Schoendienst."

"The railroad guy? From Atlanta?"

"Yeah. You know him?"

"I know *of* him. He's a big political donor—supports both Democrats and Republicans, depending on the issue."

"Huh," Skelly said. "So that's just Schoendienst's vacation house? Damn! It's huge. Must be at least ten thousand square feet. Right at the point where the bay meets the Gulf. But it's so far off the road, you can only see it from a boat. It looks like a Spanish castle."

"You party with the likes of Miles Schoendienst?" Conley asked, only half joking. "The drugstore business must be in way better shape than weekly newspapers."

"Not," Skelly said. "Family-owned pharmacies like mine are a dying breed. We can't compete with CVS and Walgreens. Not to mention the online pharmacies. I've been out to Sugar Key exactly twice—both times, come to think of it, were to drop off prescriptions for Symmes Robinette."

"You still make deliveries?"

"For old customers, yeah. Mom always said service was what separated us from the chain stores. We don't advertise it, but I make deliveries if somebody requests it."

Conley was intrigued. "What kind of stuff were you delivering to Symmes Robinette?"

"Nice try. You know about HIPAA regulations, right? There's such a thing as patient privacy."

"But this patient is dead," Conley pointed out.

"Doesn't matter. Let's talk about something else, okay? I shouldn't even have mentioned that he was a customer."

"Was Robinette sick?" Conley knew she was pushing, but she couldn't help herself. "Maybe that's why he crashed the Escalade."

"No comment," Skelly said firmly.

"You're no fun."

"That's what my ex always said too."

"Ouch. From the research I did earlier, I saw that Robinette's house in D.C. was in Georgetown. I didn't look up the tax records yet, but there's nothing cheap in Georgetown."

"What's your point?" Skelly asked. "Symmes was a lawyer. All lawyers are rich, right?"

"He's been in elected office for decades. Hasn't practiced law in forty years. So where's a small-town lawyer come up with the kind of money to own millions of dollars' worth of real estate?"

"It's not against the law to be a rich politician. Maybe he's done really well in the stock market. Are you suggesting Robinette was some kind of crook?" Skelly asked.

"Not suggesting anything. Yet. I'm just doing what my old editor called *turning over rocks*. To see what crawls out from under, you know?"

Skelly fixed her with a stern expression. "This isn't Atlanta, Conley. Symmes Robinette was a hero to a lot of people around here. With the exception of my mama. You need to be real careful about what kind of rocks you turn over in Silver Bay. It's a small town, and people take this stuff real personal."

"So . . . don't go poking any bears? Is that what you're saying?"

"If you want to put it that way."

"I'll be discreet, but if there's a story here, I'm gonna find it, Skelly. That's what I do. It's the only thing I know how to do."

"Fair enough," he said. "But what happened to kicking back at the beach? Hanging out with your grandmother?"

"Who says I can't do both? Speaking of family," she asked, trying to sound casual, "what's up with the Little Prince these days?"

"Charlie? He's a lawyer in the old man's law firm. He's a customer at the drugstore. I see him at the country club occasionally, although I haven't been over there since, well, since Danielle left. I know he hangs with the courthouse crowd. Very preppy. I think he's what they call an *up-and-comer*."

"So a chip off the old block. I wonder—"

"Oh shit!" Skelly jumped to his feet. "Mama?"

A tiny, wraithlike figure walked briskly down the sidewalk in their direction. She was barefoot, wearing an oversize white undershirt, and was, from what Conley could see, naked from the waist down.

"Patrick?" June called. Her voice was startlingly loud and shrill, coming from such a diminutive body. She stood outside the wrought iron fence surrounding Lorraine's yard, searching for her long-dead husband.

Skelly rushed to his mother's side, taking her by the arm. "Mama, what are you doing out here? What happened to your clothes?"

"I'll go get her something to wrap up in," Conley said. She went inside and came out with the first thing at hand, a crocheted throw G'mama kept in a basket by the hall closet.

She flew down the steps and handed the blanket to Skelly, who struggled to wrap the throw around his mother's waist.

"Patrick?" June Kelly gave her son a stern look. "I've been calling and calling you. Your supper is ready. Where have you been?"

"I'm sorry, Mama," Sean said. "I just came down here for a moment. Let's go on home now and get you back to bed. It's pretty late."

June brushed her son aside, letting the throw fall to the grass. Conley couldn't help but stare. What had happened to her beautiful, stylish, accomplished neighbor? Sean's mother's face was smooth and unlined, but she wore grotesquely smeared red lipstick, and her thinning white hair stood out from her head like a barbed wire halo.

"Who's that?" June Kelly demanded, pointing at Conley. "Your new girlfriend?"

Skelly shot her an apologetic look as he tried again to cover his mother's exposed lower body.

"This is Sarah Conley Hawkins, Mama. You know Sarah. She's Chet and Melinda's daughter. Lorraine's granddaughter. Come back to town to visit."

"Don't lie to me, Patrick." June batted his hands away. "Is this your girlfriend? One of the nurses at the hospital? Or one of your so-called patients? How dare you!"

June Kelly's brilliant blue eyes searched Conley's face, trying to make a connection. Conley thought about all the times Miss June had treated her to a free ice cream cone at the soda fountain. She thought about the pharmacist's immaculately starched white lab coats with her name stitched in cursive letters over the breast pocket that she'd worn over her pretty dresses. June Kelly, RPh.

"It's me, Miss June," Conley said, taking the older woman's fragile arm. "Sarah Conley. Sean's friend from down the street. Remember me?"

"Sarah? From down the street?"

"Yes, ma'am," Conley said. She picked up the throw and fastened it, sari-style, looping one end over the older woman's shoulder and knotting it securely in front before taking a step backward.

Skelly mouthed a mute "Thanks." He took his mother's arm and gently turned her back toward the sidewalk. "Let's go home. Okay? I can't wait to see what you fixed for dinner."

"Pot roast! Your favorite," June said cheerfully. "And cherry pie."

They were halfway down the sidewalk. "Thanks, Conley. I'll bring the blanket back tomorrow." Skelly's voice floated in the warm evening air.

She went back inside and tried to resume her research on Symmes Robinette. Many of the references to Robinette focused on his political life, his campaigns, and his accomplishments. There was precious little about his life back in his home district in Silver Bay.

She picked up her phone and hesitated. It was late; maybe her sister was in bed. She texted instead.

Hey, Gray. Doing research for the obit on Robinette. Can't find any online articles from The Beacon. *Help.*

Her phone rang as soon as she'd finished sending the text.

"Hey. Where are you?" Grayson asked. Conley could hear the clatter of glassware and voices in the background. Maybe a television too.

"I'm in town at G'mama's house. There's no Wi-Fi at the beach. Where are you?"

"No place special. You're not gonna find any online articles from the *Beacon*."

"We're not digitized?"

"No, we're not digitized. In case you haven't noticed, this is a small-town weekly. If you want to search the back issues for stories on Robinette, you'll have to go over to the office and look through the bound volumes."

"Ugh. That'll take forever. I don't even know what I'm really looking for. So I'm guessing there's no index either, right?"

"Nope." Grayson sounded amused that she would even ask. "Anything specific you're looking for?"

"Everything. Local color. Family. Hey, did you know Symmes Robinette was married before?"

"Before what?"

"Before Vanessa, who, by the way, is probably twenty years younger than the late congressman."

"Maybe. I don't know. You'll have to ask G'mama. She's always up on all the latest dirt. Or better yet, get with Rowena."

"Ugh. Rowena. Say, Gray, what do you know about the sheriff over in Bronson County?"

"Merle? He's only been in office a couple years. But he seems okay. He's black, you know."

"So?"

"So it might not be newsworthy in Atlanta, but it is around here."

"Do you know him?"

"Sort of. We're in Rotary together."

"Good. Call him up first thing in the morning and ask him to give your new star reporter a phone call. His deputy isn't what I'd call helpful."

"What do you want to talk to him about?"

Conley rolled her eyes in frustration. "Symmes Robinette. Duh. The accident was in your sheriff buddy's jurisdiction. I need to know why Symmes was thirty miles from his ritzy oceanfront home at three in the morning, and I need to know the official cause of death."

"Call me stupid, but isn't his death gonna be from being burned alive in a car wreck?"

You are *stupid,* Conley thought. "We don't know that. There were no other cars around. I want to know what caused the wreck and whether he was alive when the fire started."

"Okay, yeah. That makes sense," Grayson said.

"I also need to talk to the district medical examiner. I don't suppose you're in Rotary with him too?"

"Nope. But maybe George McFall would know something."

"From the funeral home?"

"Yeah, if the body's been released. George McFall has probably seen more corpses in his lifetime than any M.D. you can name."

"But what if there's, like, criminal evidence?"

"Then I think the medical examiner calls in the state crime lab. But you're not thinking there's something criminal going on with Symmes's death, right?"

"I don't know yet. It's just . . . odd. Do you think George would talk to me?"

"He'd talk to you all day long about Florida State football or the evils of cremation versus burial in a $5,000 coffin, but I have no idea if he'd talk to you about what killed Symmes Robinette," Grayson said.

"Is he in Rotary with you?"

"Yeah. He's president this year."

"Great. How about you work your way down the Rotary membership roll, call up all your good-old-boy buddies in town, and ask them really nicely to talk to your sister about how Symmes Robinette died."

"There are lots of women in Rotary now, you know. It's not just men like it used to be."

If she stayed on the phone with her sister much longer, Conley thought, she might pull her eye muscles from rolling them so hard and so often. If that was possible. This was something she'd make sure to ask George McFall about.

"Good to know," she said. "Do you have Rowena's phone number?"

"Yeah."

"Could you please text it to me?"

"I will, but you can't call her this late at night."

"Duly noted," Conley said. "One more question. When's payday?"

"Friday. But we usually hold a first paycheck back for new hires."

"Not this time, Gray," Conley said. "Not if you want my byline in next week's paper."

14

HELLO, SUMMER BY ROWENA MEIGS
MAY 1986

Reliable sources are saying that our own U.S. Representative Symmes Robinette has filed for divorce from his high school sweetheart and bride of twenty-four years, the lovely and charming Emma "Toddie" Sanderson Robinette.

Toddie Robinette is a beloved member of Silver Bay society, where she has been active in the Women's Assistance Guild, the Silver Bay Presbyterian Church, and the League of Women Voters. She is past president of the Silver Bay Elementary School PTA and the Griffin County High School Athletic Association.

Although details of the split are being kept verrrrrry quiet, Toddie's friends are heartbroken for her. The Robinettes' darling home on Spruce Street has been put on the market, and over the summer, Toddie and the children, Hank and Rebecca, will move out to the country.

Your correspondent has been hearing whispers that Symmes Robinette, who spends most of his time these days attending to government business in Washington, D.C., has an especially close "friendship" with a vivacious young brunette aide in his congressional office. We will, of course, report any forthcoming details as they emerge.

In the meantime, the good old days of summer have returned with a vengeance. Mr. and Mrs. V. B. Connors entertained members of the smart set with a dinner dance at the Silver Bay Country Club Saturday night. (V. B., or Bubba, as he is known to one and all, is the newly elected president of the state bar association, and his darling wife, Suzan, is a phenom on the tennis courts!) Tables were resplendent with gorgeous arrangements of pink mums, white tea roses, baby's breath, and cymbidium orchids. Ladies were chic in the latest summer silks and florals, and their spouses looked elegant in white dinner jackets. Is there anything handsomer than a Southern gentleman in a white dinner jacket? Your correspondent was smitten, y'all!

Conley leafed through the next few pages of the 1986 bound volume of the *Beacon* for more tidbits about Symmes Robinette's divorce, but as luck would have it, the issue was the last one in the volume she'd dragged from the sagging bookcase in the corner of the cluttered newspaper office.

Sighing, she went back to the bookshelf to look for the next volume. It was a hopeless chore. The *Beacon* had been in existence for over a hundred years—so there were dozens and dozens of heavy, leather-bound volumes—none of which were shelved in any kind of order. She spent the next half hour running a finger over the dusty spines of the books, each of which was stamped in gold with the volume number and year, but the search was useless.

She heard voices coming from the reception area.

Lillian King and Michael Torpy were settling themselves in at their desks. Each had a cup of takeout coffee and a paper plate holding a sausage biscuit.

"You guys work on Saturdays?" she asked.

"Not my idea," Lillian said. "We're doing a special end-of-the-school-year advertising section."

"Really?"

"Yeah," Michael said, looking up from his computer terminal. "Grayson had the idea to sell ads to the families of all the graduating seniors, so now I gotta come up with fascinating stories about all these kids."

"Money's money," Lillian said sharply. "Those ads are paying our salaries."

"Hey, Lillian?" Conley said. "I need the next bound volume for 1986, but it seems to be MIA. Got any clues where it might be?"

"No telling," Lillian said. "People come in and out all the time wanting to look through the back issues, but nobody around here ever puts 'em back in any kind of order."

Conley gestured at the shelves, which looked like they were about to collapse under the weight of the books. "Is that all of 'em?"

Michael rolled his chair away from his desk. "I think I've seen some more of those books somewhere around here. Did you look in the supply closet?"

"Thanks. I'll check there," Conley said. She pushed the door of the closet open and flipped the light switch. The walls of the room were lined with homemade wooden shelves that she knew had been the handiwork of her late grandfather. The shelves held boxes of office supplies that Conley reckoned had also been there since her grandfather's time and which had sadly outlived him and modern-day journalism—boxes of typewriter ribbons, reams of yellowing newsprint cut into copy paper—from the days when the staff typed their stories on first manual and then electric typewriters, spiral-bound stenographer's notebooks, and boxes and boxes of waxy red copy pencils that had once been used to mark up reporters' copy.

She spotted four or five bound volumes shoved haphazardly on the shelves, but they were all from the 1960s. She sighed heavily and went back to her desk.

"Any other ideas about where missing volumes might be?"

"Look in Grayson's office," Lillian advised. "Anything goes missing around here, I can usually find it in that rat's nest of hers if I look long enough."

Conley tried the door and looked up. "It's locked."

"Here," Lillian said, producing a key from her desk drawer. "But don't let on that I gave you that. She likes to think that office is her inner sanctum."

Grayson's desk was stacked high with back issues of the *Beacon,* file folders, page proofs of color ads, coffee cups, and soft drink cans. There was a bookcase in the corner, bulging with old books that Conley knew had been her grandfather's, but no bound copies of the *Beacon.*

It struck her how much Grayson had changed since their childhood. Conley had always been the messy, creative one whose bedroom was one empty cereal box short of a dumpster, while her older sister had insisted on keeping her own bedroom spotlessly clean and tidy. Back when they were kids, the surest way to make Grayson nuts was to trespass in her room, borrow an item of clothing, and bring it back stained, torn, or wrinkled—which was usually the state of every item of clothing Conley owned.

The only thing of interest in her sister's messy, disorganized office, as far as Conley was concerned, was the sofa. The brown leather upholstery was old and cracked and peeling. A pillow and a lightweight cotton blanket had been tossed on one end of the sofa, and draped over the arm was a pair of yoga pants and a sports bra.

"Huh," she said aloud. She opened the door to the tiny bathroom. A makeup bag was perched on the top of the toilet tank, and a glass held a toothbrush and a tube of toothpaste. The back of the door held more of what she recognized as Grayson's clothes; in fact, it looked like several days' worth of clothes. Obviously, her sister had been sleeping in the office. The question was, why?

"Interesting," she muttered before backing out of the office and re-locking the door.

She went back to her desk and began typing up the police blotter, rolling her eyes at the mostly innocent nature of the "crime wave" the town had experienced the week before.

THURSDAY, Apr. 30–4:40 p.m.—ANIMAL CRUELTY—Officer responded to call of animal cruelty at Smitty's Bait & Tackle, at Silver Bay Marina. On arrival, officer waved down by complainant Annalisa Sorenson, 19, who stated that bait shop operators were torturing live animals (bait fish) by penning them up in bait tanks. Officer advised bait fish not covered by current animal cruelty statutes. Bait shop owners requested complainant leave premises and stop harassing fishermen.

FRIDAY, MAY 1.—THEFT FROM VEHICLE—Silver Bay Country Club. Victim, reports his vehicle, 2019 Mercedes Sedan, was entered in parking lot of Silver Bay Country Club, sometime between 8 p.m. and 11:30 p.m. Victim stated car, which was unlocked, was ransacked and valuables removed. Items taken include pair of three-carat diamond and sapphire stud earrings worth estimated $36,500, also insulated Yeti coffee mug, and security transponder for victim's gated community.

SUNDAY, MAY 3.—SUSPECTED DRUG OVERDOSE. Officer and Fire and Rescue Unit dispatched to Griffin County High School football field at 1:40 a.m. Anonymous caller reported apparently unconscious person in parking lot. Officer observed group of teenagers surrounding victim but witnesses scattered upon seeing approach of emergency vehicles. Victim, white female, approximately 15 years old, pale and unresponsive, had vomited. No ID found on victim who was transported to Northwest Florida Memorial emergency room.

"Okay, I'm gonna do it," Conley announced, after she'd shipped the column to Grayson for editing.

"Do what?" Michael looked intrigued. The rookie reporter looked about fifteen. He was lanky, with freckles, wavy reddish hair, and an impossible amount of energy.

"I've got to call Rowena and ask what she knows about Symmes Robinette," Conley said gloomily.

"Cool. I mean, Rowena acts kind of batty, but she always seems to know everything that's going on in town. How old do you think she is?" the kid asked.

"Older than dirt," Lillian volunteered. "And twice as mean."

"Hellooooo," the voice on the other end of the line sang out. "This is Rowena. To whom do I have the pleasure of speaking?"

"Oh, hi, Rowena. This is Conley Hawkins."

"Conley?" There was a long pause at the other end of the line.

"Sarah Conley Hawkins."

"Oh. Sarah. How niiiiice," Rowena trilled. "How are you today? And how is that darlin' grandmother of yours?"

"I'm fine, thanks. G'mama is fine too. I'm calling because I agreed to write the obituary for Symmes Robinette for *the Beacon*—"

"Such a shock!" Rowena said. "My phone has been ringing off the wall since yesterday. In fact, I'm going to dedicate this week's column just to Symmes."

"Great idea," Conley said. "Since you're such an institution in Silver Bay and knew him and his family so well, Grayson thinks it would be a good idea if I picked your brain before I start writing."

"I think that's a wonderful idea," Rowena said. "Would you like to drop by my house for some coffee and doughnuts?"

"That would be really helpful," Conley said.

"Wonderful! I like those maple-bacon-frosted doughnuts they have at the Corner Café. And Tuffy just likes the bacon, so be a dear and bring three of those, plus whatever it is that you young girls eat these days. We'll have a lovely little talk. You know where my house is, don't you?"

"I do," Conley said.

Everybody in town knew Rowena Meigs's house. The Crispin-Meigs House, as it was known, had once been what Rowena herself would have called a showplace, a formerly stately Greek revival mansion with six massive Doric columns marching across a sweeping veranda that looked out on Silver Bay's moss-draped Lee Street, named, of course, for Robert E. Lee, who, according to unreliable local sources, had once spent the night there during the waning days of "the Late Unpleasantness."

Nowadays, the mansion resembled a crumbling wedding cake. Each of the front porch columns seemed to list in a different direction, and the porch itself sagged. The long-neglected front garden featured azaleas that had grown head-high and a towering magnolia tree whose roots had knuckled up the front walkway. The white-brick façade of the house was covered with a fine sheen of green mold.

When she reached the front porch, Conley was startled to see a large raccoon casually dining from a tin pan full of what looked like cat food.

"Shoo!"

The raccoon slinked away into the tall weeds at the edge of the porch.

The front door opened before she could ring the bell.

Rowena was dressed in a pale pink floor-length caftan with pink ostrich feathers outlining the hem, the kind her grandmother would have called a *hostess gown*. Her face was heavily powdered, her lips caked with fuchsia lipstick. She clutched Tuffy tightly under one arm, and in her right hand she held her cane, which today was decorated with a jaunty pink satin bow. "Why, Sarah Hawkins," Rowena trilled. "What a nice surprise."

"Um, you invited me here, Rowena. Remember? I wanted to ask you about Symmes Robinette."

"Of course, you silly girl," Rowena said. "You come right on in here."

The interior of the house was gloomy and dimly lit, but Conley glimpsed faded wallpaper and rows and rows of portraits of even gloomier-faced Meigs ancestors.

"I've set us up in Judge Meigs's office," Rowena said, leading her into a high-ceilinged room with dark paneling. A fireplace took up one wall of the room, and mahogany bookcases lined the other three walls. The room was hot and airless, with a single propped-open window offering the only ventilation.

"Let's sit right here and have a nice chat," Rowena said, using her cane to indicate a spindly, gilt-trimmed settee with faded crimson upholstery. She seated herself in a high-backed leather chair. A mahogany tea table rested between the chairs, and on it was a highly polished silver tea set. Beside the tea service were a pair of delicate bone china cups and saucers and a small jar of Sanka.

Conley sat and handed over the white cardboard box from the Corner Café.

"Oooh, goody!" Rowena said, lifting out a doughnut. "Bacon-maple. My favorite. Now," she said, spooning the Sanka into a cup and adding water from the teapot. "Tell me why your sister thinks I might know something of importance about poor old Symmes Robinette." She handed the teacup to her guest.

Conley took a sip of coffee and immediately wished she hadn't. The "coffee" was boiling hot and thick as maple syrup.

She set the cup on the table. "Grayson says you know everything and everybody in town."

"And where all the bodies are buried too," Rowena said, breaking off a bit of doughnut and feeding it to Tuffy, who was nestled in her lap. Crumbs showered down the front of Rowena's pink gown, and the tiny dog quickly hoovered them up.

"Exactly," Conley said. "I was reading some of your columns in the back issues of the *Beacon* for research—"

"How nice," Rowena said. She pointed at the portrait of the stern-faced, white-bearded man hanging over the fireplace mantel. "That's my great-grandfather-in-law, you know. Judge Culver W. Meigs. He was a highly influential man. Served in the Florida legislature. The party wanted him to run for Congress, but my husband's great-grandmother Lilla put her foot down and said she was not about to let the judge go traipsing off to Washington, D.C., and consort with who knows what kind of people. Did you know that?"

"I didn't," Conley said.

"Oh yes," Rowena said airily. "All the Meigses were dedicated to public service. And I like to think that in some small way, I've carried on the family tradition. I think journalism is a noble calling, don't you, Sarah Hawkins?"

"I do," Conley said. "I was reading your column from 1986, where you broke the news that Symmes was divorcing his first wife. I imagine that caused shock waves back then."

"It was a huge story!" Rowena said. "Absolutely thrilling! All the other reporters around the state were just *furious* that a little ol' society columnist from Silver Bay had scooped them. Your granddaddy was *terrified* I was going to get hired away by the papers in Jacksonville or St. Petersburg."

"I'll bet," Conley said.

"Of course, I wouldn't have dreamed of leaving Silver Bay, which has been the Meigses' home for generations, but your granddaddy didn't know that. I simply told him that I would need a substantial raise to justify staying on at the *Beacon,* and in the end, after a lot of hemming and hawing, I received a ten-dollar-a-week raise."

"Wow," Conley said. The old lady was a master blackmailer and manipulator.

"Which made me the highest-paid staffer on the paper," Rowena said smugly.

"How did you find out about the divorce?" Conley asked.

Rowena took a bite of doughnut and chewed. She dunked the rest of the doughnut in her coffee cup and stirred it around a bit until the pastry dissolved in the hot coffee, which she promptly drank.

Finally, she gave an arch smile. "A true journalist never reveals her sources," she said, giving her guest an exaggerated wink.

"It's been nearly forty years. And Symmes Robinette is dead," Conley pointed out.

"Welllll . . ." Rowena stared up at the ceiling for a moment. Conley followed her gaze and saw that the immense crystal chandelier directly above her head was caked in decades of dust and generations of spiderwebs.

"She passed away a few years ago, so I suppose it wouldn't be breaking a confidence to tell you that it was Myrtis Davis."

"I don't think I know that name," Conley said.

"She was in real estate here for years," Rowena said. "I think she and Toddie were Kappas together at Ole Miss. Or maybe it was Auburn. Myrtis was lovely. A real go-getter. Anyway, I happened to bump into her downtown one day, and she was absolutely distraught. She'd just come from the Robinettes' house. Toddie had called her to say she was selling the house because she and Symmes were getting a divorce and could Myrtis come over and give her an idea of what it should list for."

"Did Toddie tell her the cause of the split-up?"

Rowena gave her an appraising glance. "How old are you, Sarah?"

"It's actually *Conley,* if you don't mind. And I'm thirty-four. Why?"

Rowena shook her head and gave that tinkly laugh again. "I just find it hard to believe that a girl your age can't guess why a middle-aged married man, living alone in a place like Washington, D.C., in a passion pit like the United States House of Representatives, would decide to dump his boring, old, small-town, middle-aged wife."

"There was another woman?"

"How *did* you guess?" Rowena picked up the second doughnut, bit in, and rolled her eyes in ecstasy. "Aren't these just the yummiest doughnuts in the world?"

"Um, I guess."

"Symmes didn't have to look too hard to find himself a newer, younger companion when he got ready to trade in Toddie," Rowena went on. "Vanessa was, what? Twenty-four? Working as a *congressional aide* in his office. My spies told me she was really just a glorified typist."

"In a column you wrote at the time, you referred to a 'vivacious brunette.' Was that Vanessa?"

"None other," Rowena said. "Symmes, the naughty boy, didn't even try to hide the fact that they were carrying on. It was an open secret in Washington. Of course, poor Toddie had no idea. Write this down, Sarah. The wife really is the last to know."

"And that's why they split up? Because he was having an affair?"

"Well," Rowena said, her blue eyes glittering maliciously. "Toddie might could have overlooked a little dalliance. These things do happen. But she really couldn't ignore the fact that Vanessa was pregnant with Symmes's bastard child."

15

Rowena settled back in her chair, waiting to see Conley's reaction to this last gossip bombshell, idly picking bits of bacon from the last remaining doughnut and feeding them to Tuffy, nestled snugly in her lap, the pink bow on the dog's topknot brushing the bottom of the old woman's chin.

"Wow," Conley said finally. She had to let the information sink in. Charlie Robinette was a love child? It made sense, now that she thought about it. "A child born out of wedlock to a sitting congressman's secretary?" she said finally. "While he was still married to his first wife? Stuff like that's not all that uncommon now, but back then, in Silver Bay, it must have caused quite a scandal."

Rowena's fuchsia-caked lips formed a girlish pout. "It would have, but your fuddy-duddy of a grandfather wouldn't print it. The biggest story of my career, and it never saw the light of day."

"Granddaddy?" This was more of a shock than the revelation about Symmes Robinette's secret baby. "I can't believe he would choose to suppress a story just to protect a local politician."

"'We are not the *National Enquirer,* Rowena,'" the columnist said, using fingers as quote marks. "That's what he told me. 'We do not deal in salacious gossip or scurrilous rumors.'"

"That part sounds exactly like Granddaddy," Conley had to admit. Her grandfather had always been a stickler for facts.

"But it wasn't gossip!" Rowena insisted. "I made it my business to get a copy of the baby's birth certificate. I rode the Greyhound bus all the way up to Washington, D.C., and paid for my fare with my own money just to make sure it was true. Charles Symmes Robinette Jr. was born on February 15, 1986. And he weighed nine pounds and seven ounces, so Vanessa could hardly claim he was premature."

Her chin was quivering with indignation at the memory of her suppressed scoop.

"Vanessa and Symmes were married—by the U.S. House of Representatives chaplain, mind you—three months later. The day *after* the divorce from Toddie was finalized."

Conley struggled to put those facts together with what she'd already discovered about Symmes Robinette's marital history. "So it wasn't generally known around town? About the baby?"

"There was talk, of course," Rowena said. "Around the bridge table and at cocktail parties. You know how people talk in a small town like Silver Bay."

Conley's smile was brittle. She knew all too well about the corroding nature of prying eyes and whispered insinuations and always the questions about her own mother's whereabouts, couched in terms of sincere concern from those same bridge players and cocktail partygoers.

"The talk died down after Toddie disappeared," Rowena said. "She never said a word to any of her friends. One day, she and the children just up and got in their station wagon and drove away."

"Surely not," Conley scoffed. "People, especially the wives and children of prominent politicians, don't just vanish."

Rowena sniffed. "I suppose she might have told someone where they were going, but even Myrtis, her real estate agent, swore she didn't know where Toddie and the children relocated."

"And then Vanessa settled into town pretty seamlessly, right? I mean, she's a member of G'mama's church and everything."

"That woman *slithered* into Silver Bay," Rowena said, waggling unkempt eyebrows that resembled a pair of fuzzy white caterpillars. "Some people have short memories. And I suppose, for poor old Toddie, it was a matter of out of sight, out of mind."

Conley glanced down at her watch. She still had several more people to talk to before writing her story for the *Beacon*'s Tuesday deadline.

"I've taken up enough of your time today, Rowena. But I do keep wondering, what was Symmes doing out there in the country so far from home and at that time of night?"

Rowena polished off the third doughnut, chewing rapidly, and Conley realized her hostess had never offered her one.

"I really couldn't say what he was doing. But I have my sources, and you can be sure if I find out, I'll write all about it in *my* column."

Conley picked up her backpack, preparing to leave, when Rowena said, "I wrote a book. Did you know that?"

"No, I didn't. That must have been so exciting for you," Conley said, trying to feign interest.

"Oh yes. It was the most . . . empowering thing I've ever experienced," Rowena gushed. "Would you like a copy?"

"Oh no," Conley said quickly. "I mean, I'd love to read it, but I wouldn't want to put you to any trouble."

The old woman hoisted herself from the chair and tottered over to the wall of bookcases. Opening a cabinet door, she revealed rows and rows of garish pink-jacketed hardback books. She plucked one from the shelf.

"Here it is," she said gaily, thrusting a copy at Conley.

The cover of the book featured the same heavily retouched photo of Rowena Meigs as the one currently used for her column in the *Beacon*, her blond bouffant coiffure an architectural marvel, lavish false eyelashes fluttering, smiling coquettishly into the camera, a pink feather boa draped loosely around her generous décolletage, her wrists, neck, and ears decked with diamonds—or something resembling diamonds. The title was written in flowing purple script: *Rowena Remembers: Secrets of Silver Bay Society*.

"It's a collection of my columns from the *Beacon*," Rowena said. "I had the most marvelous time compiling it. So many wonderful memories." She sighed heavily. "Everyone said it was the most amusing thing they'd ever read. I really think it was the crowning achievement of my journalistic career."

"I can't wait to read it," Conley lied.

"It will tell you everything you need to know about this town. And there are quite a few mentions of Symmes and Toddie, by the way. They were just the most darling couple back then. Before that *woman* came into the picture."

"I'll be sure to look for those mentions," Conley said. She started to tuck the book into her backpack.

"That will be forty dollars, dear," Rowena said. "You can't imagine how much money it costs to publish a book with so many photographs."

Conley returned to the accident site an hour later. The grass and pavement were charred black from the car fire, and bits of broken glass and metal littered the shoulder of the road.

She pulled over, got out of the car, and paced back and forth on the lonely stretch of asphalt, with no real idea of what she was seeking. Both sides of the road were lined with fields with ragged borders of pine trees and palmettos behind barbed wire fencing. A single hawk wheeled through the air, its screech the only jarring note in the pastoral scene. There was nothing remarkable about this place, except that a man had died here a couple of days ago.

Downtown Varnedoe was even sleepier than it had before. Deputy DuPuy reluctantly showed her into the sheriff's office, where she found Merle Goggins sitting behind his desk, peering over half-moon glasses at something on a computer monitor.

"This is the reporter lady I told you about," the deputy said, turning to go.

"Your sister emailed to say I'd be hearing from you, but she didn't mention you'd show up on my doorstep today," the sheriff said.

"I did leave you several voice messages," Conley said pointedly.

Merle Goggins was a trim man, probably in his early fifties. He wore a starched khaki uniform shirt with a brass badge pinned to the breast pocket. His wary smile showed not a hint of remorse.

The office was as spartan as its occupant. The sterile, white, concrete-block walls held a bulletin board with the usual safety posters and departmental announcements, and a glass display case held dozens of embroidered patches from police departments around the country. His desktop contained the computer, a beige telephone, and a framed photograph.

"Sit," Goggins said, pointing to a straight-backed chair opposite the desk.

He pulled a manila file folder from the top desk drawer and opened it. "Grayson said you're writing a story about Representative Robinette. What do you want to know?"

"Cause of death, to start with."

"To be determined. You were at the crime scene that night, so you know the condition of the body."

"Okay," Conley said. "So are you saying there's no chance that you'll get a blood alcohol level or anything like that?"

He shrugged noncommittally.

"Is there anything at all you can tell me about the accident? I mean, it was a mild spring night—no rain, full moon, no traffic that we saw."

"We know," Goggins said.

"Was there any physical evidence at all that you can tell me about?"

"Nope."

Conley decided to try a different tack. "I know Robinette was in his seventies. Have you taken a look at his medical history?"

"We've requested it."

"From whom?"

"I can't get into that."

Conley hadn't written a single word in the reporter's notebook on her lap because Goggins hadn't given her a single fact. "Have you spoken to his family? His wife or son?"

"We've talked to the son, who's a lawyer."

Goggins spread apart the fingers of both hands, laying them flat on the open file. "We're giving Mrs. Robinette time to grieve. As a courtesy to the congressman's legacy."

Conley leaned forward to see the framed photo on the desk. It was of a much younger Merle Goggins, wearing Marine dress blues, standing next to his bride, who was dressed in a short white wedding dress. She got up and studied the framed diplomas on the walls. One was from the FBI Academy, where she knew local law enforcement officials from around the country took all kinds of forensic and investigative classes. The other was a college diploma, for a bachelor's degree in political science, from Oklahoma State University.

She sat back down. "What are you doing here?"

"Me? I'm doing my job. Protecting this community."

"No, I mean *here*. How did you wind up in this Podunk county in the Florida Panhandle?"

He cracked a semi-smile. "My wife is a Cowart. Half the people in this county are related to her. It's how I got elected. After we had our daughter, Elise wanted to raise our children around family. So here we are. And what exactly are you doing here, Sarah Conley Hawkins, formerly of *The Atlanta Journal-Constitution*, working for a Podunk weekly paper in the middle of nowhere Florida?"

"The same thing," Conley said. "I'm sure Grayson told you I'm between jobs. I came home to check on my grandmother, and my sister guilt-tripped me into helping out on this story."

"Not a very interesting assignment, compared to what you're used to. Single-car fatality. No evidence of foul play."

Conley jotted her contact information on a page of her reporter's notebook, ripped it out, and handed it to the sheriff.

"On the contrary. I find this story fascinating. And I'd appreciate it if you'll call me with any new information."

"We'll see," he said.

She was out in the parking lot, about to get into her car, when she heard someone call her name. "Hey, Sarah. Hold on."

It was the sheriff's deputy she'd met that night at the crash scene, hurrying toward her. He was dressed in sweat-stained workout clothes, black spandex bike shorts, and a sleeveless red T-shirt. She couldn't remember his name.

"Oh, hi, um—" She flashed an apologetic smile. "I'm sorry, I'm completely blanking on your name. Skelly's friend, right? Popp?"

"Walter. Poppell. These days, everybody calls me *Walt*. How you doing? Keeping busy?"

He placed a hand on her open car door. Looming over her, his presence was overpowering, as was the combined smell of sweat and a thorough drenching of his pine-scented body spray.

"I'm fine," Conley said, taking a half step backward.

"You look really nice today," Poppell said, letting his glance linger.

"Better than I looked that night out on the highway," she said.

"Yeah. That was sick, right?"

She nodded and slid into the driver's seat. "Good to see you again, Deputy. I'd better get going. Wouldn't want to make you late to work."

He stayed right where he was, with his hand on the car door. "So what are you doing here? I mean, you live over in Silver Bay, right?"

"For now. I'm staying with family. Actually, I was just checking with the sheriff about the victim of the crash."

"Why's that?"

"It's kind of my job," she said. "I'm doing a story for the newspaper."

"That's cool. You're doing a story about the wreck, huh? I guess you already know it's that senator dude."

"He was actually in the U.S. House, but yes, that's the plan. If I can get somebody to talk to me."

Poppell glanced over his shoulder at the department's front door. "The sheriff didn't talk to you?"

"He talked, he just didn't tell me anything I didn't already know."

"Like what?"

"Like the cause of death, for starters."

Poppell snorted. "The dude fried to death! You were there."

Skelly was right, Conley thought. Walter Poppell really wasn't the brightest light on the Christmas tree.

"I'm wondering what caused the crash in the first place. There were no other cars around when we arrived."

"Right. Yeah." He shrugged. "Maybe if I hear something, I'll give you a call."

"That'd be great," Conley said. She put the key in the ignition and went to fasten her seat belt, but Poppell did not remove his hand from the door.

"Maybe we could grab some dinner, have some drinks, something like that," Poppell suggested, giving her his winningest smile.

Was he hitting on her? "I'm pretty busy with this story right now and helping take care of my grandmother," Conley said, trying to be tactful.

"But you gotta eat, right? We've got a kick-ass pizza place just opened here in town. Sal's. The owner's a real Italian guy from New York and everything."

"Sounds great," Conley said. She pulled firmly on the door, and he reluctantly loosened his grip.

"Sure thing," Poppell said. "And I'll keep my ears open, in case I hear anything good."

16

The white-clapboard Victorian house was one of the most gracious buildings in town. It had twin turrets with red tile roofs that had always reminded her of little elves' caps, and gleaming black shutters, stained glass bay windows, and lush landscaping with flower beds bursting with white petunias that looked like lace cuffs on a green velvet dress.

But Conley's throat tightened as she approached the front door of the McFall-Peeples Funeral Home, her palms damp with sweat, her heart pounding. She averted her eyes, as always, from the quaint, antique, black funeral carriage which would have once been pulled by a team of horses parked on the grass near the curving brick driveway.

Don't be such a baby. It's just a building. Shit happens. People die, and their friends and family need rites and rituals to mark their passing. The circle of life and all that.

She forced herself to climb the wide, white brick steps. The front porch was picturesque too, with a row of rocking chairs and hanging baskets of ferns. The front door was slightly ajar. Should she ring the doorbell? Conley wasn't sure.

Before she could consider the question further, a small child exploded through the doorway. Conley didn't know a lot about kids, but this one looked to be somewhere between two and four, with a headful of blond ringlets. One thing she knew for sure was that this small person was a girl, because she wasn't wearing a stitch of clothing.

"Graceanne! Get back in here. Graceanne?" A petite woman with the same blond ringlets ran out onto the porch, bumping squarely into Conley.

"Excuse me!" the woman said. "But I seem to have misplaced my kid."

The child peeked out from behind a rocking chair and giggled.

"About this tall?" Conley asked, holding her hand knee-high. "Blond hair, no clothes?"

"That's my demon, all right."

Conley pointed toward the rocking chair. The child dashed forward and was promptly scooped up into her mother's waiting arms.

"I'm so sorry you had to see this," the woman said. "Not exactly the image of caring, compassion, dignity, and discretion we usually try to project around here. May I help you?"

"No worries," Conley said with a laugh. "Funeral homes kind of stress me out, so your daughter was a welcome distraction."

"A disaster is more like it," the woman said, slinging the naked child over her shoulder. "Come on inside, won't you? I'll just throw some clothes on this little imp, and then we can talk. I'm Kennedy McFall, by the way." She held out her hand.

"And I'm Conley Hawkins."

The woman tilted her head and smiled wider. "I'd heard you were back in town. But I guess you don't remember me, do you?"

"Should I?" Conley studied the younger woman, who was barefoot and dressed in a sleeveless pastel Lilly Pulitzer dress.

"Not necessarily. I mean, you were two or three years ahead of me in school."

Conley followed Kennedy through the foyer of the funeral home, pausing each time the other woman stooped to pick up a tiny pair of underpants, shorts, a T-shirt, and finally, a pair of sandals, all of which were scattered like bread crumbs down the length of the long hallway.

"In here," Kennedy said, nodding to an open door that led into a small, sunny office. The space was at odds with the gloomily formal pseudo-colonial décor in the rest of the funeral home. Kennedy's desk was a slab of glass set on chrome sawhorses. Framed family snapshots and cheerful crayon scribbles covered the pale pink walls.

She plunked herself onto an overstuffed lime-green settee and started to dress the still-squirming child. "Graceanne!" she said sternly. "Do you want to go back to time-out?"

"No!" the child exclaimed.

"Then hold still and let me get you dressed before your grandfather comes home and puts the both of us in permanent time-out."

When she'd succeeded in clothing her daughter, Kennedy reached behind a sofa cushion and pulled out an iPad. The little girl grabbed it and retreated behind the sofa, where she was soon giggling at a cartoon show.

"Call the mom police," Kennedy McFall said with a sigh. "I'm using a screen to shut my kid up."

"Whatever works," Conley said, shrugging.

"You'd better tell me what I can help you with before she gets her second wind," Kennedy said, nodding in the direction of her daughter.

"I was actually looking for George McFall. Is he your dad?"

"So they tell me. He's out right now. Anything I can help with?"

Conley hesitated. "I'm working on a story about Symmes Robinette."

"Ohhhhhh." Kennedy nodded. "For the *Beacon*, right? There's not much I can tell you. Anyway, Rowena came by a little while ago and picked up the funeral notice."

"Rowena?"

"Yeah," Kennedy said, running a hand through her unruly curls. "I was kind of surprised to see her. I mean, funeral notices aren't exactly her job. Usually, we just email them into Lillian in your office."

"No," Conley said, remembering what Rowena had said earlier in the day about her own story. "It's not Rowena's job. I think she might have gotten her wires crossed."

"You think?" Kennedy winked. "I think it's kinda cute that Grayson has let the old girl keep her column all these years, and I hope you don't mind my saying so, but she gets spacier by the minute."

"We know," Conley said ruefully. "But she's an institution around here, or so I'm told."

"I'm over that evil little mutt of hers," Kennedy said. "He actually snapped at Graceanne today!"

"So sorry," Conley said. "I'll pass that along to my sister. In the meantime, I really do need to talk to your dad about Symmes Robinette."

"He's actually gone out to the house to speak to Vanessa about the arrangements. This promises to be quite an event. Dad says it'll be the largest service he's ever handled. People are flying in from all over the country."

"When is the service?"

"Next Saturday, we hope. There's going to be some kind of official memorial in D.C. at the Capitol on Tuesday. The whole family is flying up there for that. And then, fingers crossed, there'll be the service here in town, with the funeral at the Presbyterian church and, afterward, a reception in the church parlor. Visitation hour here the night before."

"That's a lot," Conley said, remembering what had seemed like the never-ending ordeal of her own father's rather simple funeral six years earlier. "It must be very difficult for his poor wife."

"For Charlie too," Kennedy agreed. "And it doesn't help matters that the medical examiner hasn't released the body yet. Vanessa is totally beside herself about that."

"Oh?" Conley tried to sound casually disinterested.

"Can you believe it? I mean, it was an accident, right?"

"That's what I hear."

"So what's the big deal? Dad says there's some kind of law, that there has to be an autopsy because of the circumstances, but still. You didn't hear it from me, but Vanessa has been raising holy hell about it. She's called everybody from the governor to the White House, trying to pull strings to get that body released and the death certificate issued."

"And?"

"Last I heard, nothing had changed. I think Charlie's doing his best to get her to chill out, but if you know Vanessa, you know that ain't happening."

"Right," Conley said noncommittally. Her brief interactions with

Vanessa in the past had been intense and unpleasant. Intensely unpleasant. "You know Charlie?"

"We're, uh, kind of dating. Actually, more than kind of." Kennedy smiled and changed the subject. "Wow, you really have been gone from here a long time, haven't you?"

"Pretty much," Conley agreed.

"I hope this doesn't make me sound like a total loser," Kennedy confided, blushing slightly, "and I don't want you to think I'm a stalker, but I've kind of been following your career for years now."

"Really? Why?"

"You were a hotshot eighth grader when I was in fifth grade," Kennedy said. "All the teachers used to talk about what an amazing student you were and how you were going to be an important writer someday. I was a nerdy little bookworm who aspired to being a famous writer someday, so you were sort of my hero."

"Mama?" Graceanne poked her head out from behind the sofa and held out the iPad. "More."

"Just one more," Kennedy said, tabbing over to an icon and pressing a key to restart whatever video the child was watching, before handing it back.

Conley found herself blushing now. "I think that's the nicest thing anybody's ever said to me. I was such a loser in middle school. I wanted desperately to hang with the cool kids like Grayson, but I didn't fit in anywhere. It was almost a relief when my grandmother insisted on sending me away to boarding school in Virginia."

"I was the exact opposite," Kennedy said. "I *was* one of the cool kids in high school, unfortunately. Cheerleader, homecoming court, all that crap. No more nerdy bookworm for me."

"But you went to college, right?"

"Kinda. All my friends were going to Florida State, so that was a no-brainer, as far as I was concerned. I pledged the right sorority, dated the right jocks. Got a degree in advertising and followed my college boyfriend to Orlando. Got a job with an agency, married the boyfriend."

"What brought you back to Silver Bay?" Conley asked.

Kennedy yanked a thumb in the direction of Graceanne. "This one. My husband split. Just walked out on us. I tried the whole solo single-mom thing, but it's so damn hard! I don't know how women do it without family. My mom finally talked me into moving back here, and I have to say, it's been a huge relief."

"I'll bet," Conley said.

"You probably think it's weird, raising a kid in a funeral home," Kennedy said.

"You live here?" Conley didn't bother to hide her surprise.

"Upstairs. My dad's parents raised him and my aunts and uncles here, and they turned out okay. The whole second story is one huge apartment. Way more room than we ever had in our crappy little rental in Orlando. And it's free, so the price is right. My mom watches Graceanne while I'm working, and she spoils her rotten."

"But what do you do here? I mean, you don't actually . . ."

"What? Embalm bodies?" Kennedy chuckled. "God, no. I do all the marketing, some of the bookkeeping, anything that doesn't involve mortuary science."

"That's what it's called?" Conley was intrigued, despite herself.

"Yup. My grandfather and my dad graduated from a mortuary school in Atlanta. Dad made noises about sending me, but I said hell to the no."

"And you like it? Working in the family business?"

"Yeah," Kennedy said, sounding surprised at her own answer. "I actually do. What about you?"

"Me?"

"Yeah. What's it like, coming home and working for your family business after working for a big-deal daily newspaper?"

"This is only a short-term thing," Conley said. "I'd taken a job with another publication, but things didn't work out as planned. So I'm back in town, staying out at the beach with my grandmother, sending out résumés."

"And working at the *Beacon*," Kennedy said. "Must be kind of a letdown, huh? The last scandal we had around here was when the high school football coach left his wife for the girls' basketball coach. Nobody would have cared except that he had a losing season that year. Nothing exciting ever happens in Silver Bay."

"We'll see," Conley said. "I'd better hit the road. But before I do, could I get another copy of the Robinette funeral notice?"

"Give me your business card and I'll email it to you," Kennedy said.

Conley scribbled her contact information on a page of her notebook and handed it over. She stood up and peeked behind the sofa, where the little girl was busily stripping off her shirt and shorts again. "Bye, Graceanne."

"Bye-bye." The little girl waved her tiny panties as a farewell gesture.

"I'll walk you out," Kennedy said. "We've got to start setting up for a service this afternoon." She glanced behind the sofa and sighed. "Oh Lord. What am I gonna do with this child? Stay right there, Graceanne," she said sternly. "And put those clothes back on. Right now, before you give some old fart a heart attack."

Conley stared straight ahead as Kennedy steered her toward the funeral home's front door, but she still had flashbacks of standing in a never-ending receiving line inside one of the reception rooms just off this hallway, dressed in a starchy black dress, pantyhose, and heels, as somber-faced well-wishers grasped her hand and murmured condolences after her father's funeral.

"Doesn't it ever bother you, living with all this death, constantly?" she asked.

"Guess I don't think of it like that," Kennedy said. "There's sadness, yeah, but like my dad always says, we're helping families say goodbye to their loved ones. That's not a bad thing. And I get to raise my kid here and work with my family. You get that, right, working in your own family's business?"

"Have you met Grayson?" Conley grimaced. "Not so much. There's a lot my sister and I don't see eye to eye about."

"How is she?" Kennedy asked. "I've been so busy with work and the kid, I haven't made it over to the Wrinkle Room in what seems like ages."

"The Wrinkle Room? What's that?"

"You know. That's what we call the bar at the country club. We're usually the only people in there under the age of sixty."

"Ohhh. Good one. Grayson's fine. I guess."

"Tell her I said hey," Kennedy said. "And I'll let Dad know you dropped by."

17

She was on the way back to the *Beacon* office when Grayson called. "Where are you?" she asked, skipping, as usual, any niceties like a greeting.

"Just leaving the funeral home," Conley said. "Where are you?"

"I'm at the office. We just got an emailed press release from Robinette's office about the funeral arrangements, with some canned statements from a bunch of political types. Want me to email it to you?"

"You can, but I'm on my way to the office now, so I'll look at it when I get there," Conley told her.

When she arrived at the *Beacon,* she found Grayson at her desk, working her way through a stack of bank statements. The bedding and clothes she'd seen earlier were gone, and so was the rest of the staff. Grayson was dressed in a faded Griffin County High Marlin's tank top and blue spandex bike shorts. Her arms were tanned, but shockingly thin. Grayson had lost weight. A lot of weight.

Standing over the desk and looking down at her older sister, Conley noticed the number of silver streaks in Grayson's hair, and with Grayson's reading glasses sliding down the bridge of her nose, she looked like a feminine version of their father at that age.

It struck her then that Grayson was exactly the age their father had been when Melinda pulled her first of many vanishing acts.

"What happened to Lillian and Michael?" Conley asked.

Grayson shoved the bank statements aside, covering them with page proofs of the IGA's next display ad. "I sent 'em home. I can't afford to pay overtime. Lillian worked late last night, and Michael's covering a minor-league baseball game in Apalachicola tonight." She pointed at a desk in the outer office. "I had Lillian clean off a work space for you. I printed out the press release from Robinette's office."

"Thanks."

"You getting any good stuff about Robinette?" she asked.

"Depends on how you define *good*. According to Kennedy McFall, there'll be a ceremony to honor Robinette in D.C. on Tuesday at the Capitol, then the actual funeral is next Saturday, pending the medical examiner's release of the body. I've also got some juicy stuff courtesy of my session with Rowena this morning."

"How'd that go?"

"The old bird's definitely got the good dirt," Conley said. "Listen to this—she told me Robinette got Vanessa pregnant while Symmes was still married to his first wife."

"You mean with Charlie? No shit? Are you sure? I mean, consider the source."

"Rowena claims she saw the baby's birth certificate with her own eyes. Charlie was born three months before Symmes Robinette's divorce from his first wife was final. Symmes and Vanessa got married the day after the divorce was final—in the House chapel in D.C.—by the House chaplain."

"Damn," Grayson chortled. "I thought old Symmes was Mr. Christian Family Values. How come this is the first I'm hearing about it?"

"Granddaddy wouldn't run the story Rowena wrote about the kid," Conley said. "He considered it gossip and beneath the paper's dignity."

"Sounds like Pops," Grayson said. She tapped her fingertips on the desktop. "You know we can't run a story like that now, right?"

"Why not?"

"It's ancient history, Sarah. That happened, what, thirty-four years ago? Nobody cares about that stuff now. And you especially can't write about it in light of our esteemed congressman's untimely death. What? You think the *Beacon* is gonna run a story telling the world that Charlie Robinette is, literally, a bastard? The week after his old man gets killed in a car wreck? That's like lighting a bag of dog poop and leaving it on the old man's grave."

Conley stared openmouthedly at her sister. "You can't be serious."

"Dead serious," Grayson said. "Granddaddy was right. It is beneath our dignity, especially now."

"Dignity? We're a newspaper. Who cares about dignity? We publish the news. Facts. Good or bad, they're the facts. Look, I know that back in the day, the press looked the other way when politicians behaved badly. They ignored JFK's affairs, but that all changed with Bill Clinton. Symmes Robinette was an elected official. If I can prove what Rowena claims, then Vanessa was a member of his staff when she got pregnant with his kid, which means he was bonking her while she was on the government payroll."

Grayson stood up from her desk and glared at her younger sister. "In case you haven't noticed, we're not *The New York Times* or *The Atlanta Journal-Constitution*. We are the by-God *Silver Bay Beacon*. We are a tiny, struggling weekly paper, and we've managed to stay in business because this town considers us part of the community." She tapped the page proofs she'd been working on. "These ads might not seem like a big deal to you, but they're what keep the lights on and the press rolling around here. The community's goodwill keeps us in business."

Conley returned her glare, and suddenly, she felt they were right back in the living room at Felicity Street, teenagers bickering over whose turn it was to borrow their father's Buick. She took a deep breath and tried to tamp down her anger.

"So what? You want me to write a puff piece about Robinette? Overlook any inconvenient facts that might tarnish his heretofore sterling reputation?"

"Not a puff piece," Grayson said. "The facts. The police report, a statement from his office, list of accomplishments, like that."

Conley went out to her new desk and picked up the press release. It was printed on letterhead from the U.S. House of Representatives. She read it over, then carried it back to Grayson's office.

"Here," she said, her voice dripping acid. "Here's your story. Symmes Robinette, war hero, champion of freedom, defender of democracy, beloved colleague, husband, and father. Why bother paying me any of the *Beacon*'s good money? Just run this, verbatim. Or better yet, let Rowena write your story. She's already all over it. Made a trip to the funeral home just this morning to pick up the obituary."

"Damn it, Sarah," Grayson started. "What? You're quitting?"

"Damn straight," Conley said. "And for the last time, my name is Conley."

She'd driven halfway around the square, her hands still shaking with barely suppressed rage, when her cell phone rang. It was G'mama. Had Grayson already called to tattle about their fight?

"Sarah?"

"Yes, ma'am," she said wearily.

"Are you still downtown?"

"Yes, ma'am."

"Oh, good. I was wondering if you could pick up a prescription for me. Sean called to say it was ready, and he even offered to bring it out here to the Dunes, which was so sweet of him, but I told him I thought maybe you'd pick it up."

"Happy to," Conley said.

"How is your research on Symmes Robinette coming along?"

"I'll tell you about it when I get home," Conley said. She didn't feel up to explaining her sudden resignation over the phone.

"Fine," Lorraine said. "See you soon."

Kelly's Drugs hadn't changed much over the years. The big neon sign outside, in the shape of a mortar and pestle, still hung over the front door. A spinner rack near the front held comic books and paperback romance novels. The soda fountain ran along the left side of the store, and the pharmacy was at the back. The black-and-white checkerboard linoleum floor tiles were a little more scuffed, and the prices posted on the menu board by the lunch counter had of course increased, but that was about it.

"Hello there!" a woman's voice called from the back. Conley was startled to see June Kelly perched on a high-backed stool behind the pharmacy counter. "Can I help you?"

Conley stared. June Kelly seemed to be her old self today. Her white hair was freshly coiffed, her lipstick seamlessly applied. She wore the starched lab coat with her name above the pocket.

"Sarah?" Miss June said, studying the new customer. "Sarah Hawkins!" She bustled around the counter and gave Conley a warm hug. "Where have you been hiding yourself?"

"Um, well," Conley stammered, at a loss for words. "I guess I've been working."

"How's your daddy's bursitis?" she asked. "Is Chet taking the medication Patrick prescribed?"

"He's much better, thanks, Miss June," Conley said.

"What can I get for you today? How about a nice ice cream cone? With extra sprinkles?"

She was still holding Conley's hand between her own birdlike hands. Conley glanced around the store. "Right now, I'm looking for Sean."

A moment later, Skelly stepped out from the stockroom. He held up a white paper sack. "Guessing you're here for your grandmother's meds? I felt bad we didn't have this one ready earlier. Hope you didn't have to make a special trip into town."

He came around the counter and gently disengaged his mother, walking her back to her perch.

"No trouble. I was just over at the office," Conley said. "Hey, since you're a pharmacist, how about selling me a bottle of aspirin?"

"You sick?"

"No," she said. "I've just got a throbbing headache."

"I'll give you some aspirin, but have you eaten anything today?"

"Come to think of it, I haven't," she said. "But I think my headache is more from tension than hunger."

"Mom, do you think you can watch the counter while I fix Sarah some lunch?" he asked. "It's slow right now, but if you need her, Ginny is in the back room, unpacking stock."

"All right," June said calmly. She sat back on her stool and folded her hands in her lap.

Skelly handed her a paper cup with two tablets. "Cherry Coke?" he asked, his hand poised above the soft drink fountain.

"Please."

He scooped crushed ice into a tall plastic cup and squirted deep red cherry syrup nto it, then added the carbonated drink, finally plopping a maraschino cherry on top.

She swallowed the pills with a gulp of the icy concoction.

"Wow," Conley said, "talk about a trip in the wayback machine. I don't think I've had a Cherry Coke this good since the last time your mama fixed me one while I was sitting right here at this soda fountain." She glanced toward the back of the room, where the older woman was sitting placidly, leafing through a comic book.

"She just asked me if my dad was taking the meds your dad pre- scribed."

"Sorry," Skelly said. "Up until just now, I thought she was having a pretty good day. She loves coming into the store. It seems to center her or something. Her happy place, you know? Plus, it's fairly early in the day. Evenings are when the confusion and agitation usually seem to set in. *Sundowners,* the doctors call it. Now how about lunch? What'll you have? Grilled cheese, chicken salad? BLT? I've got some great-looking tomatoes. The sky's the limit as far as you're concerned."

Conley didn't have to look up at the menu board. "I'd love a Kelly burger."

"You got it."

He opened an under-counter refrigerator and brought out a stack of thick patties separated by neat squares of waxed paper and slapped two on the griddle. Then he held up a plastic tub of thinly sliced onions and another of chopped mushrooms.

"You going full Kelly?" he asked.

"Why not?"

"Think I'll join you. I haven't eaten today either. We had a busy morning."

He drizzled oil from a squeeze bottle onto the grill top and when it was sizzling added the onions and mushrooms, stirring them briefly with a broad-bladed spatula.

Conley propped her elbows on the red Formica countertop, sipped her Coke, and watched as Skelly moved behind the counter with an ease gained from long practice.

He took two seeded hamburger buns from a bag on a shelf above the grill, split them, and placed them on the grill beside the burgers, pressing down on them with the back of the spatula. Skelly added a scoop of bright orange pimento cheese to each meat patty, waited another moment, then ladled on the sautéed vegetables.

And then he was plating his creation, sliding the buns onto two plates, topping each with a burger. "All the way, right?"

She nodded enthusiastically. Skelly wiped his hands on a cotton towel, then added a juicy red slice of tomato and a sprinkling of shredded lettuce. Finally, he added the top bun, spearing the whole thing with a pickled okra slice on a long wooden toothpick. He heaped potato chips alongside the burger, then presented the plate to Conley with a flourish.

"Lunch is served," he announced.

She bit into the burger, chewed, and sighed happily. "Now I can tell all those snippy eighth-grade girls I finally went all the way with Sean Kelly!"

Skelly, mid-bite, choked, then began laughing. "As if."

They worked their way through their lunch, laughing and trading reminiscences about their childhood exploits.

"How's the headache?" he asked, polishing off the last potato chip on his plate. "Any better?"

"A little," she said. "That burger was definitely a good idea for the headache, but the main problem I'm experiencing is a pain in the ass called Grayson Hawkins."

"You two knocking heads again? What's Gray done now?"

She filled him in on her sister's opposition to the story she wanted to write.

"Seems to me Grayson has a point," Skelly said. "Maybe Robinette wasn't a saint, but so what? He's dead now. Let it alone, why don't you?"

She drained the last of her Cherry Coke and considered his question. Why couldn't she let it be? Why did she have to keep turning over rocks and poking at trouble?

Before she could form an answer, June Kelly drifted over, slipping onto the barstool next to hers at the lunch counter.

"What are you two talking about?" she asked. "You both look so serious."

Skelly shrugged. "Sarah's been working on a story for the newspaper, Mama. About Symmes Robinette."

Miss June's face clouded, and her eyes narrowed. "Him! What's he done now?"

"He's dead, Miss June. He was killed in a car crash over in Bronson County, Monday night," Conley said.

"I'm glad," the older woman said. "Serves him right for how he did Toddie."

"Mama!"

"He was a horrible, horrible man." Her soft voice rose in indignation. "He got that girl pregnant, and then he divorced Toddie so he could marry that whore. And then Toddie moved away and took the children." She turned to Skelly, looking perplexed. "Son, where did Toddie go?"

"I don't know, Mama. That was a long time ago."

"Maybe she's at the farm," Miss June said. "The children love that farm. Hank and Rebecca. They had horses and a mule. You tried to ride the mule one time, remember, Seanny?"

"Maybe," Sean said. "I was just a little kid back then, and all Toddie's kids were older than me."

"Where was Toddie's farm, Miss June?" Conley asked, intrigued.

Her face clouded, and tears sprang to her eyes. "I miss my friend so much."

"What about the farm?" Conley repeated.

"Don't!" Skelly said sharply under his breath. "Can't you see you're upsetting her?"

Conley's face flushed with shame. "You're right. I'm so sorry." She took out her billfold to pay for her lunch, but Skelly waved the money away. "On the house."

She pressed a five-dollar bill into his hand anyway. "I always like to overtip the help. And Skelly? I really am sorry. I got carried away."

He shrugged. "Five minutes from now, she won't remember you were here."

"Bye, Miss June," she said, touching the older woman's arm. "I'll see you soon."

The tears had vanished as quickly as they'd appeared. "Oak Springs!" she said, perking up again. "I remember now. It was Oak Springs. I'll get Seanny to take me there. And you can come too."

"I'd like that very much," Conley said.

18

Conley's cell phone dinged to signal an incoming email. Maybe all those emails and résumés she'd sent out were triggering a job offer.

She tapped the email icon and her hopes sank. Again. Not a job of- fer, she saw. Just an email from Kennedy McFall from the funeral home: "Here's the Symmes Robinette obituary. We'll send over the photos the family requested to run with the obit later today. Let me know if you need anything else. Enjoyed seeing you today."

Resting in the arms of his Savior: The Honorable U.S. Representa- tive C. Symmes Robinette was taken, suddenly, from this earthly plain on Thursday near Varnedoe. Symmes, a lifelong Floridian, was a U.S. Marine Corps veteran, a war hero, an attorney, and an elected public servant, first as a state legislator and then as an eighteen-term member of Congress. But he would be the first to say that his most important role in life, and the one he cherished most, was devoted husband to Vanessa and father to C. Symmes "Charlie" Robinette Jr.

Born in 1943 to Marva Franklin and Clyde D. Robinette, Symmes was an only child whose father died tragically young. Later, Marva, who went to work at the Varnedoe Denim Assembly

Mill, married Gordon Pancoast, the manager who raised Symmes as his own. Symmes enlisted in the Marines at twenty-two, served honorably in Vietnam, and was awarded the Bronze Star for heroic service in a combat zone. Symmes became the first member of his family to attend college, at Florida State University, where he went on to earn a BA in government. He graduated from Florida State University College of Law in 1974.

Symmes opened his private practice in Silver Bay immediately after law school, and it was not long before leaders in the community recognized his intelligence and deep commitment to public service. He was first elected to the Florida House of Representatives in 1978 and was later tapped to run for Congress from the Thirty-fifth District. Among his notable achievements over many years of service to his community was the awarding of over $40 million in earmarked public funding for local highway improvements, water treatment facilities, and, in 1999, completion of the C. Symmes Robinette Veterans' Administration Hospital in Bronson County, which he regarded as his crowning achievement during a lifetime of public service.

An Eagle Scout, Symmes was awarded many honors over his lifetime, including Florida Rotary Man of the Year, U.S. Chamber of Commerce Friend to Business Award, Christian Family Values Ambassador, and Florida Bar Association Award of Excellence.

Symmes was a member of the VFW, the American Legion, the Silver Bay Rotary Club, the Seminole Boosters Club, the Silver Bay Country Club, and Silver Bay Presbyterian Church.

Following a memorial service in the U.S. Capitol, there will be a celebration of life at Silver Bay Presbyterian Church on Saturday at 2:00 p.m. Reception to follow at the Baptist church gymnasium. Family visitation hour will be Friday night at McFall-Peeples Funeral Home.

Resting in the arms of the Savior. The phrase made her chuckle. At her first reporting job at the *Belvedere Bugle* in Louisiana, Conley's weekly responsibilities included gathering, rewriting, and editing the obituaries submitted by local funeral homes. The paid death notices, which were priced according to word length, were a lucrative revenue stream for the paper, so funeral homes and the bereaved were encouraged to get as flowery as possible.

She'd been given a list of sappy death euphemisms to use when writing the obits and invested much time and energy into padding them as colorfully as possible.

Angels carried her away, Joyfully singing with Jesus, Promoted to glory, Fell asleep in the cradle of death, Advanced to eternal life, and *Breathed her soul into her Savior's arms* were some of the more popular euphemisms she employed in her carefully crafted death notices, but her favorite euphemism was one that she'd seen only once, when the grieving family of a bayou fisherman had written that their beloved father had "slipped anchor."

Slipped anchor, she thought, had a nice, simple ring to it, although it had not been a big moneymaker for the *Belvedere Bugle,* circulation 2,617.

Conley drove around the square and parked in front of the former Silver Bay Savings and Loan building. The 1920s-era art deco, two-story building had been painted a tasteful light gray and transformed into offices for the Robinette Law Firm.

She sat in the car for five minutes, trying to find a reason not to go inside and confront a part of her personal history she'd just as soon forget. And that was the thing about being back in Silver Bay, she realized. For every happy memory, like watching a Gulf sunset from the porch of the Dunes or sipping a Cherry Coke at the lunch counter at Kelly's Drugs, there was also the reality that with every block she turned in this town, it seemed, she bumped up against a sharp corner of her painful past.

A somber wreath of white lilies with trailing white satin ribbons hung from the law firm's plate glass doors. The door was locked, but there was a discreet intercom button on the casing.

She pressed the button, and a moment later, a man's voice answered, "Who's that?"

She was so startled, it took a moment to gather her composure.

"Uh, hi. It's Conley Hawkins. With the *Beacon*?"

There was a pause. "Come on in."

The intercom buzzed, and she heard the lock click. The bank's former lobby, where, accompanied by her father, she'd opened her first savings account at the age of eight, had been turned into a reception area.

Charlie Robinette was waiting for her just inside the door. He looked like an ad agency's idea of a young lawyer; straight blond hair brushing his eyebrows, horn-rimmed tortoiseshell glasses, untucked blue oxford cloth dress shirt, skinny jeans, and polished oxblood loafers.

"Here," he said, handing her a piece of paper.

It was a copy of the obit she'd just read in her car.

She tilted her head and waited. Nothing. "You don't know who I am, do you?"

"Should I? Connie something, right? With the paper?"

"Not Connie. *Conley*," she said, enunciating slowly. "Sarah Conley Hawkins."

He let out a slow exhalation of breath. "Holy shit. Sarah!"

"That's me."

Charlie ran a hand through his hair. "Man! This is crazy. I never would have recognized you. I mean, you look awesome. Really. I like your hair like that. How long has it been?"

She straightened her shoulders. "Let's see. I believe it would have been the summer before my senior year of high school."

His face colored, and he laughed uneasily. "Well, that accounts for my memory lapse. I don't know about you, but most of my summer that year was lost in a haze of Jägermeister and cheap weed. Up in smoke, right?"

"My memory of our last meeting was probably more vivid than yours," Conley said coolly. "Let's see. I went out with you two or three times at the beginning of the summer, when I got home from boarding school. I thought you were funny and cute. But when I refused to 'put out,' as you phrased it, for revenge, you told everybody in town that I'd—what's that graphic phrase for group sex you used? 'Pulled a train'? So cute and colorful."

"Oh, man," he said. "Kids, huh? If I really did that, I'm sorry."

"You really did do it. And more." Conley said. She wiped her sweaty palms on her jeans, willing herself not to go batshit postal on Charlie Robinette. Batshit was not why she was here. She had a job to do. The past was the past. Ancient history.

Until the guy who'd ruined your teenage life didn't even recognize you as an adult or have the grace to acknowledge the damage he'd done to your life.

He shrugged. "I'd do a lot of things differently now, if I had the chance."

"Would you?" she asked.

"Hell yeah. Look, you can't judge somebody by the stupid shit they did at the age of eighteen."

Her head was starting to throb. She had to let it go, had to put the past firmly in the past, where it belonged.

"I didn't come here to talk about this stuff," she said. "Let's start over, shall we? First, I'm sorry for your loss."

"Whatever." He was obviously annoyed that she'd dredged up ancient history. "You came for the obituary, for the *Beacon*? Now you've got it."

"Thanks, but Kennedy McFall just emailed it to me. I was actually hoping to speak to you about a story I'm writing about your dad for the paper."

He sighed dramatically. "There's not much I can tell you. We're still in shock. It hasn't really sunk in yet. What else do you need?"

"For starters, I was wondering if you have any idea why the medical examiner hasn't released the body or determined the cause of death."

"Who told you that?"

"The funeral home."

His pleasant face reddened. "They had no business telling you something like that. We don't know why there's a holdup. Typical bureaucratic incompetence. The kind my dad battled his whole career."

She nodded.

"My father was killed in a single-car wreck," he went on, growing animated. "He was basically incinerated. Nothing else matters, okay? We don't need this shit."

"I'm sorry for your loss," she repeated. "It must be incredibly painful. When I spoke to Sheriff Goggins over in Varnedoe—"

"Why would you talk to the sheriff?" he cut in.

"Because that's part of my job. Your father was a prominent figure in this community, Charlie. In this state. Given the nature of his death—"

"Given the nature of his death, I find it totally inappropriate for you to show up at my office asking these kinds of questions," Robinette said. "And since when does a crappy weekly like the *Beacon* run this kind of shit?" He took a step toward her, his fists balled up. "What the hell are you trying to insinuate?"

Conley stood her ground. "I'm not insinuating anything."

"I think you need to leave here now," Robinette said. "Despite the fact that I've tried to apologize, you've obviously still got some kind of personal ax to grind with me. I'm warning you, Sarah, if you come up with some kind of bullshit story about my dad's death, I will grind you and that pathetic excuse for a paper into dust."

She smiled. "Good to see you again, Charlie."

19

Conley spent another ten minutes sitting in the front seat of the Subaru, trying to calm down after the confrontation with Charlie Robinette.

She was still sitting there when he emerged from the bank building and locked the door behind him. She slid down in the seat, hoping he wouldn't spot her, but he went straight to a car parked at the curb, got in, revved the engine, and quickly backed up and drove off. He was driving a black Porsche Cayenne. When they'd dated all those summers ago, he'd driven a candy-apple-red Porsche 911. Same old Little Prince.

When the Porsche was out of sight, she drove away with more questions swirling around in her brain. Her innocuous questions about the congressman's death had struck a raw nerve with Charlie. She'd been stupid to bring up their past, but after the searing pain and humiliation of the way he'd treated her all those years ago, the confrontation was inevitable, if unwise. He'd practically thrown her out of his law office. And she hadn't even gotten around to asking the thing she was most curious about: Why had the family's official obituary omitted any mention of Symmes Robinette's other survivors, including his first wife and their children?

She had a lot of research to do, but there was no way she could go back to the *Beacon* office and the (very) temporary work space Grayson had allocated her. Grateful that she'd brought her laptop along, she drove back to Felicity Street and let herself into G'mama's house.

While she was setting up her work space on the dining room table, she googled the name of the Panhandle district's chief medical examiner.

Theodore Moriatakis, she learned, had been appointed to his position by Governor Lawton Chiles in 1995. It was Saturday, but she reasoned that since death doesn't take weekends off, perhaps the medical examiner's office didn't either. She tapped the number listed on the county's website and wasn't surprised when her call was routed to voice mail.

The pleasant recorded voice directed her through a series of prompts for all the reasons a caller might need to reach the medical examiner's office. The last prompt allowed her to leave her name and phone number and the reason she was requesting a callback.

"Hello. My name is Conley Hawkins. I'm a reporter for *The Silver Bay Beacon,* and I'm calling to inquire about the cause of death for Symmes Robinette. Please return my call as soon as possible."

She disconnected and went back to the browser bar, mainly to satisfy her own curiosity.

It didn't take long to find Symmes's marriage and divorce records online. In 1962, in Varnedoe, Florida, at the age of nineteen, he'd married Emma Todd Sanderson, age eighteen. Their divorce decree was issued in May 1986. No surprise, Rowena Meigs's account had been wrong. It had actually taken two days for Charles Symmes Robinette, age forty-three, to marry Vanessa Renee Monck, age twenty-five, in Washington, D.C.

As she'd suspected, there was no way to access Charlie's birth record. When she checked the District of Columbia's vital records page, she was informed that birth records could only be accessed by the person in question, a parent, or a legal representative.

On a hunch, she pulled up Charlie's Facebook page. His profile photo was a professionally done headshot, showing Charlie dressed in a conservative coat and tie.

The Little Prince bore an uncanny resemblance to his father. He had the same slight, receding chin, flat cheekbones, and high forehead. They even shared the same nose.

Charlie wasn't what she'd call active on the social media site. There were a couple of old postings—Charlie being sworn in to the Florida Bar with his proud father looking on; Charlie at a Tallahassee tailgate party, dressed in a fraternity jersey, clinking a beer bottle with similarly dressed guys; and Charlie, dressed in hunter's camo, kneeling beside a huge buck he'd killed three years earlier. He hadn't posted anything new in two years.

On a whim, she typed Vanessa Robinette's name into the Facebook search bar and was mildly disappointed to see that Vanessa's account was private.

What now? She drummed her fingertips on the mahogany dining room table and stared absentmindedly at the floral-patterned wallpaper.

What about Symmes Robinette's house? Skelly, who'd delivered prescriptions there, had described his waterfront mansion in an exclusive gated golf and tennis community as gigantic, worth probably more than $2 million. Again, she was curious about how a country lawyer turned career politician, whose official congressional salary was $174,000, could afford such lavish digs.

Conley navigated to the website for the county's tax assessor to see if she could look up the value of the congressman's property. She typed Robinette's name into the search bar only to be rewarded with NO RESULTS FOUND.

Now what? She really needed Robinette's address. It wasn't likely she'd find an elected official's home address online. She considered calling Skelly but quickly discarded the idea.

She couldn't even get a plat number to estimate the appraised value of the other homes at Sugar Key without the address of somebody who lived there.

What she needed was what she didn't have anymore, which was an expensive, expansive database—the kind maintained by a big-city newspaper—much like the one where she'd been most recently employed.

Conley picked up her phone and dialed her former office husband, Butch Culpepper, whose number she knew by heart.

When he answered on the fourth ring, he was out of breath, and she heard echoing footsteps and muffled shouts and grunts in the background.

"Sare Bear!" he exclaimed. "What's up?"

"Where are you?" she asked. "It sounds like you're in a gym or something."

"I am in a gym."

"No way," she said flatly. Butch was the most proudly sedentary human she knew, someone whose idea of a workout was a trip to the refrigerator for another pint of Cherry Garcia.

"Way. Benny's team is in the NAGVA finals. We're out in Seattle."

"What the hell is NAGVA?"

"Sare Bear, we've been over this. It's the North American Gay Volleyball Association. Benny is the star outside hitter."

Several lame jokes came to her mind, but she immediately shelved them. "So I guess there's no way you can get to the newsroom to do a little research for me, huh?"

"Afraid not, hon. We don't go home until Wednesday. What's up?"

"I think I'm on the trail of a hot story, but I keep running into dead ends. I need access to some databases."

"A hot story in Silver Bay? What? Somebody rigged the goat rodeo?"

"That's hilarious, Butch," she said. "But I've got a dead congressman and a lot of questions."

"Oooh," Butch said. "Now you've got me all hot and tingly. And speaking of, why not just give Kevin a call?"

"Absolutely not."

"Get over yourself. The poor man's been mooning around since you left. He's probably in the newsroom right now, staring at your photo and pining away."

"Stop. I can't just up and call Kevin out of the blue and ask for a favor like this. Never mind. I'll call Tiana instead."

"You could, but I know for a fact that she's in Memphis for her cousin's wedding."

Conley sighed heavily. "Okay. You two have fun."

"We always do," Butch said.

She stared down at her phone for a full five minutes, trying to think of another way to get the information she needed. In the end, she scrolled through her contact list and tapped Kevin's name.

He picked up after the second ring. "Conley? Hey."

"Hey, Kev. How are you?"

"Good. How about you? How are things down in Florida?"

"They're different. I'm kinda working for my sister right now. Or I was."

"At the newspaper? Wow. How did that happen?"

"It's complicated. And I sort of already quit, but I'm onto a story, and I just gotta keep going."

"Same old Conley," he said without rancor. "Go ahead. I'm listening."

That was one of the things that had drawn her to Kevin Rattigan. It was the thing that made him so good at his job. He was a world-class listener.

She recounted the details of Symmes Robinette's death and filled him in on the hostility her rudimentary questions had triggered from the locals, including her publisher/editor.

"I think I saw an Associated Press wire story about your congressman's death. How can I help?"

"I hate to ask," she began.

"Just tell me what you need. I'm on my way to the office right now."

"Okay," she said eagerly. "I need some more info on Robinette. I guess I forgot to mention that I was there—at the accident."

"Really?"

"Yeah. It was past three in the morning, so as you can imagine, the timing is one of the things that made me suspicious. My friend and I were driving back to town, and we came across this black Escalade. It had rolled over. We could see a man trapped inside. Then smoke was pouring from under the hood, and Skelly tried to break the window with a tire iron—"

"Who's Skelly?" Kevin interrupted.

"Just a guy I grew up with. And then the car caught on fire, and the heat was so intense we had to back away—"

"You're dating this dude? That was fast. Even for you."

"I am *not* dating Sean Kelly. I'm not dating anybody. Jesus! I haven't even been home for a week. We grew up two doors apart, okay? I happened to run into him at a bar the first night I was home. I'd had a couple of drinks, so he offered to drive me back to town in my car."

"It's not really any of my business," Kevin said quietly, and Conley knew she'd hurt him. Again.

"Kevin," she said. "I swear. He's like a brother. In fact, he's more Grayson's friend than mine. Look, I know things ended badly between us. And that's on me. I screwed up. I treated you like shit. And I'm sorry for that. I'm just not good at this stuff."

"That's the understatement of the year," he said finally. "Okay, let's get back on topic. Tell me exactly what you need."

"One of the things I'm interested in is how a career politician can afford what's been described as a waterfront mansion worth millions—on a congressman's salary."

"Maybe he inherited money?"

"I don't think so. Up until a few years ago, he lived in a nice house not far from my grandmother's place. And then some developers come to town about five years ago, and they buy this little spit of land. It's called Sugar Key. When I was a teenager, it was where kids went to watch the submarine races."

"Huh?"

"It's where teenagers went to drink rotgut and screw in the back seat of somebody's Honda," she said. "Nothing out there back then but scrub pines and palmettos. And mosquitoes. Lots of mosquitoes. From what I hear," she added.

"I'll bet."

"They built a gated golf and tennis community with only like ten lots. And Symmes owns a house out there."

"You should be able to just look that up in the county tax maps online," he said.

"I should be, but I tried doing it with just Symmes's name and came up with zip. I need an address. And that's not easy to come by for a sitting member of Congress."

"Okay, I think I should be able to get that. I can always call somebody up in the D.C. bureau."

"While you're at it, see if you can find out where Symmes lived in the district. And how much that place is worth."

"Anything else?"

"My source tells me that Symmes was tight with the developers of Sugar Key. I'm thinking if we find out who the corporate officers are, maybe that'll give us some insight into what kind of relationship he had with them."

"You're thinking a real estate developer killed a member of Congress? In a single-car accident on a country road?"

"I don't know what I think," she said. "I'm just doing what I know how to do. Turning over rocks."

There was a long pause at the other end of the line. "You're asking for a lot, Conley."

"I know. But there's a story here, Kev. I can smell it. It's just out of my reach. And it's so damn frustrating."

"Down the rabbit hole you go, huh?"

"Only if I can get somebody to help me dig that hole. And it ain't gonna be anybody around here. It's like Robinette is some sacred cow. Get this—he was married with a couple of kids, and when he was in his forties, he got his secretary pregnant. While he was in office! Somehow, he managed to hush it up, divorce the first wife, and marry the baby mama, who was a couple decades younger. And nobody in Silver Bay even raised an eyebrow. A columnist for the *Beacon*—she's this ancient crone named Rowena—got wind of the story, wrote a piece, and my granddaddy killed her story, because he said it was beneath the paper's dignity."

"When was this?"

"Back in the eighties," Conley said. "But it might as well be today, because my sister insists it's still not a story."

"She's worried about pissing off the family? Or losing subscribers?"

"Both of the above. Plus pissing off the few advertisers we have left. According to my grandmother, Grayson has been shopping the paper to sell."

"Are people actually buying newspapers these days? I thought print journalism was circling the drain."

"I can't have this discussion right now. It's too depressing. Do you think you can help me?"

He let out a prolonged sigh. "Yeah. I'll see what I can do. In the meantime, start with Robinette's campaign finance disclosure documents. If there's something fishy with his financials, that's the place to start."

She smacked her own forehead. "Duh! Oh my God. Of course. Why didn't I think of that?"

"You would have, eventually. I'll call you back when I know something."

20

When her cell phone rang, Conley didn't recognize the number, but since it was a local area code, she answered anyway.

"Conley? Hey. It's Winnie." The housekeeper's voice sounded strained.

"What's wrong?" Conley asked.

"I think you need to get out here," Winnie said. "Your grandmother took a fall a little while ago. She'd been out working in the garden, and I hollered at her to come on in the house and get out of that heat, but when she came inside, she was acting kind of funny. Her words were blurry, and her face was white as a ghost. She walked in the kitchen and just fell out."

"Oh my God. Is she conscious? Do you need to call an ambulance?"

"I wanted to," Winnie said. "I got a cold dishcloth and put it on her face and helped her sit up, and she come back around after a minute or two, and the first words out of her mouth were, 'Don't you dare call 911.'"

"Where is she now?" Conley grabbed her backpack, shoved her computer and notebooks inside, and dug out her car keys.

"I cleaned her up and got her into her bed, but she was fighting me the whole way. Said she was fine, just got a little overheated and light-headed is all. I managed to make her eat something and drink some water, and she just now dozed off, so I thought I'd better call you."

"You did the right thing. I'm on my way," Conley said. "Keep an eye on her, okay?"

"I'm sitting in a chair right outside her room, and I check in on her every five minutes or two, just to make sure she's breathing."

"Did she hit her head again? Do you think she has a concussion? Maybe we should call her doctor." Conley's words came out in a jumble as she raced toward the front door. "I don't remember his name. Wait. It's on the prescription I picked up from Kelly's today. I'll call him."

"Better not," Winnie warned. "She will have your hide, and mine too. She made me swear not to tell you, but I figured when you get here, you could just act like you don't know nothing."

"Okay, we won't call yet," Conley said. "I'll get there as fast as I can."

She ran through red lights, blew through stop signs, with her foot hard on the accelerator as soon as she cleared the square.

This is my fault, she thought. *I told Gray I'd watch over G'mama. I promised to take care of her. This is on me. And if she dies, it's all on me.* The loop played endlessly in her head, alternating with prayers to a God she thought she'd long ago discarded.

Granddaddy's Wagoneer was parked with the rear bumper poking nearly a foot onto the street in front of the Dunes. She pulled the Subaru up next to it and took the stairs to the second floor two at a time, her footsteps slapping against the worn wooden treads.

Winnie was sitting on a kitchen chair parked outside the bunk room that Lorraine had claimed for her bedroom.

"Is she awake?" Conley was out of breath, her heart pounding in her chest.

"Who's that?" her grandmother called.

Conley forced herself to act calm. She poked her head inside the bunk room door. G'mama was struggling to sit up.

"It's just me," Conley said. "How are you?" She stepped inside the room, and Winnie was just a step behind.

"Winnie called you and told you to come home, didn't she?" Lorraine glared at her housekeeper, who glared right back.

Her grandmother's voice was thready, almost wheezy.

"Hell yes, she called me," Conley said, sinking down onto the bed. "Somebody around here has to show some common sense. She told me you fell. Passed out!"

"It was just a little sinking spell," G'mama protested. "Nothing for everybody to get themselves all worked up about."

There were large Band-Aids on her grandmother's exposed forearms and another on her right cheek.

Conley tapped Lorraine's sunspotted arm. "What happened here?"

"Just a scratch from the garden," Lorraine said, swatting her hand away. "Nothing for you to worry about."

"She got cut when she fell," Winnie said. "Bled so much I thought she was dying."

Angry blue-black bruises were already blossoming on both of Lorraine's arms. "I suppose I tried to catch myself when I had that sinking spell." She held out her arms to survey the damage herself. "This old skin of mine is like tissue paper," she complained. "If I as much as brush up against something, this happens."

"What did you have to eat today?" Conley demanded.

"I ate like a fat old pig," Lorraine said. "I had breakfast—"

"Black coffee and a piece of leftover pecan pie," Winnie volunteered, poking her head around Conley. "I told her she can't eat like that, but she never pays attention to what I say."

"You just mind your own business," Lorraine snapped. "I'm a grown woman, and I can eat whatever I like."

"No. You can't," Conley said. "According to Gray, your doctor says you're prediabetic. You've got to limit your carb intake, eat protein, balance your diet, and drink plenty of fluids. Preferably not black coffee. Do you even drink water? Did you take your meds today?"

"And what medical school did you attend, young miss?" Lorraine asked.

"I attended the school of common sense." Conley pressed her grandmother's bony hand between her own two hands. "Damn it, G'mama. This isn't funny. If you don't start eating right and taking your meds, you're going to kill yourself, and Gray will blame me. Do you want that on your conscience? Because I don't. You're all I've got, you know."

Lorraine studied her granddaughter's stricken expression. "That's not quite true," she said quietly. "You've got your sister. And your mother is still alive. She might not be around, but she cares about you. I know she does."

Conley bit her lip and looked out the bedroom window. It had gotten late while she was in town. The sun was starting its descent toward the horizon. A palmetto frond rasped in the breeze outside, and a small green lizard crept across the window screen. The sun's rays slanted across the rumpled blue-and-white-striped sheets on the bed and illuminated the network of fine lines on her grandmother's narrow face.

She looks old, Conley thought. Not indestructible. Aged. Aging. Not yet fragile, but no longer the indomitable force of nature Lorraine Du-Bignon Conley had always represented.

"If Melinda cares so much, why didn't she come home when Dad died? Do you even know where she is these days?"

Lorraine turned her head toward the pillow. "I'll try to do better," she said finally, avoiding, yet again, any discussion of a topic she disliked. Her voice was muffled. "No more pecan pie for breakfast."

"We need to get you in to see your doctor," Conley said, seizing the moment. "And when you go, I'm going to be right there in that room so I can really understand what's going on with your health."

"All right," Lorraine muttered. She managed to raise herself to a sitting position and, to Conley's amazement, swing her feet over the edge of the bed.

"What are you doing?" Conley protested. "You need to rest."

"I've been resting," Lorraine said. "It's nearly suppertime. I'm going to take a nice, cool bath and wash off this garden muck. Then I intend to eat something healthy, as you insisted, and drink some water." Her voice turned steely. "And then you and I are going to have a talk, young lady."

"About what?"

"Help me up," G'mama commanded, holding out her hand. "Bath first. Then we talk."

. . .

Lorraine allowed Winnie to run her a bath and lay out a clean set of clothing for her before shooing her and Conley away.

"I'm not convinced she doesn't need to see a doctor," Conley fretted to Winnie once they were out in the kitchen.

The housekeeper was chopping up the chicken she'd roasted earlier in the day, placing it on a bed of salad greens, then adding thick, deep red slices of tomatoes and hard-boiled eggs.

"Me either. But you heard her. She thinks she's just fine. Nothing but a sinking spell."

Winnie shook her head. "Never saw such a stubborn old fool." She went to the refrigerator and brought out a jar of her homemade buttermilk ranch dressing.

"I've got an idea," Conley said, reaching for her cell phone. "He's not a doctor, but she loves him, and maybe he can kind of check her out and see if she really does need medical attention. Do we have enough for one more mouth for supper?"

Winnie gave her a look. "Have you ever known me to run out of food?"

"I was just going to call you," Skelly said. "I shouldn't have jumped down your throat today. I know you didn't mean any harm, asking Mama questions."

"I shouldn't have upset her like that," Conley said. "Sometimes I lose track of boundaries. You were right to rein me in. I'm sorry I went too far."

"It's forgotten," Skelly said. "I was going to call and ask if I could take you out to dinner, to make it up to you."

"And I was calling you for sort of the same reason. G'mama had another spell today. She'd been out working in the garden in all this heat, and when Winnie finally made her come inside, she passed out cold on the kitchen floor."

"Good God! Were you there? What did you do?"

"I'm ashamed to say I was still in town, at Felicity Street, working on this damn story," she admitted. "Winnie managed to get her up and make her eat and drink something. G'mama insists it's nothing, and she absolutely forbade Winnie to call an ambulance or even to call me."

"That's not good, Conley," Skelly said. "Sounds to me like her blood sugar was out of whack."

"Had to be. The only thing she had to eat today was a slab of pecan pie and a cup of coffee for breakfast."

"What can I do?" Skelly asked. "Do you want me to have a talk with her? Try to get her to understand how serious this is?"

"She probably won't listen to a lecture. But maybe if you just showed up at the Dunes, like at cocktail time, on some kind of a pretext, she'd invite you to stay for supper because she adores you. Is there any way you could do that?"

"If I know your grandmother, she'll see right through the pretext, but I'm willing to give it a try."

"Oh, wait. What about Miss June? Can you leave her for that long?"

"She'll be fine," Skelly said. "Her favorite cousin comes over to visit on Saturdays to give me a break, and they have movie night. Anita usually sleeps over. What time should I just innocently drop by?"

"As soon as you can get away," Conley said. "Thanks, Skelly. I owe you one."

Winnie had fixed a tray with fruit, cheese, and crackers.

Conley helped herself to a cube of cheddar. "Any idea what G'mama wants to talk to me about? Sounds like I'm fixing to be in the doghouse."

"It's this damn Symmes Robinette thing," Winnie said, sinking onto her favorite step stool. "Your sister called her up, and then I know she got a couple of other calls too. Folks in this town are riled up because they don't like you asking questions about him. They all think that old man's shit don't stink."

"But you don't agree?" Conley popped a green grape in her mouth and chewed.

Winnie pressed her lips together tightly. "No, ma'am. I been knowing his kind all my life." She glanced in the direction of the hallway that led to the bunk room. "He's the reason my sister didn't live to see her babies grow up. There's a whole lot of bodies in the graveyard over in Plattesvile that he's responsible for, and a lot of other people that are still walking around alive, but messed up inside because of him. Symmes Robinette can rot in hell as far as I'm concerned."

She wiped her hands on a dish towel and placed the cheese plate on a wicker tray, along with glasses, the ice bucket, and the cocktail pitcher.

Conley was too stunned by Winnie's outburst to respond at first. "What did Symmes have to do with Nedra's death? I thought she had cancer."

"Winnie?" Lorraine stood in the doorway. She was wearing pale lilac cotton slacks, a white blouse with long sleeves that hid the cuts and bruises on her arms, and a silk scarf with a swirly design in blues, pinks, and lavender draped across her narrow shoulders. Her thinning silver hair was still damp from her bath, but combed back and fastened with a silver clasp. She'd applied makeup over the bruise on her cheekbone. She was once again the queen of the Dunes.

"I've got the drinks tray all ready," Winnie said.

"But you're sticking to water or iced tea, at least until we figure out these sinking spells of yours," Conley said.

"Ridiculous," Lorraine said. She turned to the housekeeper. "Winnie, if you don't mind, Sarah and I have some family matters to discuss."

"Suits me," Winnie said, turning on the aqua radio. "Guess I'll see if I can get me a ball game to listen to."

21

Lorraine waited until they were in their assigned seats on the porch. Conley poured her grandmother some unsweetened iced tea and served herself a sunsetter.

Suddenly, Lorraine whipped out her obsolete flip phone and brandished it at her granddaughter as though it were a switch and the screened porch was the woodshed.

"Sarah, what on earth have you been up to today?"

Conley took a sip of her cocktail, strictly to bolster her courage. "Who called?"

"The question is, who didn't? I have been on this phone off and on all afternoon, listening to complaints about you."

"Grayson called, right? Did she tell you I quit?"

"She said you quit a hot second before she was about to fire you."

"I told you this wasn't going to work," Conley said. "Grayson won't listen to me. She just wants a puff piece about Symmes Robinette's death. And I'm not about to put my byline on that kind of cotton candy bullshit."

"We'll get to that in a moment. I also heard from Charlie Robinette. He'd worked himself up into quite a lather after your visit."

"G'mama, I only asked him the questions I'd ask anybody else in the same circumstances."

"I don't fault the questions you asked, Sarah. It's your technique. Or lack thereof. You apparently went charging into the law offices of a man who just lost his father this week. And the first thing you do is tell him you find his father's death highly suspicious! You tell him you've called the sheriff and the funeral home, asking them all kinds of inflammatory questions. How did you think he was going to react?"

Conley's cheeks burned because not only did her grandmother's criticism sting, it rang true. Seeing Charlie after all these years, so smug and entitled, so dismissive. She hated the word *triggered,* but that's how she'd felt. She'd lost her objectivity. Maybe if she'd tried to seem sympathetic, even obsequious, she could have lulled Charlie Robinette into giving up the information she was seeking.

"Didn't you learn anything at all from growing up in this family?" Lorraine pressed. "How many times have I told you that you'll always catch more flies with honey than vinegar?"

Conley stared out at the Gulf. The bright turquoise shade of the water had deepened, and a light breeze ruffled a stand of sea oats atop the dune line.

"You're right," she murmured.

"What's that? Sit up and speak up, child."

"I said, 'You're right.' I should have taken my time, buttered Charlie up, and laid it on thick about what a great public servant and war hero his father was. And then asked about the death certificate."

"At the very least," Lorraine said. "And you had no business telling him that Kennedy McFall had given you any information about the service or about the lack of a death certificate. You betrayed a confidence from someone whose business depends on discretion. My God, Sarah. That's Journalism 101, and I never went to journalism school."

"I guess being married to Pops was like going to journalism grad school," Conley said.

"Being his granddaughter and being brought up in the newspaper business should have done the same for you," Lorraine fired back.

"So now what?" Conley asked. "Just have Grayson run Rowena's piece and be done with it?"

"Don't be absurd," her grandmother said. "If there really is a story in Symmes Robinette's death, I want us to get to the bottom of it."

"You're not worried about pissing off his family, alienating the community, and losing subscribers?"

"Of course I worry about it. Your sister worries about it too. But that's Grayson's job. It's your job to go out and get the real story. What's that thing you're always saying?"

"Turning over rocks and kicking up dirt?"

"I am worried about something else, though," G'mama said. "Charlie alluded to some kind of bad blood between the two of you. He claims you're trying to settle an old score because of some silly teenage prank."

Conley's face grew hot. "He called it a silly teenage prank?"

"His exact words. I wasn't even aware you knew him. I'd heard Symmes and Vanessa shipped him off to military school because of some bad behavior on the boy's part. What kind of prank is he talking about?"

"I don't want to get into all that," Conley said. "All you need to know is that Charlie was a pig. When I started asking him questions about Symmes's death today, he threatened to 'grind us into dust.' What's that tell you about him?"

"It tells me there's something he's trying to hide, but it also tells me we need to be absolutely certain any story we print is impeccably sourced and fact-checked."

"It will be," Conley said.

Lorraine nibbled on a cracker with a slice of cheese. "What makes you so sure there really is a story here? And I'm not talking about the fact that Symmes fathered a baby by his secretary while he was still married to Toddie. It might be true, but it is no longer noteworthy or germane to his untimely death."

"Unless it is," Conley insisted. "Remember how Granddaddy had us all sit down together to watch *All the President's Men*, way back when he bought his first VCR?"

"He wanted you children to watch a story about two intrepid reporters bringing down a corrupt president so that you could understand the power and potential of great journalism," Lorraine said. "I just liked looking at Robert Redford." She fanned herself and smiled. "I liked him better in *Butch Cassidy and the Sundance Kid.*"

"Who didn't?" Conley said. "I never forgot that scene when the confidential informant meets Bob Woodward in that dark parking garage and tells them to 'follow the money.' That's what I intend to do. Follow the money."

"What money is that?"

"Symmes Robinette owns a house on Sugar Key, where, from what I'm told, waterfront houses start at two million. His house in D.C. is in Georgetown. I looked it up. The median price of a home there is one-point-six million."

"Good Lord! I had no idea. How can any of these politicians afford to live like that and maintain a house back in their district?"

"That's what I want to know. Robinette didn't come from a wealthy family, right?"

"Not really," Lorraine said. "Symmes's mother was widowed when he was quite young, I believe. She worked in the mill, over in Plattesville, and her second husband was a plant manager."

"Where's Plattesville?" Conley asked. "I keep hearing about it, but I know I've never been there."

"It's mostly gone now," Lorraine said. "But at one time, it was a thriving neighborhood on the west side of Varnedoe. There was a blue jeans factory and a big railroad switchyard. You could ask Winnie about Plattesville. She grew up there. Most of the homes and churches were torn down in the early nineties, after it was condemned by the state due to chemical contamination from the industries there. There were all kinds of lawsuits and accusations about cancer-causing agents in the water."

"So that's what Winnie meant when she said Robinette was responsible for Nedra's death?"

Lorraine looked startled. "When did she tell you that?"

"Just now," Conley said.

"Winnie almost never talks about Nedra or what happened to her." Lorraine toyed with the hem of her scarf. "It was a terrible thing. The railroad operated a huge switchyard in her neighborhood. For decades, they stored hundreds of barrels of caustic chemicals there. Eventually, they abandoned the site, but there was a retention pond on the property, and over the years, the chemicals seeped into the soil and leached into the water. Winnie told me there were drainage ditches that wound all through the neighborhood. Winnie and Nedra and the neighborhood children played in that water. Their grandmother grew vegetables in that contaminated soil."

"And that's what gave Nedra the cancer?"

"It was so horrible," G'mama said, shuddering. "Nedra's husband, Ed, was a no-account drifter. By the time she was thirty, she was raising those three little boys by herself. And then she got sick. I can't remember the kind of cancer, but it was quite rare. She was having excruciating abdominal pain. By the time she was correctly diagnosed, the cancer was so advanced, there wasn't much they could do. As it turned out, there were other, similar cancers diagnosed in people who'd grown up around Plattesville and that chemical dump."

"A cancer cluster," Conley said.

"There was a young lawyer, a woman who worked for some environmental action organization. Randee something. She heard about the cancer cases, organized the families who'd been affected, and started filing suits against the railroad."

"Let me guess. Symmes Robinette represented the railroad."

"Of course," Lorraine said. "He was already making a name for himself around this part of the state. And he was in the state legislature by then. Politically connected through and through."

"What happened to the lawsuits?"

"Some of them were settled out of court. Those people were poor, and most of them were poorly educated. Their family members were sick and dying, so it was easy for the railroad to throw a few dollars their way and make them go away."

"And Nedra's case?"

"If you think Winnie is stubborn, you should have met Nedra! As sick as she was, she refused to settle, because by then, it was a matter of principle. So Symmes played the long game. He was a master at foot-dragging. Every time the judge would set a date for a hearing, Robinette would claim he had to be in Tallahassee on state business, and the judge, who, I suspect, was one of his cronies, would grant him a continuation. Poor Nedra died before she ever got her day in court."

"That's so sad," Conley said.

"Winnie told me the state came in and paid all the families a nominal amount of money for the homes that they tore down. Nedra was always certain that she'd prevail in court and that her boys would be provided for after her death, but none of that happened."

"No wonder she hates Robinette," Conley said.

G'mama craned her neck and looked toward the stairway to make certain the housekeeper wouldn't overhear the next part of their conversation.

"There was an incident . . ."

They heard heavy footsteps on the stairs, and Lorraine stopped talking. But when she spotted their visitor, her bruised face was wreathed in a smile.

"Sean Kelly! Oh my goodness. What a nice surprise!"

Sean carried a bouquet of brightly colored zinnias in an old jelly jar in one hand and a bottle of white wine in the other. He put the jelly jar on the table, leaned over, and kissed the cheek that Lorraine offered. "I was in the neighborhood and thought I'd drop in to make sure Conley delivered your prescription." He touched the bruise on her cheek. "Have you taken up boxing since I saw you last, Miss Lorraine?"

"Just a silly fall earlier today. I got overheated after working in the garden." She pointed at a wicker armchair. "Sit down there and fill me in on what's new in town."

Sean pulled the chair up closer to his hostess. "Did you hit your head when you fell?"

"Not really. You'll stay for dinner, of course. I know Winnie has fixed enough to feed the whole town. Why don't you go back downstairs and tell her you'll be joining us?"

"She already invited me, and of course I said yes. I never pass up an offer for a home-cooked meal. Miss Lorraine, how were you feeling before you passed out? Did you have a headache? Were you dizzy? Had you eaten?"

G'mama regarded her granddaughter and Skelly with growing suspicion. "I should have known," she said angrily. She pointed at Conley. "You put him up to this. You've been sneaking around behind my back—"

"It was my idea," Skelly said hastily. "When Sarah was in the store this morning, we had a disagreement. I called to apologize, and she happened to invite me to dinner. It was all completely innocent, I can assure you."

"There's nothing innocent about this girl," Lorraine said. "She told you about my stupid fall and asked you to come out here and check up on me."

"You wouldn't go to the hospital, and you won't let me call your doctor. I'm worried about you, G'mama," Conley said. "Do you want me to call Grayson and get her in on this conversation?"

"That won't be necessary," Lorraine said coldly. She turned to the pharmacist. "To answer your questions, I very foolishly didn't eat properly this morning. I was gardening outside in the heat, and I was feeling a little dizzy when I came in, and that's when I had my spell. No, I don't have a headache. I know I don't have any broken bones, because I was able to walk out here, unassisted."

"No vomiting or funny metallic taste in your mouth?" Skelly asked. "Your eyes aren't sensitive to light?"

"No and no. Can we talk about something more pleasant now?"

"If you insist," Skelly said. "The good news is, I don't think you have a concussion. But you definitely need to see Dr. Holloway and discuss this latest episode with him."

Lorraine pointed out the window. "Now look what you've gone and done, Sean. You almost made me miss the sunset."

It was true. The sun hovered just slightly above the quivering waters of the Gulf, bathing everything in a coral-tinged light. A string of pelicans soared past, silhouetted in the dying purple light.

Lorraine held up her glass. "Quickly, Sean. Pour yourself a drink. It's bad luck not to toast at sunset."

Skelly did as instructed, dropping cubes into a glass and pouring himself a cocktail.

Lorraine clinked her glass against Conley's and then against his. "Here's to the light. Here's to the sunset."

"Here's to old friends," Conley added, touching her glass to Skelly's.

"And here's to your health," he added, tapping Lorraine's glass.

They all drank, then paused, watching as the last golden glimmer slipped out of sight.

"How is June?" Lorraine asked as they were finishing up their dinner.

Skelly poured the last of the white wine into Conley's glass and then his own.

"Physically, she's fine. I took her to the store, and she recognized Conley right off, although she forgot both Conley's and my dad are both dead. Then, by tonight, when her favorite cousin, Anita, arrived for their regular Saturday night movie date, Mama didn't know her. She thought Anita was her own mother."

"I'm sorry, Sean," G'mama said. "It must be very hard for you to watch her decline. Your mother was such a smart, vibrant woman."

"It's hardest on her," Skelly said. "She gets so frustrated sometimes. She'll come into the store and sit behind the counter, and it's all familiar. Her favorite part of being a pharmacist was compounding drugs for patients. She said it was like cooking. Now she looks at the tools and she can't remember how they work."

He put his fork carefully on the side of his plate. "That was the best meal I've had in a long, long time. I'm afraid my bachelor cooking leaves a lot to be desired."

Winnie came in from the kitchen and began clearing the dishes. "You should taste her cooking," she said, nodding at Lorraine. "Can't even scramble an egg without burning it."

"It's true," G'mama admitted without rancor. "We'd all starve without Winnie." She touched her granddaughter's hand. "The only thing my mother ever fixed was franks and beans on the cook's night out. But Sarah is quite a good cook, aren't you?"

"I get by," Conley said.

"One year, after she'd been to Italy on vacation, she came home and made osso buco. From memory! It was the most marvelous thing I'd ever tasted. And she's a wonderful baker, aren't you, Sarah? My goodness, she can make cookies and pies. She used to bake her daddy a chocolate silk pie for his birthday—"

Conley stood up from the table and began gathering the rest of the plates. "Come on, Skelly. Let's give Winnie a hand."

"No, no," Lorraine protested. "I'll help Winnie. It's your first Saturday night at the beach. You young people should go have some fun."

Conley turned to Skelly and rolled her eyes. "Is it my imagination, or is my grandmother trying to set me up with you?"

Skelly grinned. "It might work, if you'd bake me a chocolate silk pie."

22

Effectively banished from the kitchen, Conley and Skelly stood, uncertain, on the screened porch.

"Where shall we go?" Skelly asked. "Back to the American Legion?"

"God, no!" Conley shuddered at the memory.

"I was kidding. We don't have to go anywhere if you don't want to. I mean, your grandmother can't *make* us go out on a date."

"You mean, like your mother *made* you ask me to the country club teen dance all those years ago?"

"For the last time—"

"I was kidding too," Conley said, playfully tapping his arm. "I know you said you don't think G'mama has a concussion, but I think I probably need to stay close to home."

"How about a walk on the beach, then?"

"Sounds perfect."

They kicked off their shoes at the dune line and followed the worn path down to the water's edge.

Skelly waded out until the water lapped at his ankles. "Want to hear something pathetic? I think this is the first time, in at least two years, that I've been anywhere near the beach."

"Since Danielle left?"

"Maybe before that. She hates sand."

"That's not pathetic. It's sad." Conley waded out to join him. She let her feet sink into the soft sand, feeling the hundreds of tiny coquinas burrowing away from her toes. "You wanna hear pathetic?"

He nodded.

"I came out and went swimming after I moved G'mama in here the other day. And it was the first time I'd set foot in the Gulf since before my dad died."

"Really? You used to be such a beach bunny. You never came out here all those times you came back to visit over the years?"

"No," she said simply. "As Grayson reminded me, I've been blowing in and out of Silver Bay, in a strictly perfunctory way, for years now."

"It's not such a bad place to live," he said, gazing appreciatively back at the lit-up profile of the Dunes.

They saw the silhouettes of the two older women, Winnie and Lorraine, standing side by side at the kitchen sink, bathed in the soft, yellow light of the kitchen.

"It's not that it's a bad place. It's just not necessarily a good place for me," Conley said. A wave rolled up, splashing water on the hem of her pants, so she walked back up to the beach.

He followed a moment later, and they walked slowly along the waterline. When a row of huge, close-set houses appeared ahead, she stopped and stared. There were four of them, pale pink stucco, vaguely Moorish revival in appearance, four stories tall, each house bristling with balconies, rotundas, and rooftop cabanas. The turquoise swimming pools behind each house glowed in the gathering dusk, and laughter and music drifted through the air.

"What the hell is that?"

"That, my friend, is Villa Valencia." Skelly said the name with a pronounced Spanish accent.

"Where did those monstrosities come from? Didn't the Cooleys used to live there? And your aunt and uncle? Didn't they own that cute little yellow cottage your family used to stay in every summer?"

"After my aunt and uncle died, my cousins couldn't agree on what to do with the cottage, so they sold it. The Cooleys sold out too, and so did the people who owned that squatty little brown concrete-block house."

"I remember that place. We used to call it *the shit house*," Conley said.

"A developer came in, knocked everything down, and built those 'villas' in their place."

"They must cost a small fortune. They're huge!"

"I'm surprised Miss Lorraine hasn't complained about them to you. Everybody on the beach has been up in arms about the villas."

"Because they block out the sunlight?"

"That too. Somehow, the developer got the county to grant a height variance. They're now the tallest structures on the beach, which means they effectively block the view of the houses across the street from them."

"That'd piss me off," Conley said. "Of course, G'mama's house is big too, but it's only two stories, raised up off the ground, and it's been there since the 1920s."

"It's not just the view that has people riled up. None of those owners are local. They built those houses as investment properties. Each one has ten bedrooms and ten baths. They're rented out through Airbnb, which means every weekend, and all week long during tourist season, as many as ten cars descend on each house. Sometimes lots more. People rent them out for frat parties and weddings and corporate functions. Sometimes there'll be a hundred people or more, spilling out on those patios, partying in the pools 'til dawn, blasting music, clogging the street with illegally parked cars."

"Ohhhhh," Conley said.

"The neighbors are righteously pissed," Skelly said. "To them, it's like somebody plunked down motels right in the middle of their quiet, quaint little street."

"And there's nothing anybody can do about it?"

"The neighborhood association hired a lawyer who complained to the county, and they've made noise about trying to get an ordinance passed prohibiting multifamily rental units, or at least putting a moratorium on more of them. But the Villa Valencia homeowners have a lawyer too. You'll never guess his name."

"Not Symmes Robinette?"

"Close. Like blood close. Charlie Robinette."

Conley felt her phone buzzing in the pocket of her shorts. She pulled it out, looked at the caller ID screen, and turned to Skelly. "Sorry. I gotta take this."

"Hi," she said softly. "Thanks for calling me back, Kev."

"Where are you? Are those waves I hear?"

"I'm taking a walk on the beach," she said, deliberately omitting the fact that she wasn't walking alone.

"Sounds nice. Our D.C. correspondent did some asking around and managed to get your guy's address in Georgetown and down there in Florida. I'll text it to you. I also got you the names of the corporate officers of Sugar Key Partners, Ltd."

"Who are they?" she asked eagerly.

"The names don't mean anything to me," he said curtly. "Guess you'll have to do your own legwork. Okay, bye. Have a nice walk."

Kevin had every right to hang up on her. But she couldn't deny that it hurt when he did.

She sighed and put her phone away.

"Business call?" Skelly asked.

"Yeah. A friend at the paper. I'd asked him to help me with some research about Symmes Robinette."

He raised one eyebrow. "A friend or a special friend?"

"Former special friend. That was the guy I told you about. Kevin Rattigan, my ex-boyfriend. He has access to a lot of databases and sources that I don't have down here."

"He's helping you out even though you dumped him?"

"It's a newspaper thing, Skelly. We were colleagues before we were a couple. That's what colleagues do in our business."

"Seems weird to me," Skelly said. He walked on, then stopped. "Any chance the two of you will get back together?"

"Why all the questions about my past?"

"Maybe I'm trying to figure you out. That's all."

"Let me know when you do," Conley said. She dipped her hand in the water and flicked it at him.

They left the lights of Villa Valencia behind and finally reached the south end of the island, the point where Silver Bay flowed into the Gulf. A long line of weather-beaten pilings jutted out into the water, the last remains of the Fisherman's Pier that was blown away in a hurricane in the late 1990s. Pelicans roosted on several of the pilings, their heads folded under their wings as though tucked in for the night.

By unspoken agreement, Conley and Skelly trudged through the soft, white sand toward a swinging bench that stood at the edge of the dune line. The wind was up, and there were whitecaps on the waves. Her dark hair blew in the breeze and ruffled the fabric of her blouse.

"Remember when we all used to go shark fishing out there on summer nights?" Skelly asked, pointing at the remnants of the long-gone pier and stretching his left arm across the back of the bench.

"Did anybody ever catch a shark?" Conley asked.

"I think somebody caught a little nurse shark one time. Mostly, I think we just sat out there, drinking and smoking until the old guys who ran the bait shop ran us off."

Conley turned her face skyward and gazed up at the stars. "Back then, I always thought summer would last forever. Like, I never even knew what day it was. We'd move out here to the beach right after school got out. Grayson and I had our bikes and a little bit of spending money from doing our chores, and every day, we'd wake up, eat breakfast, and then take off. G'mama's only rule was that we had to check in with her at lunchtime."

"Same with all my cousins and me. We'd roam from our place, to y'all's, to the LaMonacos', to the pier, and sometimes, if we had money, to the arcade," Skelly said. "Don't think we put on shoes—or underwear, for that matter—from June 'til September, when we had to go back to school."

"Halcyon days," Conley said, smiling at the memory. She and Grayson had been the only girls in the pack of boys that included the Kelly cousins, right up until puberty struck. After that, after she'd gone away to boarding school, things changed. She was suddenly an outsider. And she'd been one, she realized, ever since.

"Halcyon," Skelly said, turning the word over in his mouth. "I've seen that word in books but never really knew what it meant."

"I've always thought *halcyon* means a time of sweetness and contentment, of happy times remembered," Conley said. "But let's ask the Googles."

She pulled her cell phone out and typed the word into the search engine.

"Huh," she said reading the definition. "I never knew that."

"What?"

"It's a word that comes from Greek mythology, referring to a bird—a kingfisher, actually—who had the magical power to calm the wind and waves at the winter solstice so that she could breed in a nest floating at sea."

"Halcyon days," he repeated. "I guess you don't know you're living them until years later, looking in the rearview mirror." After a moment, he said, "I can't remember. Did your dad come out to the beach with y'all in the summertime, or did he stay in town for work?"

"Up until my mother left, the whole family stayed at the Dunes for the season. Dad kept what he called *summer hours* at the bank. He'd get off work at two and then come out and spend the night. He only worked half days on Friday."

"My dad did the same thing," Skelly said. "He'd tell his nurse not to schedule any patients after two in the summertime, unless it was an absolute emergency. He'd come out to my aunt and uncle's house, change out of what he called his *town clothes* and into this ratty pair of orange Bermuda shorts with blue flamingos embroidered on them."

"Oh my God! I totally remember those shorts. I don't ever remember seeing him on the beach when he wasn't wearing them. They'd faded so much they looked pink."

"My mom tried hiding them, but he always found them. It was like a running joke between them. Finally, one year in August, she enlisted all us kids in her plot. She sent him to Mr. Tastee for ice cream, and while he was gone, she rigged the pants to some rope and she ran it up the flagpole on the front of the cottage. When he got back with the ice cream, we were all standing on the front steps, saluting his shorts. I've still got a photo of it somewhere."

Conley pointed at the brightly colored shorts Skelly was wearing.

"I was wondering when you'd suddenly gotten so sporty—these aren't the same shorts, right?"

He laughed. "No, but they're as close as I could find. I guess I have gotten sporty in my middle age. After wearing a white lab coat at the store all day, this is my way of changing gears. Maybe that's how my dad felt too, after wearing his white lab coat all day."

"Your dad was such a good sport," Conley said. "I always thought he and your mom made a great team. They were always laughing and joking around. You could tell they liked each other."

"I never really thought about that before," Skelly said. He looked over at Conley. "I guess things weren't so great between your parents, huh?"

She shrugged. "We never even knew there were any problems until the first time she left."

Her phone pinged, signaling an incoming text. She glanced down, glad of the distraction, then stood so abruptly the swing hit her in the back of the knees, nearly sending her sprawling. "I need to get back to the house."

"Something wrong?" he asked, trying to match her pace as she strode through the sand.

"The text was from Kevin. He sent me the information I need for my story."

He reached out and grabbed Conley's hand. "It's Saturday night. I thought we were having a nice time. You told me there's no internet out here. What's the rush?"

"The *Beacon*'s deadline is Tuesday. I've got to get a handle on this Robinette thing so that I can convince Grayson there's more of a story here than just a politician's tragic accident."

"I thought you said you quit the *Beacon*," Skelly said.

"I did. But G'mama wants me to see it through. Besides, if this story turns into a thing, it could be my ticket to a real job at a real paper. If it has national implications, I could freelance it out to the *Times* or the *Post*. At the very least to my old paper."

"What if it's not a thing?" he persisted. "What if it's just a run-of-the-mill accident on a lonely country road? What then?"

She turned around to face him. "Then I find another story or, better yet, another job. I have to work, Skelly. I'm a journalist. It's who I am. It's what I'm good at."

He watched her striding away, back down the beach toward her grandmother's house. He took one last look at the remains of the pier and the dozing pelicans. "Halcyon days," he murmured.

23

"She's asleep," Winnie reported when Conley got back to the Dunes. The housekeeper had dragged a chair into the hallway outside Lorraine's bedroom and was sitting there, looking half-asleep herself, with a battered Nora Roberts paperback novel open on her lap.

Conley opened the door and tiptoed inside. Her grandmother was propped up on her pillows on the bottom bunk bed, glasses perched on the end of her nose, softly snoring. The bruise on her cheek made an ugly dark stain on G'mama's pale skin. Conley reached out and removed the glasses, placing them on the nightstand, then leaned down and lightly kissed her cheek before turning off the reading lamp and exiting the room.

"You go on to bed too," Conley told Winnie, pointing at the small bedroom across the hall. She was already having second thoughts about driving back to town for the night, especially after G'mama's fall earlier in the day. Skelly was right. The story would have to wait.

When she heard a slight knock at the front door, she flew down the steps and opened it.

Skelly stood there, holding the sandals she'd forgotten out on the beach.

"I figured Cinderella might need her slippers," he said, handing them over.

She looked down at her sandy bare feet. "Whoops."

"Want me to follow you back into town?"

"There's been a slight change in plans. I'm staying here tonight," she said, stepping outside. "If G'mama's feeling okay in the morning, I'll go in."

"What changed your mind?" he asked, clearly surprised.

"I guess you did. There's nothing I could do tonight that I can't do tomorrow. And in the meantime, if something happened, if G'mama had another spell, I'd never forgive myself for not being here when she needed me."

"You'll want to call her doctor Monday and let him know what's going on," Skelly said.

"I will," she promised. And then she placed both hands on his shoulders, stood on her tiptoes, and impulsively kissed him square on the lips.

He took a half step backward and looked at her quizzically.

"That's for being my Prince Charming," she said.

He bowed from the waist. "My pleasure."

Conley changed into her pajamas and carried her things downstairs, noiselessly slipping into the boys' bunk room and climbing into the top bunk using the wooden ladder her grandfather had built by hand.

The beds were probably relics from the fifties or sixties, she thought, with maple wagon-wheel headboards and footboards to fit in with the vaguely cowboy-meets–Beach Boys decorating theme. The wall-mounted sconce on the top bunk featured a brass horse head, but the slightly musty-smelling chenille bedspreads had a tufted design of seashells, waves, and anchors.

She switched on the light, and the brass chain pull came off in her hand. She shook her head, looking around the bunk room. This had been the hangout for generations of boy cousins, and she hadn't been in here in decades.

In the dim light from the sconce, she could see that the ceiling was mottled with large water stains. The wheezy air-conditioning unit in the bedroom's only window dripped water onto the floor, where the boards were beginning to warp.

The Dunes was showing its age, and the effect, even in the semi-darkness, was not flattering.

She picked up her cell phone, and using the flashlight app, she began leafing through the book she'd chosen for her bedtime reading—the collected wit and wisdom of Rowena Meigs.

The paper was shiny and the print small. It was evident that the book's publisher had merely photocopied Rowena's old columns instead of resetting them in more readable type.

Conley flipped pages until one of the hundreds of boldfaced names caught her attention.

HELLO, SUMMER
OCTOBER 28, 1984

*A good time was had by all last Saturday as friends and family of **Toddie and the Honorable U.S. Rep. Symmes Robinette** gathered for a delightful harvest-time "hoedown" at **Oak Springs Farm**, the family's country estate in Bronson County.*

Toddie, always the "hostess with the mostest," transformed the farm's rustic horse barn using hay bales, jack-o'-lanterns, and scarecrows aplenty, into a magical party setting, complete with square dancing and cocktails for the grown-ups and hayrides, a pumpkin-carving contest, face painting, and bobbing for apples for the kiddies.

In keeping with the party theme, Symmes, who is our handsome and outgoing congressman for the Thirty-fifth District, and Toddie wore fetching his 'n' hers denim overalls and plaid flannel shirts, while their teens were dressed in dungarees and T-shirts emblazoned with VOTE FOR MY DAD. A little birdie informed your correspondent that Toddie, as talented with a needle as she is with a saucepan, designed and whipped up the entire family's costumes herself.

Spotted among the partygoers were the cream of Silver Bay po-

*lite society, including **George and Winkie Covington.** George is chairman of the Symmes Robinette for Congress committee, and Winkie is a whiz on the tennis courts. **Luther and DeeDee Najarian** were among the square dancing set. Luther does important things for the railroad, and DeeDee owns a darling boutique in downtown Silver Bay called Shoe Business. Later in the evening, Symmes and Luther were seen outside the horse barn, "holding court" with the **Honorable Judge Beckett Martin,** no doubt plotting how to keep progress moving in our fair community.*

*A "frightful" event marked the fifth birthday party of your correspondent's own great-niece, Tara Torrence, at the **Piggy Park Bar-B-Q Ranch** in downtown Silver Bay. Entertainment was provided by a skeleton-costumed bluegrass group who proclaimed themselves as the Crypty Kickers. (Don't tell the kiddies, but your correspondent happened to recognize Tara's talented daddy, Tommy Torrence, as the fiddle player.) The Piggy Park chefs departed from their usual fare and delighted the young guests with such Halloween-themed delicacies as "spaghetti and eyeballs," and "Frankenweiners" franks and beans, "Ghoulish Green Punch," and chocolate-covered "Black Cat Cupcakes." At party's end, Tara's little guests were each given specially made pumpkin goodie bags full of take-home treats.*

Conley read only a few more of Rowena's columns before closing the volume. Oak Springs Farm, she'd learned, was in Bronson County. Bronson had been a mostly rural area in the Florida Panhandle when she was growing up, a place of quail-hunting plantations and cattle farms. She'd taken horseback riding lessons at a stable there as a preteen, in her horsey phase.

Earlier in the day, June Kelly had said Oak Springs might have been where Toddie Robinette and her children moved after her divorce from Symmes. Maybe, Conley thought, Toddie was still there.

And if she did still live there, would she have anything interesting to say about her recently deceased ex-husband? Would she have any light to shed on the circumstances surrounding Symmes's death?

She stared up at the ceiling, pondering her next move.

G'mama's breathing, from the bunk below, was steady and even, punctuated by muffled, snuffling snores. She felt her own breathing fall into rhythm with her grandmother's. As a child, Conley loved slipping out of her own bed in the bunk room she shared with Grayson and tiptoeing upstairs, where she'd noiselessly slide under the covers, spooning up against G'mama. She'd loved the scent of her grandmother's night cream, the feel of the pink satin pillowcase she always used to keep her hair from being mussed. Falling asleep with her grandmother's breaths tickling the back of her neck, she'd felt safe, secure. Loved.

24

She was floating in the warm waters of the Gulf, her body lifting and falling with each movement of the tide. Above, the ink-black night was spattered with numberless stars and just the sliver of a moon. Her father's voice was calling. "Sarah. Sarah. Where are you?" She turned over, limbs flailing, trying to get a bearing on his location.

"Dad?" She spun around. "Dad?"

He called once more. "Sarah. Where are you?"

She struck out swimming, desperate to find him. Her strokes were awkward and uneven. She'd never been a graceful swimmer. She swam for so long! Her arms and legs burned from fatigue, and she struggled to keep her head above water. Now she was sinking, pulled down by the weight of her own body. "Dad?" she whimpered.

"Sarah! Sarah!"

She sat upright, gasping for air, yanked abruptly from one world to another.

G'mama stood by the side of the bunk bed, tugging at her arm. "Sarah Conley Hawkins! What on earth are you doing up there?"

Conley blinked and looked around the room and then back at her grandmother, her mind racing to come up with a plausible explanation.

"When I came in from walking on the beach, I was too tired to go upstairs to my own room, so I just decided to climb up here."

Lorraine pushed aside the sheet Conley had pulled up to her neck. "But you weren't too tired to go upstairs and change into your pajamas?"

"Busted," Conley said sheepishly.

"I told you, I'm fine. I don't need a babysitter or a bodyguard," G'mama said. She picked up the bound volume of Rowena's columns from the foot of the bunk, where Conley had shoved it before falling asleep. "Where did you get this?"

"Rowena gave it to me yesterday."

"Gave it? I never heard of that woman giving anybody anything."

Conley hopped down from the bunk. "You're right. She charged me forty bucks."

"Why, that old bandit!" Lorraine exclaimed. "Pops had those books printed for her. I think we used to sell them for ten dollars apiece. Of course, we didn't sell but maybe two cases, and most of those were to Rowena's relatives."

Conley chuckled as she headed upstairs toward her own room.

"Wouldn't you like to go to church with us this morning?" G'mama called after her. "We're having a pancake breakfast afterward."

"Another time, maybe," Conley said, pausing on the staircase. "But wait. You're not thinking of driving yourself into town, are you?"

"We're going to beach church," G'mama said, referring to the non-denominational service held on Sundays at Kirby's Karaoke Café, where the family had attended summer services for years. "And Grayson is picking me up. I think you should go too. I want to clear up this unpleasantness between the two of you."

"No, thanks," Conley said, turning to go. "I've got work to do in town this morning."

Upstairs, she turned on the shower in the tiny claw-foot tub and stripped out of her pajamas. But she yelped at the shock of the cold water streaming from the showerhead. She turned the nozzle on the hot water up all the way, got out of the tub, and waited five minutes, until finally, she gave up and took the fastest shower of her life.

Wrapped in a towel, she plugged in her hair dryer and turned it on—

at which point the light fixture overhead sparked. A glance at the wall socket showed scorch marks. She cringed, thinking of how close she'd just come to electrocuting herself. And setting the house on fire.

When she got back downstairs, she found her grandmother waiting for her ride to church, dressed in what passed for casual in Lorraine's world, a colorful floral-print shift, pearl earrings, hot-pink ballet flats, and a straw handbag, which hung loosely from her wrist.

Opie sat at Lorraine's feet, sensing, from his mistress's apparel, that she was about to leave without him.

Her grandmother wrinkled her nose at the sight of Conley's own outfit—gym shorts, a T-shirt, and tennis shoes.

"You're going into town looking like that?" She touched her grand-daughter's damp hair. "On a Sunday?"

"I'm working, G'mama," Conley said. "Nobody's going to see me. By the way, is the hot water heater broken? I had to take a cold shower just now. And I think I might have shorted out the electrical panel up-stairs when I plugged in my hair dryer."

"Oh," Lorraine said, waving her hand. "I should have warned you. It takes a long time for hot water to travel all the way up to there. And I was taking my shower too, so I'm afraid I might have hogged all the hot water this morning. Sorry, dear."

"That's okay. But have you had the wiring checked lately?"

G'mama shrugged. "I'll speak to Grayson about it. She handles that kind of thing." She then reached into her pocketbook and brought out a small white envelope. "I have something for you."

Conley took the envelope and ran her thumbnail under the flap. A key ring with a circular brass fob slid onto her palm. "What's this?"

"It's the key to the *Beacon* office. In fact, this happens to be Pops's old key."

Conley turned the key fob over and saw her grandfather's mono-gram. "Why give this to me? Why not give it to Grayson? She's running the paper, not me."

"Your sister has her own key," Lorraine said. "I wanted you to have this one. To remind you of your place in this family and in this company. I want you to understand what's at stake here."

"You know I'm not going to stay in Silver Bay permanently, G'mama. This is strictly a temporary situation, until I get a job . . ."

"You mean at a real paper?"

"That's not what I was going to say," Conley protested.

Her grandmother's piercing blue eyes stared her down. "You won't find anything more real or as rewarding as your hometown, Sarah. And you won't find a community that needs a real newspaper as much as Silver Bay. You can make a difference here. If I didn't believe that, I wouldn't ask you to stay."

Conley sighed. "G'mama, I just don't—"

A horn sounded from outside. Opie went to the door and started scratching at the screen.

Lorraine peered through the door's glass sidelights. "There's Grayson. I'd better go. Think about what I said, will you, please? And, Sarah?"

"Yes, ma'am?"

"It would be lovely if I didn't have to receive any phone calls about you today. And be a good girl and take Opie with you, please? I think he's feeling neglected."

As she rounded the courthouse square downtown, she saw the faithful drifting out of Sunday services at the Methodist, Baptist, and Presbyterian churches, the women dressed in summery floral dresses, the men in short-sleeved shirts, jackets slung over their shoulders, children skipping along behind, clutching their Sunday school art projects. The square was otherwise deserted, except for a frail-looking elderly woman seated on a bench, feeding popcorn to pigeons near the Confederate statue.

Conley parked at the curb outside the *Beacon* building and turned to the Jack Russell, who'd rode into town in the passenger seat, staring out the window, wagging his tail in enjoyment of the impromptu ride-along.

"C'mon, Opie," she said, and the dog hesitated but then hopped down onto the pavement.

The *Beacon* office was dark and silent.

She flicked on the lights, and after unpacking her laptop and re-search supplies, she sat down at her assigned desk and consulted the text message Kevin had sent the night before, with Symmes Robinette's local address—21 Sugar Key Way.

She typed the address into the search bar on her laptop and waited. The first hit came up on the county's tax rolls. It showed that the title to the home at that address had conveyed to Vanessa Robinette two years earlier, which meant that the sale had been completed after Robinette's last congressional campaign.

The county records showed that the seller, Sugar Key Corp. Ltd., sold a 4,228-square-foot home on a half-acre waterfront lot with five bedrooms, five baths, a three-car garage, and a swimming pool to Van-essa Robinette for the sum of $260,000.

"Damn. I want a deal like that," Conley murmured aloud.

Opie, who'd been dozing at her feet, looked up and thumped his tail in agreement.

For comparison, she typed in the addresses for the lots on either side of the Robinettes' bargain beach house.

The house at 19 Sugar Key Way sold six months prior to Robi-nette's, for $1.95 million, and the house at 23 sold in November of 2018 for $2.1 million.

Checking Robinette's financial statements from 2016, she saw that for a man who'd spent his last forty years in public service, the congress-man had managed to amass an impressive fortune.

He had a SEP account with a balance of $3.3 million and had stocks that, at the time of the filing, were worth another $6 million.

She ran a finger down the list of stocks Symmes owned, noting that most were blue-chip stocks, with a modest number of tech stocks and bank stocks, along with stock in a company called, oddly enough, Sugar Key Holdings.

Among his personal assets, he'd listed a home at 2331 Trinity Street in Silver Bay, which he'd purchased in 1980, for $32,000. She knew the house must be only a few blocks from G'mama's house on Felicity Street.

According to the assets list, Robinette also owned a home on eight hundred acres of land in Bronson County, with a valuation of $2 million. Was that Oak Springs Farm? She jotted down the address of the property. If so, where had Toddie moved after the divorce? Surely she wasn't renting from her ex?

Conley went to the Bronson County tax assessor's website and stared at the screen for a moment. She typed in the address for the parcel of land listed as an asset by Robinette in his last financial disclosure statement, and when the deed listing came up, she had to blink and reread the listing twice.

Symmes Robinette, it appeared, had conveyed title to the eight-hundred-acre parcel, plus a house, to Emma Todd Sanderson, as of May 8, less than a week before he'd died in a fiery car wreck, for the sum of one dollar "plus other considerations."

Emma Todd had to be Toddie Robinette, who'd probably reverted to her maiden name after her divorce from the congressman.

"Son of a bitch," she whispered.

She looked around the office for the printer, then realized she didn't know how to sync it up to her laptop to print. Instead, she took a screenshot of the property assessor's card.

Her stomach growled, and she did a silent fist pump. It never failed; whenever she was working on a story and hitting on all cylinders, she became ravenously hungry. And, she realized, she hadn't had any breakfast. Or lunch.

She prowled around the empty office, looking for something to eat. The break room refrigerator was disappointingly barren except for a suspicious-looking carton of greek yogurt and a soggy, half-eaten sandwich. Of course there were no vending machines, and she knew, without looking, that nothing would be open around the square on Sunday morning.

Her eyes lingered on the closed door of her sister's office. As a kid, Grayson had been a notorious snack hoarder. Winnie complained bitterly over all the times she'd found random bags of half-eaten Cheetos under Grayson's mattress and Snickers bars hidden in her underwear drawer.

Luckily, the door to Grayson's inner sanctum was unlocked. In her starved condition, Conley would have picked it without a single pang of guilt.

She walked directly to the desk and pulled open the deep middle drawer. Jackpot! Strewn among the stray paper clips, Post-it notes, and pencils, she found a veritable snack smorgasbord. There were Cheetos and Snickers, of course, because they were her sister's classic childhood comfort foods, but in addition, she'd stockpiled granola bars, bags of peanuts, even those cute little prepackaged cheese-and-cracker combos.

There was, Conley thought, a *lot* of snackage here. She swiveled around in Grayson's desk chair and spotted a mini-fridge under the console table behind the desk. Opening the fridge, she found containers of orange juice, bags of grapes, baby carrots, packages of sliced turkey, and tiny, round, red-wrapped cheese wheels.

She thought back to the previous day, when she'd spotted a pillow and blanket on the sofa here. She got up and opened the door to the room's tiny coat closet. The pillow and blanket were neatly folded on the closet shelf, but the clothes rod held a plastic dry cleaner's bag containing several dresses, skirts, blouses, and suit jackets. A laundry basket on the floor held more folded clothing, including lingerie and gym clothes. Four pairs of shoes were lined up on the floor.

In the bathroom, she spotted her sister's hair dryer and curling iron, as well as a bag of toiletries.

Grayson, she realized, was living here. In her office. Not just taking the occasional power nap or grabbing a meal because she was too busy to go home to Tony.

Conley sat down on the sofa, ripped the wrapper off a granola bar, and began chewing nervously.

What was going on between Tony and Grayson? She and Tony had never been especially close, but she'd always thought Tony, whom Grayson had met during her last year of law school at Stetson, was a good match for her sister. G'mama approved too, especially after Tony had been so understanding about moving back to Silver Bay to allow Grayson to take over running the paper after their grandfather's death.

Tony was corporate counsel for a software company based in Texas, so he traveled a lot for business, and since, according to Grayson, he wasn't into "family stuff," Conley seldom saw him outside of major holidays and family funerals.

How like Grayson not to say a word about whatever was going on in her marriage. In addition to being a snack hoarder, as a child, she'd been so secretive, Conley never knew what was going on in her sister's life.

Whatever it was, Conley decided, it would be up to Grayson to decide when to reveal the details of her personal life. She finished off the granola bar and swept a few telltale crumbs from the sofa before tiptoeing back to the outer office.

She'd just settled herself in front of her laptop again when her cell phone pinged with a text message. It was from Skelly.

Mama's having a good day. Want to come over for lunch?

The half-formed idea in her head suddenly blossomed.

Sure thing. How about a drive in the country after that?

Conley watched the little bubbles that meant he was typing a reply.

Okay. What are u plotting?

25

"Sorry," Conley said when she arrived on the Kellys' doorstep at noon. She gestured down at Opie, who was already straining at the leash to go inside the house. "When you invited me, I neglected to say I had a plus-one."

"It's fine," Skelly said. He leaned down to scratch Opie's ears, and the terrier immediately rolled onto his back to allow for a thorough belly scratch. "Mom loves dogs. She misses Buford something awful."

"Awww. Buford. What a good boy he was," Conley said, smiling at the memory of the Kelly family's golden retriever. The dog had been their constant companion in their childhood. "But he's been gone a long time, Skelly."

"I know. But Mama doesn't," he said. "C'mon in. Lunch is ready. Nothing fancy."

Conley followed Skelly down the hall and into the dining room. Miss June was seated at the head of the mahogany table, which was covered by a grand damask tablecloth. Three places were set with fine bone china, crystal, and slightly tarnished sterling silverware. A cut glass bowl in the center of the table was filled with a riot of colorful zinnias, cosmos, and sunflowers, and pink tapers burned in the silver candelabras.

"How pretty you look today!" Conley exclaimed as she leaned down to kiss Miss June's cheek.

The older woman wore a bright blue housedress with snaps up the front and had tucked a sprig of pale blue plumbago behind one ear.

"You look nice too, Sarah," Miss June said diplomatically.

"Whoops! I'm sorry to show up at your beautiful table dressed like what G'mama would call a *ragamuffin*, but I didn't know I was going to be the recipient of such a lovely lunch invitation," Conley said.

"And who is this?" Miss June cried, spotting Opie, who was busily sniffing her ankles.

"This is G'mama's dog, Opie," Conley said. She scooped the dog into her arms and held him out to the older woman, who beamed, letting the dog lick her chin and face.

"That's enough now, Opie," Conley said, trying to sound stern. "I'm going to put him in the backyard for now, or he'll be pestering us for food all during lunch."

"Oh no, let him stay," Miss June protested. "He can sit on the floor right here by me. And he'll be a good boy, won't you? What did you say his name was, Sarah dear?"

"Opie," Conley said. She touched the rim of one of the dinner plates. "This is so elegant. Much too elegant for the likes of me."

"Seanny did all this. Just for me," her hostess said happily. "I do like things to look nice, especially on Sundays."

"It's beautiful, Seanny," Conley said teasingly.

"Do *not* call me that," he said under his breath. "She's been so excited about having company for lunch. Do those flowers look familiar?"

She turned and scrutinized the centerpiece. "Are those . . . ?"

"I figured your grandmother wouldn't miss a few flowers from her garden, now that she's out at the beach. She usually sends Winnie down with a bunch every week."

"I know she'd love knowing your mother is enjoying them," Conley said, following him into the kitchen. "Now what can I do to help? Did I mention I'm starving?"

"You can help me carry in the salad. Everything's ready. Nothing fancy over here at Chez Kelly. Just a green salad and spaghetti and meatballs."

He went to the stove and lifted the lid of a huge saucepan, and the smell of oregano, garlic, and tomatoes filled the kitchen.

"Smells divine," she said, picking up the plates he'd already filled with tossed salad.

An hour later, she was washing dishes in the kitchen while Miss June sat in a chair in the living room, petting Opie and feeding him treats.

"Where'd you learn to make red sauce like that?" she asked her host, who was filling plastic quart containers with the leftover spaghetti.

"I had a friend in pharmacy school. He was from a big Italian family in New Jersey. We'd have these communal study groups on Sunday nights, and he'd always bring what he called his *nonna's Sunday gravy.*"

"If you ever get tired of running a pharmacy, you could probably open a restaurant with a recipe like that," she said.

"Not a chance," Skelly said, putting the last container in the refrigerator. "I don't get a chance to cook that often, but when I do, it's strictly for relaxation. I make this spaghetti all the time. It's one of Mom's favorites, and it's easy for her aides to warm up for lunch and dinner. She's fine with eating the same thing every day, because she never remembers she had it the day before and the day before that."

"She seems pretty alert and happy today," Conley said. She hesitated. "I was going to ask—do you think she'd be up for a Sunday drive out in the country?"

"You mentioned that in your text. I know you, Sarah Conley Hawkins. What's up? It's got something to do with Symmes Robinette, right?"

"Guilty," Conley said. "I've been poking around, looking at Robinette's most recent campaign finance statements. In addition to the house on Sugar Key, I found the address for what I think must be Oak Springs Farm. Looks like a pretty rural part of Bronson County."

"Why is this important to your story?"

"I looked up the property on the Bronson County tax assessor's website, and I couldn't believe what I found. Symmes deeded the farmhouse and eight hundred acres of land back to Toddie."

"So?"

"He did it a week before he died, Skelly. He just handed his ex-wife, whom he divorced thirty-four years ago, a gift worth two million."

"What do you hope to accomplish by driving out to that farm?"

"It's a beautiful day for a drive in the country," Conley said, trying to look and sound innocent. "Fresh air, beautiful scenery. Your mom can sit in the back seat and hug Opie, and I'll even let you drive!"

"And you can sit up front with me and try to figure out something nefarious about the death of a politician," he said, shaking his head.

"Exactly!"

"Where are we going?" Miss June asked, looking out the window from the back seat of the Subaru.

"Remember, Mama? We're going for a Sunday drive," Skelly said.

"Wonderful!" It was the third time she'd asked the question since they'd left the neighborhood, and they'd barely cleared the Silver Bay city limits.

"I saw a photo on the county website of the farmhouse Symmes deeded back to Toddie," she told Skelly. "It's two stories, with big, wide porches. Looks like something out of a magazine spread. Quite a difference from the photo I saw of the house she got in the divorce settlement."

"How so?" he asked.

"I think she must have been living in the caretaker's cottage or something. Not a shack or anything. The property card said it was fifteen hundred square feet. But it was modest compared to the big house. The reason I'm so puzzled is, why give her that big house—and all that land—now? They've been divorced all this time."

"Maybe Robinette was feeling guilty. Seems to me that he got the gold mine and she got the shaft when they split up in the eighties."

"Maybe," Conley said, sounding dubious. "I looked up his finance records from his last campaign. He was rolling in the dough. He had six million in cash and stocks, plus the Sugar Key house, plus a town house in Georgetown. And that land and house he gave to Toddie."

"I had no idea being a congressman was so lucrative," Skelly said. "I'm in the wrong racket, owning a little country pharmacy."

"Robinette might or might not have been feeling guilty, but he was definitely feeling generous in this last month or so," Conley said. "He also 'sold' his old house—the one that's right around the corner from yours and G'mama's—to his son, Charlie, also for a dollar. The house was assessed at over half a million dollars."

"I know Charlie's been living in that house since Symmes and Vanessa moved out to the beach at Sugar Key," Skelly said. "I guess the old man decided he might as well give it to his kid."

"And again, the question I have is, why now?"

Skelly looked out the window at the passing scenery. "Maybe . . . he was feeling his own mortality."

"Or maybe he knew he had some kind of terminal illness and wanted to assuage his own guilt," Conley said.

"I wouldn't know."

Conley, who'd been watching his expression, pounced. "You *do* know something. You're the only pharmacy in town. If Symmes Robinette was sick, you'd know what it was. How bad it was."

"HIPAA," Skelly said. "I can't have this conversation with you, Conley. It's a violation of my professional ethics."

"Sorry," she said, chastened. "The last thing G'mama said before she left to go to church with Grayson this morning was that she didn't want to get any more phone calls complaining about her pushy granddaughter."

Skelly had typed the address for Oak Springs in the GPS of his phone, and they were about fifteen miles outside the Silver Bay city limits when he suddenly slowed the Subaru and pulled off the side of the road.

He pointed to a spot on the pavement just a few yards ahead. It hadn't rained, and the asphalt was still coated with oily black soot, the shoulder littered with glittering pieces of red plastic from the shattered taillights.

"Does this look familiar?" he asked.

Conley's mouth went dry, and her stomach knotted as she remembered the night of the wreck and the glowing orange of the car fire. "I came past here the other day, but everything looks so different in the light of day." She gazed out the window and saw the roof of a small house protruding above the tree line. "I didn't notice that house before. Wonder who lives there? I wonder if those people saw or heard anything that night?" she mused.

"Good question for the cops," Skelly said, steering the car back onto the road and resuming normal speed.

"The map says we're getting close," he announced a few minutes later. They passed a small billboard proclaiming WELCOME TO BRONSON COUNTY—THIS IS QUAIL COUNTRY.

They heard a soft noise from the back seat. Conley turned to see that Miss June was napping, with Opie sprawled on his back across her lap, also asleep.

"You see that?" she asked.

He glanced in the rearview mirror and smiled. "I think maybe you should bring Opie by to see her more often."

Five minutes later, they saw a long row of white-painted fencing. "Okay, that's Riverdale Farm. If I remember correctly, that's the first one of the big plantations along this road. There are smaller ones scattered around the county, but half a dozen of the biggest ones are right along here."

"It's pretty," Conley said, admiring the rows of neat fencing, the stately, moss-draped oaks, and pristine pastures dotted with cattle, horses, and the occasional mule.

"You've never been out here?" he asked, sounding surprised.

"Don't think so. My dad didn't hunt at all. And Pops was more into deer hunting than quail. He said quail hunting was like horse breeding. A rich man's game."

"He was right about that," Skelly muttered. "Not many of these places are owned by locals anymore. A lot of these plantations belong to big-money tycoons. They fly in on their private jets during dove or quail season with their billionaire friends, knock down some quail, sip some bourbon, then jet back up north."

"It's a nice lifestyle," she said.

They were passing another plantation now. "I haven't been out here in ages," Skelly said, "but now that I see the landscape, I do remember coming out to Oak Springs with my parents when I was a little kid."

They passed two more plantations, Buie's Creek and River's Edge. Eventually, he pulled over at another impressive entranceway. A pair of tall brick columns held a pair of elaborately scrolled wrought iron gates. A discreet sign on one of the pillars announced OAK SPRINGS FARM, EST. 1902.

"Wow," Conley said, letting out a low whistle.

Skelly backed the Subaru up a little, then began to pull away.

"What are you doing?" she asked, alarmed. "Stop!"

He stopped the car and gestured at the gate. "You said you wanted to see it. You've seen it. We had a nice ride out in the country on a beautiful Sunday. Mama got to hold a dog and take a nap. I call that a win-win."

"I thought we'd go see the house," Conley said. "You know, maybe let your mom have a little visit with her old friend."

"I'm not up for trespassing," Skelly said. "Not even for you."

"It wouldn't really be trespassing," Conley pleaded. "We could just drive down to the house, maybe knock on the door, pay our respects. I mean, Toddie was your mom's best friend."

"Toddie?" They both turned to see that Miss June was awake. "What is this place?" she asked plaintively. She craned her neck to see out the window, and before they knew it, she opened the door, climbed out of the back seat, and walked, with surprising speed, toward the gate.

"Mama?" Skelly called.

His mother pointed at the sign, her face animated. "I know this place," she said. "This is Toddie's farm." She gave the iron gate a push, and the hinges squealed in protest.

"Shit," Skelly said, flashing Conley an annoyed look. He got out of the car and approached his mother.

Miss June used her shoulder and pushed the gate open a few more feet. "Toddie lives here," she told her son.

"Now, Mama," he started to say, but just then, Opie gave a short yelp of excitement, jumping out of the car and trotting over to join his new friend.

"Opie," Conley called, following behind. "C'mere, boy! Come here!"

The terrier paused and gave her a backward glance, followed by an enthusiastic wag of his somewhat stubby tail.

"Good boy, Opie," she called encouragingly, creeping slowly toward him. "C'mere, Ope."

He wagged his tail furiously. Then the little Jack Russell scampered past Miss June and her son, down the driveway as fast as his brown-and-white-spotted legs could go—which was surprisingly fast for an elderly dog whose usual speed was tortoise-like.

"Opie!" Conley yelled. "Come back!"

Skelly took his mother by the arm and guided her into the back seat of the Subaru while Conley clambered into the seat beside him.

"You did that on purpose," he said, starting the car and rolling through the now open gate.

She knew better than to protest.

26

The Oak Springs Farm driveway wound through an arching canopy of moss-covered oaks and towering pines, but Conley was oblivious to all of it. "Follow that dog," she instructed Skelly as he drove down the sandy lane. "If something happens to Opie, G'mama will kill me. And then she'll kill you too."

Every few hundred yards, the dog stopped to rest. Skelly slowed the truck and Conley jumped out to approach the dog on foot, but each time she came close enough to grab him, Opie trotted off, playing his own game of keepaway with the pursuers. At the end of the lane they finally spotted a white, two-story farmhouse with wide porches tucked behind a pair of spreading live oaks.

A tall, white-haired woman stood on the porch, her arms firmly wrapped around the squirming brown-and-white Jack Russell terrier, while half a dozen dogs circled around her, barking and whining.

"Thank God," Conley breathed. Skelly had barely put the Subaru in Park before she was out of the car and running.

"Is this your dog?" the woman called. She had light blue eyes and weather-beaten skin and was dressed in faded blue jeans, mud-spattered work boots, and a navy-blue T-shirt.

"Opie!" Conley said, holding out her arms. "You bad boy!" She turned to the woman. "Thanks so much for catching him." She looked down at all the dogs surrounding her. "They wouldn't hurt him, would they?"

"No, they're just curious. Bird dogs are the nosiest creatures you'll ever meet. And they're a little jealous."

"They're beautiful," Conley said of the elegant dogs. "What breed are they?"

"They're all English setters. Llewellyn setters, if you want to get technical." The woman stuck out her hand. "Don't mind the dirt or the dogs. I'm Toddie, by the way."

"And I'm Conley." She turned to gesture toward Skelly and Miss June, who were standing beside the car. "I believe you might know those folks?"

Toddie fished a pair of glasses from the breast pocket of her shirt and stared. "Good heavens! Can it be? Is that June Kelly?"

"It is," Conley said.

"She looks . . . different. Smaller."

"She's suffering from dementia," Conley said quietly. "That's her son, Sean. He runs the pharmacy now, and Miss June has been talking about you lately. We thought—well, *I* thought it was such a nice day . . ."

Before she'd finished the sentence, Toddie was striding toward the car, arms outstretched. "June Kelly!" she called. "Come here and let me give you a big old hug!"

"Toddie?" June said. She looked at her son. "Is that really Toddie? She looks old!"

"Mama!" Skelly said.

"She's right. I do look old. I *am* old." Toddie enveloped the smaller woman. "Oh, June, my old friend. How I've missed you." She left an arm slung around June. "And Sean! The last time I laid eyes on you was when you were crying to get away from one of my mules."

Skelly grinned. "I've been trying to live that down for more than thirty years. And I'm still not crazy about an animal that could kick you in the head and kill you."

"Seanny works at the store now, Toddie," June said proudly. "He's a big help to me."

"I'm sure he is," Toddie said. She looked past the Kellys at Conley, who was hanging back, not wanting to interrupt the reunion.

"Is this your wife, Sean?"

"Uh, no, Mrs. Robinette, er, Toddie. That's Sarah Conley Hawkins. Her family lives two doors down from Mama's house. Maybe you remember them?"

"Lord, I've been living out here in the country, away from civilized society in Silver Bay, for so long you'll have to remind me of their names," Toddie said.

"Why, Sarah is Lorraine's granddaughter," June said. "Lorraine Conley. You know, them; Lorraine and Woodrow, they run the newspaper."

"Of course," Toddie said, nodding. "That would make you Melinda and Chet's daughter, right?"

"Yes, ma'am," Conley said, feeling suddenly awkward.

"I hope your parents are well," Toddie said. "It's been a long, long time."

"Melinda ran off some time ago, and we don't know where she is," June volunteered. "And Sarah's daddy's dead. Like my Patrick. Did you know my Patrick died, Toddie?"

"I didn't know that." Toddie nodded gravely at Conley, with just a hint of a twinkle in her cornflower-blue eyes. "But my condolences to both of you."

Skelly's face blushed crimson as he glanced from Toddie to Conley. "Sorry, y'all. Mom's, uh, sort of unfiltered these days."

June pointed a bony finger at Toddie. "Whatever happened to that sorry husband of yours, Toddie?"

"Why, he ran off with a younger gal who didn't sass him half as much as I did," Toddie said good-naturedly. "That's when I said good riddance to bad rubbish."

"Oh my God, Mama!" Skelly pulled her by the hand. "I think maybe we need to be getting you home for a rest." He turned to Toddie. "I don't know what to say, Toddie. I'm mortified. Truly."

"Don't give it another thought, Sean," Toddie said, putting a hand on his shoulder. "I feel badly that I've let so much time go by without connecting with people from my old life. It's just that we stay so busy out here at the farm, I lose track of time."

"It's just as beautiful here as I remembered from when I was a kid," Skelly said.

"Thank you. My son, Hank, works here right beside me, and of course, Rebecca lives on the property now too since her divorce, in what we call the *little house*. Her girls are teenagers now, if you can believe it. How about you, Sean? Do you have kids?"

"No, ma'am," Skelly said. "Divorced too, unfortunately."

Skelly nodded at Conley and then, pointedly, in the direction of the car. "We'd best be getting her home now. Mom loves getting out and seeing people, but when she gets overtired, I never know what's going to come out of her mouth."

"My granny was like that when she got dementia," Toddie said. "She once told our pastor he oughta pass around the collection plate and buy a new set of teeth for himself and a larger size dress for his wife."

"Ouch."

"It was good seeing you again, Sean, and June, of course. Any special reason why y'all came all the way out here today?"

"I'm gonna get Mama settled in the car," Skelly said. "Here, Conley. I'll take Opie and put him back there with her." He put the wriggling terrier under his arm and led his mother back to the Subaru.

"He's embarrassed," Conley told Toddie once he was out of earshot. "I'm afraid I should admit to you that I dragged them out here today under false pretenses."

Toddie cocked her head. "Oh? How's that?"

"Well, I'm currently working at the *Beacon*. Temporarily. And the thing is, I'm working on a story about your ex-husband. About his death, I mean."

Toddie's smile faded.

Conley rushed on. "I'm sorry for your loss. It must have been a terrible shock for your family."

"My family?" Her voice grew frosty. "If you're looking for a story about my ex-husband, you'd best contact his wife. Symmes and I parted ways more than thirty years ago."

"Vanessa—I mean, Mrs. Robinette—submitted an obituary for the *Beacon*, and the thing is, it only lists her and her son as the congressman's survivors. There's no mention of you, which I guess isn't unheard of, or the children you had with the congressman."

Toddie's lips clamped tightly. "That's not surprising," she said finally. She looked away and then back at the Subaru. "I'm sorry you made the trip here for nothing, Sarah."

"I was wondering," Conley said, rushing now. "It's just that in my research, I saw that the congressman deeded this farm over to you only a week before his accident. And I found that unusual—"

"I don't have anything else to say to you about this matter. Thank you for bringing June to see me today. But if you'll excuse me, I've got dogs to train and a farm to run."

"That was incredibly awkward," Conley said as they drove away from the farmhouse.

"What did she say?" Skelly asked.

"Basically, she said, 'Here's your hat, what's your hurry?'" Conley turned in her seat and saw that Miss June was already dozing, with Opie draped contentedly across her lap.

"The good news is that Toddie's been out of touch for so long, she probably doesn't have your grandmother's phone number," Skelly pointed out.

"I guess I need to apologize to you again," Conley said, sighing.

"Not to me," he said.

She leaned her head against the window and closed her eyes for a moment, but sat up straight after she remembered a question that had been bothering her since that morning. "Skelly, do you know what's going on between Grayson and Tony?"

He kept his eyes on the road and was slow to answer.

"What do you mean?"

"Whenever somebody answers a question with a question, I start thinking they have something to hide," Conley said. "I mean, my sister has been sleeping in the office. Basically living there. Are they separated? Did she run Tony off?"

"Ask her," Skelly said.

She rolled her eyes. "You know Grayson. She's so . . . uptight. Tight-lipped. And we've never really talked about family stuff."

"Not at all? Like, well, like about your mom?"

"Nope."

"Do you ever open up to her about what's going on in your life? Does she know you broke up with your live-in boyfriend before you came back home?"

"Whose side are you on here?"

"I don't take sides. I'm neutral," he said.

"That's bullshit," she said under her breath.

A few more miles of pastures and farmland rolled past before he spoke up again.

"Before Danielle left, this last time, when we were still trying to save our marriage, we went to counseling. And the therapist—who was a guy, by the way—said something that clicked with me," Skelly said.

"I can't wait to hear it."

Skelly ignored her sarcasm. "He said that seventy-five percent of the issues people have in their relationships—the reason they end up in therapy—is because they just assume things. They assume their partner knows what they want in life. They assume they both share the same values and goals. But you can't do that. You can't expect even the person who's closest to you to know what you're thinking unless you open up and talk about it in an honest and open way."

"And did that help?" Conley turned in her seat to face him. "With you and Danielle?"

"Obviously, it wasn't enough to save our marriage. Once we did start talking, it turns out that I assumed she wanted to stay married to me and live in Silver Bay, maybe even start having kids together. But Danielle didn't. She assumed I knew she felt trapped—in our marriage, in the situation with my mom, running the family business, all of it."

"So opening up to each other didn't really help," Conley said.

"In a funny way, it did. Not with the marriage, but it helped me clarify things. What I wanted, for instance, and what was important to me. I realized that even if I did what she wanted, things wouldn't really change between us." He gave her a sideways glance. "If you tried to really talk to Grayson, you might be surprised at what she has to say. Running that paper and looking out for your grandmother . . . I know from my own experience that things can get overwhelming."

"My sister doesn't want to talk to me," Conley said. "She thinks I'm an entitled brat because I got to go off and have the career I wanted, while she stayed home to save the *Beacon*. You don't really know my sister, Skelly. She enjoys being a martyr. She should have been a Catholic instead of a Presbyterian. Saint Grayson. Our Lady of Perpetual Sacrifice. That's my big sister."

"Isn't that kind of harsh?" he asked, raising an eyebrow. "If her marriage is in trouble, if she and Tony split up, she's probably feeling pretty damn lonely. And vulnerable."

"Grayson Hawkins? Vulnerable?" Conley said with a hoot. "Get real."

27

When she came downstairs Monday morning, Conley found Winnie alone in the kitchen, stemming and slicing strawberries into a colander.

"Where's G'mama?"

"Gone to the store," Winnie said, shaking her head in disapproval. "One of the ladies at church brought her a gallon of these strawberries from their farm, and she's determined to make jam today."

Conley poured a mug of coffee from the battered aluminum percolator resting on the front burner of the stove. "You let her go by herself?"

"I tried to get her to let me drive, or wait until you were up, but she's wanting to get going before it gets too hot. She does look a lot better this morning. That knot on her head is almost gone. Anyway, she was just going to the IGA, and it's not but a few blocks from here."

Winnie's turquoise transistor radio was sitting on the windowsill. An announcer was reading the local news, most of it, Conley realized, cribbed directly from last week's issue of the *Beacon*. A zoning commission meeting was coming up; construction was slated to begin on an annex to the jail. The Lutheran church was sponsoring summer day camp for needy kids, and the weather was expected to stay the same, hot and sunny.

"In other news, WSVR has learned, Florida's late congressman Symmes Robinette will be memorialized Tuesday, when his body will lie in state in the rotunda of the U.S. Capitol. Dignitaries expected to attend the service will include all the members of the Florida congressional delegation, the Florida governor and lieutenant governor, and, reportedly, the president and vice president. A contingent of Silver Bay residents will also attend the service, including Robinette's widow, Mrs. Vanessa Robinette, and his son, Charles Robinette Jr.

"This community has been in mourning since last week's tragic accident claimed the life of the eighteen-term congressman—"

Winnie reached up and snapped the radio off. "Not everybody is mourning," she muttered.

Conley regarded the housekeeper over the rim of her coffee mug. "Winnie, can I ask you a question?"

Winnie turned and wiped her berry-stained hands on a dish towel. "About him?"

"Yeah. G'mama never would say what exactly happened, you know, that time you got in trouble."

"Lorraine likes to call it *an unfortunate incident*," Winnie agreed. "You know your grandmother. She likes to tippy-toe around the unpleasant stuff."

"Must be a family trait," Conley said. "Do you mind talking about it? I've always been curious."

"There's not a whole lot to tell," Winnie said. "I did something the law says I ought not to have. Went to prison for twenty months."

"What, exactly, did you do?"

Winnie looked out the kitchen window. Bright sunshine streamed in, seagulls cried, and waves crashed on the nearby beach. Just another morning at the beach.

"You know my sister, Nedra, the boys' mama, died of cancer when she wasn't even thirty yet. Cancer she got from that railroad switchyard over in Plattesville, where we grew up. The railroad stored barrels of chemicals there for years and years, chemicals they knew caused cancer. Those barrels rusted, and the chemicals leaked out, so the poison went into the lake us kids used to play in. It washed into the drainage ditches where we used to catch tadpoles and into the dirt where my mamaw grew her garden."

"So you were living on a toxic waste dump," Conley said.

"We didn't know no better at the time. Then folks started getting sick. Nosebleeds, headaches, gut problems. Women were having miscarriages. Or worse." Her hand rested lightly on her own abdomen, an unconscious gesture. "People were dying. Even little kids. Nobody put it together until this lady lawyer, Randee, showed up. She'd been looking at the statistics in the neighborhood. Putting pins in a map to show who got the cancer and where they lived."

"A cancer cluster. But the railroad never accepted responsibility for it, right?"

"No. Randee did her best. She filed lawsuits, but the judges around here? They were in cahoots with the railroad. And of course, the railroad hired Symmes Robinette to go to court for them. The best judges and lawyers money could buy. What chance did we have? We were just a bunch of white trash from the wrong side of town. They brought in doctors that said we'd gotten sick from smoking cigarettes, or drinking, or just because."

Conley sipped her coffee slowly and glanced at the clock above the stove. She needed to get to work.

"Did the *Beacon* ever write any stories about what went on in Plattesville back then?"

"Not that I remember," Winnie said. "But then, I was busy working for y'all, plus taking care of my sick sister and her kids."

"When's the last time you talked to that lawyer, Randee?"

"Probably the day she went to court with me to try to talk the judge out of sending me to prison," Winnie said. "Didn't do any good. But I didn't hold that against her."

"What exactly did you do?" Conley repeated.

Winnie rubbed her thumb and forefinger together, and her face took on a dreamy expression. "I used to smoke. Did you know that? Not inside your house, because your grandmother didn't allow it. Drank a good bit too, after Nedra died. Most of the time, I don't miss it. But when I think about those dark times? I kinda get the taste for a cigarette and a beer." She took her coffee mug and refilled it, then sat down at the table opposite Conley. "One day, after he'd gone and gotten elected to Congress, I heard on the radio that Symmes Robinette was coming back down here from D.C. for some groundbreaking hoo-ha they were doing for the new Veterans Administration clinic. Nedra had been dead a couple of years, and times were so hard. I was lonely. Bitter too. Wasn't thinking straight. I packed up Jesse. I think he must have been home sick from school, and I took him with me out to where they were getting ready to build the clinic."

"Jesse's the youngest, right? And he's still here in town?"

Winnie nodded. "I kind of had a plan, but I was scared. I drank a couple of cans of beer in the car to get my courage up. Okay, maybe I had three. That part was wrong. Me drinking when I shoulda been watching out for that little boy. Then me and Jesse got as close as we could to the front of the crowd, listening to the speeches. Robinette spoke, so puffed up about how he'd brought so much money back to his 'beloved community.' All the time he talked, I was thinking about Nedra, about her boys being raised orphans, how sick she'd been at the end, how she suffered, begging to die. So I did it. When Robinette came down from the stage, for all his shaking hands and kissin' babies bullcrap, I crept right up next to him. He patted Jesse on the head, and I just stuck my hand down in my pocketbook, got a big old handful of ashes, and flung 'em right in Robinette's face."

"Ashes?" As soon as she said the word, Conley realized what ashes Winnie meant.

"Nedra's ashes. Her 'cremains,' the funeral home called 'em. I wish you'd seen the look on Robinette's face. It was hot, and he was sweatin' like a pig anyway, so those ashes stuck to him like flour on a biscuit."

Conley shuddered at the image.

"Some lady screamed, because I guess they thought maybe I had a gun or something. There were cops all over the place, and one of 'em grabbed me and knocked me onto the ground." Winnie's eyes dropped to her hands, clutching the mug. "They handcuffed me. Jesse was right there. He saw all of it. Lord Jesus, I will never forget the look on that boy's face. When the cop was handcuffing me, Jesse started kicking at him, screaming for him to let me go."

"Oh, Winnie," Conley whispered, touching her wrist.

"Lorraine and your granddaddy came and got me out on bail, did everything they could for me, even paid Randee to defend me, but the judge who sentenced me, he was set on making an example of me. Plus he was one of Robinette's cronies. He said I'd made 'terroristic threats.' So I went to prison. The worst part? Nedra's no-account husband, Ed, and his sorry mama got that judge to give them custody of the boys while I was away. They only wanted the kids because the county gave 'em food stamps, which Ed sold to buy drugs."

Conley knew bits of the rest of the story—how the two older boys had run away from their father, ended up committing petty crimes and being sent away to Florida's notorious juvenile detention center in Marianna.

"I was away at boarding school, but I remember how upset G'mama was about what happened to Jason and Jerry," she said.

"It's a miracle they didn't end up getting killed or worse at that hellhole," Winnie said. "You know the state shut it down about ten years ago. As soon as I got out of prison, your granddaddy helped me get my boys back."

"Despite all that, they turned out to be wonderful young men," Conley said. "You should be so proud of that, Winnie."

"No," she said emphatically. "Anything they made of themselves was despite me messing up their lives. Those twenty months I was in prison? They were in their own prison, first living with Ed and then getting sent to Marianna. And that was all on me. Because I messed up. They suffered because of me." Winnie dabbed at her eyes with the edge of the dish towel. "Now you can see why I'm not sorry Robinette died. I know the Bible says I've got to forgive, but it doesn't say *when* I've got to forgive him, right?"

"Right."

They heard the clank of the elevator rising from the ground floor, and when the door opened, Lorraine emerged, carrying her canvas tote of groceries.

"Don't you start fussing at me for driving," she warned as Conley took the bag and began unloading the sacks of sugar, Sure-Jell, and lemon. "Anyway, aren't you supposed to be at work this morning?"

"Am I?"

Lorraine took an apron from a nail on the back of the pantry door and fastened it around her waist.

"After church yesterday, I reminded Grayson that she'd be a fool to let somebody as talented and hardworking as you to quit over a little family spat," she said. "So she's expecting you this morning. I never did get a chance to ask you last night about your research. Did you find out anything interesting?"

"I found out Symmes Robinette died a rich man," Conley said. "Just from his last campaign finance reports, I saw that two years ago, he had six million in stocks and bonds. And real estate holdings including his house in town, the Gulf-front mansion on Sugar Key, and a town house in Georgetown."

"My goodness," G'mama said. She reached into a cabinet and brought out a blue graniteware stockpot, then dumped in the strawberries and the sugar.

"Symmes's people were not wealthy. I mean, his stepfather was a manager at the plant, but they were middle class at best. How did he get so rich?"

Winnie snorted. "Blood money. He made all that money off legal fees from the railroad after they poisoned all of us. How much money do you think he got paid?"

"But that was so long ago," Lorraine said. "He's been in Congress all these years. I don't think congressmen are allowed to make money outside of speaking fees and things like that. So he only had his salary, right?"

"Which was about 174,000 dollars a year," Conley added.

"The rich get richer," Winnie put in. "He probably got stock tips every time he went to dinner with those Washington lobbyists."

"I found out he deeded a quail-hunting plantation with a farmhouse and eight hundred acres of land to his ex-wife a week before he died."

"Toddie? He just up and gave her that farm? Oak Springs, over in

Bronson County?" Lorraine had been cutting up a lemon. She put her paring knife on the cutting board. "That doesn't sound like the Symmes Robinette I know. The man was so tight his shoes squeaked when he walked. He wouldn't even buy an ad in the *Beacon* to congratulate the high school graduating class for the special section we did every May. And I know Toddie used to sew the children's clothes—and hers too— because he didn't see any need for them to have store-bought when she could make them so much cheaper."

"Apparently, he had a change of heart. According to the Bronson County tax assessor's office, that was a gift worth two million. And he didn't stop there. He also deeded over his old house, around the block from your house, G'mama, to Charlie around the same time. The place was worth over half a million."

Winnie turned on the burner under the pot of strawberries and added water, picking up a wooden spoon to stir. "A lot of good all that money does him now," she said with a glint of malice in her eye. "Like my mamaw always said, you don't ever see a Brink's truck in a funeral procession."

"No," Lorraine said thoughtfully, taking the spoon out of the housekeeper's hand. "But now Vanessa Robinette is a very wealthy widow. And since she's almost twenty years younger than Symmes, she'll have plenty of time to spend all that loot he left behind. She knows how to spend it too. I've never seen her dressed in anything but the latest designer fashions, and I know for a fact that she gets a new Mercedes every other year."

"G'mama!" Conley said, feigning shock. "I can't believe you just said something that catty."

"Well . . ." Lorraine had the grace to look a little ashamed. "Call me a narrow-minded, judgmental old biddy, but I guess I never did forgive her for sleeping with another woman's husband. It sticks in my craw. It really does."

28

As soon as Conley entered the *Beacon*'s outer office, Lillian King was at her side. "Heads up. You've got a visitor waiting to see you in Grayson's office."

"Who is it?"

"She just showed up here five minutes ago, demanding to see the manager. I don't know her name, but she looks rich. And she's definitely pissed about something."

"Conley?" Grayson stuck her head out of her office door. "Need to see you."

The visitor was seated on one end of the sofa in Grayson's office. She was slender, dressed in black slacks and a sleeveless V-necked black top that showed off tanned, well-toned arms. She'd gone redhead since the last time Conley had seen her.

She'd had some work done too, Conley thought. The nose was shorter, the chin line sleeker, the lips were much plumper, but the changes were subtle. And expensive. The only jewelry she wore was a platinum wedding band and an enormous diamond solitaire engagement ring.

Grayson was clearly flustered. "Conley, you remember Vanessa Robinette, right?"

"Of course," Conley said.

"Ladies, I'm going to have to leave you to chat, because I have a meeting to get to," Grayson said. And then she fled the office as though pursued by a pack of rabid dogs.

"I'm sorry for your loss, Mrs. Robinette," Conley said, seating herself on the other end of the sofa. "But I'm actually glad you dropped by, because I was going to call you today. I'm working on a story about your husband's death—"

"So my son tells me," Vanessa said. "He said you ambushed him at the law firm and that you've been asking a lot of intrusive and embarrassing questions around town. I thought I'd just drop by today and get some things straight."

"Intrusive?" Conley blinked. "The questions I was asking were pretty straightforward."

"Hounding Charlie about the cause of his father's death? Dear God! We haven't even buried Symmes yet. Don't you people have any sense of decency?"

"As I said, you and your family have my condolences. But your husband was a highly visible public figure in this community. And his death, and the circumstances surrounding it, are news. I merely asked Charlie if the medical examiner had determined the cause of death."

"He burned to death in his car!" Vanessa snapped. "The sheriff over in Bronson tells me you were a witness to the accident. What part of this don't you understand?"

"As you said, I was there. I didn't witness the accident, but I must have arrived shortly afterward. So I don't understand a one-car accident at three in the morning on a clear, cloudless night," Conley said quietly.

Vanessa turned her engagement ring so that the stone was facing the palm of her hand. "He's been very ill." Her large brown eyes filled with tears. "We thought we'd have more time together. Time to plan things out. He was diagnosed in September. The doctors were cautiously optimistic."

"What kind of illness?" Conley asked.

"Non-Hodgkin's lymphoma." She twisted the ring around and around.

"You never made his condition public?"

Her head snapped up. "Why would we do that? This was a private family matter."

"Because he was an elected member of Congress? Don't the voters here in the district have a right to know—"

"No. They don't," she said flatly. "Symmes was treated at Walter Reed and got right back to work. He never missed an important vote or committee meeting. Even with the chemo. It was brutal, but he was determined to keep going. Most men his age would have given up, but most men weren't like my husband."

Conley thought back to the previous week. "Isn't the House currently in session?"

Vanessa glared at her. "He had business back here. Look. I've tried to be helpful, because after all, this was Symmes's hometown paper, but I won't continue to be treated in this unprofessional, disrespectful manner."

For a moment, Conley felt like a preschooler who'd just been given a demerit for biting or hair pulling.

Vanessa stood up and smoothed the fabric of her slacks. "I'd hoped that if we chatted in person, you'd understand the enormity of my husband's legacy to this community. All the things he achieved. The VA clinic, highway improvements, his work on elder abuse . . ."

"Of course I'll be writing about all that," Conley said.

"Symmes did so much good for the people here," Vanessa said, tearing up again. "You have no idea of his commitment. He had a brilliant legal career before he was asked to run. He could have gone into practice anywhere—in New York, or Miami, or LA. Instead, he chose to go to Washington, to fight for his people back home."

"You met while you were working as an aide in his office, is that right?" Conley asked.

"That's right. I was young and just starting out. Symmes was so kind and generous. He was always one to encourage young people."

"And he was married at the time, right?"

Vanessa's tears vanished. "Technically, yes. If you can call what they had a marriage. It had been over for years. His alleged wife wouldn't step foot in D.C. He was lonely and so unhappy. He'd been asking for a divorce for years, but she refused because she liked the prestige of being married to a congressman, that's all. It was always about the money with her. He made her a very generous settlement offer because of the children."

"And also because you were pregnant?" Conley asked.

"We've never made a secret of that," Vanessa said. Her voice was calm, but her cheeks flared red. "This isn't the Victorian era. Most people didn't give it a second thought." She headed for the door. "I really have to go. There are arrangements to be made. My husband's service in D.C. is tomorrow."

"One more question, please." Conley followed her to the door. "The obituary that you submitted through the funeral home? There was no mention in the list of survivors of your husband's ex-wife or their two children."

Vanessa raised her chin. "Damn straight I left them out. They weren't mentioned because they weren't a part of Symmes's life. You know what? I don't even know their names. I doubt my husband could remember them either. *That's* how estranged he was from all of them."

"And yet," Conley said, "he deeded over the title to Oak Springs to Toddie the week before he died."

Vanessa had her hand on the door but stopped and turned to stare at Conley. "What did you just say?"

"I said he deeded over the title to a farmhouse and eight hundred acres of land in Bronson County to his first wife, Emma Todd Sanderson—that would be Toddie, right?"

"That's not possible," Vanessa said, shaking her head. "He's allowed her to live there for years now, rent-free, out of the goodness of his heart, but he would never deed that property to her. I don't know what that woman has told you, but it's impossible. Symmes would never have done something like that."

"Toddie refused to discuss it with me. I found the notice of deed transfer in the county tax records," Conley said. "For the sum of one dollar and other considerations."

"If he did do something like that—and I'm not saying he did—it was the chemo. He hadn't been himself lately. That's why he was home, because I wanted him to get some rest. But he was confused and disoriented. *Chemo brain,* the doctors called it. He'd get up in the middle of the night and just drive around for hours. It was terrifying."

"Do you think that's what happened the night he died?" Conley asked.

Vanessa shook her head violently like a mule shaking off a pesky fly. "If you have any more questions, I suggest you call my lawyer." Her eyes narrowed. "Charlie tells me there's some sort of bad blood between the two of you. So if this rag of yours prints one derogatory word about my late husband, I will personally make sure that you come to regret that decision."

She brushed past Lillian King as she was hurrying through the office, jostling the office manager as she went, causing her to drop a handful of papers. "Excuse me," Vanessa said with a curt nod.

Conley walked slowly back to her makeshift work space, where she was soon joined by Lillian.

"Seems like Miss Thang there had kind of a bee up her butt," Lillian said. "Who was she, anyway?"

"That was the widow Robinette," Conley said grimly. "And I think that's an accurate description of her current mood."

Lillian handed her the sheaf of papers she'd managed to retrieve.

"What's this?" Conley asked.

"Rowena's latest masterpiece," Lillian said. "Your sister said I should give it to you for 'tweaking.'"

"Nooooo," Conley moaned. "I've got my own story to write."

"I'm just the messenger," Lillian said. "But wait 'til you see this mess."

29

HELLO, SUMMER

By Rowena Meigs

Cupid's quiver must be mighty empty this week, as your correspon-dent received notices of no fewer than three recent engagements! Re-grettably, we will not be announcing these upcoming nuptials, due to the fact that the brides-to-be have been living with their intendeds without benefit of clergy for several months now. Your correspondent realizes that this is an increasing fact of modern life, but we do not intend to publicize or sanctify such arrangements.

*We are, however, delighted to announce that one of Silver Bay's most talented young students, **LizaJane Hooper,** recently won second place in the **United Daughters of the Confederacy** speech contest. This year's topic was "Democracy: What It Means to Me." LizaJane is a rising junior at Griffin County High School and the daughter of Mr. and Mrs. Stephens Hooper. LizaJane's maternal grandmother, **Arthureen Gresham,** is vice president of the North Florida chapter of the UDC. LizaJane's prize was a dozen roses from Francine's Florals and a gold-tone UDC medal.*

What a delightful time was had by all at the elegant soirée hosted *by the children of **Harkness and Jinxy Westphail** in honor of the blessed couple's fiftieth wedding anniversary. Golden and silver centerpieces of mixed mums and daisies decorated each table, and guests feasted on fried shrimp, fried catfish, hushpuppies, coleslaw, and a specially prepared wedding cake with a cake topper bearing an uncanny likeness of the honorees, crafted from Rice Krispies and colored frosting by talented granddaughter **Sonia Castleberry**, who also decorates cakes at the Silver Bay Bakery.*

*A late note: Silver Bay was deeply saddened by the tragic death this week of longtime congressman **Symmes Robinette**. Your correspondent will have all the news of the funeral in next week's column. In the meantime, deepest condolences to the family.*

Conley glanced down at Rowena's copy. "I can't," she said, tossing the papers onto her desktop. "I haven't had enough coffee yet to tackle this."

"Take it from me. There isn't enough coffee in Colombia to make sense of Rowena Meigs," Lillian said. "But your sister was real specific that this needs to get done today."

"I'll rewrite it when I get back," Conley said, heading for the door.

"Back from where?"

"Scene of the crime," Conley replied.

She'd intended to make another visit to Bronson County sheriff Merle Goggins, but she slowed down as she approached the accident site on the county road where Symmes Robinette had died. Traffic was heavier this time of day, and with a pickup truck close on her rear bumper, she pulled onto the shoulder of the road about a hundred yards from the spot, spying, for the first time, a break in the barbed wire pasture fencing and a narrow dirt road that led through the field.

Conley parked the Subaru just inside the entrance to the dirt road, got out, and walked over to the crash site. The scorched pavement, still littered with bits of red taillights and shattered glass, made her stomach clench just as it had the previous week.

It apparently hadn't rained lately in this part of the county. She saw several sets of heavy tire-tread marks crisscrossing in the hard-packed dirt and weeds along the shoulder. Probably from all the rescue vehicles that had responded to the 911 call, she thought. When she saw a break in the traffic, she darted across the two-lane road. The grassy weeds here were more matted down, with heavier tire imprints. The shoulder was strewn with cigarette butts and empty plastic water bottles, more evidence of the rescue crews who'd battled the car fire.

She crossed back to where she'd parked the Subaru and leaned against the rear bumper, swatting at mosquitoes and watching cars and trucks whiz by as she wondered exactly why she was drawn, yet again, to this macabre scene.

Her musings were interrupted by the putt-putting of a motor. As she turned, she saw a dust-covered, olive-green four-wheel Ranger vehicle like the ones used by local hunters approaching. But this one was driven by a woman, with a large dog riding shotgun in the seat beside her.

"Can I help you?" the woman called as she drew nearer. Conley saw that the driver was older, in her seventies maybe, with steel-gray hair topped with a white sun visor.

"Oh, uh, no. I'm okay," Conley said when the ATV stopped a few feet away.

"You're parked on my property," the woman said pointedly. "Having some kind of car troubles, are you?"

Up close like this, Conley saw that the dog looked to be some kind of hound mix. He had large, floppy ears, a grayed muzzle, and big, droopy brown eyes filmed with cataracts.

"Oh no. My car is fine." Conley found herself unaccountably flustered. "I'm, uh, a reporter, and I'm just trying to figure out what happened here last week."

"The night that poor man burned to death?" Her blue-gray eyes traveled to the scorch marks on the pavement. "That was an awful thing."

"It was," Conley agreed. "If this is your property, do you live around here?"

The woman waved in the general direction of the fields behind her.

"Right back there. How about you? What kind of news outfit do you work for?"

"I'm a reporter for *The Silver Bay Beacon*. My name is Conley Hawkins."

The woman tilted her head and studied her. "Kin to Chet Hawkins, are you?"

Conley slid easily into the Southern speech patterns she'd lost during her years in the city. "Yes, ma'am. He was my daddy."

"Well, your daddy was a nice man. When my husband was alive, we did business with your daddy's bank. He was always square with us."

Conley knew this about her father, but it was nice to hear from a stranger. Her father valued being square. He'd always talked about and tried to exhibit qualities like integrity and honesty and loyalty. These weren't just words for a DAR speech contest for Chet Hawkins. She liked to think maybe those qualities were ones she'd inherited, along with her great-grandmother's aquamarine ring and a box of tarnished sterling silver flatware that she'd left behind in a rented storage unit in Atlanta.

"I'm glad to hear that," she said now. "About last week. Did you see or hear anything that night?" She slapped at a mosquito that had landed on her forearm.

"It's blazing hot out here," the woman said. "Why don't you come on up to the house, and we'll talk. Might as well leave your car here."

The woman patted the dog on the rump. "Scoot over, Sport. We got company."

The dog opened one eye, gave a baleful sigh, and slid onto the floor of the Ranger.

The field spread out before them with crops that had already grown two feet high in the hot Florida sun.

"Is all this land yours?" Conley asked.

"Yes, but we lease this part to a hunting club. Farther back on the property, we grow peanuts and soybeans. Well, *I* don't grow any of it anymore; my sons and I lease it out. Stopped farming after Alton died." She turned and offered Conley a weather-beaten hand. "I'm Margie Barrett, by the way."

They drove past a decaying wooden farmhouse with a collapsed front porch and saplings growing through the rusted-out tin roof. Bales of hay were visible in the open doorway.

"That's the old homeplace," Margie commented. "Alton and I lived there when we were newlyweds, but after that, I told him I wasn't bringing my babies home to a house where you could see clean through the floorboards."

The house would have made a beautifully evocative black-and-white photo, Conley thought as they passed, but she had to agree with Margie's housing preferences.

The Ranger rumbled along the dirt road, and then they were approaching a tidy concrete-block house. It was painted pale turquoise and had an abbreviated front porch with a pair of rocking chairs and hanging baskets of ferns. A tabby cat scampered away into the yard at the sound of the approaching vehicle. The house stood in a patch of carefully tended green lawn, with beds of red, white and blue annuals.

Margie parked the Ranger and tenderly lifted the old dog and set him on the grass. "Sport's almost fourteen years old. He doesn't move around so good anymore. Like me. Come on inside, and I'll get us a couple of Cokes."

Conley settled on a sofa in a wood-paneled living room whose walls were dotted with family photos. The furniture was maple, reproduction early American. There was a worn brown vinyl recliner facing a flat-screen television. Sport parked himself on the green shag carpet near her feet.

"Here we go," Margie said, handing her a glass. She set a small bowl of water in front of the dog, but he was already dozing.

"About last Thursday morning," Conley said, easing her notebook out of the pocket of her jeans. "I was asking you if you saw or heard anything?"

Margie reached down and absentmindedly scratched the old dog's ears. "Sport here is about blind, but his hearing is still pretty sharp. He got me up way after midnight. I'm not sure of the time, but I know I'd fallen asleep in the recliner, watching TV. I took him outside to pee, but after a while, he was pacing and kinda growling and yipping to be let off the leash. I usually keep him leashed outside at night 'cause I'm scared he might hear something and take off running. Blind as he is, and old as I am, I might never find him again." She chuckled and patted the dog's head. "We can't have you getting lost, can we, Sport?"

"Did he hear something?" Conley asked.

Margie nodded. "At first, I thought it was probably just a possum or a raccoon, but then I heard it myself. Voices. Coming from up the road by the highway."

She pointed to a large picture window that looked out on the field. Conley could just barely see the gleaming metal roof of her car in the distance.

"Folks, especially townsfolk, don't realize how far voices carry out here in the country. But once I got Sport quieted down, I heard two men's voices. They were arguing, and it was pretty loud."

Intrigued, Conley leaned closer, her pen poised over her notebook. "Could you make out what they were saying?"

"Not really, but I could tell from the tone that they were spittin' mad. After a while, I heard a woman's voice too. Now I could hear her a little better, because she was screeching. Something like 'Stop! Just stop it!' Then the voices got a little lower. Not too long after that, I heard car doors slamming."

"How many?"

"Two? Three? I'm not really sure. At least two, anyway. Then I heard a car tear off outta there. *Peeling rubber,* my boys used to call it when they were teenagers."

"Huh." Conley thought about it for a moment, wondering if the fight had anything to do with Symmes Robinette's wreck.

"Could have been just some old drunks pulling off the road to settle a score," Margie observed. "There's a juke joint bar up the road, and we get our share of drunk drivers coming from there late at night. Couple of years ago, I heard a commotion and found a fella had driven clear off the road, through my fence, and into the pasture."

"I know the place. The American Legion bar," Conley said. "My friend and I were there that night, headed home when we came up on the wreck."

"I'll be," Margie said.

"You didn't hear the wreck yourself?" Conley asked.

"Guess not. I got Sport back inside and went on to bed. My room's at the back of the house, and I've got a window air conditioner that kind of drowns out everything else. I fell back asleep, and at some point—maybe an hour later?—Sport heard all the sirens from the fire trucks and ambulances, and he woke me up yowling at 'em."

"You didn't see or hear anything at all?" Conley repeated.

"Not until the fire trucks got there," Margie said. "After that, I got dressed and took the Ranger up to the road to see what had happened." She shuddered. "I wish I hadn't seen what I did. That poor man. Did the police ever say what happened?"

"Not so far," Conley said. "Have you told the sheriff's office about hearing those voices, and the fight, earlier in the evening?"

Margie shrugged. "Hadn't even thought about it 'til just now. They sent somebody the next day—a deputy—to ask if I'd seen anything that night, and I said I hadn't."

"What did the deputy look like?"

"Big ol' fella. A white boy," Margie said.

Conley was fairly sure she'd met that deputy the night of the crash and afterward too.

She scribbled her name and phone number on a page of her notebook, ripped it out, and handed it to her hostess. "I was on my way to the sheriff's office when I stopped here earlier. Guess I'd better get going. If you think of anything else from that night, anything at all, could you give me a call?"

"Be glad to," Margie said. "I'll take you on back to your car now."

As the Ranger bumped along the dirt track road, Conley spotted a pair of huge black birds hovering over something up ahead among the green stalks of sunflowers. Sport, again sprawled on the floor of the vehicle, raised his grizzled snout, sniffed, then went back to sleep.

"Ugh," Margie said, pointing at the birds. "There's a big ol' dead deer over there. I'll be glad when those buzzards pick that poor thing clean."

Conley stared at the birds in mute horror. As the Ranger approached, she saw a lumpy brown form sprawled on its side. Two buzzards hopped on the ground, tearing at the corpse, while two more circled closer and closer in the air above.

She turned her head and averted her eyes. True, she'd been raised in a small Southern town, had seen her share of roadkill—although not since she'd moved to Atlanta—but the sight still filled her with revulsion.

Her phone buzzed in the pocket of her jeans. She took it out and glanced at the caller ID. The area code was local, but she didn't recognize the number, so she disconnected and put the phone away.

"Here we go," Margie said, pulling alongside the Subaru.

"Thanks for the ride and the cold drink," Conley said, stepping down. She leaned over and scratched the old dog's ears. "Bye, Sport."

30

Conley was pulling into the parking lot behind the sheriff's office when her phone rang. It was the same number that had just called, so she didn't answer. But it rang again a second later from the same number, and this time the caller left a voice mail.

It was Michael Torpy, the young reporter at the *Beacon*. He sounded breathless. "Hey, Conley. It's Mike. Grayson told me to tell you to call back. It's important."

She hit the callback button on her phone.

"Hi, Mike. What's up?"

"Sorry to bother you, but I just got back from city hall, and I heard something I thought you'd be interested in, and Grayson agreed."

"Okay. Hit me."

"Charlie Robinette just announced he's going to run for his father's seat in Congress," Michael said.

"Who'd you hear that from?"

"Unfortunately, Buddy Bright broke the news a few minutes ago," Michael said. "When I got to city hall, everybody was talking about it. I don't think anybody saw it coming. He's formed a campaign committee and everything. But it gets better. You'll never guess who else is getting ready to announce for Robinette's seat." He didn't bother to wait for an answer. "It's Robinette's wife."

"Vanessa? She's going to run for Congress? Against her own son? Where did you hear that?"

Michael hesitated, then lowered his voice. "I've, uh, been dating this girl who works in the county clerk's office. She was running copies for one of the lawyers in town this morning, and she overheard him talking on the phone."

"Hmm. Thirdhand. Not so reliable."

"No. It's true," he insisted. "I checked around. One of my old classmates at FSU works in the governor's office as an assistant to Roy Padgett's director of communications. The governor is going to call for a special election to fill Robinette's seat, and according to Jill, Vanessa Robinette started calling his office late last week to ask him to support her."

"Can you get anybody to go on the record that she's going to run?" Conley asked.

"Grayson's working her contacts in Rotary," Michael said.

"Call up Vanessa," Conley said. "Just ask her flat out, 'Are you running?' If she says yes, that's a hell of a story. Unless damn Buddy Bright already broke that too?"

"He hasn't so far," Michael said. "I've got the radio on in the office right now."

Conley stared out the window of the Subaru, absentmindedly watching the front door of the sheriff's office. "Is Grayson in the office now?"

"Yeah."

"Okay. Hang up and tell her to call me back ASAP."

"Gray?" she said when her phone rang a minute later. "This is a hell of a story, if we can confirm it."

"I know. Amazing, right?" For a change, her sister sounded just as breathless as her young staff member.

"If we can break this story ahead of everybody else, especially Buddy Bright, it could be huge," Conley said. "The wire services and the national press will be all over it. But we've gotta nail it down and go with it, like, right now."

"We don't go to press until tomorrow night," Grayson reminded her.

"Doesn't the *Beacon* have a digital edition?" she asked.

"Sure. We run local calendar listings, high school scores, the Humane Society's pet of the week, that kind of stuff."

"But you never run actual news stories?"

"Sometimes we run briefs, like on an Election Day. We have a hard enough time putting out the actual paper," she said, sounding defensive.

"That changes now," Conley said. "Gray, this is important. If we can nail down a story saying Symmes Robinette's widow is going to run for his seat—against her own son—it's crazy good. This is some seriously Shakespearean shit. Even if we just break it on the website, it means the *Beacon* owns the story. Not some crappy radio station. *We* do."

"I'm not even convinced anybody pays attention to the digital *Beacon*," Grayson said.

"They will," she vowed. "After you left this morning, Vanessa admitted to me that Symmes was diagnosed with non-Hodgkin's lymphoma back before Christmas. They'd kept it a secret from the public, probably to allow Charlie to begin quietly building up a campaign war chest to run for his father's seat in Congress. I'm over at the sheriff's office in Bronson right now. Start working those phones. If Charlie has started raising money, he will have had to have filed some kind of financial disclosure. We've gotta get Vanessa on the record that she intends to run too. If it's for real, Michael needs to get his friend in the governor's office to try to get a quote from Padgett about whom he plans to support. He'll probably try to weasel out of endorsing either one at this point, but we need to at least have a 'no comment' comment."

"I'll see what I can do," Grayson said warily. "Man, what a morning! What's going on at the sheriff's office? Has Goggins been at all helpful?"

"He hasn't had a chance to shut me down yet," Conley said. "But that's only because I just got here."

Merle Goggins donned a pair of half-moon-shaped reading glasses and looked down at a document on his desktop, then back up at Conley Hawkins.

"You seem to think there's something sinister about Congressman Robinette's death. Why is that?"

"I have questions," Conley said. "That's my job. I assume it's yours too."

"That and keeping the peace and running the jail and fighting with the county commission to give me enough funding to do my job," Goggins said. "But yes, I have questions too. Tell me yours, and I'll answer to the best of my ability."

"No bullshit?"

He smiled. "As little as possible."

"Okay. First, do you have a cause of death from the medical examiner?"

He tapped the document on his desktop. "It's still preliminary, but it looks like Symmes Robinette suffered a fatal head injury consistent with the impact of his vehicle flipping over at high speed. Probably sustained when his head hit the steering wheel or dashboard. As you know, the subsequent fire left very little other evidence."

"About the crash. Any thoughts on what could have caused it?"

"Again, the fire didn't leave us a lot to work with as far as the vehicle was concerned. We talked to the dealer in Tallahassee who sold the car to the congressman. It had been serviced regularly. A local mechanic who did minor maintenance said everything was in order with the Escalade when Robinette brought it in for an oil change last month."

"Okay. So. Relatively new car. No traffic that night. Do you get why I'm seeing sinister?"

"I didn't say there was no traffic that night," Goggins protested. "You told one of my men you didn't see any other cars as you arrived on the scene. That doesn't mean there weren't any."

"Correct." She tapped the end of her pen on her open notepad. "Did your man talk to Margie Barrett?"

"That's the widow lady who lives on the property near the crash site?" Conley nodded.

"Yes. He talked to her. She told him she didn't hear the crash or see anything. That house is a good ways off the highway, according to Poppell."

"I just came from there myself," Conley said. "At first, she told me the same thing. Then she remembered that when she took her dog outside to pee way after midnight, he was agitated. The dog is mostly blind, so she thought he was hearing or smelling a possum or a raccoon in the trees. But then she heard two men arguing loudly. And then a woman's voice. After that, she heard car doors slamming and a car racing off."

"She told you that?" he said sharply. "Wonder why she didn't tell my investigator?"

"We kind of hit it off," Conley admitted. "It turns out she and her late husband used to bank with my dad."

His leather chair creaked as he leaned back in it and reached for the cell phone on his desktop. He tapped a key. "Poppell? I need to see you in my office."

Five minutes later, Walter Poppell, the deputy who'd interviewed her the night of the crash—and who'd hit on her during her last visit—strolled through the sheriff's door.

He glanced over at Conley, then did a double take. "Oh, hey," he said, smirking.

"Poppell, you remember this lady? Sarah Conley Hawkins? She was a witness at the scene of Symmes Robinette's wreck," Goggins said. "And she's a reporter for the newspaper over in Silver Bay."

"Yes, sir," Poppell said. His right hand rested lightly on his holstered weapon, and his broad face looked anxious.

"Margie Barrett, that lady who lives in that farmhouse near the crash site, just told Ms. Hawkins here that she heard two men arguing that night, up by the highway. And a woman's voice too. Did she mention anything about that to you?"

"No, sir," Poppell said, shaking his head vigorously. "Said she was asleep when the wreck must've happened and couldn't hear from her bedroom because of a noisy air conditioner."

"This was earlier in the night," Conley said. "Sometime after midnight."

He shrugged. "She never said nothing like that to me."

"I reckon you need to go back out there and interview her again," Goggins said, his face stern. "And make sure you ask her about all night. What did she hear earlier? Or see? Go ahead and canvass the whole area again. Knock on doors and ask questions. Find out if anybody else heard or saw two men arguing that night. They might have had a woman with them."

"But I already talked to everybody out that way," Poppell objected.

"Talk to 'em again. Just do it."

"Yes, sir," Poppell said. He slunk out of the office, leaving the door ajar.

"Dumb-ass," Goggins muttered under his breath. He returned his attention to Conley. "What else?"

"Did you know Robinette had terminal cancer?"

He blinked. "Where did you hear that?"

"Vanessa Robinette told me this morning, when she came into the office to complain about my intrusive questions. She said her husband was suffering from chemo brain and couldn't sleep, which was why he was driving around way out in the country at three in the morning."

"What she told us too," Goggins said. "Gotta say that's a new one on me."

"Sheriff, have you or Poppell talked to the rest of Robinette's family?"

"We talked briefly to the son, Charlie. He wanted to be present when we spoke to his mother. He didn't have a whole lot to say. He was understandably broken up by his father's death."

"I meant his other family," Conley said.

"I'm not getting your drift."

"His ex-wife, Toddie, and their two kids. I forget their names. They live right down the road here in Bronson County on a quail-hunting plantation called Oak Springs Farm."

"I know the place," Goggins said cautiously. "They invite me and my department out for a dove shoot every fall. Nice folks. You say she used to be married to Symmes Robinette? I'll be damned."

"The marriage broke up in 1986 when Robinette got his twenty-five-year-old congressional aide pregnant," Conley said.

Goggins raised an eyebrow. "And that'd be the present Mrs. Robinette? I'm surprised this is the first I'm hearing about that."

"The divorce and remarriage was apparently hushed up at the time," she said. "Toddie and the children were exiled out here to Oak Springs, and Vanessa and her kid stayed in Silver Bay."

"Well, then, that's old news," Goggins said. "Don't see it has any bearing on Symmes Robinette's death."

"You'd think so," Conley agreed. "Except for the strange fact that a week before he died, Robinette suddenly deeded over a farmhouse and a big chunk of valuable timberland to Toddie, for one dollar 'and other considerations.' But before you tell me the congressman was just tidying up his affairs before his impending death, you should know that when I asked Vanessa about it this morning, she acted shocked. And pissed."

Goggins gave her a patronizing smile. "Are you suggesting that Vanessa Robinette had something to do with her husband's death? On what basis? That she was pissed that he literally gave away the farm to his ex-wife?"

"I think it's worth noting," Conley said. "I went out to Oak Springs this past weekend. It's what, five miles from here?"

"If that."

Conley was tapping her pen on her notepad again. "I'm wondering if Symmes was trying to reconcile with his first wife."

"And I'm wondering how you think Vanessa Robinette managed to arrange her husband's death in a one-car accident when she was miles away, asleep in her own bed."

Conley jumped on that last statement. "How do you know she was at home?"

"She told me. Once we got the accident victim's identity verified from the license tag, I drove over to her house at Sugar Key myself, to notify her what had happened."

"And what time was that?"

"Probably around 8:00 a.m."

"Five hours after the wreck," Conley said. "Plenty of time if you were doing something sinister."

"You're skating on thin ice," Goggins warned. He scribbled something on the margin of the report he'd been looking at. "Since you're here, let me ask you a question. I understand your grandmother employs a woman named Winifred Churchwell?"

"Winnie. Yes. She's worked for us most of my life. She helped raise my sister and me. Why do you ask?"

He held up a sheet of paper, then whisked it back into the folder on his desk. "Were you aware that she did a stint in federal prison for assaulting Congressman Robinette?"

"Yes," Conley said. "What about it? You're not trying to say Winnie had something to do with Robinette's death, are you? That's crazy."

"It's been brought to my attention, that's all."

Conley felt her face grow hot. "Does that piece of paper you're looking at tell you how Winnie 'assaulted' Robinette?"

"Nope."

She recounted the story of the cancer cluster and how it had directly affected Winnie and Nedra and their neighbors, who'd been exposed to the contaminated soil and water in Plattesville, and Robinette's role in defending the railroad.

"About a year after Winnie's sister died from cancer, leaving Winnie to raise her three little boys, Winnie went up to Robinette at a ribbon-cutting ceremony for a VA clinic and tossed a handful of her sister's ashes in his face," Conley said. "He had her arrested and charged with assault. And for that, she spent twenty months in prison."

He winced. "But, as you say, it's interesting."

"Winnie had nothing to do with Robinette's death," Conley said. "I was with her when we got the news that the wreck victim had been identified. She was as shocked as we were."

"I'm not saying your housekeeper is a suspect. I'm not saying anybody's a suspect," Goggins said. "It's still an open investigation."

She heard her phone ping with an incoming text message. Glancing down, she saw the text was from Grayson.

Need you back here ASAP.

"Gotta go," she said, stowing her notebook in her backpack. "Will you let me know if Poppell turns up any information on the mysterious men arguing in the nighttime?"

"Possibly," Goggins said. "And you'll do me the same courtesy?"

"Possibly."

31

Lillian King pulled Conley aside as soon she as entered the *Beacon*'s tiny reception area. "It's your lucky day," she said, keeping her voice low. "Vanessa Robinette this morning and now Rowena Meigs in the afternoon."

"Noooo," Conley groaned. "Why didn't Grayson give me a heads-up?"

"She was probably afraid you'd turn tail and run all the way back to Atlanta," Lillian said. "They're in her office now, waiting for you."

"What's Rowena want? She already turned in her column this morning. I haven't even had time to fix that."

"From what I could tell by eavesdropping outside Grayson's door, Rowena has got herself a hot tip about Vanessa Robinette. She wants us to run it on the front page."

Rowena was sitting in a chair facing Grayson, with her back to the door. Conley stood there and, catching her sister's eye, put her forefinger to her temple and mimed pulling a trigger.

"Here's Conley now," Grayson said, a little too heartily.

"Hello, Sarah Conley," Rowena said, giving her a curt nod of acknowledgment. She'd been holding her Pomeranian in her lap, but the tiny ball of fluff gave a small yip of protest and jumped down onto the floor.

Rowena was dressed in a hot-pink tracksuit, blindingly white Velcro-fastened tennis shoes, and her customary string of pearls.

"Hi, Rowena," Conley said. "Lillian tells me you have another story for us?"

"Yes," Rowena said. "I was just explaining to Grayson here that I won't be filing my exclusive unless she can guarantee me front-page, above-the-fold placement."

"Oh?" Conley grabbed a chair from the outer office and rolled it in to sit beside the paper's society columnist. She set her backpack on the floor. "What's the big story?" she asked, feigning ignorance.

"Why, it's just the biggest scoop this paper has ever seen," Rowena said. "Much bigger than the time the PTA treasurer embezzled all the money from the school's fruitcake sale to pay for her breast implants."

Grayson gave her sister a weak smile. "Rowena managed to get an interview with Vanessa Robinette today."

"An exclusive interview," the columnist put in. "Vanessa is going to run for Symmes's seat."

"Really?" Conley said. "That's quite an achievement. How'd you manage to pull that off, Rowena, if you don't mind my asking?"

"I don't mind at all. I ran into Vanessa at Mignon's, not even an hour ago."

"Mignon? Is that someone in town who I should know?"

"Mignon's Salon de Beauté," Rowena said. "Of course, the actual Mignon's been dead for years now, but yes, dear, you should know about the hair salon. It's never too early for a girl like you to start think-ing about covering up those pesky little gray hairs."

Conley wasn't sure, but she believed she'd just been insulted.

"Anyway," Rowena went on, "Vanessa was getting a blowout, because she leaves bright and early in the morning for Symmes's memo-rial service in Washington, and I was in the chair next to her, getting my rinse, and we just started to chat. I told her how sorry I was about Symmes and asked about her plans for the future. I'm a widow too, you know, and as I said to Vanessa, I've been through the same experience she's going through."

"I'm sure she appreciated your wisdom," Grayson said.

"She really did," Rowena agreed. "She told me that Symmes was dying of cancer! I had no idea, did you?"

"She, uh, mentioned it when she was in to see me this morning," Conley said. "I guess I'm surprised she didn't mention her plan to run for Congress while she was here."

Rowena favored Conley with a pitying smile.

"I'm afraid Vanessa doesn't like you very much, dear. It's possible you alienated her with all your pushy, big-city tactics."

"Pushy?" Conley said.

Grayson gave her sister a warning shake of her head, signaling that Conley should stand down.

"Vanessa told me that once Symmes got sick, he started grooming young Charlie to run for his seat. But Charlie, although a very dear boy, I'm sure, is a bit headstrong. Symmes was having second thoughts."

"Did Vanessa say why?" Grayson asked.

"Some family matter," Rowena said. "I'm not sure Vanessa and Symmes approved of the girl Charlie has been running around with." The old woman lowered her voice. "She's newly divorced. With a young child. Not very suitable."

"Pot meet kettle," Conley said. "Remember, Symmes was 'not yet divorced' with *two* young children when he married Vanessa."

"Anyway," Rowena went on, "according to Vanessa, Symmes had his doubts. He thought Charlie needed some life experiences before he'd be ready to go into government and that it would be a disservice both to his constituents and his family to put his son in a position he wasn't really ready to assume."

"And Vanessa told you she is ready to assume those responsibilities?" Conley asked.

Rowena shrugged. "Why not? I'm a little surprised at a career girl like you, Sarah Conley, for expressing doubts that a woman should run for Congress."

Conley gnashed her molars for a moment before deciding to ignore

Rowena's quaint "career girl" comment. "I don't have an opinion on Vanessa's qualifications as a candidate, Rowena. Grayson and I just need to make absolutely sure that Vanessa Robinette went on the record with you that she intends to run for her late husband's seat. Against her own son."

"Of course," Rowena said, bristling. "Despite what you might think, I am a seasoned, professional journalist."

"Did you ask her to go on the record about why she's running for a seat her son has just declared for?" Conley asked.

Rowena fiddled with a loose thread on the cuff of her jacket. "Of course not. That would be rude. I can't insult a woman who's just lost her husband like that." Leaning heavily on her cane, decorated today with a red, white, and blue ribbon, Rowena heaved herself from the chair. "You have my story."

She snapped her fingers at the Pomeranian, who'd been sniffing the perimeter of the office. "Come, Tuffy," she called. "Mommy has an important meeting to cover."

Tuffy scampered toward his owner's outstretched arms, pausing before lifting a leg and releasing a vigorous stream of urine on Conley's backpack.

"Oh my goodness," Rowena said, scooping up the dog. "Naughty boy!" She plucked a handful of tissues from her pocketbook and dabbed ineffectively at the damp bag. "There," she said. "All fixed."

32

EXCLUSIVE TO THE SILVER BAY BEACON
FROM ROWENA MEIGS

SILVER BAY, FLORIDA—Following the tragic death last week of her husband, Thirty-fifth District U.S. Rep. Simms Robinette, Mrs. Vanessa Robinette revealed in an exclusive interview with this correspondent that she will mount a campaign to run for the remainder of her husband's term in Congress.

Simms Robinette died in a one-car accident on County Road 321 last Thursday night.

"Of course, I am heartbroken over the sudden loss of the love of my life," Mrs. Robinette told the Beacon *this week. "But public service has long been the focus of my life with Simms, and I can think of no better way to honor his legacy than to seek to continue serving his constituants in Congress."*

Mrs. Robinette said the entire family will travel to Washington, D.C., on Tuesday, where Rep. Robinette's body will lie in state in the Capitol Rotunda. Among the important dignitaries expected to honor our eighteen-term congressman are the president and First Lady, the vice president, Florida governor Roy

Padgett and Florida First Lady Heidi Padgett, the Speaker of the
House of Representatives, and others.

The memorial service will be presided over by the House chap-
lain. Mrs. Robinette divulged that she will wear a simple black
Chanel suit, a black hat and veil, and black Louboutin pumps
for the service. Her only jewelry will consist of her late husband's
gold wedding band and his FSU fraternity pin, as well as a jeweled
American flag broach, which was a recent birthday gift.

Conley stopped reading aloud. "You're not really going to run this
drivel, right?"

Grayson spread her hands apart in a gesture of surrender. "What
choice do I have? You heard her. Rowena thinks her exclusive is the
biggest scoop since the sinking of the *Titanic*."

"You can't run this crap," Conley repeated. "She didn't even spell
Symmes correctly. Or *constituent*. Or *Louboutin*. Or *brooch*. Rowena's
right about one thing. It is a big story. But she's buried the lede. She
doesn't even mention the fact that Vanessa plans to run against Charlie."

"What do you want me to do?"

"Fold her story into mine. Her byline can run above mine. This once.
I'll write a new lede, saying that we've learned, exclusively, that Vanessa
will run for the seat, against Charlie, who's already established a campaign committee and started raising money. And we'll add that Symmes
was diagnosed with cancer late last year, a fact he hid from the public."

"Rowena will pitch a hissy if we do that," Grayson said gloomily. "She'll
probably get her damn nephew to take the legal ads away from the paper. If
we lose that revenue, Conley, I don't think the *Beacon* can survive."

"If we don't *own* this story, cover it aggressively and professionally,
we deserve to lose the legals," Conley said. "But if we jump out ahead
on this, show the community that we do hard-hitting, quality journalism here, then I think we'll gain ad revenue. And subscribers."

"And what if that plan doesn't work? It's fine for you. You're not
planning to stick around here and save the ship. You'll be outta here
with the first job offer that comes across the transom. But I'm the one—
me—Grayson Hawkins, whose name is on the masthead as publisher

and managing editor. And I'm the one who'll get to take the blame for running our family business into the ground after over a hundred years. I'll be the one left to put a for sale sign in the window and lay off Lillian and Michael." She pointed toward the ceiling. "I'll be the one to turn off that stupid fucking lighthouse."

Grayson buried her head in her hands. Her voice was muffled. "It's all on me."

Conley was shocked by the despair in her sister's voice. She stood behind Grayson's chair and awkwardly patted her back as though soothing a colicky baby. "Come on, Gray," she said softly. "It's not that bad. We can do this. I'll help. We're gonna write an amazing story, and all of us—you, me, Michael—we'll kick ass. Look. As soon as Mike gets us a reaction statement from Charlie Robinette, I'll put the story together."

She looked up. "I appreciate it, but I just don't think—"

"I haven't even had a chance to tell you yet," Conley added. "I talked to a woman who lives near the wreck site. She heard voices sometime after midnight that night, coming from up near the road. Two men arguing loudly. And a woman telling them to stop. Not even the sheriff knew about that. And don't forget, I've got those photos of the fire. Hell, I nearly forgot—I've got video!"

"What good's video gonna do?" Grayson asked.

"If we put out a digital edition tonight, which we totally should do, we can embed the video of the car fire. Have you got any idea how many more people look at video than just still photos?"

She shrugged. "Not really."

"Gawd," Conley groaned. "Gray, I love you, and I don't want this paper to fail. But we have got to get you and the *Beacon* into the twenty-first century."

"You don't think it's too . . . disrespectful? Or macabre? I mean, Symmes Robinette died in that fire."

"Newspapers and television broadcasts have been using photos and videos of fatal accidents for decades and decades," Conley said. "Think of the *Hindenburg*. Or the Zapruder film of the Kennedy assassination. It's news. Sad and tragic, but nonetheless noteworthy."

"Okay," Grayson said reluctantly. "Call Michael and see if he's gotten any statement from Charlie Robinette. Lillian usually sends out our digital news briefs. I'll let her know we're doing one today."

Conley had another thought. "You run ads in the digital updates. Right?"

"No. I never thought of that."

"Think of it now," Conley urged. "Make a list of your biggest advertisers. The Island IGA, for sure, right? And Mort's Liquors? And the Lamplighter? Call 'em all. Or better, go out and see them. Offer them a combined ad buy for . . . what? Maybe an extra fifty bucks? They get display space in tonight's digital edition, plus whatever they usually do in the print edition."

"I'm just not sure," Grayson said. "You can't believe what a hard sell these businesses are. I'm practically giving away ad space as it is."

Conley was nearing the end of her patience. "Take a look at the online editions of other dailies, if you don't believe me." She pointed at her desktop computer. "Go ahead. Call up the *Tampa Bay Times, Tallahassee Democrat, Orlando Sentinel, Miami Herald*. They've all monetized their online editions. They use flashy graphics, video, all kinds of stuff to get eyes on their ads. That's what we've got to do too."

Grayson tapped some keys and stared at the screen. "Hmm."

"Just do it, okay?"

Grayson sighed a heavy, embattled sigh.

Conley's stomach growled loudly. It was after two, and she'd missed lunch. "Hey," she said, whirling around. "What about Kelly's Drugs? Do they advertise with us?"

"Nope," Grayson said. "As far as I know, they never have."

"Why not?"

"I guess our former ad sales manager just neglected to put the hard sell on them."

"Who was our former ad sales manager?"

"That'd be me," Grayson said. "It felt awkward, trying to sell something to Miss June."

"But we've always done business at Kelly's. For as long as I can remember, G'mama's had an account there."

Grayson shrugged.

. . .

Skelly was behind the pharmacy counter but looked up when Conley entered the store, his face lighting up when he saw his newest customer.

"Hey," he said. "What can I get you?"

"Some lunch? I haven't eaten, and I'm starved."

He finished filling a bottle with a creamy white liquid, capped it, and slapped a label on it. "Let me bag this and call the patient to tell him it's ready, then I'll meet you over at the soda fountain and get you fixed up."

Conley set her backpack on the floor and twirled around on the stool, surveying the luncheonette as though she'd never seen it before. Nothing had changed since she'd first started coming here as a child.

"What's your pleasure?" Skelly asked when she spun around to face him.

"Hmm. Do you still make the pulled pork with that tangy sweet sauce?"

He nodded. "Yep. George still smokes four or five pork butts for me every Sunday. He makes the sauce from my mom's old recipe. I usually sell out by Thursday or Friday morning at the latest. I have a couple of dozen customers who put in standing orders to pick it up on the way to their beach houses every week."

"Pulled pork, definitely."

"How's your coleslaw? You don't serve that vile creamy mayonnaise-drenched mess, do you?"

He pretended to be shocked. "Mayo in my slaw? What kind of joint do you think this is? We do sweet-sour vinegar slaw. And George's wife hand grates the cabbage and onions herself. None of this pre-shredded crap you buy at the store."

"Coleslaw, then. And coffee, if you've got any. We've got a long night ahead of us."

He fetched two mugs and poured one for her and one for himself. He dumped sugar and a creamer into his own mug and sipped. "Breaking news, right? I heard Buddy Bright this morning talking about Charlie Robinette's announcement."

Conley made a face. "That damn guy! He's everywhere. He might have gotten the jump on Charlie's announcement, but we've got an even better story. We're going to put out a special digital-only edition later today."

"The *Beacon*? You guys do that?"

"Grayson says they sometimes do it for elections or big football news, but this is too good a story to hold for another day, so yeah, we're gonna go for it." She tapped her fingernail on the countertop. "Which reminds me. Grayson says Kelly's Drugs doesn't advertise in the *Beacon*. Mind if I ask why not?"

Skelly took another sip of coffee. "It just never came up. Mom used to handle all that stuff. When I came home to work here, I just kinda kept up with what she'd been doing. I know we buy space in those cheesy coupon mailers, but I think that's all the advertising we do." He gave her a quizzical look. "So now you're the ace reporter plus ad saleswoman?"

"Not by choice," Conley said. "I'm trying to drag my sister into the brave new world of digital news. Newspapers don't make money on subscriptions, you know. In fact, we lose money on them. Most papers depend on revenue from advertising. And if we can sell ad space in digital editions, it's a win-win. More eyes on your ad, more money for us."

"I guess I could try doing an ad buy in the *Beacon*," he said. "Tell Grayson to come see me, okay?"

"Do you have the graphics for the ads you run in that mailer?" she asked.

"Yeah."

"Okay, email them to Grayson. She can send you the rates, and if you decide to do it, your ad can run in tonight's digital—which should get a lot of hits."

"Why's that?"

She waggled her eyebrows. "I could tell you, but then I'd have to kill you. No, really. This story is starting to take off in ways I'd never imagined."

"You're not even gonna give me a hint, are you?"

"Nope. Now about my lunch?"

33

When Conley got back to the *Beacon* office, Lillian was at her usual post in the reception area. The radio was on, and she was listening to Buddy Bright, who was talking excitedly about the county commission zoning meeting. Conley reached over and turned the volume down.

"I've had about enough of that guy," she groused. "When does he sleep?"

"I go to church with a lady who works at the Waffle House out on the county road," Lillian said. "Melissa told me that Buddy Bright's in there all the time, at all hours of the night. Guess he really is a night owl."

Conley sat back down at her desk and was trying to craft a lede for the story that would be combined with Rowena's exclusive when Michael Torpy burst into the tiny newsroom, holding his cell phone in one hand and a grease-stained paper sack in the other. He wore faded blue jeans, a rumpled short-sleeved shirt that had seen better days, and unlaced Converse high-top sneakers. As always, the earbuds for his iPhone dangled from around his neck.

"I got Charlie Robinette to give me a statement," he announced, grinning. "He confirmed that he's running for his father's unexpired term. And," he added, "I videoed the interview, just in case."

He rolled his desk chair up alongside hers. "Take a look." He tapped the photo icon on his iPhone and held it out for Conley to watch.

Charlie Robinette was already assuming the mantle of a mature politician. His neatly barbered hair showed a few strategically placed gray hairs at the temples. Conley cynically wondered if he'd had his barber tint his hair just for the occasion. He was wearing a white button-down shirt with a loosely knotted red, white, and blue tie, the shirtsleeves rolled up, as though notifying the voting public that he was ready to get down to work in Washington.

He looked steadily into the camera. "All my life, I've looked up to my dad as a role model. And I modeled my life plan after his, graduating from the same university and law school, practicing law in the family firm, and working summers during college as a congressional aide in his office. Dad and I had many late-night discussions on the topic of public service and the best way to serve his constituents and address the changing needs of the district."

"Uh, so, does that mean your dad was grooming you as his successor?" Michael asked off-camera.

"Yes," Charlie said. "That's why I'd begun having conversations with some of Dad's closest political advisers over the past year. My father made it clear to me, even before his recent illness, that he believed I would be the best candidate to represent the Thirty-fifth District. Of course, we'd hoped I wouldn't have to announce before his retirement, but cancer has a way of cheating the best-laid plans."

Michael's voice could be heard off-camera. "Can we back up? You're saying he knew the cancer diagnosis was terminal? But kept that diagnosis secret?"

Robinette's smooth, tanned face flushed. "We felt it was a private, family matter. Dad felt well enough to be in Washington, attending to the people's business in Congress, right up until the end of his life."

"Did you know your mother intended to run for your father's seat?"

Robinette's expression was blank. "No. She didn't discuss her decision with me or with anyone else in his close circle of associates as far as I know."

"Won't this strain relations in your family?" Torpy asked.

Robinette shrugged. "My mother is her own woman. Clearly, I think my father's decision that I should run for his seat, should he not be able to complete his term, is one that should be respected."

"So no family feud?" Torpy asked.

Robinette cracked a smile, displaying beautiful, white teeth. "Thanksgiving could get a little awkward, but we're a political family. My dad always cooked two turkeys on the holiday—one on the smoker, the other in the oven—so that my mom could make her famous giblet gravy from the pan drippings. We're used to finding ways of compromising."

The video ended, and Conley jumped up and flung her arms around the young reporter, whose face blushed as bright as his auburn hair. "Mike! That was brilliant! Exactly what we needed," she said.

"What's exactly what we needed?" Grayson walked through the front door just in time to hear Conley praising the paper's junior staff member.

"Mike not only got Charlie Robinette on the record as saying he's running—against his own mother—he got it on video," Conley said, still beaming with pride.

"Good work, Mike," Grayson said. "You'll write the piece about Charlie's announcement. Give me about twenty inches. Get some reaction comments from a couple of Symmes's party cronies, and see if there are any Democrats sniffing around and testing the waters to oppose the GOP candidate. Conley, you'll do the story you suggested, wrapping Rowena's story into yours. Write it as a second-day piece, since the accident happened last week. Thirty-five inches, max."

Conley nodded, then turned to Lillian. "Grayson tells me you usually send out the digital news updates. We're aiming to send out a big updated story about Robinette's death—and the fact that both Charlie and Vanessa have announced they're running—by five o'clock today. You can handle that, right?"

Lillian did a double take. "I send out the emails with the election results and football scores, but we haven't won a game in a while. And I've never messed with video."

Michael opened his paper sack and began inhaling a chili dog. He paused mid-bite. "I can help you with that, Lillian."

"I've got some news too," Grayson said. "I just sold Sean Kelly a three-month contract for advertising, both in the print paper and the digital edition. And I managed to talk the IGA, Silver Bay Motors, and Gulf Coast Orthodontics into doing a digital ad buy too."

For the first time since she'd come home to Silver Bay, Conley thought, her sister seemed animated, excited even. It was the first glimpse she'd had of the old Grayson.

Lillian's jaw dropped. "Now we're running ads with the announcements? Who's gonna make that work?"

Grayson draped an arm around Michael. "You know how to do digital layout, right?"

"Sure," Michael said. "I was production manager on the college paper. We embedded video, music, and advertising graphics all the time. No problem."

Conley regarded her colleague with frank admiration. "How old are you, Mike?"

Michael was seated at his desk, eating limp french fries and tapping away at the keys on his computer. "Twenty-three."

"They taught you all that in journalism school?"

"Some I learned in class, some I picked up from my friends working on the staff of the school paper. But a lot of stuff I figured out from watching YouTube videos."

"Maybe sometime you'll teach me," Grayson said. "But not today."

Conley spent the next two hours on her story, combining the more lucid details of Rowena's "exclusive" with her own, while tall, skinny Michael kept jumping around, pacing the room between paragraphs, radiating a kind of crackling energy that lit up the shopworn newspaper office. He had his earbuds in place, and she could hear faint notes of the rap music he favored.

As they tapped away at their computer keyboards in tandem, she found her young colleague's enthusiasm contagious and welcomed the adrenaline buzz that came from working on a hot story on deadline.

She was her own worst critic, always, and as she reread her story, she wished again that she'd been able to interview Vanessa Robinette and again regretted that she still didn't have answers to her nagging questions about the nature of Symmes Robinette's fatal accident.

But that was the nature of news gathering. There were always more questions, not enough time. What her story really needed, she decided, were photos that illustrated the schizophrenic nature of the late congressman's complicated domestic life.

"Lillian?" she called.

The receptionist looked up from her own computer. "What now?"

"Can you look in our photo files and see if we have any old photos of Symmes Robinette with his family? Maybe at a ribbon cutting? Or some local function?"

"I'll look," Lillian said warily. "But those files are a big mess. We had a leaky roof a couple of years ago, and some of 'em got wet and ruined. No telling what's in there." She got up and walked slowly toward the bank of ancient gray file cabinets flanking the right side of the newsroom.

Finally, Conley was satisfied with her work—or as satisfied as she would ever be. She yawned, got up, walked around the room, and looked over Michael's shoulder as he was working on his own story about Charlie Robinette's announcement.

"I found this," Lillian said, tossing a couple of black-and-white photos on her desk.

In the first photo, dated 1984, Symmes Robinette had a full head of dark hair and was standing in front of an American flag, his hand on a Bible held by an attractive woman beaming up at him. Taped to the back of the photo was a typed-out cutline: SILVER BAY RESIDENT C. SYMMES ROBINETTE SWORN INTO CONGRESS WITH WIFE EMMA TODD ("TODDIE") AT HIS SIDE.

"This is perfect," Conley said. She picked up the next photo, dated 1988, which showed Robinette, standing with a group of men, holding a ceremonial shovel. The cutline for this one said: U.S. REP. SYMMES ROBINETTE MARKS CONSTRUCTION OF NEW VETERANS ADMINISTRATION CLINIC.

It struck Conley that this must have been shortly before Winnie had flung a handful of her sister's ashes at Robinette.

"That's all you could find?" Conley asked.

"I was lucky to find these," Lillian said.

"Wish I had a photo of Robinette with Vanessa and Charlie," Conley said.

"Oh, we got something like that," Lillian said casually. "The funeral home sent it over to run with the obituary. I told Kennedy Mc-Fall that was gonna be an extra $150, but she said that's what Vanessa wanted and she didn't care what it cost. I'll email it to you."

She went back to her own desk, and a minute later, Conley was looking at a black-and-white wedding photo of Symmes and Vanessa Robinette, staring blissfully into each other's eyes. Symmes wore a suit and tie with a white boutonniere and had his arms wrapped around Vanessa, who wore a short white dress and a floral headpiece. The Capitol Rotunda was in the background.

"Jackpot," Conley said, rubbing her hands together. She clicked to see the second photo, which was of the Robinette family gathered around a Christmas tree. Charlie was a gawky preteen, with traces of acne and braces on his teeth.

At four o'clock, Grayson strolled into the newsroom. "How's it coming?"

"I'm done," Conley said. "I just shipped my story over to you."

"I need five more minutes," Michael chimed in. "Waiting on a callback from Charlie Robinette's campaign chairman. He knows I'm on deadline."

"You got it," Grayson said. "I've already laid out the page. As soon as I've copyedited both pieces, you can show me how we upload your video."

Michael continued typing, nodding his agreement. He held up his cell phone, indicating he had an incoming call.

"Done!" Michael yelled five minutes later. "I just have to double-check the spelling of *Miles Schoendienst*."

"Schoendienst?" Conley looked up from her computer. "He's Charlie's campaign chairman?"

"Yeah. You know him?"

"Not personally," Conley said, "but I know he's the retired president of the railroad and that he was one of the developers of Sugar Key—and that he built the mansion Symmes and Vanessa live in there for a ridiculous bargain price."

Michael looked up at Grayson. "Should I put that in my story?"

"Not for tonight," Grayson said. "Let's get the digital edition out, then you can follow up on that for tomorrow's print version. Right now, I need you to sit in my office and walk me through this video stuff."

"I'll hang out here in case you've got any questions," Conley volunteered.

Shortly after six, Grayson and Michael emerged from the office, grinning and high-fiving.

"It's done," Grayson said. "We pulled the switch. It's out there in the ozone."

"Does that mean I can go home?" Lillian picked up her pocketbook and headed for the door. "My husband's been texting wanting to know what's for supper."

"Go on, get outta here," Grayson said. "You guys go on too," she added, gesturing at Conley and Michael. "Great job, team. I mean it. I didn't know if we could do this digital thing, but this feels good. Really good."

"Um, maybe I shouldn't ask, but do you know how many folks are on your email subscriber list?" Conley asked.

"Last I checked, we had about six hundred," Lillian said.

"That's all?" Grayson's face fell. "I thought it would be at least twice as many as that."

"We might want to work on our social media marketing," Michael said tactfully. "Like, does the *Beacon* even have a Facebook page? Twitter account? That kind of stuff?"

"Not really," Grayson admitted. "We had a summer intern who started a Facebook page a couple of years ago, but then she went back to school, and nobody here knew the password for the account."

"Oh-kay," Michael said. "Tomorrow, first thing, I'll scrub the old page, and we'll put up a new one that all four of us can post to. Then after we get off deadline for the print edition, we'll tackle Twitter. If that's okay with you?"

"If we gotta, we gotta," Grayson said resignedly. "It just seems like a lot of extra work, you know? I mean, who's gonna write whatever we put up? Who's gonna read it?"

"We can all write posts," Conley said. "Once you get used to it, social media doesn't really take that long. And believe me, it works. Most papers have whole departments that do nothing but social media. We need to let our readers know what stories we're working on. What's going on in the community. And we need to hear from them about what they want to know. The more interactive we are, the more readers—and subscribers—we'll get."

"More subscribers mean more advertising," Michael pointed out.

"I guess." Grayson looked unconvinced.

"Hey," Conley said. "We just did something here. We put out a real digital edition. With breaking news. That's huge. What do you say we go celebrate? Michael? Have you got plans tonight?"

"Not really," Michael started to say.

"Not tonight," Grayson said hastily. "I've got some stuff to take care of."

"Like what?" Conley asked.

"Tonight doesn't work for me, okay?" Grayson said. "Maybe later in the week. Now, all y'all scoot. We don't have the budget for overtime."

34

Michael turned to Conley after the boss had left the building. "Should my feelings be hurt that she doesn't want to celebrate with me?"

"I don't think it's you she's avoiding. It's me. Sibling rivalry, plus I think she's got some personal stuff going on."

Michael nodded. "You mean like the reason she's sleeping in her office every night?"

"You figured that out, huh?"

"I came in early one morning a couple of weeks ago and caught her sacked out on the sofa in there. She made up some kinda lame excuse about how she'd stayed late working. But it wasn't the first time. Kinda weird, though, that she wouldn't tell her own sister if she's having issues."

"You obviously don't have any sisters," Conley said, laughing.

"I've got a couple of brothers, but they're way older than I am," Michael said.

"Grayson and I are not what you'd call *close*," Conley admitted. "Part of the issue is that my grandmother pretty much forced her to hire me. She's pissed about that, but she's also pissed because she knows I'm only working here temporarily."

"So you're really actively job hunting, huh?"

Conley sighed. "Yeah. I made it clear from the start that this was just a temporary gig. And Grayson made it clear she didn't want me to work here. It was our grandmother's idea. She thought Grayson would welcome the help and that once I got settled, I'd want to stay. But I'm too old to live with my grandmother, and I can't make a living working at the *Beacon*."

Michael started gathering papers into his backpack. "Damn. Well, selfishly, I wish you'd stay. Today was great. Awesome! But I get it. I'm sure it's a huge step down for you after working at a big-city daily paper, working at your family's crummy little weekly."

She smiled wistfully. "You know what? Just now, working on this Robinette story, writing a mile a minute, the adrenaline pumping? That wasn't crummy. It reminded me of why I got into the business."

"I'm glad," he said. "Guess I'll go home, grab a beer, and watch the ball game. See you tomorrow?"

"Maybe I'll head out myself and take a long walk on the beach. Maybe I'll even fix myself a drink and watch the sunset. But I'll be here in the morning. Bright and early," she promised.

But she didn't head for the beach. Not right away. Something was definitely going on with her sister. She'd been elated, effusive—for Grayson, anyway—but then, suddenly, her mood shifted and she was once again distant and evasive.

Grayson and Tony lived in a two-story colonial revival white frame house in a subdivision called Bay Manor. All the 1960s-era houses were variations on the same theme: bleached brick or wood frame, colonial-revival style with impressive doorways with leaded-glass sidelights and bay windows, two-car garages, and small but immaculate lawns.

Conley cruised slowly past Grayson's house on Jasmine Way. Kids were riding bikes on the sidewalks, dodging the sprinklers, women were gathering in a neighbor's driveway, gossiping and sipping from plastic cocktail cups. A father and son were playing catch in the front yard at the house across the street from Tony and Grayson's.

But there was no sign of life at their house. On a normal day, both Tony's Lexus and Grayson's BMW would have been parked in the driveway because the garage was too narrow to fit their cars. Tonight, the driveway was empty, both garage doors closed. No lights burned from behind the windows. More important, the grass was overgrown, and the shrubs were ragged.

Definitely something was off. Tony was famously anal-retentive about his yard, mowing and blowing and pruning and planting every weekend. No stray leaf was ever safe for long on Tony Willingham's lawn.

It was clear to Conley that her brother-in-law was gone. It was true he traveled for work all the time, but no matter how frequent his business trips, it was a point of pride for Tony that he'd won the subdivision's Yard of the Month plaque so often, his neighbors had officially declared him out of contention.

Which still didn't explain why Grayson was sleeping in her office.

She thought back to Kennedy McFall's chance remark about seeing Grayson at the bar at the country club—the Wrinkle Room, she'd called it.

Conley steered the Subaru toward the Silver Bay Country Club. The golf greens stretched out on both sides of the road, which was lined with moss-draped oak trees. The sun was setting, and the sky was growing a deeper blue. A few stragglers were headed for the clubhouse on their golf carts, and as she turned in to the parking lot, she counted a couple of dozen cars, including Grayson's BMW.

"Errands, my ass," Conley muttered. She had half a mind to park, stroll into the bar, and confront Grayson right there. Make her come clean about the state of her marriage.

But she knew she wouldn't do that. That wasn't the Hawkins way. In their family, they didn't talk of such things. Abandonment, betrayal, estrangement, depression? These emotions did not exist in her family. Or if they did, they were tamped tightly down. Way down.

She stopped at the IGA for supplies. The wine offerings were miserable—cheap sauvignon blanc, sour-tasting pinot grigio, and a Riesling so Kool-Aid sweet, one sip would rot your teeth. She'd managed to discover a passable chardonnay, so she piled three bottles in her cart, then headed over to the deli counter, where she picked up some pita chips and her favorite pimento cheese. Maybe she really would take a walk on the beach for a little sunset picnic.

"I'm home," she called after she'd tromped up the stairs at the Dunes. She found G'mama and Winnie in the kitchen, seated at opposite sides of the enamel-topped table with a one-thousand-piece jigsaw puzzle spread out between them.

"What's that supposed to be?" Conley said, leaning down to give her grandmother a peck on the cheek.

Winnie held up the top of the puzzle box. "It's either Venice or Florence. I forget which."

Conley pointed at the picturesque gondola gliding down a canal. "I'm betting it's Venice."

"You're home late," Lorraine said. "Is there a big story brewing?"

"The Robinette thing is heating up," Conley said, unloading her groceries on the counter. "Charlie made an official announcement that he's running for Symmes's unexpired term, and then, lo and behold, Rowena ran into Vanessa at the beauty parlor, and Vanessa told her she intends to run too!"

"Against her own son?" Lorraine looked up, startled.

"Sounds just like that family," Winnie said. She picked up a piece, and her hand hovered over the puzzle as she considered its placement.

"Yup. Did you know Symmes had cancer?"

"No! Where'd you hear that?" Lorraine asked.

Conley found a canvas tote bag in the cupboard and began loading it. Wine bottle, opener, plastic cup, chips, cheese dip, spreader.

She quickly filled the two women in on the day's developments. "We sent out a digital edition of the *Beacon* a little while ago," she added.

Her grandmother looked confused. "Digital? Like television?"

"A little bit," Conley said. "It's our print content, but because this is such hot breaking news, we sent it out on the internet to our mailing list. And it's got embedded video too, thanks to our hotshot young gun, Michael. Here. I'll show you."

She reached into her small cross-body pocketbook for her cell phone but came up empty.

"Must have left my phone in the car," she said.

But a thorough search of the console and the floor of the Subaru failed to turn it up.

G'mama was waiting by the kitchen door when she got back upstairs, holding up her own ancient flip phone. "Sean Kelly just called me," she said. "You left your backpack—and your phone—at the store today."

"Thank God!" Conley exclaimed. "I was starting to panic. That phone has my whole life in it. Guess I'd better head back to town to get it, though."

"No need," G'mama said. "Sean said he'd just drive it out to you." She gave her granddaughter an exaggerated wink. "I think that boy's got a crush on you, Sarah Conley Hawkins."

"Stop with the matchmaking! We're old friends, G'mama, and that's all. I'm going upstairs to change, then. As soon as Skelly drops off my phone, I'm going to go for a walk on the beach."

"Put on something cute, like a sundress, and do something with your hair," G'mama instructed. "Sometimes I think you forget you're an attractive single girl."

"Lalalalalala," Conley said, putting her hands over her ears and starting for the staircase. "I can't hear you."

"Seems like it'd be kind of rude for you to just grab your phone and ask him to leave after he went to the trouble to drive all the way out here," Winnie commented. "Your grandma and me already had our supper, but I can warm up something for the two of you, if you want."

"Not you too, Winnie," Conley said.

35

Conley didn't put on a sundress, but she did take the time to pick out a pair of white shorts that showed off her legs, and a scoop-necked coral-pink tank top. She ran a brush through her hair and, in a begrudging concession to her grandmother, put on a pair of dangly silver earrings and some peachy-coral lipstick.

She was in the kitchen, pouring herself a glass of chardonnay, when she heard Skelly's feet on the staircase outside.

"Your boyfriend's here," Winnie whispered from her seat at the table.

"Stop it!" Conley ordered.

G'mama moved with surprising swiftness toward the living room and the front door. "Sean Kelly, come on in here," she said loudly.

She ushered Skelly into the kitchen. He had Conley's navy-blue backpack slung over his right shoulder and was holding out a bottle of wine.

"I was getting ready to lock up the store, but I kept hearing this buzzing noise. I thought I was going crazy, then I spotted this backpack on the floor by the lunch counter."

"Oh my God, thanks!" Conley eagerly unzipped the bag and rummaged around until she found her cell phone. The screen was black.

"I think the battery died while I was on the way out here," Skelly said.

"I'm just glad to have it back," she said, plugging it into an adapter near the kitchen counter.

"I bet you're hungry after that long ride out here from town," Lorraine said, beaming at him. "Why don't you sit right down and let us fix you some supper?"

Conley shot her grandmother a warning look, which was ignored. "Sean probably needs to get back home to look after Miss June, right?"

"Actually, her aide is staying over with her tonight," Skelly said. "Thanks for the offer, but I already grabbed a sandwich before leaving the store." He turned to Conley. "But I wouldn't mind a short walk on the beach."

She grabbed the wine tote she'd already packed, adding an extra plastic tumbler. "You read my mind."

"You look pretty serious," Conley said as they trudged down the path through the dunes. "What's wrong?"

"I got the digital issue of the *Beacon*," he said. "I guess it took me by surprise. I mean, Gray told me y'all were putting out a special issue, but geez, Conley, that story about Symmes Robinette, dying under 'mysterious circumstances' and all that stuff about him giving his farm to his first wife and then Vanessa running against Charlie? Was all that really necessary? It seems like pretty private family stuff to me."

"He was an eighteen-term member of Congress who died in a one-car crash at three in the morning," Conley said. "And the medical examiner's office still hasn't ruled on the cause of death."

"You make it sound so sinister," Skelly said.

"We've talked about this, Skelly," Conley said. "None of what Michael and I wrote is gossip. It's not conjecture. It's news. And before you ask, yeah, it is relevant. And what's news—and especially relevant—is the fact that the family hushed up Symmes's terminal cancer diagnosis last year so that he could start quietly setting up his son as his anointed successor."

Conley ticked off the talking points she'd used to persuade Grayson that the stories were credible, relevant, and important to their community.

But Skelly still didn't look convinced.

"Are you regretting your decision to make that ad buy with the *Beacon*?"

"Maybe I'm just not used to seeing anything controversial in the paper," Skelly admitted. "But I will say I think the ad should bring in some new business for Kelly's Drugs. Besides, if I want folks in Silver Bay to shop local—at Kelly's instead of the damn chain stores—I need to walk the walk."

"Attaboy," she said, patting his back. "Maybe if a bunch of other local businesses see Kelly's advertising with us, they'll decide to do the same thing."

They reached the edge of the dunes. Conley was already barefoot, but Skelly kicked off his loafers, and they dropped the tote bag near a weathered cedar swinging bench. Conley uncorked the bottle of chardonnay and held it up to show him.

"Wine?"

"Don't mind if I do," Skelly said, holding up his tumbler.

Conley dug her toes into the sand. "This is what I missed, living in Atlanta. Going barefoot. The smell of the ocean."

"All the things we take for granted living on the Gulf coast," Skelly agreed.

The sky turned a soft violet, shot through with streaks of orange. The Gulf was quiet tonight, sending gentle rolling waves washing along the beach. They walked north without speaking, wading out just far enough to let the warm water lap against their ankles.

As the sky darkened, they saw lights switching on in the houses just above the dunes.

Conley held up her empty tumbler when they'd walked all the way to the pier, a healthy half-mile stroll. "Ready to head back?"

Skelly nodded, and they pivoted and walked south.

The Hawkins family called the area where the swing was located *Pops's Cove*. It was the spot where her grandfather liked to "pitch camp," as he put it, spreading out the picnic blanket, the cooler of cold drinks, the hamper of sandwiches or fried chicken, and the folding aluminum lawn chairs.

In the winter, they'd build a fire here and roast Apalachicola oysters, which they'd smear atop saltine crackers doused with Tabasco sauce.

This was the spot where the family gathered after Pops's funeral and after Conley's father's funeral too. Later, G'mama had commissioned a local carpenter to build a six-foot-long swing hung from two A-frame posts. A small brass plaque on the back proclaimed it dedicated to the art of "sitting around, doing nothin'," which her grandfather always claimed was his only hobby.

Skelly held the swing still while Conley refilled their tumblers, then they both sat down, staring out at the deepening sky.

"I took a ride by Grayson's house on the way out to the Dunes today," she told him. "I'm pretty sure Tony's gone. His car's not there, and the yard looked pretty raggedy."

"Sad," Skelly said.

"Even sadder is the fact that my own sister can't be straight with me. I wanted all of us to go out for drinks after we got off deadline to celebrate our first big digital experiment, but Grayson said she had stuff to do. Then I saw her car at the parking lot at the country club." She shook her head. "Why can't she just be honest and tell me what's going on?"

"Maybe she's embarrassed," Skelly said. He stretched his arm along the back of the swing. "I know the last time Danielle left—for good—I didn't tell anybody. I kept thinking, maybe she'd change her mind. It's stupid, but I guess I thought if I didn't admit we were getting divorced, it would keep it from happening. I wouldn't have to admit that our marriage was a failure. And so was I."

"Denial is a powerful emotion," Conley said, sighing. "It must be a generational thing. From the time I was a little kid, nobody ever leveled with me about what was going on with my mom when she up and disappeared."

"When she left, she was gone for long stretches of time, right?" Skelly asked.

"Yep. And the times got longer over the years."

"What did your dad tell you and Grayson?"

"The first time, he said she was going to graduate school. Someplace out west."

"But that wasn't true?"

"No. I think she was actually in rehab. But nobody has ever admitted that to me. Later, as I got older, I figured out that things weren't working in their marriage. They never fought as far as I could tell. She'd just . . . vanish."

He let his palm rest on her shoulder, and after a momentary shock, she realized his touch was welcome. Reassuring even.

"Must have been hard on your dad," he said.

"The worst," she agreed. "Every time she came home, he was so happy! I'd hear him humming to himself. He'd bring home little presents for her in the middle of the week—some flowers, a bottle of her favorite perfume, maybe a piece of jewelry." Conley sighed and took a sip of her wine. "But the rest of us, G'mama and Pops and Grayson—even Winnie—we were all . . . holding our breath. Everybody knew it was just a matter of time before she left again. Everybody but Dad. And then, when she was gone, he just got so quiet. And sad. So very goddamn sad."

Skelly tilted his head toward her, absorbing her words. He was a good listener, which she found to be a precious quality in a man. His eyes were a deep blue green, and they were bracketed with crow's-feet.

"I'm sorry," she said suddenly. "This must hit awfully close to home for you. Anyway, it's old history. Let's talk about something else."

"No, it's actually a relief to talk about it," Skelly said. "I went to a therapist for a while after Danielle left, but once she filed for divorce, eventually it felt like a waste of money. Like, she's not coming back, so why keep beating a dead horse?"

"Would you take her back again if she decided to try to make it work?" Conley asked.

"No," he said quickly. "Too much has happened. And not just with her. With me too."

"Like what?"

He looked away and blushed slightly. "You really want to know?"

"Yes."

"Don't laugh. You moved back home."

"Oh God, Skelly," she started to say.

He tapped his fingertip gently to her lips. "Let me finish. When you walked into the bar at the Legion last week, my brain lit up like a pinball machine. Endorphins, whatever. And then when we danced together . . ."

"We'd both been drinking," Conley said. "Me, especially."

"No," he said stubbornly. "I had two beers. It wasn't the booze talking. At least for me it wasn't."

"I'd forgotten what a great dancer you were. Are," she corrected herself. She found herself thinking back to the only other time she'd danced with Sean Kelly. God, how she'd looked forward to that night. She'd gotten her first professional manicure and pedicure, even talked G'mama into taking her shopping at the mall in Tallahassee for her dress. She'd had a huge crush on Sean Kelly, one that she'd never confessed to a single soul.

"What?" he asked, leaning closer. "You're still mad at me for taking you home early, and then, after . . . you know, with Steffi . . . I was an idiot. A horny, teenage idiot. You'll never know how many times I wished that night had ended differently."

"Me too," she said simply. She took another sip of wine and then another. "As long as we're dabbling in true confessions here, maybe now is the point when I tell you that you broke my silly girlish heart that night."

He closed his eyes and buried his head in his hands. "Gaaaaaah," he groaned. "I was such a pig. Such a loser."

"I had the night all built up in my mind," she went on, liberated by the wine and the passage of time. "I was the only girl in my class at boarding school who was still a virgin. Okay, maybe the others were lying, but I was convinced that I was the only virgin left in the world. So I decided it was high time to . . . you know . . . become a real woman. And I'd made the decision that the most perfect boy in the world to give it up to was . . . Sean Kelly. The world's cutest boy next door."

He raised his head and regarded her with sad puppy dog eyes. "You're totally making this up just to torture me."

"Nope," she said sadly. She mimed an *X* over her chest and repeated the oath she and Grayson—and Sean—had shared as kids. "Cross my heart and hope to die, stick a needle in my eye."

"You're killing me here," Skelly said.

"I had the whole evening all planned out. We'd dance the night away. You'd wrap your arms around me during the slow dances, and I'd press my miniature breasts up against your masculine chest, and you'd be so swept away with passion, you'd kiss me right there on the dance floor."

Skelly took a long gulp of his own wine. "Go on."

"That's about it," she said, shrugging. "At one point in the evening, I went to the ladies' room, and some girls had a flask of Southern Comfort. I took three or four swigs, and then, when I went back out to the ballroom to start my big seduction, you were dancing with Steffi. And you had your hands all over her ass."

"She asked *me* to dance," Skelly protested. "And for your information, she was grinding on me like a cat in heat. Also, now that you mention it, the guys in the men's room were passing around some stuff that night, but it wasn't Southern Comfort. I guess I was semi-buzzed, because if I'd been sober I never would have had the nerve to grope Steffi whatshername right there in front of God and the chaperones."

"You broke my heart that night," Conley said. "I found Grayson and begged her to get her date to take me home, but they had plans of their own, so I just had to sit there, watching you dry hump the biggest slut in Silver Bay."

"I'm sorry," Skelly said. He took both her hands in his. "Teenage boys should not be allowed out in public. They should be chained until their hormones are under control and they learn how to be decent human beings."

Her mind wandered to Charlie Robinette and the excruciating humiliation he'd inflicted upon her only a year or two after that night at the country club with Skelly. They'd both been horny teenagers, but the difference was that Charlie had gone out of his way to hurt her.

"That's a little extreme, don't you think?" Conley said, looking down at their entwined hands. "Anyway, in retrospect, it's probably all for the best. No telling how long that condom I stole from Grayson's dresser drawer had been in there."

Skelly's eyes widened. "You brought a condom? To the country club dance? For real?"

"It was in my evening bag with my lipstick, a roll of Certs, and a quarter for the pay phone. My mama might not have been around a lot, but she did sit me down when I turned thirteen to explain the facts of life," Conley said primly. "Her only words of advice before my freshman year of college were to never let a stranger buy me a drink in a bar and to get myself to the student clinic and get on the Pill."

"Well, damn," Skelly said. "Just . . . damn."

"I know," she agreed. "You didn't even kiss me at the front door. All my fantasies died that night."

Skelly leaned his forehead against hers. "If only there were a way I could make it up to you now," he murmured, tilting her chin until his lips hovered over hers. "If only I knew your big sister wasn't hiding in the bushes, waiting to beat the crap out of me for making a move on you."

Conley's lips curled into a smile. "I happen to know that at this moment, Grayson's ensconced at the bar at the club, and I'm the last thing on her mind. What the hell. Give it a shot."

"Really?"

She took his face in her hands and kissed him, long, slowly, deliberately.

He pulled away for a moment. "So that's a yes?"

Her response was to wrap her arms around his neck and pull him closer. "Do you need a permission slip?"

His first kiss was gentle, tentative, like a prolonged sigh. He wove his fingertips through her hair, kissed her earlobes, then the hollow of her throat. He rained kisses on her bare shoulders, then worked his way back up to her mouth, parting her lips with his tongue.

"Okay?" he asked, his lips still against hers.

"Skelly?"

"Mmm-hmm?"

"You're doing just fine."

His kisses grew more urgent, and Conley responded in kind. By mutual agreement, they tumbled, giggling, out of the swing and onto the soft sand below. At some point, she realized that the sky had grown darker, violet deepening to purple.

"Hey," she said, sitting up suddenly. She pointed toward the horizon. "The sun's about to set."

Skelly propped himself up on one elbow, dropping a kiss on her bare shoulder. He gazed out at the orange fireball poised to disappear. "Beautiful. Like you."

"I've missed this," she said.

"What? Making out on the beach with the cutest boy next door?"

"I was gonna say *sunsets*. I can't remember a single night, living in Atlanta, that I stopped what I was doing just to watch the sky turn this amazing color. But making out with you on the beach is pretty amazing too," she said, smiling down at him.

He sat up and wrapped his arms around her chest, kissing her neck and shoulders, and she leaned back into his embrace. Finally, the sky was an inky blue black, scattered with stars and a waning crescent moon.

Skelly pulled her back down into the sand, tugging at her clothes with renewed urgency, nudging her knees apart with his own. She pulled his shirt over his head, and he obligingly removed her top. He easily removed her shorts. She found his zipper and slowly inched it down, stroking him as she went.

They reclined on their sides, facing each other, their legs entwined, touching, stroking, kissing.

"Um, Conley?"

She was kissing his chest, working her way down his abdomen, enjoying how ragged his breathing got the farther south she moved.

"Did you by any chance keep that condom you stole from Grayson?"

She stopped what she was doing. "A twenty-year-old condom? Um. No. But what kind of pharmacist doesn't keep birth control in his pocket for emergencies like this?"

"The newly divorced kind. The kind who's convinced he'll never have sex again."

She kissed him lightly, then pulled him on top of her. "Lucky for you, I was a Girl Scout. And I'm always prepared."

. . .

"Wow," Skelly said, draping an arm over her side. "What was in that wine?"

"Nothing special," Conley said lazily.

"Unlike you," he said, nuzzling her neck. "I can't believe what just happened here. Sarah Conley Hawkins jumped my bones."

"I seem to remember that you made the first move," Conley said, reaching for her top and pulling it over her head.

"I was trying to restore your faith in humanity. To make all your teenage fantasies come true," he said.

She chuckled. "I'd say my fantasies were more than realized."

Skelly sat up and gazed around. "I didn't want to say anything because I didn't want to spoil the mood, but for a while there, I kind of had this creepy feeling that we were being watched. You, uh, you don't think your grandmother could see us from the house, do you?"

"No way," she said flatly. "I can see the cove from my room, but G'mama sleeps downstairs. What time is it, anyway?"

He consulted his watch. "Nearly nine."

"Then G'mama and Winnie are either bent over their jigsaw puzzle or fast asleep. I'd vote for sleeping."

"Hope so," he said, pulling on his shirt. "I don't want her chasing me down with a shotgun for besmirching her granddaughter."

She handed him his pants and donned her own panties and shorts. "Don't be so dramatic. The besmirching was mutual. Anyway, my grandmother adores you. Always has."

He put one leg into his pants and then the other before pulling her to her feet. "And what about you?"

Conley busied herself brushing the sand from her bare legs, arms, and neck. "God. I'm a mess. I've got sand in places I didn't know I had."

"Me too," Skelly said. He reached for her hand. "You haven't answered my question."

"Skelly." She drew out his name. "What do you want from me?"

"Never mind," he said curtly. "What was I thinking? We literally had sex on the beach here a few minutes ago, but how self-involved am I to think you might indicate you have some kind of feelings for me?"

"I do have feelings for you," she protested. "I wouldn't be here if I didn't. But this—you and me? This is so new. I'm just out of a relationship, you're newly divorced . . ."

"Were you in love with this guy Kevin? The reporter in Atlanta?"

"No," she said slowly. "I cared about him, but it hadn't gotten that far."

"Well, I've been divorced for almost a year," Skelly said. "And Danielle and I were off and on separated for the last five years of our marriage. This isn't some rebound thing for me, Conley."

"Oh, Skelly," she said softly. "Give me some time, please?"

He picked up his shoes and started walking up the path through the dunes. "I don't have much choice, do I?"

36

FAMILY DRAMA FOLLOWS MYSTERIOUS DEATH
OF CONGRESSMAN ROBINETTE
By Rowena Meigs and Conley Hawkins

Silver Bay, Florida—Both the widow and son of U.S. Rep. Symmes Robinette (R-Florida) have announced that they will run for his unexpired term, a development that is sending shock waves through Silver Bay and the Thirty-fifth District.

The seventy-seven-year-old, eighteen-term congressman died last week in a fiery, early-morning, single-car crash in rural Bronson County. Bronson sheriff Merle Goggins said the incident remains "under investigation."

On Monday, Robinette's widow, Vanessa Robinette, in an exclusive interview with The Beacon, *confirmed her intent to run in a special election, which will be held in November.*

"Of course, I am heartbroken over the sudden loss of the love of my life," Mrs. Robinette told the Beacon *on Monday. "But public service has long been the focus of my life with Symmes, and I can think of no better way to honor his legacy than to continue serving his constituents in Washington."*

Earlier on Monday, Mrs. Robinette disclosed that Robinette received a diagnosis of end-stage non-Hodgkin's lymphoma last September. Although the congressman was treated at Walter Reed National Military Medical Center, his diagnosis was kept a closely guarded secret.

A few hours earlier, Mrs. Robinette's only son, Charles S. "Charlie" Robinette Jr., announced that he has already formed a campaign committee, headed by Miles Schoendienst, a retired railroad executive and top political fund-raiser in North Florida.

"My father made it clear to me, even before his recent illness, that he believed I would be the best candidate to represent the Thirty-fifth District," Robinette said. "Of course, we'd hoped I wouldn't have to announce before his retirement, but cancer has a way of cheating the best-laid plans."

Charlie Robinette, a partner in the Robinette Law Firm in Silver Bay, said his mother's announcement took him completely by surprise.

"She didn't discuss her decision with me or with anyone else in the family or [Symmes Robinette's] close circle of associates as far as I know. . . . My mother is her own woman," Robinette said. "Clearly, I think my father's decision that I should run for his seat, should he not be able to complete his term, is one that should be respected."

He downplayed the potential for a family feud stemming from clashing political ambitions.

"Thanksgiving could get a little awkward, but we're a political family. . . . We're used to finding ways of compromising."

Charlie Robinette defended his father's decision to hide his cancer diagnosis from voters. "We felt it was a private, family matter. Dad felt well enough to be in Washington, attending to the people's business in Congress, right up until the end of his life."

The body of Charles Symmes Robinette, a fourth-generation native Floridian, will lie in state Tuesday in the Capitol Rotunda, where government officials, including the president, vice president, Speaker of the House, and Florida governor Roy Padgett,

*along with other dignitaries, will gather to pay tribute to Robi-
nette's decades of public service.*

*Following the memorial in Washington, D.C., services will be
held this Saturday at Silver Bay Presbyterian Church. The family
will receive Friday night at McFall-Peeples Funeral Home.*

*But in the meantime, Robinette's sudden death has revealed
long-hidden cracks in the façade of the family life of the decorated
Vietnam veteran and conservative congressman who also served in
the Florida senate.*

*The obituary written by Robinette's widow, Vanessa Monck
Robinette, fifty-nine, and submitted to the* Beacon, *lists as sur-
vivors, in addition to Ms. Robinette, his thirty-four-year-old son
Charles.*

*No mention is made in the death notice of Robinette's older
children from his marriage to his first wife and high school sweet-
heart, Emma Todd "Toddie" Sanderson Robinette, who married
Robinette in 1962, when he was nineteen and she was eighteen.
Hank Sanderson Robinette is fifty-two. and Rebecca Robinette
Bouillotte, age fifty.*

*"Damn straight I left them out," Vanessa Robinette said when
asked about the omission. "They weren't mentioned because they
weren't a part of Symmes's life. You know what? I don't even know
their names. I doubt my husband could remember them either.
That's* how estranged he was from all of them."

*But according to Bronson County tax records, Symmes Robinette
transferred title to Oak Springs Farm, a working quail-hunting
plantation that includes a 3,500-square-foot farmhouse and eight
hundred acres of timberland, to Toddie Sanderson for one dollar
"and other considerations," the day before his fatal accident.*

*On the same day, Robinette also transferred title to his for-
mer home in Silver Bay to Charlie Robinette, who has resided
at the Trinity Street home since his parents moved into their
4,200-square-foot oceanfront mansion on Sugar Key, the gated
country club subdivision developed in 2017 by Miles Schoendienst,
Robinette's longtime business associate and campaign contributor.*

Vanessa Robinette was apparently blindsided by the news of her late husband's largesse in deeding the farm to his first wife.

"That's not possible," Vanessa said when told of the deed transfer. "I don't know what that woman has told you, but it's impossible. Symmes would never have done something like that."

Toddie Sanderson, who has lived at Oak Springs Farm since her 1986 divorce from Robinette, declined to comment for this story.

Charles Symmes Robinette Sr. was the only child of Marva Franklin Robinette and Clyde D. Robinette. He grew up in the Plattesville community where, following the death of her husband at the age of forty-two, Mrs. Robinette worked at a now-defunct textile mill. Mrs. Robinette met and married her second husband, Gordon Pancoast, who was a plant manager, when Symmes Robinette was twelve.

Robinette enlisted in the U.S. Marines in 1965 and, following a tour of duty in Vietnam, returned home to Silver Bay in 1967. He received his undergraduate and law degrees from Florida State University.

He was elected to the Florida senate in 1978 and ran for his first term in the U.S. House of Representatives in 1984.

During his terms in Congress, Robinette was instrumental in delivering tens of millions of dollars in federal funding to Florida and the Thirty-fifth District, including funds for new wastewater management systems, highway improvements, and the establishment and construction of a new Veterans Administration clinic in Silver Bay.

During his first term in office, Symmes Robinette hired a vivacious brunette named Vanessa R. Monck as a legislative aide.

According to Vanessa Robinette, a romance soon blossomed between the then forty-three-year-old legislator and his twenty-five-year-old protégée. "I was young and just starting out. Symmes was so kind and generous. He was always one to encourage young people," she recalled this week.

Mrs. Robinette stated that the congressman's marriage to Toddie Robinette "had been over for years. His alleged wife wouldn't step foot in D.C. He was lonely and so unhappy. He'd been asking for a divorce for years, but she refused."

But when Vanessa Robinette became pregnant with the congressman's child, the divorce was quickly granted. The two were married in a private ceremony in Washington, D.C., in 1986, three months after the birth of Charles S. Robinette Jr.

According to several longtime residents, by the time Symmes Robinette brought his new bride and infant son home to Silver Bay, his first wife had withdrawn her children from local schools and moved with them, forty-five miles away, to Oak Springs Farm in Bronson County.

The farm is less than ten miles from the secluded stretch of county highway in Bronson County where Symmes Robinette died last Thursday.

At three o'clock that morning, two witnesses encountered a late-model black Escalade SUV, which had flipped upside down. The driver of the vehicle appeared unconscious and trapped inside the vehicle. The witnesses called 911, but their attempts to free the driver were unsuccessful, and when the Escalade caught fire, they were driven back by the flames. Fire rescue units from Bronson County responded to the 911 call, but the driver, later identified as Symmes Robinette, was unresponsive.

The witnesses said they saw no other cars in the vicinity. The weather that night was clear. Bronson sheriff Merle Goggins said that the cause of the accident remains under investigation. And although the congressman sustained massive head injuries, the district medical examiner's office still has not determined the cause of death.

Vanessa Robinette blamed her husband's accident on what she called "chemo brain," saying that his cancer treatment made him "confused and disoriented," and that in recent weeks, he'd begun to awaken in the middle of the night and go for long drives. "He hadn't been himself," she said. "That's why he was home . . . to get some rest."

That same impairment, she said, would be the only reason her husband would have deeded such valuable property to his long-estranged ex-wife.

37

Conley was sound asleep when her cell phone rang shortly before six Tuesday morning. She groped for it in the dark, dropped it onto the floor, and finally answered on the sixth ring.

"Nice story, Hawkins." It was Roger Sistrunk, her former editor in Atlanta.

"Roger?" She yawned, still groggy from a restless night. "What are you talking about?"

"Isn't this your byline in *The Silver Bay Beacon*? It's seven o'clock. Did I wake you up or something?"

"Hell yeah, you woke me up. The Florida Panhandle is in a different time zone from Atlanta. Are you talking about the Robinette thing? Where'd you hear about it?"

"Google Alerts," Sistrunk said. "Hell of a story."

She swung her legs over the bed. "Yeah, it's gotten kind of crazy with the widow and her son both declaring they're gonna run for Robinette's seat."

"I was gonna send Felker down there to do a follow-up, but then I thought, why not hire Conley?"

That got her attention. "Me? I thought you had a hiring freeze."

"We do. I'm talking about freelance. I want to hire you to write me a Sunday piece. Say, eighteen hundred words? And we want that video and your still photos to go with it."

"Which video? The car fire or the video of Charlie Robinette? I shot the car stuff because a friend and I were the first ones on the scene that night. My colleague Michael Torpy scored the video of Charlie Robinette."

"Both," Sistrunk said. "The video makes the story. Especially the part where the son talks about his mom ruining Thanksgiving by running against him. You guys own the video, right?"

She went to the closet and started pulling out clothes. She was wide awake now, and the wheels were turning. If Sistrunk was waking her up at seven his time, they had a bona fide hot story on their hands. And she'd need to stay cool to leverage it into more than a one-shot Sunday reader piece.

"Yes," she said, laying clothes out on the bed. "The video is ours. But if you want it, you're gonna have to pay for it. What kind of a rate are we talking about?"

"Like $750. Don't break my balls over this, Hawkins. You know the kind of freelance rates we pay."

Her phone beeped, indicating an incoming phone call. The number had a 404 area code, meaning it was from Atlanta.

"That's ridiculous," she snapped. "Hang on a sec, Roger. I've got an incoming call I need to take."

She clicked over to the incoming call. "Hi. This is Conley Hawkins."

"Conley!" The woman's voice was warm and vaguely Southern. "This is Selena Kwan. I think we met years ago at a press club forum. I'm the NBC bureau chief in Atlanta, and I want to talk to you about this sensational Robinette story of yours."

"I remember you," Conley said warily. "From when we both covered the Atlanta public school cheating scandal, right?"

"Good memory," Selena said. "I'm gonna cut right to the chase here. We're really interested in this story about your dead congressman."

"Uh-huh."

"This would normally be too regional a story for us, but the angle of the mother and son running against each other for Robinette's seat is too good to pass up."

"I agree," Conley said.

"So couple of quick questions. Who owns the rights to that video?"

"I shot the car fire video myself," Conley said. "My friend and I were the first ones on the scene after the wreck. Well, the first that we know of. And my colleague at the *Beacon,* Michael Torpy, shot the interview with Charlie Robinette."

"Okay. Perfect."

"The story is still developing," Conley said quickly. "Vanessa Robinette as much as told me that *if* Symmes deeded over the quail-hunting plantation to Toddie, his first wife, it was the cancer meds talking. I wouldn't be surprised if things get nasty in a hurry down here."

"Better and better," Selena said, chortling. "Who doesn't love a messy family drama? So here's what we'd like to do. The Washington bureau is going to send a camera crew to cover the memorial service at the Capitol today. Hopefully, we can get the widow and the son staring daggers at each other, with the flag-draped coffin in between."

"At the very least," Conley agreed. "Vanessa is not your typical tea-and-cookies political wife, and she is not the type to fade into the woodwork."

"But in the meantime," Selena continued, "we'd like to buy the rights to both videos. For onetime use, I can pay $500, or better for you, $1,000 for exclusive, cable-wide use on all our platforms for the rest of the month."

Conley hesitated. "Just the video?"

"What else did you have in mind?" Selena asked.

"As I said, the story is just heating up. The cause of Robinette's accident still hasn't been determined."

"Didn't the sheriff tell you he died of head trauma or something?"

"Yeah. But what caused that accident? I was right there. Clear night, no other cars around. It was three-o-freakin'-clock in the morning, and he was a good forty miles from home. The car was a six-month-old Escalade."

Selena was quiet for a moment. "Can I ask you a personal question?"

Conley knew what was coming, but she waited.

"What's a pro like you doing working for a tiny weekly paper in a town I can't even find on a map? Didn't I hear you left the *AJC* for a gig in D.C.?"

"The job in D.C. didn't pan out," Conley said. "My family owns the *Beacon,* so I came home to spend time with family and to send out job applications, and this story exploded in my lap the second night I was in town."

"Lucky you," the producer said. "Okay, would you be willing to freelance consult with us on the story?"

"I would be, but I should tell you that I was on the phone with my old boss at the *AJC* when you called. He wants the video and for me to freelance a print piece for them."

"We don't care about print, so go ahead with that if you want," Selena said quickly. "But we would want an exclusive on that video."

Conley's phone beeped with another incoming call from a 404 area code.

"Can you hold for a minute, Selena? I've got another call I need to take. Be right back."

She clicked over to the new call. "Hi. This is Conley," she said.

"Conley Hawkins!" the man's voice was a little too loud, a little too boisterous for such an early hour in the morning. "Peter Elkhaly, senior executive producer at CNN. Don't we know each other?"

Even though CNN was based in Atlanta, Conley knew only a handful of journalists who worked there. Most of the old barriers and animosity between print and broadcast had faded in recent years, but the economic ones still existed. Print journalists were paupers compared to the salaries broadcasters made in a major market like Atlanta.

"Don't think so," Conley said. "What can I do for you, Pete?"

"It's Peter. I'll be brief. We want that Robinette story you guys ran last night. Especially that video."

She smiled. "The thing is, I've got my old boss at the *AJC* and the Atlanta NBC bureau chief, both on hold. I'll be brief too. What's your offer?"

"A thousand, and it's ours exclusively."

"That's all you got?"

"What else do you want? We like the video, we like the family feud angle, but I'll be honest with you. This is an election year, Conley. We got stories exploding all over the place. That's about the best I can do."

"Okay," she said. "Thanks for calling." She disconnected and went back to her previous caller, hoping that the NBC bureau chief hadn't hung up or given up. "Selena?"

"Still here. What's your thought on my offer?"

"Well," Conley said slowly. "That was Peter Elkhaly from CNN on the other line . . ."

"That tool? I hope you didn't cut a deal with him."

"I told him I'd think about it," Conley lied.

"I had a chance to talk with my boss while you were busy," Selena said. "He likes this story as much as I do, and we agree that it could have legs and that having you on the ground down there following up as things develop will give us a nice edge. So. We'll figure out an associate producer contract for you, and in the meantime, we'd like to lock up the exclusive on both those videos. How does $2,000 sound?"

It sounded like four car payments on the Subaru and a windfall for Michael Torpy. But more important, if the associate producing gig happened, maybe it could work into an actual job down the line—and a ticket out of Silver Bay.

"Sounds fine," Conley said. "I'll have to speak with my colleague who shot the interview with Charlie Robinette, but I'm pretty sure he'll agree. And I'll need to clear the deal with my managing editor."

"Do that," Selena said. "I'll email you the contract as soon as legal gets it to me. And, Conley?"

"Yes?"

"Welcome aboard. I think we're gonna have some fun with this one."

She clicked back over to Roger Sistrunk, who was still on hold, but he'd disconnected.

38

G'mama was talking animatedly on the phone when Conley walked into the kitchen.

Winnie's transistor radio was propped on the windowsill, and Buddy Bright was prattling on about the upcoming memorial service in Washington for Symmes Robinette.

Conley went to the cupboard, found a box of strawberry Pop-Tarts, tore open the foil wrapper, and took a bite of the corner of the pastry.

"At least let me put that in the toaster for you," Winnie said, but Conley resisted.

"I like 'em this way. It's even trashier than if it's toasted."

Winnie rolled her eyes in response.

Conley leaned against the kitchen counter, unashamedly eavesdropping on her grandmother's telephone conversation.

"Harriet, Harriet. Let me stop you right now," Lorraine said. "Is there anything in that article that's untrue? You might not like what we published, but that does not make it filth. So no, I'm not going to fire my granddaughter, who happens to be an award-winning investigative journalist. And I'm not going to 'make' Grayson publish a retraction. She's the managing editor, not me. And I happen to trust her judgment implicitly."

"She's been getting calls like this all morning," Winnie whispered. "Can't even drink her coffee in peace."

G'mama listened patiently. "I'm sorry you feel that way. The *Beacon* values all its subscribers, but of course, if you don't want to get the paper anymore, we'll cancel your subscription. Which means you won't get any more grocery store coupons. No, I don't think we do offer refunds. All right, Harriet. Love to Smitty. See you at church."

G'mama put the phone down and penciled a hash mark on the back of an envelope. Conley counted eight of them.

"Winnie says you're having a rough morning?" She pointed at the envelope. "Are those all cancellations?"

"No. These are people I'm making a note to shun after this. Harriet Steinmach is the only one who actually canceled."

"Well, thanks for sticking up for freedom of the press," Conley said, brushing a kiss on her grandmother's cheek. "Are you mad at us for running the Robinette thing?"

"Of course not! That special edition you all put out last night was wonderful! It's making people sit up and take notice, which we haven't done in a long time. Pops used to say that was a newspaper's job—not just to report the facts but to get them thinking about the facts, asking questions, get 'em riled up. I loved the ads too, once I got used to them flashing and blinking at me."

"That's all Michael's doing," Conley said. "He really is a whiz kid."

"I'm sorry I wasn't awake when Sean left last night," G'mama said, picking up her coffee cup. "Did you two have a nice walk?"

Conley poured her own coffee, avoiding meeting her grandmother's probing eyes. "Very nice. We sat out on the beach for a long time, just drinking our wine and watching the sunset."

"I saw he finally bought an ad too," G'mama commented. "Maybe that'll make some of our other local businesses do the same."

"Hope so," Conley said, swallowing her coffee. "I'd better get in to the office. Lots to do before the print deadline tonight."

"Wonder if they'll show Symmes Robinette's funeral on television," Lorraine said.

"I happen to know NBC will have somebody at the service today,"

Conley said. "And that reminds me. We'll need to pull photos of the memorial service off the wire."

She rinsed out her coffee mug and set it on the counter.

"When are you seeing Sean again?" G'mama asked.

"Not sure. I've got a crazy-busy week ahead." She debated whether to tell her grandmother about the deal she'd worked out with the Atlanta paper and the network but decided to clear her arrangement with Grayson first.

She was driving down Main Street, headed for the office, when she saw a blue-and-white Bronson County sheriff's vehicle parked in front of Kelly's Drugs. She parked beside the cruiser and pushed through the door, setting the bells tied to the door handle jingling.

Skelly was behind the pharmacy counter, deep in conversation with the deputy she remembered from the accident scene and from her later encounter at the sheriff's office, Walter Poppell.

Poppell looked up and gave her a smirking finger wave. Conley sat down at the soda fountain counter and turned her back to him, although she could still see the conversation in the back-bar mirror.

After a moment, she got up, went behind the counter, and fixed herself a glass of water. Ten minutes later, she saw Poppell leave, and Skelly walked over slowly, installing himself behind the counter.

"What was that all about?" she asked.

Skelly fiddled with a stack of laminated menus. "I guess it's okay to tell you. I mean, he didn't say not to. They wanted a list of all the prescriptions I filled for the Robinettes, going back for the past two years."

She leaned in. "Really? Plural? Symmes and Vanessa? Did you give it to him? I mean, are there any HIPAA regulations prohibiting that?"

"He said it's a criminal investigation."

"I know you can't tell me anything about Vanessa's meds, but what about Symmes's? He's dead now, so the rules don't apply anymore, right?"

He poured himself a mug of coffee. "Want one?"

"Thanks, but I'm already buzzed, and it's got nothing to do with caffeine. Come on, Skelly," she pleaded. "Vanessa herself told me about

Symmes's cancer and said he was on chemo. She even blamed 'chemo brain' for the fact that he'd get up in the middle of the night and go driving around. She said he wasn't thinking right when he deeded over the quail-hunting plantation to Toddie."

Skelly tugged at his ear, a nervous gesture she remembered from their childhood.

"No," he said, shaking his head. "This doesn't feel right. It's an invasion of his privacy. I'm sorry, but I really can't tell you anything without Vanessa's permission."

She gave him a sheepish grin. "I figured you'd say that, but I had to ask, just in case."

Skelly touched her hand. "Can we talk about last night for a minute? I'd really like to understand these mixed signals I'm getting. I mean, one minute we're rolling around on the sand and you're ripping off my pants, and five minutes later, it's like nothing even happened."

"God, I hate this stuff," Conley muttered.

He raised an eyebrow. "Stuff? Like talking about emotions? Admitting you care for somebody and want to be with them?"

"I should never have told you any of that juvenile stuff about my crush and the condom. Any of it. It was teenage fantasy."

"Then why did you?" He didn't look away, so she did, gazing out through the drugstore's plate glass window at people strolling by on the sidewalk outside.

Conley glanced at the old red Coca-Cola clock on the wall, with its the PAUSE THAT REFRESHES logo.

"Grayson's gonna kill me if I'm late to work," she said. "It's deadline day, and we're still chasing a huge story."

He clamped his hand over hers. "Can you at least answer my question before you run off to chase your Pulitzer Prize?"

"I don't know. Talking about old times, maybe I was feeling sentimental."

"Nope," he said. "Not buying it."

"Okay. Maybe I was still curious. About what I'd missed out on that night at the country club dance."

"That is a completely lame, bullshit answer." His hand didn't move.

"Skelly." Her voice was pleading. "I know you're looking for more. You deserve more. But right now, I need to concentrate on work. I wasn't going to say anything earlier, but this Robinette story is blowing up. My old boss at the *AJC* called this morning and wants me to freelance a Sunday piece about it. While I was on the phone with him, the NBC bureau chief in Atlanta called. She wants me to cover the story as it unfolds. And then CNN called too. Their offer was bullshit, but still . . ."

He slowly lifted his hand, releasing hers. "What you're saying is this story is your ticket out of Silver Bay. And the *Beacon*. And your family drama. And it's a one-way ticket, party of one. Right?"

"Maybe. I don't know. What I do know is, there are no jobs in print journalism right now. Nobody's hiring, at least at my career level. I'd sort of halfway thought about trying to make the switch to broadcast, but that didn't seem realistic. Now there's a possibility that this NBC thing could work into something more. Like a real, full-time job with boring stuff like benefits."

"And way more prestige than working for your family newspaper in some swampy Florida backwater," Skelly said.

Conley slid off the barstool, snatched her backpack off the counter, and hitched it over her shoulder. "Ambition isn't a crime, Skelly, and I won't let you make me feel guilty for having it."

The bells jangled noisily as she pushed her way out the front door.

"Neither is loyalty," Sean Kelly said to nobody in particular.

She was about to make the turn into the *Beacon*'s parking lot when she spotted the Bronson County sheriff's vehicle half a block ahead, making a left into an auto body shop. She sped up and parked the Subaru on the street.

The lot in front of the shop was lined with relics from another time. There was a rusting black hulk of a 1950s-era pickup with a white scripted SILVER BAY AUTO BODY logo on the door—complete with a four-digit telephone number. An olive-green 1970s fastback Mustang rested on four rotted-out tires, and a perky little orange 1960s VW bug missing its doors sat beside it. The bug's rounded bumpers sported fading but groovy pink and yellow daisy decals, and the interior of the car had been completely stripped. She'd always lusted after that car.

Conley's phone buzzed, and she glanced down. The text was from Grayson.

WHERE THE HELL ARE YOU? SHIT IS HITTING THE FAN.

Her fingers flew over the keyboard. *Working on Robinette story. Talk soon.*

She checked her emails, hoping to see some kind of correspondence from Selena Kwan about the NBC offer. Her phone buzzed with an incoming text. It was from Roger Sistrunk. One sentence.

Do we have a deal or what?

She bit her lip. She didn't want to burn any bridges with her old boss, just in case, but she also needed Sistrunk to recognize her value. She began typing.

I've had an offer from NBC, but since I talked to you first, here's what I can offer the AJC. Onetime use only of the Charlie Robinette video, a Sunday piece, including my firsthand account of being first on the scene of the fire and still photos of the fire. I'm willing to file follow-up pieces as the story unfolds, for a price to be determined. My price is $1k. My colleague Michael Torpy, who shot the video will need $250. Let me know what you decide. Best, C.

She went back to watching the front door of the auto body shop. What was a Bronson County sheriff's deputy doing in Griffin County? It couldn't be a coincidence that the same deputy had just visited Kelly's Drugs looking for a list of Symmes Robinette's meds.

Her phone buzzed. She read the incoming text from Sistrunk and smiled.

Damn it, Hawkins. It's a deal. Twenty inches, $1k, by 5:00 p.m. Thursday. Tell Torpy he's got a deal too. Don't fuck this up. Okay?

Okay, she typed back. *Love you too. Xoxo.*

When she looked up again, Poppell was emerging from the auto body shop. He held a large brown paper grocery sack in his meaty hand. The top of the bag had been folded over and secured with bright red tape. He placed the bag on the seat of the cruiser, closed the door, and drove away.

She recognized the bag and the tape from her days covering cop shops. They were used to secure evidence.

Jesse Bayless wore wrinkled blue coveralls. He was standing in a work bay near the crumpled remains of a late-model black Escalade, wiping his soot-blackened hands on a shop towel. She recognized the car too. It had become Symmes Robinette's funeral pyre.

"Hey, Jesse," she said.

He looked up sharply. "Oh, hey, Sarah. Didn't see you standing there."

Jesse was the youngest of Nedra's sons. He had a fringe of graying bangs cut straight across, Buster Brown–style, and dark brown eyes that drooped at the corners. Even the bands of tattoos protruding beneath the cutoff sleeves of his jumpsuit didn't make him look menacing. He looked, she thought, like the human embodiment of a Bassett hound.

"I just came in. Right after that sheriff's deputy left."

"Nothing's wrong with Aunt Winnie, I hope."

"Nope. I just left the house an hour ago. She's as ornery as ever."

"You'd be ornery too if you'd had to raise a bunch of sorry characters like the three of us," Jesse said with a chuckle.

"Don't forget she helped raise me and Grayson too, so make that five kids," Conley said. "Hey, what was that deputy from Bronson doing here? Was it about that?" She pointed at the Escalade.

He picked up a tool from the workbench and began wiping it with the shop rag. "Yeah."

"I saw he was carrying an evidence bag. What was in it?"

"Not sure I'm supposed to say," Jesse replied. "Anyway, you were there that night, right? You and Sean Kelly?"

"Not when it happened, but right afterward," she said.

"You think Robinette was already dead? Before the fire started? I asked that Poppell dude, but he said it was none of my business."

"He wasn't moving," Conley said. "His head was slumped forward. I could see some blood, but whether he was just unconscious or dead, I don't know."

"Kinda hope he was alive," Jesse said, his gentle demeanor putting the lie to his words.

She had no response to that, remembering Winnie's equally harsh response to the news of Robinette's gruesome death.

"Bet I know what he was doing over there in Bronson County that night he was killed," Jesse said.

Conley raised an eyebrow. "Really? What's that?"

"Booty call. The old shitbird was chasing after some young blond chick."

"Come on, Jesse," she said. "He was seventy-seven and dying of cancer."

"I'm telling you, I saw him myself. At the Waffle House, two or three weeks ago. They were holding hands."

He went back to the workbench, picked up his cell phone, and scrolled through his camera roll until he found the frame he wanted. He held it up so she could see it.

The photo was a blurry side view. A gaunt, older, balding man was seated in a booth, the younger woman across from him. A curtain of blond hair concealed half her face, but yes, the couple's hands were intertwined on the tabletop.

"What do you think this proves?" Conley asks.

"Speaks for itself," Jesse said. "I was there. I seen the way he was looking at that girl." He wiped the phone on the seat of his coveralls and put it back on the workbench. "And now I'm not the only one who's seen it."

"You still hate Robinette." It was a statement, not a question. "You sent that photo to his wife?"

The mechanic shrugged. "If he'd done to your family what he did to mine, you'd hate him too," Jesse said. "My mom's been gone close to thirty years, but I'll never forget how sick she was, the way that cancer ate up her insides. Robinette got rich off the money the railroad paid him to cover it up. But my family? My mama got the grave, and Aunt Winnie got sent to prison. So yeah. *Hate* ain't a strong enough word."

"Fair enough, I guess," Conley said. And then she repeated her earlier question. "I'm still wondering what was in that evidence bag the deputy was carrying."

"Huh? Oh. Yeah. It was the driver's-side mirror. It was hanging halfway off anyway."

"Did Poppell say why he wanted it?"

"I didn't ask."

"What's the Escalade doing here anyway?" Conley asked. "The accident happened in Bronson County."

"Yeah, but we've got a towing contract with them. Griffin County too," Jesse said. "After they peeled what was left of the old bastard off the upholstery, they called, and we towed it over here to the garage."

Conley shivered, thinking of the visual. "What happens to the car now?"

"Poppell said it'll probably get towed to the state crime lab for more tests. His wife don't want it, so if the state doesn't come get it, we'll sell it for scrap."

"Did Poppell ask any other questions about the car?" Conley asked.

"He wanted to check the glove box, but like I told him, if there was anything in there, it got burned up in the fire."

Her phone buzzed with another text from Grayson.

?????

"I'd better get to work," she said, stashing her phone in her pocket. "Thanks, Jesse," she said, extending her hand, but he shook his head. "Naw. You don't wanna shake hands with a nasty old grease monkey."

She took his hand anyway, pumping it vigorously. "Always a pleasure, Jesse."

He followed her through the shop and out into the parking lot. It was just after nine o'clock, and the air was already as thick and hot as tomato soup.

"Hey, Conley," he said as she was about to get into her car.

She whirled around, hoping he'd thought of some other nugget of information. "Yes?"

"That Subaru. Does it get good mileage?"

"Gets great mileage," she said. "Don't forget to call me if you think of anything else about that Escalade."

39

Grayson called when Conley was half a block from the *Beacon* office.

"Hey," her sister said. "Charlie Robinette is having a press conference at the courthouse, starting in ten minutes. Get over there right away."

"What's it about?" Conley asked.

"Don't know," Grayson said. "We just got an email from his *communications director* promising that it was a breaking news event."

A small but growing crowd was already gathering on the courthouse lawn. Conley counted two television vans parked on the sidewalk, one from Pensacola and one from Tallahassee, and of course, she spotted Buddy Bright's gleaming white Corvette with a homemade working press vanity plate on the front. The normally quiet streets around the square were lined with cars. She pulled into a vacant spot in front of Kelly's Drugs, hopped out, and hurried across the street.

A small wooden platform had been erected near the Confederate war monument. Draped with American flags, it held a podium and a microphone. The television reporters, with tripod-mounted cameras, were set up directly in front of the podium, and a couple of dozen people milled around. Half of them, Conley noticed, were wearing bright red T-shirts and baseball caps emblazoned with I'M WITH CHARLIE—ROBINETTE FOR CONGRESS 2020.

Always a cynic, she wondered how recently the campaign gear had been ordered and distributed.

The heavy plate glass doors to the courthouse lobby were open, and Conley could see employees with lanyard IDs around their necks, standing inside, craning their necks to get a view of the action.

Conley wove her way through the crowd and managed to wedge herself in between the dueling television reporters. "Hi," she said breathlessly to the tall male Latino reporter manning a camera with the CBS logo. "Any idea what's going on?"

He shrugged. "No idea. We were shooting a story about beach erosion, and the producer called and told us to swing by to shoot a press conference. Who is this guy, anyway?"

Before Conley could answer, a cute blonde in a navy-blue pantsuit and tall spike heels walked onto the platform, followed by Charlie Robinette, in his campaign casual dress shirt with the rolled-up sleeves and loosened tie. Conley recognized the blonde. It was Kennedy McFall, from the funeral home. She tapped the microphone and began speaking.

Conley whipped out her cell phone, swiped through to her camera, and began recording video.

"Hi, everyone, and thanks for being here on short notice. I'm Kennedy McFall, communications director for your next U.S. representative, Charlie Robinette. Charlie has a brief statement to make, and then he'll take questions."

Charlie put his arm around Kennedy's waist briefly and nodded at the small press contingent.

"I should tell y'all that Kennedy is also my fiancée. Anyway, that's not what I came here to talk about today. What I do want to talk about is transparency, which I think is vital for a public servant." He gulped and ran a hand through his immaculately coiffed hair. "This isn't a move I make lightly. And it's something that I've been reluctant to address, but I believe that recent events have made my actions unavoidable. As you may know, last week, we lost my father, a decorated Vietnam War vet and your dedicated congressman of over thirty years."

"Rest in peace, Symmes," a man's deep voice called from behind Conley.

"Yes, definitely," Charlie said, his face solemn. "What most of you don't know is that Dad had been diagnosed with non-Hodgkin's lymphoma last year. He received treatment at Walter Reed, but the prognosis was dire. It was Dad's wish that we keep his condition a private, family matter. His intent was to continue working for the great Thirty-fifth District and his treasured constituents as long as his health allowed. In the meantime, after many heart-to-heart conversations, Dad impressed upon me that his deepest wish was for me to succeed him in office, and after some consideration, I was honored to accept the challenge. Of course, we all hoped that time would come after his retirement from the term to which he was recently elected, but per my dad's request, I began to assemble a campaign committee."

Kennedy nodded sympathetically, touching his arm lightly.

"Although Dad continued to fulfill the obligations of his office in Washington, in recent months, his condition worsened. Three months ago, against the advice of his specialists in Washington, my mother insisted that Dad return home to Silver Bay for treatment."

Charlie tugged at the knot of his tie. "Since that time, my mother slowly managed to isolate Dad from his closest associates and from the rest of his family. She resisted my suggestion that he return to Walter Reed for treatment from the doctors there who routinely work with cancer patients, saying he was too ill to travel. Eventually, she forbade me to visit Dad, saying that his immune system was too weakened from chemo to allow visitors. Since my parents reside in a gated community, she was able to instruct security guards not to allow me entrance. She also confiscated Dad's cell phone, cutting off my only other means of communication with him." He paused. "In effect, my father became a prisoner in his own home."

"That's terrible," a woman behind Conley murmured.

"Tragic," her friend agreed.

"Still," Charlie continued, "through admittedly devious means, which I won't go into here, I managed to see my father, despite my mother's best efforts. Two weeks before his death, I was shocked by my father's appearance. He looked emaciated and seemed . . . somewhat confused. When I confronted my mother with my impressions of Dad's rapid decline, she flew into a rage, accused me of disloyalty and dishonesty, and informed me that as a result of what she called my 'disobedience,' I would not see or hear from my father again. After that, my mother stopped speaking to me. At all."

He stared off into space for a moment, blinking back tears. "After consulting some of my father's oldest, most trusted advisers, I came to a very difficult decision. Two weeks ago, I filed a complaint with the Adult Protective Services division of the Florida Department of Children and Families, due to my concerns that my father was the victim of elder abuse, being perpetrated by his wife, Vanessa Robinette."

A small, collective gasp ran through the crowd.

"This is an incredibly painful, agonizing action for any child to take," Charlie said. "Believe me, I take no joy in any of this. But what kind of a son would I be if I allowed my father's suffering to go unreported? What kind of citizen would I be if I merely looked the other way at an instance of abuse? Sad to say, elder abuse is on the rise in the state of Florida, with over two thousand reports of elder abuse just in our region of the state in recent years. An even sadder statistic is that nearly sixty percent of alleged abuse cases are perpetrated by family members of the elderly victims."

Conley turned and panned with her phone to capture the reactions on the faces of the mostly middle-aged crowd, as did the broadcasters standing on either side of her.

"Following my report, a caseworker began investigating my allegations," Charlie said. "I haven't yet been made privy to their findings, because less than two weeks later, my father was killed in a one-car wreck, the cause of which is still under investigation by local authorities."

"Holy shit," the CBS cameraman whispered under his breath.

"Damn," the pretty blond Fox reporter muttered.

"In light of this tragedy, it would be easy for me to stay silent about my concerns, if only for the sake of keeping the family peace. But I can't in good conscience do that. Not when the welfare of our elderly neighbors, people like my ailing seventy-seven-year-old dad, is at stake."

Charlie clasped his hands in front of him. "This is the last, best thing I can do for my dad. Thank you all for coming." He took a half step back from the podium, and Kennedy hugged him briefly.

"Charlie will take a few questions now," she announced.

"Charlie!" A high-pitched voice called out from the far-right side of the podium.

Heads turned, and the crowd cleared a path for a wizened man dressed in all black. Conley groaned. Buddy Bright.

"Charlie, are you saying you suspect that your mother had something to do with your father's death?"

"Not at all," Robinette said firmly. "I thought it was my duty to report my concerns about my father's welfare to state authorities. I will leave it to them and to related law enforcement authorities to carry out their investigations."

Conley opened her mouth to ask her own question, but Buddy Bright beat her to the punch. "Why do you think your mother was keeping your father a prisoner in his own house?"

"I have no idea," Charlie said. "You'd have to ask her that question."

Conley waved her hand over her head. "When was the last time you saw your father? And what were the circumstances, since you say Vanessa blocked you from entering Sugar Key?"

Robinette's faced flushed slightly. "I'm not going to talk about that right now."

She plunged on with her next question. "Yesterday, Vanessa told *The Silver Bay Beacon* that your father had decided you weren't mature enough to run for Congress and that he'd urged her to run for his seat. Did your dad tell you that he'd changed his mind and was supporting her as a candidate?"

"My father never told me any such thing," Charlie shot back.

"So if your mother says that, she's lying?" the CBS reporter called.

"No comment," Charlie said.

Kennedy tugged at Charlie's sleeve and whispered something in his ear. He nodded and cleared his throat as she stepped back to the microphone.

Sensing it was her last chance, Conley called out a final question.

"What's this mean for your father's memorial service in Washington? Shouldn't you be on your way there right now?"

Charlie and his fiancée had another whispered exchange.

"Out of respect for my father's memory and a desire to maintain a dignified atmosphere at this memorial of my father's legacy of service to our country, I made the decision not to attend the ceremony in the Capitol Rotunda today. Of course, I'll be paying my respects at the service to be held here in his hometown this weekend, with the rest of our extended family."

"That's it for today," Kennedy announced. "But you can expect to hear more from Charlie in the coming weeks and months as we launch his campaign for the U.S. House of Representatives. We'd like to thank y'all for coming out today."

She quickly hustled Robinette toward the steps at the rear of the platform. Conley tried to follow, but her progress was slowed by the two broadcasters, who stepped in front of her to start disassembling their gear.

"Move, damn it," she growled at the CBS cameraman.

He turned around, startled. "Who the hell are you?"

"I'm from the local paper, and you're in my way," she replied, whipping around him to see which way Robinette had gone.

Just as she reached the edge of the square, she spotted her quarry standing on the passenger side of a white SUV. "Hey, Charlie," she called. He looked up, but when he saw her, he shrugged, got into the car, and closed the door. The SUV drove off.

Conley raced back to her Subaru and called Grayson from the car.

"Anything good?" Grayson asked anxiously.

"Charlie Robinette just stood up on the courthouse square, with his fiancée-slash–press secretary, who also happens to be Kennedy McFall, and announced that two weeks before Symmes died, he filed a claim of elder abuse against his mom with the state."

"Say again?"

"He said Vanessa had been holding his dad hostage in his own home, isolating him from all his colleagues, friends, and family. Took away his cell phone and ordered the security guards at Sugar Key not to allow Charlie onto the property."

"Tell me you've got that on tape," Grayson said.

"I videoed the whole thing," Conley assured her. "Charlie claimed Vanessa brought Symmes home three months ago, against the advice of his doctors at Walter Reed."

"Oh my god. This is so great," Grayson said.

"There's plenty more," she promised. "I'll tell you the rest when I get there."

40

"No, ma'am," Lillian was telling the caller. "We are definitely not affiliated with the *National Enquirer*. Yes, I'm positive. Okay. I'll be sure to tell Ms. Hawkins she's gonna burn in hell for running that story about our good Christian congressman. Yes, ma'am, I'll tell her sister too. And her grandmama. You have a blessed day, okay?"

The *Beacon*'s receptionist / office manager set the phone delicately back on its receiver. "You owe me," she told Conley.

"Busy morning?" Conley asked.

"That phone hasn't stopped ringing," Lillian said. "Emails, phone calls. We haven't had that many calls since we quit running the horoscope column. All because of that story of yours and Michael's." She handed over a stack of pink message slips. "Most of these people just want you to call 'em back so they can bitch you out personally."

Conley riffled through the stack. "That's all? Just fourteen? G'mama had eight phone calls before nine."

Lillian pursed her lips. "That's not counting the ones who started off saying, 'Listen, bitch,' at which point, I hung up on 'em. Y'all don't pay me enough money to put up with that cussing shit."

Conley tore the message slips in half and handed them back. "File those, will ya?"

. . .

Grayson was on the phone too. Her expression was pained. She looked up when Conley entered the office. "Okay. I can't get into this right now." She spun around in her chair so that it faced the wall. She lowered her voice. "You know it's my deadline day. I'll call you tomorrow, after the paper's out."

She spun her chair back around and placed the cell phone facedown on the desktop.

"God, what a day!"

"Yeah, Lillian told me the haters are out in force," Conley said.

"It hasn't all been bad," Grayson said. "I hate to admit it, but you were right about the video and putting out the digital edition. The response has been unbelievable. The last time I checked, those videos had been viewed nearly two thousand times. And Michael's idea to put in a special subscription coupon was genius. We've gotten thirty-two new subscribers. He set up the new Facebook page as soon as he got in this morning and made us all administrators so we can all post to it."

"Cool," Conley said. "Hey, there's something I need to let you know about—"

"But like you said, the haters are coming out of the woodwork," she said. "At last count, Lillian said we've had nine subscriptions cancelled. And I was parking out front this morning when a big old white Cadillac came cruising really slowly past me. The passenger-side window rolled down, and these two old geezers both leaned over and flipped me the bird!"

"That's a badge of honor," Conley said. "My old city editor at the *AJC,* Roger Sistrunk, used to say if a newspaper isn't pissing people off, it's not really doing its job."

"Easy to say in a big city like Atlanta, where the readers don't know your address and phone number and have no compunction about getting right in your face to tell you what they think of you," Grayson said. And then she grinned. "But I gotta say, this story has been the most fun we've had around here in a long time."

"It's a thrill, right? And wait 'til you see the video I shot of the press conference."

She handed over her cell phone and tapped the arrow to show the video. Grayson's eyes widened as she heard Charlie Robinette's accusations against his mother.

"Unbelievable," she said when the video ended. "He comes this close to accusing Vanessa of having something to do with his father's death. And is that our Kennedy McFall, from the funeral home?"

"One and the same."

"Huh," Grayson said. "I had no idea. She's a little older than he is, right?"

"I think so. Rowena said Vanessa and Symmes didn't approve of her because she's divorced and has a kid. Maybe the age thing is part of it. Again, unbelievable irony. This thing is exploding, Gray. There were camera crews there from television stations in Tallahassee and Pensacola. And get this—despite what your buddy Merle Goggins says, I don't think the cops believe that accident was entirely accidental. They've asked Skelly for records of all the prescriptions he'd filled for Symmes—and Vanessa."

Grayson frowned. "Skelly told you that?"

"On my way to the office this morning, I saw the police cruiser parked outside Kelly's, so I went inside and sat down at the soda fountain. Weirdly, it was the same deputy who showed up at the crash that night. After he was gone, I kinda wormed it out of Skelly. Also, Robinette's wrecked car was towed to Silver Bay Auto Body, where Winnie's nephew Jesse works. That same deputy showed up at the body shop. After he left, Jesse told me the deputy collected what was left of the driver's-side mirror."

"Did Jesse have any idea what the cops are looking for?"

"No, but I intend to call the sheriff ASAP and ask."

"Good work," Grayson said.

"One more bit of trivia. Jesse saw Symmes holding hands with an attractive young blonde at the Waffle House not far from the crash site two or three weeks ago. He even showed me a picture of them."

Grayson crossed her eyes. "We definitely can't run anything about that. Photo or no photo."

"Agreed," Conley said. "I just thought it was interesting." She paused and cleared her throat. "Hey, uh, speaking of my old boss, Sistrunk called me this morning. He wants me to freelance a piece on the Robinette thing for this Sunday's *AJC*."

Grayson's smile faded.

"Don't worry. I'll file my stories for the *Beacon* first. He doesn't need my piece until Thursday afternoon."

"I guess that's okay," Grayson said.

"There's more. While I was on the line with Sistrunk, I got a call from the NBC bureau chief in Atlanta. We met briefly years ago at an Atlanta Press Club thing. Anyway, Selena saw my byline on the version of the story that went out on AP, and now they want me to string for them on this story."

"You're gonna be on television?"

Conley laughed. "Don't worry. I'm not gunning to be the next Anderson Cooper. What they want is somebody local with a handle on the Robinette story that can consult. Strictly off-camera. And it doesn't hurt that I've got that video of the car fire. They want an exclusive on that."

"What's that mean for the *Beacon*?" Grayson scowled. "You've got a hot story, so now you're just gonna walk away because Hollywood is calling?"

"I just told you, it's not Hollywood, it's Atlanta calling. I'm not walking away; I'm staying right here. I'll still cover the story for the *Beacon*, but I'll freelance on the side for the network. And probably the *AJC* too, if this story has the legs we think it does. Print reporters do this all the time, Grayson, especially when there's a breaking story that's off the beaten path."

"What are they paying you?" Grayson demanded.

"That's none of your business. I will tell you, it's a lot more than you're paying me."

"Of course. And the fact that your family happens to *own* this newspaper? That means nothing to you, right?"

Conley planted both hands on Grayson's desk and leaned forward. "Can I remind you? G'mama had to *force* you to hire me. And can I also remind you that as soon as I started making waves with this story, you threatened to fire me?"

"Let me remind *you*," she countered, "I gave you this job when you showed up here, unannounced, because you had no place else to go to."

"Look," Conley said, exasperated. "I don't understand why you're so pissed about this. You've known all along that I didn't plan to make a career here at the *Beacon*. I never hid that from you. And I'm not hiding the fact that I'm entering into a stringing gig with NBC and the *AJC*. I told you that as a professional courtesy."

"And what am I supposed to do with that? I don't have a choice in the matter."

"You could be grateful," Conley snapped, "that you've got an experienced reporter on staff who's been on this story since Skelly and I rolled up on Symmes Robinette's flaming Escalade. You could realize that you and the *Beacon* stand to gain readers and advertisers from all this, not to mention the prestige of scooping the rest of the world on this Shakespearean drama unfolding right in front of your eyes. But no, you can't appreciate what you've got here. You've got a stick up your ass because you had to admit I was right and because your husband has walked off and left you."

Grayson's face paled. "Who told you that?"

"Nobody told me, you silly twit. You think I haven't noticed you're living in this office? That you spend your evenings drowning your sorrows at the Wrinkle Room at the country club? Jesus, Grayson! It doesn't take a Woodward and Bernstein to figure out that Tony's gone. Now. Do you wanna tell me what's really bugging you?" Her face softened. "I hurt for you, sis. I do."

"I don't need your pity," Grayson said, picking up a neat stack of papers and re-neatening them. "We're going through some stuff, that's all. It'll work itself out. It has no bearing on your work here at the paper."

"This isn't about the paper. You're my sister. I care about what happens to you. Please talk to me."

Grayson massaged her temples with her fingertips. "Do you have any idea how much of my life I spend here? This place is like a gigantic boulder. Every day I push it uphill, and then overnight, it rolls back down, and I start all over again. When Pops ran the *Beacon,* he had an advertising salesman, a circulation manager, and an office manager. He had a managing editor who also did layout and pasteup, four reporters, and two full-time photographers. We owned our own printing plant, and we had a battalion of kids on bikes delivering it every week.

"Now? It's just me. And Lillian. With the crappy salaries I can afford to pay, I can only afford either burnouts or kids right out of journalism school, most of 'em green as grass and biding their time before moving on to a bigger paper. The fact that I managed to find a gem like Michael Torpy is a friggin' miracle. I sell the ads, edit the copy, worry over circulation, and design the pages. We couldn't afford to modernize our old press, so now, as soon as we put the paper to bed, I drive ninety minutes away to the printing plant in Milton. Tonight, I'll probably sleep in the front seat of my car so I can be the first one at the loading dock in the morning. Once I've got the papers loaded, tomorrow I'll head back to Silver Bay and start driving around town to fill all the paper boxes."

There was a silver-framed wedding photo of Grayson and Tony on the credenza behind the desk. Grayson picked it up, stared at it, then put it back, facedown. "According to Tony, I spend every waking hour of my day at the office anyway and I never have time for him. He travels, I work, and when I'm not working, I'm worrying. About the paper. About G'mama. About money." She shrugged. "He got fed up. He's been renting a condo in Houston."

"How long ago did he leave?" Conley asked.

"About a month ago. I don't have much of an appetite, so I eat dinner in the bar at the club most nights. And going home to an empty house is depressing, so I sleep here. Any other questions?"

Conley was too stunned to speak at first. "Why didn't you say something? Does G'mama know the kind of pressure you're under?"

"She knows we're in a financial bind and that I've talked about selling out to that chain from Kansas City, which, of course, she's opposed to. I don't want her worrying about me. And I'd appreciate it if you'd keep the stuff about Tony to yourself."

"I'm not gonna go tattling to her about your marriage," Conley said.

"If you'll let me, I'd be happy to pitch in and help out with the other stuff."

"Since we're putting all our cards on the table, I guess I should tell you we're gonna have to do something about G'mama's finances."

Conley looked up sharply. "Are you saying she's broke?"

"Not broke, but she's not exactly the dowager countess of Silver Bay these days," Grayson said. "I really think we're gonna have to sell one of the houses."

"You're kidding!"

"I wish. The house on Felicity Street is in okay shape, but the Dunes is in terrible shape, and the maintenance is killing us. The last hurricane did a number on the roof. I had it patched, but the whole thing needs to be replaced."

"There's something going on with the hot water heater too," Conley said. "And the wiring."

"That house is a firetrap," Grayson said, her face gloomy. "I tried to tell you it wasn't safe to have G'mama out there, but you wouldn't listen."

"No, you didn't tell me it was unsafe," Conley countered. "You just accused me of parachuting in and screwing everything up. What are we gonna do about all of this? It'll break G'mama's heart if we have to sell the Dunes."

"For right now, we do nothing. It would take tens of thousands of dollars to get the house into shape to sell it. Money we don't have."

"I'm sorry, Gray. I wish you'd told me. About Tony. And the house."

Grayson shrugged. "Shit happens. Let's drop it for now, okay? I'm sorry I blew up at you about this stringing gig. I can't blame you for wanting to make a living and for thinking about your career. It's just that, this past week or so, I'd gotten my hopes up that maybe we can keep this place afloat. I know that's not realistic, but what can I say? Maybe I've got printer's ink in my blood after all."

"Welcome to the club," Conley told her.

41

After the commercial break, Buddy cued up his theme music and leaned into the microphone.

"Hello again, Silver Bay. It's the ten o'clock hour, and if you're just tuning in, this is *Up All Night with Buddy Bright.* The phone lines are open, and I'm waiting to hear from my favorite listeners."

He tapped a button on the computer screen, and a woman's voice with a deep Southern drawl filled the room.

"Hey, Buddy. Longtime listener, first-time caller Sonya. I watched that press conference on Channel 4 today, and I just about busted a gusset. I am a wife and a mama and a grandmama, but when I heard Charlie Robinette tell all those lies about his sweet mama, it really raised my hackles. I mean, I wanted to puke! Talk about an ungrateful little punk. I voted for Symmes Robinette every time he ever ran for anything, and I just know he is rolling in his grave right now at the way his son is disgracing the family name. You can bet that whenever they have that special election, I'll be voting for Vanessa Robinette. In the meantime, the flag on my front porch will by flying at half-mast."

Buddy leaned back in his chair and stared out the window at the now-darkened streets of downtown Silver Bay. After being called in early to work the hastily called Robinette press conference, he'd had to stay on for the afternoon shift too, after the afternoon jock, Shanelle, called in sick. Drunk was more like it.

It made no difference to him. Extra shifts meant extra money in his pay envelope.

Another call was waiting.

"Hi, Buddy. It's Pooh Bear from over here in Bronson County. I've been listening to you ever since we retired and my wife and I moved down here to Florida, and it finally dawned on me why I enjoy your program so much. I swear, I remember you, what, like, seven, eight years ago. Didn't you used to work under another name at a radio station up in Detroit?"

Buddy froze. He cleared his throat. "Well, now, Pooh Bear, I've worked in lots of different places over the years. That's the nature of the radio business. But the one place I haven't worked is Detroit." He chuckled. "Guess you've got me mixed up with some other devastatingly handsome and talented disc jockey."

"No," the caller insisted. "I was in town the other day, and I happened to walk by the station while you were on the air, and I saw you sitting right there on the other side of that big plate glass picture window. See, years ago, my wife and I went to the grand opening of a new shopping center in Bloomfield Hills, and that's when we saw this deejay who looks and sounds exactly like you."

Buddy felt the blood rush to his face. He had to get this guy off the air. "They say everybody's got a twin somewhere, right, Pooh Bear? Okay, thanks for listening, and thanks for calling in tonight."

He cut the caller off and cued in the next block of commercials with shaking hands. He needed a cigarette in the world's worst way. God, how he missed the days before all the do-gooders and tobacco Nazis ruined the world.

Neal, the station owner, was a reformed smoker, and his kind were the worst tobacco Nazis of all. Every wall in the tiny station had a NO SMOKING sign tacked up. But it was after ten now, and there was nobody else around.

He tapped a cigarette out of his pack, lit up, and inhaled deeply, flicking the ashes in the dregs of his coffee mug. It ended up taking two more cigarettes before his nerves settled back down.

He flipped the mic on again. "Okay," he said finally. "Let's see what everybody else in Silver Bay thinks about the state of the world."

"Hey there, Buddy! It's me, Alice. I can't believe I finally got through to you. Feels like I've been trying for forever. Am I on the radio right now?"

He could hear her voice playing on her own radio at home.

"If you turn down the volume, Alice, I'll be able to hear you a lot better."

"Oh." She giggled. "All right. I usually keep it turned up because I'm a little bit hard of hearing."

"That's better, sweet Alice. Now what's on your mind on this beautiful night?"

"My goodness, Buddy. I can't even believe what's going on in this wicked world we live in. I think if more people would read their scripture, we wouldn't have all these troubles. I couldn't believe that lady who called in earlier. And I want to say, for the record, that I would not vote for that home wrecker Vanessa Robinette even if she were running for dogcatcher."

Lillian was working quietly, listening to the radio on her desk. Michael had left to meet up with friends for an evening of video games. Grayson was gone too, probably for dinner at the Wrinkle Room.

Despite her animosity toward Buddy Bright, Conley would grudgingly admit she'd gotten used to his easy, late-night patter with his listeners. She was still chuckling over the last caller's dogcatcher comment.

She wasn't unused to hard work and long hours—it was part of the business—but this had been one of the longest days in recent memory.

Once she'd gotten Grayson's reluctant agreement that she could freelance for the *AJC* and the network, she'd called both news outlets to alert them on the latest twist in the ongoing Robinette family drama.

She'd stopped work briefly while everyone in the office watched cable coverage of Symmes Robinette's memorial service in the Capitol Rotunda. It was an appropriately solemn occasion, what with the flag-draped coffin, and lines of somber-faced politicians filing past and shaking hands with Vanessa, who was pale-faced and striking in her black Dior suit, her late husband's fraternity pin twinkling from her lapel.

Earlier in the day, Conley had handed off the story about Vanessa's and Charlie's dueling congressional campaigns to Michael so that she could concentrate on the elder abuse allegation. It had taken the better part of the day to fight her way through the thicket of bureaucrats at the state's Department of Children and Families to find someone willing to speak on the record about Charlie Robinette's explosive claim.

"We can confirm that a family member has issued a formal complaint, but we have no further comment until our investigation is completed," a caseworker supervisor told her.

She'd finally managed to reach Symmes Robinette's former political patron—and his son Charlie's campaign chairman—late in the afternoon. Miles Schoendienst was clearly reluctant to talk on the record, but she'd finally managed to pin him down.

"I understand you live next door to Symmes and Vanessa Robinette," she said. "Were you aware that Vanessa was deliberately keeping friends and family away from the congressman?"

He let out a long sigh. "Vanessa was very protective of Symmes. Frankly, my wife and I thought she was going a little overboard. Since they'd moved out here, we'd had a sort of standing Saturday night supper club. Very casual, just three or four couples. But after she brought Symmes home from the hospital, she made it clear that he couldn't have visitors. We thought she'd turned into a germophobe."

Conley was typing as rapidly as she could. "Were you surprised when he left Washington and came home for treatment?"

"God, yes," Schoendienst said. "Those docs at Walter Reed are supposed to be some of the best in the country. I tried to broach the subject with her, but Vanessa is a very strong-minded woman. She basically told me to mind my own damn business. So that's what I did. Still, it pained me to see how rapidly Symmes declined."

"When was the last time you saw him?"

He chuckled. "Maybe a month or so ago? Vanessa had gone into town. He drove over here in his golf cart, and we sat and had a beer and watched an inning of the ball game. He didn't stay long, because he tired so easily, plus he said he didn't want the warden to know he'd escaped from solitary."

Conley typed the word in all caps. "He called his wife *the warden*? And he said he was in solitary?"

"It was his idea of a joke. Symmes had a quirky sense of humor."

"How did he look a month ago?"

"Not too good. He couldn't walk very far without getting out of breath."

"Did you know she was keeping Charlie from visiting or speaking to his father?"

"Charlie and I talked about it," Schoendienst said. "As you might know, Symmes had asked me to guide Charlie in the process of mounting a campaign committee. I've known Charlie his whole life."

"So Symmes was grooming Charlie to run for his seat?"

"Look, I feel like this whole business is disrespectful to Symmes's memory so soon after his death," Schoendienst said. "Been nice talking to you." He disconnected.

An hour before deadline, her cell phone rang. To her surprise, the caller was Vanessa, who didn't bother with a greeting.

"I assume the *Beacon* won't be printing the outrageous and slanderous accusations my so-called son hurled at me today," she said. "Because if you do, my lawyer will sue you for every last dime you people have."

"Do you deny you were keeping the congressman isolated from family and friends?" Conley asked. "Has a caseworker from the state contacted you about the allegations?"

"I'm not going to dignify this crap by responding to it," Vanessa said. "I loved my husband and did everything in my power to make his last days peaceful and pain-free. The same can't be said for his so-called friends and family members."

It was the second time that day she'd been hung up on, which made Conley believe she was getting close to the truth.

Ten minutes later, Lillian strolled over and dropped a fax on her desk. "This just came," she said.

"We've got a fax machine?" Conley asked, impressed.

"Mm-hmm."

The document had a letterhead from Alexandra Watters, press secretary for the Vanessa Robinette for Congress Campaign.

Today, in our nation's capital, a widow mourned and saluted the memory of her beloved husband, the honorable U.S. Representative C. Symmes Robinette, in a ceremony attended by his colleagues from the House and Senate, along with the vice president, First Lady, and hundreds of everyday citizens whose lives were bettered by this dedicated public servant.

But in a deliberately cruel and outrageous action, Mrs. Robinette's estranged son chose this day to sabotage his recently widowed mother.

That Charlie Robinette would choose to exploit what should be a private family matter in such a way speaks volumes about his own character, or lack thereof.

Vanessa Robinette vehemently denies these baseless allegations. In the meantime, she looks forward to launching a vigorous congressional campaign that will bring her issue-focused message to the voters of the Thirty-fifth District, whom she served alongside her husband of thirty-four years.

The final version of Conley's story ran to nearly thirty column inches. Grayson had arranged to buy photos of the Washington service, with Vanessa shaking hands with the president, standing beside the flag-draped casket, and she'd designed the *Beacon's* front page with the cell phone photo of Charlie Robinette's press conference right beside the photo of the widow Robinette.

As soon as her copy had been edited, she called Selena Kwan in Atlanta.

"I saw the piece that ran on the wire earlier today. This story is absolutely nuts," Selena said. "If I'd known the son was gonna accuse the widow of trying to kill his dad, I would have sent a camera crew down there."

"Nobody had any idea he was going to do this. The CBS reporter said he just happened to be nearby doing another story when his editor called and diverted him over to Silver Bay, just in case. This came completely out of left field," Conley told her. "I just filed my piece for the paper. I've got a strong denial from Vanessa, not to mention a lawsuit threat, confirmation from the state that 'an unnamed family member' has filed a complaint—although they won't comment on an investigation until it's completed—and some juicy quotes from Symmes's neighbor and one of his oldest friends."

"Define 'juicy,'" Selena said.

"The neighbor, who also happens to be Charlie's new campaign chairman, Miles Schoendienst, said that Symmes referred to Vanessa as 'the warden.' He said the last time he saw Symmes was a month ago, when Symmes 'escaped' while Vanessa was out of the house. I asked if he was 'surprised' that Vanessa brought Symmes home to Silver Bay instead of letting the docs at Walter Reed continue his care and his response was 'God, yes.' That day Symmes snuck over to see him, Schoendienst said it pained him to see how weak Symmes was."

"Okay, can you send me your story that you just filed? And your video of the son's press conference today?"

"I will."

"Great. I finally got the okay for your contract. I just emailed it to you. Sign it and send it back, and we'll get you on the books."

Conley felt a flutter of excitement, like a racehorse that had finally been let out of her stall.

But by midnight that night, with the office quiet, every ounce of energy was drained from her body. She tucked her laptop into her backpack, slung it over her shoulder, and prepared to lock up the office before her long drive out to the beach. She only hoped she could stay awake.

The night air felt cooler, less humid as she walked outside to the Subaru. She tossed her backpack in the passenger seat and started the car. On a whim, she drove slowly around the square. The Confederate soldier on the memorial statue was lit up and a solitary pigeon perched on his shoulder. On the flagpole beside the courthouse, the American flag hung limply, at half-mast, while the Florida state flag fluttered below it. She found herself slowing in front of Kelly's Drugs and realized, to her own chagrin, that she'd been hoping maybe she'd glimpse Skelly inside, flicking off the lights and closing up shop, as she'd just done.

As tired as she was, Conley realized, she craved companionship, craved the sensation of talking over the day's events, sharing her minor frustrations and semi-major victories. She missed having somebody to talk to. But only the neon Kelly's Drugs sign was still lit up.

42

At midnight, Buddy began his own routine of packing up. Since he'd worked two shifts already, Neal had left it up to him about whether to work the overnight. Ever since that harrowing caller, Pooh Bear, the dude from Detroit, his nerves had left him jittery and anxious.

He needed to get out of the station, to clear his mind, think, and reassess his situation. He'd landed in this fly-speck burg in the Florida Panhandle because it was a place where nothing ever happened. And that had been true until a week ago, when Symmes Robinette's car had flipped and burst into flames. The death of the congressman and the ensuing circus was shining a national spotlight on Silver Bay.

Was it time to pack up and move on? He hoped not. After six years, he'd grown fond of this place.

Just before he left, he cued up the tape of one of his "Best of Buddy" programs.

As he was pulling the Corvette onto Main Street, he spotted the blue Subaru as it idled in front of the drugstore. He recognized the car and the driver. Conley Hawkins, the hotshot reporter who'd moved to Silver Bay under her own set of mysterious circumstances. She was the competition, and he should have resented her. Instead, he admired her gumption and her drive. She reminded him of himself, back when he was young and hungry and burning up with ambition. Before Detroit.

Half a block before she reached the drugstore, he saw the black Ford pickup slide onto the street, keeping back a little, right until the moment when she slowed to a near stop. The driver braked, then held back until he was a few car lengths behind.

Buddy recognized the truck and the driver, although he didn't know the guy's name.

He'd seen the driver quite a few times, saw him walking into the Waffle House late at night, flirting with the waitresses, loitering in a booth while he idly stared down at his phone. He'd spotted him again earlier in the day, hanging around the shadows of the courthouse square, during the press conference. Now he was back, apparently following Conley Hawkins.

Common sense said he should mind his own business and go on home. Curiosity drove him to tail both the Subaru and the truck as they drove west, in the direction of the beach.

For once, Buddy wished he were driving something less noticeable than the 'Vette. Everybody in town recognized his flashy car with the WORKING PRESS vanity plate. He'd liked that, liked being the closest thing to a celebrity in Silver Bay. Driving the 'Vette made him feel like a big shot. But now, if the truck's driver bothered to glance in his rearview mirror, there could be trouble. The kind of trouble he didn't need.

When they reached the causeway that led to the beach, he almost did a U-turn. But something made him keep going.

The Subaru and the black truck slowed at the beach road, with its twenty-mile-an-hour speed limit. For the second time, he fought the urge to turn around. He inched along in the wake of the two vehicles, the only ones on the road at this late hour. He saw the Subaru's brake lights flare red, and she pulled into a crushed-shell driveway in front of a rambling old wood-frame beach cottage. The faded lettering on the mailbox said THE DUNES, EST. 1923.

The truck kept going, but only for about half a block. Then it slowed and turned into the sandy drive of a half-built house under construction.

Buddy drove on for another block, then did a quick U-turn, pulling onto the shoulder of the road with the Vette facing the truck.

He watched while the driver pulled as far forward as possible, until a construction dumpster nearly concealed it. The driver got out of the car, looked around, then slipped quickly down the sandy path through the dunes.

Buddy waited, wrestling the urge to flee. He had no business here, and whatever happened next was none of his business. He was tired and needed to think.

When he got back to his snug garage apartment, he parked and went around to the trunk. He pulled out the vinyl dustcover and lovingly placed it over the Vette, as he did every night.

Inside the apartment, he moved quickly through the tiny rooms, gathering books, clothes, and his album collection. He went into the bathroom and dumped his toiletries into a plastic zip baggie.

Something brushed against his ankle, and he nearly screamed. But looking down, he saw that it was only Hi-Fi, his black cat.

She meowed loudly and rubbed her hindquarters against his ankles. He closed the commode cover, sat down, and scooped her into his arms, stroking her fur repeatedly.

"Did you think I'd leave you?" he whispered into her ear. She purred, and he hugged her. "I would never."

Holding Hi-Fi always made him feel calmer, more centered. He walked into the living room and sank down into the sofa cushions with the cat in his arms.

Buddy looked around the room. Over his years on the run, he'd winnowed out his possessions to just the things that would fit in the trunk of the Vette. By design, the sum of his belongings could be packed in less than twenty minutes. All his business dealings were on a cash basis.

He could leave right now and be several states away by morning. When he was good and clear of Silver Bay, he could place an anonymous call to the newspaper and alert Conley Hawkins to the shadowy dude who was following her. He'd gotten good in his role as the anonymous tipster. Too good, maybe.

Payday was another week away. He could stay and watch and listen. He'd keep his head down, hoping that nobody would turn around and watch the watcher.

43

Grayson emerged from her office around midmorning, beaming, clutching a champagne bottle in one hand and a stack of Styrofoam cups in the other.

"Hey, y'all," she said loudly. "Attention, everybody!"

Lillian hung up the phone. Michael stopped posting photos to the new Facebook page, and Conley rested her hands on the keyboard of her laptop. All three of them were startled by the sight of their usually gloomy managing editor in a state of euphoria.

"What's up, boss?" Lillian asked.

"What's up is, I just got word we have a complete sellout of this week's edition of the *Beacon*." Grayson's voice cracked with emotion. "I checked with my grandmother, and she says that's never happened before. After we shipped to our mail subscribers, I found that every paper box in town is empty. The stores that sell us—the IGA, the 7-Eleven, and the Kwik-Stop, Kelly's Drugs, Tommy's Bait and Tackle, all three gas stations in town—every retail outlet is sold out."

"So that's what's goin' on," Lillian said. "I been on the phone all morning with people calling, wanting to come by and pick up a paper."

Grayson pointed at her. "Lils, call the printer in Milton and tell 'em we need a second print run."

"Are you crazy? You want to print twelve hundred more copies? Who do you think is gonna buy all those papers? Also, did you just call me *Lils*? Ain't nobody who ain't related to me can call me *Lils*."

"Sorry," Grayson said. "I got carried away. Okay, maybe run five hundred more. But before you do that, we're gonna celebrate."

She loosened the wire champagne cage, and the cork shot across the room, bouncing off the framed oil portrait of Arthur "Dub" DuBignon, the newspaper's founder, dour-faced in a stiff white collar, neatly parted hair, and wire-rimmed glasses.

"Drink up, guys," Grayson urged. "Warm champagne sucks. And cheap warm champagne sucks even more."

Michael looked over at Conley, who nodded her approval. He stood up and collected a cup, and the boss poured. Conley got a cup and let her sister fill it.

When all four staff members were holding their champagne, Grayson raised her own cup.

"Here's to all of us. The hardest-working staff in the business. Here's to fighting the good fight, and as old Dub DuBignon used to say, 'shining the light of truth.'"

They touched cups and sipped the cold, bubbly wine. They drained the bottle, then got back to work.

Conley was reading back through her notes of the phone conversation with Miles Schoendienst when her cell phone rang. She glanced at the caller ID and grabbed for it.

"Hey, Skelly."

"Hey there," he said. "I know you're probably on deadline or something, but there's someone here at the store who'd like a few minutes of your time. And I've got a feeling you'd like to talk to her too."

"Who is it?"

He lowered his voice. "It's Toddie Robinette."

. . .

Skelly met her at the door. Two or three customers were in the store, one waiting near the pharmacy counter. "She's back in the office," he said. "I thought the two of you might want some privacy."

"Did she say what she wants?" Conley asked. "Does she look pissed?"

"She's carrying a big grocery sack, but I don't think she's packing heat," Skelly said, cracking a smile. "I wouldn't say she looked pissed. More like, serious."

He helped her navigate the narrow, cluttered aisles of the stockroom, stopping at the open door of a small office. Toddie Robinette sat on a metal folding chair across from a battered steel tanker desk. He poked his head inside.

"Here's Conley. Can I get you ladies some coffee or something?"

"Not for me," Conley said.

"No, thanks," Toddie said.

"Then I'll leave you to it. Make yourselves at home."

"Thanks for reaching out to me, Mrs. uh, Robinette," Conley started, sitting behind Skelly's desk.

"It's Ms. Sanderson, but everybody calls me Toddie," she said quickly. "I haven't been *Mrs. Robinette* in over thirty-four years."

Toddie had obviously taken pains with her appearance. Unlike the day they'd dropped in on her at Oak Springs Farm, today she was dressed in tailored beige slacks and a white silk blouse. Her silver hair was pulled back from her face with a pair of tortoiseshell clasps, and the only makeup she wore was a bit of lipstick. A bulging shopping bag sat near her feet.

She crossed, then uncrossed her legs. "I know I told you I didn't want to comment about Symmes's death, but since that article you wrote in the *Beacon,* my children have convinced me that I should, I don't know . . ."

"Set the record straight?" Conley suggested.

"Something like that."

Conley took her cell phone from her backpack and set it on the desktop. "Would it be okay if I taped our conversation?"

"Is that really necessary?"

"I won't if you object," Conley said. "It's mostly to make sure I quote you accurately. I'm going to take notes too."

Toddie wore a wide white gold band on her left ring finger. She twisted it around and around. "I suppose that's okay," she said. "This is really about my kids," she added. "When Vanessa told you Symmes had no contact with them and that he didn't even remember their names, that was incredibly hurtful to them. They were so damn mad! Especially Rebecca. They'd just lost their dad. And to see Vanessa spout lies like that." She shook her head.

"Are you saying that Symmes *wasn't* estranged from y'all? That you had a good relationship with him?"

"Up until very recently, it's true, he'd had very little contact with me or the kids. But that was the way Vanessa wanted it, not the kids. She absolutely forbade him to have contact with them. And I only contacted him through his attorney."

"Why was that?" Conley asked.

"I think she wanted to rewrite history. Make it so that she was his first and only love and their son was his only child."

"And the congressman was okay with that?"

Toddie's smile was bitter. "Have you met that woman? What Vanessa wants, Vanessa gets."

Conley scribbled notes in her reporter's notebook, because she didn't really trust tape recorders and because she wanted to detail observations about Toddie's demeanor.

"Can I ask you something?" she said, looking up. "A couple of people who were close friends of yours, back before the divorce, say that when it happened, you just packed up and moved out. Overnight. Your oldest friends and neighbors told me you'd vanished, and they had no idea where you'd gone or why. They were blindsided."

"That was a condition of our divorce settlement. Symmes's attorney, a man I thought of as a very close friend—his wife was Hank's godmother—showed up and handed me a piece of paper. Wesley told me

that it was a good offer. I'd get child support, the children's college education would be taken care of, and I'd get health insurance and alimony
for the rest of my life or until such time that I remarried. I'd get my car.
Symmes would keep the house in town, which was important, because it
was in the district, and the children and I could move into the farmhouse
at Oak Springs."

"That does sound generous," Conley commented.

"Except that I got no share of our investments, or cash assets, which
I'm pretty sure he hid from me, no property of my own—he got to keep
the title to both, and my alimony was capped. It was barely enough to
pay my bills. Everything was contingent on my settling quickly, without
any fuss. And most important, keeping my mouth shut."

"And you agreed?"

"What else could I do? I had no money of my own to hire a lawyer
to fight him, and I hadn't worked since I had the children, didn't even
have a college degree."

"Whose idea was that?"

"Symmes was always adamant that he didn't want his wife to work
outside the home. His own mother was widowed when he was a young
child, and she'd had to go to work at a textile mill here. He was ashamed
of that."

"You were what, nineteen, when you married?."

"Eighteen. Symmes was a year older. I took some night classes at
the community college, before I had kids, and worked days at an insurance company. I'd always wanted to be a veterinarian. Right after we got
married, Symmes moved us to Tallahassee so he could finish his under-
grad degree. I got another job, but then I got pregnant with Hank during
his first year of law school. Two years later, Rebecca came along."

"Must have been tough times," Conley said.

"We were as poor as church mice," Toddie said. "Especially when he
was in law school. We lived in married student housing, and he had the GI
Bill to pay tuition. My parents helped us out. They even gave us the money
for our first house here in Silver Bay. They loved Symmes. Thought he
could do no wrong."

"How did he get into politics?" Conley asked.

"Symmes always had a knack for making friends with the right people, for making you think you were important. His law practice in Silver Bay took off right away. He got the job doing all the legal work for the railroad. That was huge for a young lawyer. He ran for an unexpired term in the state senate and won easily, because he had the backing of people like Miles Schoendienst. So then he was in politics, and the law practice was thriving, and he was making a good living. For the first time in our marriage, he bought me a new car of my own."

Conley raised an eyebrow. "Seriously?"

"It sounds absolutely quaint today, but back then, I had a weekly allowance. I didn't even have my own checking account or credit cards."

"And then he decided to run for Congress," Conley interjected. She was aware of the minutes ticking by. She needed to derail Toddie's sentimental journey and steer her back toward current events.

"People were telling him he was a 'rising star on the political firmament.' For his birthday that year, I got him a sterling letter opener engraved with that," Toddie said. "I wonder what ever happened to that? Probably Vanessa melted it down years ago."

"What happened when Mr. Robinette went to Washington?" Conley asked.

"It was the biggest fight of our marriage. The only fight, really. I thought we had a good marriage. Not perfect, but good. Solid. I was an idiot."

"According to Vanessa, you hated Washington and refused to step foot there."

"Another lie," Toddie shot back. "Symmes didn't want me there. The children were still there, and we'd just bought the house in town. It was such a financial stretch that my parents gave us the down payment as a gift. Symmes said we couldn't afford the house here and a place in D.C. that would be big enough for the whole family. We fought over it, but he won."

Conley nodded as she scribbled another note. "When did you find out about Vanessa?"

"Ahhh," Toddie said, thinking back. "I'd gone up to D.C. for the National Prayer Breakfast. I flew up a day early because I wanted to surprise Symmes. He was renting a pretty drab 'bachelor apartment,' so I even booked us a room at the Willard, thinking we'd have a sort of lost weekend."

Conley paused from her note taking to watch Toddie's face, anticipating the story to come.

"I cabbed over to his place and talked the maintenance guy into letting me in, which he was clearly reluctant to do. I had to show him my driver's license to show him that I really was Mrs. Robinette—which should have been my first clue."

Conley waited.

"The place was neat as a pin—which was my second clue. Symmes was always a slob. His clothes were hung up, and the bed was made." Her lips twisted into a bitter smile. "There was a makeup bag in the bathroom and a filmy pink nightgown hanging from a hook on the back of the door. And a bottle of prenatal vitamins on the bedside table."

"You must have been devastated," Conley said.

Toddie's eyes welled up with tears. "Sorry," she said, dabbing at them with a tissue plucked from her pocketbook. "You know, this is the first time in all these years I've ever talked about this."

"You didn't tell your girlfriends? Or your mom? Or your lawyer?"

"God, no. It was so humiliating. At first, I didn't know what to do. I kept thinking there had to be a rational explanation."

"And then?"

"I kind of lost my mind. I threw her stuff in a bag and cabbed over to the House office building. I walked into Symmes's office unannounced, and his secretary's eyes nearly bugged out of her head. She said the congressman was in a committee meeting, and I told her I wasn't looking for my husband. But I did have urgent business with Vanessa Monck."

"How did you know her name?" Conley asked.

"It was on the label of a bottle of antibiotics. Right next to the prenatal vitamins. That poor secretary! She babbled something about Vanessa not being available, so I said I'd wait. Two hours later, Symmes showed up, and he was even more flustered than the secretary."

"Did he try to deny the affair?"

"Not after I threw the nightgown and pills in his face," Toddie said.

"It was all so ugly and sad. He said he'd made a mistake and let things go too far with Vanessa. Claimed he still loved me and the children. He said he wanted to do the decent thing by her. I think he actually believed he could stay married and keep me and the children down here in Florida and be a D.C. daddy to Vanessa and their baby."

"Have his cake and eat it too?" Conley asked. "I'm still astonished how this didn't cause more of a scandal. I mean, a sitting, married U.S. congressman impregnates an aide nearly half his age?"

"It was a different time back then. This was way before the Bill Clinton scandal. Before social media. I'm sure the Washington press corps knew about the baby, the same way they knew about all the other politicians who'd had affairs, but I guess that wasn't considered fair game."

Conley's phone dinged softly. She glanced at the screen. It was a text from Roger Sistrunk.

How's my story coming?

As fascinating as this interview was, she needed to wrap things up.

"After the divorce, did Symmes see the children? Did you share custody?"

"Not really. They were teenagers by then. For the first couple of years or so, he'd come out to the farm and see the children occasionally when he was back in the district. Bring them birthday gifts, maybe take them out to dinner. He'd drop off gifts on Christmas Eve, always alone. Then the visits tapered off. Hank pretended not to care, but in fact, he resented Symmes so much that he'd refuse to talk on the phone or even see Symmes on his irregular visits, which infuriated Symmes. The whole situation broke Rebecca's heart. She'd always been such a daddy's girl."

"And then the visits stopped?"

"Yes. There was one last Christmas Eve, probably in the late nineties; he called the day before to say he was coming. Even Hank was looking forward to it. They waited all day, and finally, at ten o'clock, we all realized it wasn't going to happen. He wasn't coming. No call, no show."

"You said earlier that your children weren't estranged from him. But it certainly sounds like . . ."

"Everything changed after his cancer diagnosis last year," Toddie said.

"Who told you about the cancer? Both Charlie and Vanessa said it was a closely guarded secret."

"Charlie's fiancée reached out to me," Toddie said.

"Kennedy McFall?"

"That's right. It was back in March. Out of the blue. She told me about Symmes's diagnosis and said that she'd been nagging Charlie to let Symmes's other children know how sick he was."

"Did you talk to Charlie?"

"Eventually, yes. I guess he listened to his girlfriend. Until that day, I'd never spoken to him. I'd seen photos, of course, over the years, but that was all."

"Did Vanessa know you were in touch?"

Toddie hooted. "God, no! She never would have allowed that. As I say, Kennedy private-messaged me on Facebook, and after I said I was willing to talk to Charlie, he called."

"How did that go?"

"Surprisingly well. Charlie said he thought his half brother and half sister should know that their dad was diagnosed with cancer and that the prognosis wasn't great. He didn't want either of his parents to know he'd reached out to us."

"What did you do next?"

"Nothing. I told Hank and Rebecca. The news made them sad, but I don't think it really hit them that Symmes was going to die. Then six weeks later, my cell phone rang, and it was Symmes. You could have knocked me over with a feather. It had been so long, I didn't even recognize his voice."

She slid the wedding band up and down her ring finger. "He told me Vanessa had moved him back down here, to their house on Sugar Key. He said the doctors at Walter Reed were opposed to that, but she insisted she could take care of him better at home. And he asked if I thought the children would be willing to see him. He said he wanted to make amends."

"How did your kids react to that?" Conley asked.

She let out a deep sigh. "Hank wanted nothing to do with his dad.

We've always been really close, and I think he thought it would upset me. Rebecca, on the other hand, agreed right off the bat. Charlie agreed to act as the go-between to make it happen."

"How did you work around Vanessa?"

"When they first moved back down here, it wasn't that difficult. Symmes would make up some excuse to Vanessa, and Rebecca would meet him in some out-of-the-way spot. She was ecstatic! She's a single mom these days, and it meant the world to her to reconnect with her dad."

"What about Hank?"

"He was a much tougher sell. So stubborn!" Toddie said. She laughed. "But Rebecca guilt-tripped him into going with her for a meet-up. Hank works with me on the quail plantation, and Symmes was a big hunter back in the day, so I think they were happy to discover they still had something in common."

The minutes were ticking away, and Conley still had so many questions.

"Toddie, I have to ask. How did Symmes come to deed Oak Springs Farm over to you? And only two weeks before he died?"

44

Toddie slid the wedding band off her hand and held it up for Conley
to see.

"I quit wearing this after my kids were grown. Put it away in my jewelry box. I told myself it was pathetic to hang on to a symbol of a marriage that had been over for decades. But my hand felt so naked without
it! It was like my finger had atrophied where the wedding band was. So
I put it on again. I wear it now to remind myself that those years mat-
tered. That we had kids and a life together, and *she* doesn't get to erase
that."

"Why did Symmes deed over the farm to you? That's a pretty valuable piece of real estate."

"I bet it's driving Vanessa nuts, isn't it?"

"She didn't believe me when I asked her about it," Conley said.

"Too bad, so sad," Toddie said. "Oak Springs Farm has been in my
family for nearly a hundred years. My granddaddy bought it during the
Depression, when you couldn't give away farmland around here. It was
our family's happy place. We'd get together with all the cousins and
aunts and uncles there every holiday. But then, in the eighties, my dad
had made some bad investments, and my mom got sick and he needed to
sell it. I had to beg Symmes to buy it so we could keep it in the family."

She reached down and pulled a bulging photo album from the grocery bag, flipping pages until she came to a faded photo of a young couple on the porch of a rustic cabin. Toddie's hair was blond, and she wore a bikini top and cutoff jeans, and she stood on tiptoe, kissing an impossibly young Symmes, who sported sideburns and a wispy mustache, tight blue jeans, and an unbuttoned shirt. She tapped the picture with her fingernail. "That's the summer we got engaged."

There were many more photos—Symmes in military fatigues, Toddie and Symmes on their wedding day, Symmes and Toddie smiling into a camera as their young son blew out birthday candles, the family sitting on the edge of the cabin porch, dressed in plaid flannel shirts, Symmes and a preteen boy, posed together on the deck of a boat, holding a stringer of fish. Even one of Symmes being sworn in for his first term of office in the Florida Senate. Toddie tapped the photo with a finger. "I sewed him that suit," she said. "Sewed the dress I wore that day too."

"Could I borrow a couple of those photos for my story?" Conley asked. "Maybe the photo of you guys at the farm and the one of you and Symmes the summer of your engagement? I promise I'll get them back to you."

"You'd better," Toddie said, handing over the album. As she did, another photo fluttered out. This one was printed on cheap white copy paper. Toddie held it up for Conley to see.

Symmes Robinette, hollow-eyed and unshaven, was seated on a rocking chair on the cabin porch. He stared into the camera, flanked on either side by his now-grown, middle-aged children. Rebecca sat on a chair pulled up to her father's, his hand clasped in hers. Hank stood awkwardly on the other side, holding a shotgun.

Toddie let out a long sigh. "That's the last photo we have of our whole family. The next-to-last one was taken about twenty-eight years ago."

"Symmes came out to the farm?" Conley asked.

"Yeah."

"When was this?"

She shrugged. "Maybe a month before the accident? Charlie was acting as the go-between. He called and asked if it would be okay. It was a Sunday morning, and I remember Charlie joked that 'the warden' was at some kind of out-of-town function. I assumed Charlie would drive him, but Symmes came alone. He looked like death warmed over." She stared down at the photo, her palm resting lightly on it.

"It was strange, you know?" Toddie said. "Seeing him like that after so many years. He'd always been larger than life, and that day, he looked so diminished. Thin and sick. But he wanted to tour the farm and see the dogs and the old cabin. Hank drove him around on the ATV. I'd fixed lunch, but he didn't eat much. He gave Hank that shotgun he's holding in the picture. It's some special edition with sterling mounts. Probably cost thousands. Symmes said he felt bad that he hadn't been there when Hank got his first eight-point buck. He gave Rebecca a little diamond ring that had been his mother's."

"And what did he give you?" Conley asked.

"After the kids left, and it was just the two of us, I was kind of teasing, and I said, 'Your son got a shotgun, and your daughter got a ring. Don't you have a present for me?' That's when he told me that he intended to deed the farm over to me."

"Were you shocked?"

"Flabbergasted," Toddie said. "You have to understand, Symmes was never what you would call generous. It's true he let me and the kids live there rent-free, but I was responsible for the property taxes and the maintenance. It had been a hobby farm when we were married, but after the divorce, I turned it into a working quail-hunting plantation, and Hank and I have worked our butts off making it a success. As soon as the farm started turning a profit, Symmes began charging us rent on the land. For years, I'd been after him to sell it to me, but he never would." She scowled. "I guess maybe I can thank Vanessa for loosening up the old tightwad. He certainly did well by her, with all the jewelry and clothes, fancy cars, the house in Georgetown, and the oceanfront mansion."

"Did he say why he was suddenly feeling so generous?" Conley asked.

"It was obvious. He felt guilty."

There was a light knock, then the office door swung open, and Skelly poked his head inside. "Hate to interrupt, but Toddie, Mama's aide just brought her over. I told her you're here, and she really wants to see you."

"It's fine. We were just finishing up," Conley said. "Thanks, Toddie."

"Don't forget to get those pictures back to me," the older woman said as she hurried out through the stockroom.

Skelly lingered while Conley stood and stowed the photos in her backpack.

"Well?" He raised a questioning eyebrow. "Did you get what you need for your story?"

"More than enough. Toddie was amazingly frank. I have to admire her. Symmes Robinette walked off and left her with two teenagers to raise, for a woman twenty years younger. Typical of that time, he had all the money, so he had all the power when it came time for the settlement. And yet, she managed to take care of business despite all that."

"Toddie Robinette was no shrinking Southern belle," Skelly agreed. "She could be tough as nails when she had to be."

Conley patted her backpack. "With the quotes I got and the old family photos, I've got stuff now that no other reporter has access to. She was a gold mine. Thanks again, Skelly."

He shrugged. "It was her idea." He turned to go, but she reached out and touched his wrist.

"Skelly? I hate this."

"What?"

"This! This awkwardness. I wish we could just go back to the way things were before."

"You mean before the other night, when we were on the beach, and you couldn't keep your hands off me, and we had a great time, then you announced you were already over me?"

Stung, she took a step backward. "I never said I was over you."

"You could have fooled me," he said.

45

By Conley Hawkins—special to The Atlanta Journal-Constitution

Silver Bay, Florida—The life of the honorable U.S. Rep. C. Symmes Robinette, seventy-seven, may have ended in a fiery one-car crash in the early-morning hours of last week, but his mysterious death has ignited a smoldering hometown soap opera that seems equal parts Dynasty *and* Dallas.

Within days of the accident, which is still under investigation, Robinette's widow, a fifty-six-year-old former congressional aide, whom he met and impregnated 34 years ago while still married to his first wife, and their son and namesake, thirty-four-year-old C. Symmes "Charlie" Robinette Jr., both declared intentions to vie for the congressman's unexpired term in an upcoming special election.

"Thanksgiving could get a little awkward," Charlie Robinette quipped at the time, "but we're a political family. . . . We're used to finding ways of compromising."

And then things got nasty. Local voters, still divided over whether to side with Team Charlie or Team Vanessa, were further stunned this week when Charlie Robinette, who is managing part-

*ner in his father's former law firm, took to the steps of the Griffin
County Courthouse at a hastily called press conference to announce
that, prior to his father's death, he'd filed a formal complaint of
elder abuse against Vanessa Robinette, alleging that his mother
deliberately kept his terminally ill father, who was suffering previ-
ously undisclosed non-Hodgkin's lymphoma, a virtual captive in
his own home, isolating him from friends and other family members, and depriving him of skilled medical care.*

Conley rested her head on her desktop. It was only Friday and she
was already tired. Her eyes burned, and her shoulders ached. There
was so much more to this story. There always was, because the news
never ended; it just paused, hopefully long enough for someone to ob-
serve, analyze, and report.

She pushed Send on her keyboard just as Grayson walked up to her
desk. She tossed a batch of typewritten copy onto Conley's desk. "If
you're done with your freelancing gig, maybe you can do some work for
the *Beacon*."

"Noooo," Conley groaned as she looked at the byline. "I can't deal
with Rowena today."

"If I have to, you have to," Grayson said.

Her cell phone rang. It was Roger Sistrunk. She was being book-
ended by editors, not a feeling she enjoyed.

"Just read your story," Sistrunk said. "It's too long. It's too wordy,
too speculative, too gossipy. And FYI, nobody but livestock breeders
use the word *impregnate* in this century."

She spent the next thirty minutes making fixes to her *AJC* story, cutting, pasting, and nitpicking word choices with Sistrunk, whose hatred
of adjectives was well documented among the hundreds of reporters
who'd worked for the veteran editor over the years.

Finally, he pronounced the story fit to print. "We're done," he said
abruptly. "Hey, Hawkins, you might have a future in this business." He
chuckled at his own joke and disconnected.

With a heart full of dread, she turned her attention to Rowena's latest
Hello, Summer column.

*The Women's Circle of the Silver Bay Presbyterian Church went into emergency session this week following the tragic death of our favorite local congressman, the honorable **U.S. Rep. Symmes Robinette**.*

*Anticipating an overflow crowd at Saturday's funeral, Women's Circle president **Sylvia Bevin** announced that the after-service reception has been moved to the much larger gymnasium at First Baptist Church.*

*Rumor has it that in addition to **Florida governor Roy Padgett**, the Florida House Speaker, state attorney general, and a large delegation of other dignitaries from Tallahassee are expected to attend Symmes Robinette's service.*

*All eyes will be on young **Charlie Robinette**, whose announcement this week that he would run for his late father's seat—as well as his allegations of elder abuse against his mother, the vivacious and popular **Vanessa Robinette**—has divided the loyalties of family and friends.*

Your correspondent has learned that Charlie Robinette had assumed he would succeed his father in Congress, reportedly at his father's request, until recently, when the thirty-four-year-old attorney began squiring an attractive local divorcée to local social events.

The divorcée, who has a young daughter and has only recently split from her husband, reportedly did not meet with the approval of the younger Robinette's parents. Vanessa Robinette has told friends that she and her husband recently began having doubts that their son was ready to take the national stage.

Of course, your correspondent will be attending both the after-service reception and the private, invitation-only dinner, which will be hosted by Mrs. Robinette later that evening at her lavish oceanfront home on Sugar Key.

*Our sources tell us that one name that won't be on the invite list for Vanessa's dinner is retired railroad executive and longtime family friend **Miles Schoendienst**, who has accepted the role of campaign chairman for Charlie Robinette.*

*Coordinating floral tributes for the reception will be **Agnes Ryan and Babs Tillery**.*

Conley's thoughts returned to her own story and Vanessa Robinette's assertion that "chemo brain" was to blame for her husband's lack of sleep and out-of-character generosity in giving away the family farm.

She decided that if Merle Goggins over in Bronson County was interested in what kind of drugs Symmes Robinette was taking, she was interested too.

On a whim, she emailed an old friend from college, Carol Knox, who'd switched majors their sophomore year and had eventually become an oncology nurse. They'd stayed in contact over the years since, mostly through Facebook.

She knew Carol now lived down in St. Pete.

"Hey, gurlll. Can you give me a call? Working on a hot story and could use some research help," she wrote, adding her phone number.

Conley turned back to Rowena's column, typing it into the system, editing, refining, and generally trying to make it not so Rowena-ish. For the second time that morning, she pushed the Send button.

When her cell phone rang, and the number on the caller ID had a 727 area code, she grabbed for it.

"Carol? How are you? Thanks for getting back to me so fast."

"Good to hear from you," Carol said. "I'm actually sitting at the airport, and I've got nothing better to do."

They exchanged a few pleasantries, catching up on each other's lives, with Conley promising to get down to St. Pete soon for a visit, and Carol promising to read Conley's stories online.

"Here's what I'm working on," Conley said. "You know who Symmes Robinette is?"

"The congressman, right? From up in the Panhandle. He died recently, right?"

"Yeah. He was killed in a one-car crash, forty-five miles from his house, at three in the morning. And according to his wife, he had end-stage cancer."

"How old was he?"

"Seventy-seven. He was diagnosed with non-Hodgkin's lymphoma last fall, treated at Walter Reed, but then his wife decided to bring him back home to Silver Bay."

"That's a little odd in itself," Carol said. "But if he was in his late seventies and terminal, yeah, I suppose it could be okay. Was he in hospice?"

"Don't think so. His wife was keeping him isolated from everybody, including his own son, but that's another story. Meanwhile, the cops down here have asked the local pharmacy for a list of his medications," Conley said. "So I'm thinking they're thinking what I'm thinking."

"Which is?" Carol asked.

"Maybe he was impaired when he had the wreck? First off, if he was terminally ill, what's he doing driving around that time of night? His wife told me his meds gave him insomnia, that he'd wake up in the middle of the night and just drive aimlessly around. She called it 'chemo brain.' But I thought if you had end-stage cancer, the docs would really dope you up."

"Hmm," Carol said. "You can't quote me on any of this, okay? I'm not a physician, and I don't know any of the particulars of this case. All I can give you is general observations. That said, my first thought is that if he's end stage, he's probably not doing chemo anymore. His docs are doing palliative care, just trying to keep him comfortable."

"What kind of drugs does that involve?"

"Maybe a transdermal patch, fentanyl, or buprenorphine. They're both heavy-duty opioids and commonly used for cancer patients."

"Wouldn't those dope him up to the gills?"

"Not necessarily," she said. "Long-term users, especially cancer patients, can metabolize the drugs at a different rate. For instance, a dose of fentanyl that would knock you or me on our asses, maybe even be lethal, might not have that same effect on the cancer patient."

"Huh," Conley said. "Would he be on any other meds? Something for sleep, for instance?"

"Maybe. But buprenorphine especially can have pretty serious, negative interactions with other drugs and even alcohol."

"Like what?"

"Dizziness, wooziness, and the biggie. Death."

"Would all those drugs show up in his body afterward? Even if he was pretty badly burned in the car fire?" Conley asked.

"They should," Carol said. "But I'm not a pathologist. That's a question for the medical examiner."

"I've got lots of questions for the medical examiner," Conley said. "But he's not too keen on talking to reporters."

"Whoops! They're calling my flight. Good luck," Carol said. "And come see me."

After sitting at a desk writing all morning, Conley was anxious to get out of the office. She put in a call to Vanessa Robinette, but her call was immediately rolled over to the widow's voice mail.

"Hi, Vanessa," she said, trying to sound friendly, even deferential. "I'm working on a story about some last-minute details about the congressman's service, and I'd appreciate if you'd give me a call back."

Probably, she thought, Vanessa would return her call when hell froze over. She decided it was time to start knocking on doors.

She stepped inside Grayson's office.

Grayson was reading a document on her computer screen and looked up. "Rowena's column is much better. Almost literate. Thanks."

"I'm headed out for a while," Conley said. "Gonna go over to Bronson County to see if I can get your friend Merle Goggins to answer some questions. And I might make a couple of other stops too."

"Speaking of cops, I need you to stop by the Silver Bay PD and pick up the police reports," Grayson said. "Be good if you could put that together in the morning, since you'll probably be busy covering the funeral on Saturday."

"Ugh," she said. "Can't Mike cover cops this week? I'm kind of covered up."

"He's covered up too," Grayson said. "No whining, okay?"

The front desk at the Silver Bay Police Department was manned by a light-skinned black woman named Claudette, who had deep dimples and a fondness for nail art. Every time Conley stopped by to pick up copies of incident reports, her nails were different. Today, each nail was painted a bright blue, with tiny yellow smiling sunrays emanating out from each tip.

"Hey, Claudette," Conley said, bellying up to the front counter. "Love your nails."

"Oh, hey, Conley," Claudette said. She fanned her fingers out, admiring them herself. "My girl Sue really outdid herself this week, didn't she?" Without being asked, she plucked a file folder from a tray on her desk and handed it over. "There's your reports. I made copies for you."

"How come you're so nice to me?"

Claudette grinned, showcasing her dimples. "All us single ladies got to stick together," she said, laughing.

"Anything good in here?" Conley asked, riffling through the reports.

"No murders or bank robberies," Claudette replied. "Same shit, different day."

After leaving the cop shop, Conley stopped by the bakery next to the hardware store and picked up a pound cake. "Could you wrap up the box with some ribbon?" she asked the salesclerk. "It's for a gift."

Afterward, she took the causeway toward the beach until she spotted the discreet green-and-white signs to Sugar Key. As she grew closer to the development, the landscape transitioned from scrub pines and palmettos to emerald swaths of bermuda grass, sabal palms, ferns, and oleanders. A wide median strip divided the road in two and was landscaped with a riot of pink, blue, and white annuals. Hard to believe that twenty years ago, this area had been a sandspur-studded, mosquito-infested swamp known to every teenager in the county as "the Goonies," the preferred location for dope smoking, underage drinking, and sweaty, back seat shenanigans.

Half a mile down what was now Sugar Key Boulevard, she spotted a red-tile-roofed guard shack that had been built in the center of the road. To the right was the entrance, a two-lane road, each lane protected by a high, wrought iron gate. Arrows directed residents to one side and visitors to the other.

Conley slowed the Subaru and pulled onto the shoulder of the road. A pickup truck loaded with landscape equipment passed her on the left, and she watched as it slowed and then stopped at the visitor's gate. A uniformed security guard stepped out of the shack and approached the truck. She saw the driver stick his head out of the open window and converse with the guard, who held a clipboard, which she now consulted. After a moment, she handed the driver a white-and-green pass and waved him through.

Five minutes later, she watched as an Audi convertible zoomed past, barely slowing as it approached the residents gate, which swung open on the Audi's approach.

"Might as well give it a shot," she muttered to herself.

She stopped at the visitors entrance and waited. The same security guard walked over to her car at a smart pace. She was petite, with military bearing, and wore her white-blond hair pulled into a tight bun at the nape of her neck. Her uniform was spotless—sharply creased navy slacks, shiny lace-up black oxfords, white tailored shirt with faux gold epaulets, hash marks on the sleeve, even a shiny tin security badge pinned over her breast.

"Yes, ma'am?" the guard said, peering into the car and scrutinizing her closely, probably checking for concealed nuclear weapons, Conley thought.

"Hi! I'm Conley Hawkins, and I'm here to visit Mrs. Robinette," she said.

The guard frowned. "Is she expecting you? Did she leave you a visitor's pass?"

"Uh, well, not exactly. I go to her church, and I wanted to drop off a cake."

"A cake?" This appeared to be a foreign concept.

"Yeah. You know, like a bereavement gesture, to show my condolences. I figure she probably has enough chicken casseroles."

The guard did not laugh at Conley's little joke, nor did she smile. She held up her clipboard for Conley to see. "Mrs. Robinette isn't expecting guests. And she's not accepting any kind of condolence cakes."

"Oh."

The guard pointed to a narrow, curving drive just inside the gate. "You can turn around here and go through the exit." She did not offer a bye-bye wave, but stood stiffly, watching as Conley pulled the Subaru around and out of the subdivision.

Conley drove a few hundred yards, then pulled onto the shoulder again, turning around to examine the guard shack. As she did, she noticed a tall metal utility pole, bristling with cameras. She also noticed the blond guard, who came out of the shack and stood in the road, staring at the Subaru. Conley gave her a backward wave, then drove on.

46

A cloud of dust rose up as the Subaru bumped down the narrow dirt road to Margie Barrett's little turquoise cottage. The old dog tottered toward her as she approached the house, and Conley leaned down and scratched his ears. "Hey, Sport," she crooned. "Hey, Sporty boy."

The screened door opened, and Margie Barrett stepped out onto the porch. For a moment, she looked puzzled, then she smiled in recognition of her visitor. "Chet Hawkins's girl, right?"

"Yes, ma'am. It's Conley. Sorry to bother you again, but I wanted to ask you a few more questions about the night of the wreck."

"No bother at all. I'm glad to have the company," Ms. Barrett said. She turned to the dog. "Sport, you stay outside for a while and stretch your legs some more."

She fussed around, filling glasses with ice cubes and Cokes and telling Conley she'd read her story in the *Beacon*. "I've got a sister-in-law who lives over there in Silver Bay, and she carried me a copy of the paper this morning when we met for coffee," Margie said. "My goodness, can you imagine, your own son accusing you of locking up your husband?" She clucked her tongue in disapproval. "And just imagine, he had those other two children he hadn't seen in all these years. Sometimes I wonder what gets into men like that when they get some money and some power."

"The Robinettes are quite the political dynasty," Conley said tactfully.

"Now what else can I tell you, honey?" Margie asked. "I mean, I'd like to help, but there just wasn't much to what I saw and heard that night."

"I'm curious. Did a sheriff's deputy call or come around and ask you about that night, after I talked to you?"

"No. Hadn't been anybody from the sheriff's office come by. But I was over at my daughter's house for a couple of days this week, so maybe somebody came while I was away."

"Maybe so," Conley said. "Okay, I was hoping you'd just walk me through it again."

Margie folded her hands in her lap and closed her eyes. "It was way after midnight, and I fell asleep right here in this recliner. Sport needed to go outside to do his business, so I walked him outside, and he was kinda growling and straining at his leash. He can't hardly see anymore, but his hearing is still sharp. After a little bit, I heard these men's voices, yelling. And then a woman was telling them to stop. And then I heard car doors slamming and a car peel off."

"And you said you didn't hear the crash at all."

"Didn't hear a thing until Sport started yowling because the sound of the fire trucks and ambulance hurt his ears. That's when I rode up there to see what had happened."

Conley sipped her Coke. There was a scratching at the screened door, and Margie heaved herself out of the recliner.

"Oh, Sport!" she cried. "Bad boy! Not again!" She slammed the door, and the dog crouched outside, on the other side, whining.

The sick, sweet smell of rotting flesh wafted into the small room.

"He's gone and found what's left of that dead deer up in the pasture and rolled all around in it," Margie said, holding her hand over her mouth. "He loves nothing better than getting stinky. Does your dog do that too?"

Conley's mind drifted back to the ride she'd taken on the Ranger on her last visit and the deer carcass they'd spotted, with the vultures circling overhead.

"Margie, was that deer there before the night of the wreck?"

"I don't know," the older woman said slowly. "Let me think. No, I don't believe it was." She sighed heavily. "I can't stand that smell. I guess I'd better see about getting the stink washed off." She went into the kitchen and came back with a bucket and a bottle of dish detergent.

Conley followed her onto the porch, holding her hand over her own nose, choking back the urge to gag.

"What can I do?" she asked, her eyes watering.

Margie clipped a leash to Sport's collar. "We'll take him over to the side of the house and turn the hose on him. If you can hold him still, I'll soap him up real good."

The dog's cloudy brown eyes were downcast in shame as Conley grasped him by the shoulders while he was hosed and soaped, rinsed and soaped, and rinsed again. Finally, Margie shut off the hose, and Sport shook himself vigorously, spraying water on both of them.

They took the dog back inside, and Margie toweled him off, scolding him good-naturedly.

"Margie, do you think maybe Robinette's crash happened because he hit that deer?" Conley asked. "Could hitting a deer cause a wreck like that?"

"Oh, sure. My boys have both hit deer a couple of different times coming home on that road," Margie said. Her face colored slightly. "Happens more often in what they call *rut season* when the bucks are chasing after does, but not always. A couple of summers ago, one big ol' buck's antlers came clean through my older boy's windshield. He coulda been killed," Margie said, shaking her head at the memory. "I been passing that doggone carcass twice a day, every day, going back and forth to my mailbox up on the road. Don't know why I didn't think about it causing that wreck 'til you asked just now."

"And I don't know why somebody from the sheriff's office never came to talk to you," Conley said. "Maybe if they had, they'd have spotted that deer."

Before she left, she crouched down on the floor beside the damp, bedraggled dog. "Sport," she said, cradling his muzzle between her hands. "If we're right, I believe the sheriff's office needs to swear you into the department."

• • •

"Hi, Sheriff," Conley said after she'd been ushered back to his office by the desk sergeant.

"Miss Hawkins," Merle Goggins said, nodding. "Did I miss something? Did you have an appointment for an interview with me this afternoon?"

"I was in the neighborhood and thought I'd drop in and say howdy," Conley said. She set the bakery box with the pound cake on his desk. "I even brought a hostess gift. Because I'm such a nice, proper Southern girl."

"Since I know you were raised in Griffin County, I'll give you the Southern girl thing," Goggins said. "But I'm gonna call bullshit on nice and proper." He untied the ribbon and lifted out the cake, breaking off a piece and tasting it. "For me? You shouldn't have."

"To be perfectly honest, I bought that to take to Vanessa Robinette. But the security guards at Sugar Key say she's not accepting visitors. Or condolence cakes."

"We'd like to talk to her again too, but she's kind of hard to pin down these days," Goggins said. "And I imagine you're not real popular with her either."

He gestured toward the chair opposite the desk. "As long as you're here, you might as well sit down."

"Can I have a hunk of that cake?" she asked. "I didn't get lunch today."

"Neither did I, come to think of it," the sheriff said. "Want some coffee with that?"

"If you're buying," she said, surprised at his hospitality.

"I'd have it with creamer and sugar if I were you," he advised. "Otherwise, it's like crankcase fluid." He came back from the break room with two mugs of coffee, two paper plates, and a plastic knife. He served her a generous portion of cake, and they sat, sipping their coffees and enjoying the pound cake.

"Hard to find good pound cake these days," Goggins said. "My mother-in-law makes a sour cream pound cake so good it'll make you slap your mama."

"Our housekeeper, Winnie, makes a good one," Conley said. "She does a glaze with fresh-squeezed oranges."

"Now tell the truth," Goggins said, wiping his hands with a napkin and disposing of his plate. "What really brings you out here today?"

"Symmes Robinette," she said promptly. "I've got questions. Has the medical examiner signed off on cause of death?"

"Like I told you, massive head injuries," Goggins said.

"And yet I saw your deputy Poppell in town earlier this week. I know he went to Kelly's Drugs to get a list of Robinette's prescriptions, and then he went over to the body shop and took the driver's-side mirror from the congressman's Escalade."

"Don't you have anything better to do with your time than follow my deputy around?" Goggins sounded annoyed.

"Not really. This is a big story." She reached into her backpack and brought out the latest edition of the *Beacon* and slid it across his desktop.

"Thanks, but I read the online version. It's always interesting to read about rich white folks' problems."

"Wait 'til you see my next story," Conley said. "I had a long conversation with Toddie Sanderson, the original Mrs. Robinette this morning. Seems like she's much more willing to talk than the second Mrs. Robinette."

Goggins clasped his hands behind his neck. "I guess she still feels like she's the injured party. Even after all these years."

"Have your deputies talked to Toddie?"

"They had a brief conversation, right after the accident," Goggins said. "Did she tell you anything worth repeating?"

Conley smiled. "Is this the part where I tell you what I know and you tell me what you know?"

"No," Goggins said. "It's the part where I tell you that I can't comment on an active investigation."

She decided to try another tack. "I really did try to get into Sugar Key to speak to Vanessa Robinette before I came over here, and I noticed the video cameras at the entrance gate. Have you looked at the footage from the night of the crash?"

"Yes," Goggins said.

"Do they show Symmes Robinette leaving? Was he alone?"

"Can't comment on that," Goggins said.

"Did you check out Vanessa's claim that it wasn't the first night Symmes got up and drove around in the middle of the night because he had 'chemo brain'?"

"We check out all leads," he said blandly.

"The reason I ask is that Toddie Sanderson told me her daughter met with Symmes, in secret, more than once in the weeks leading up to the crash. She claims he even came out to Oak Springs Farm to tell her he'd deeded it over to her."

"Interesting," Goggins said.

"What I think is interesting is that Charlie Robinette is the one who acted as the go-between for that meeting. His fiancée reached out first, then he called Toddie, alerting her about Symmes's cancer diagnosis, even before Vanessa moved him back to Sugar Key, saying he thought his half siblings should know that their father's prognosis wasn't good."

"Are you saying there's something nefarious about the son's wanting to help his father make peace with his kids?" Goggins asked.

"Charlie had never met Toddie or his half siblings. And Toddie said Vanessa eventually forbade Symmes to see his kids after their divorce."

"Too damn bad. But you see a lot of that these days. What are you trying to get at here, Miss Hawkins?"

"Just drop the 'miss,' please. It's Conley. And I'm still trying to understand what would have motivated Symmes Robinette to be driving around out here, this far from home, in the middle of the night. I don't buy that it was random. Why Bronson County? I think he came out here again to go to Oak Springs Farm."

"You're entitled to your theories," Goggins said, sipping his coffee.

Conley's frustration boiled over. "Look, the last time I was here, I asked if your deputies had re-interviewed Margie Barrett, the woman whose farm is directly adjacent to the crash site. I went to see her again today, and she said she still hasn't been contacted by your department."

"No?" Goggins frowned. "I'll have to check on that."

"You really should," Conley said. "You should also check out the rotting deer carcass in the pasture about a quarter of a mile away from the crash site. Ms. Barrett says it wasn't there before the crash. You know what I think? Again, just another of my 'theories.' I think it's possible Robinette hit that deer when it ran out into the roadway."

Goggins set his mug on the desktop and reached for his phone. "Curtis?" His voice was sharp. "Have dispatch radio Poppell. I want him back to the station immediately. Send him back to see me as soon as he gets here." He looked over at Conley and shook his head. "Dumb-ass."

"Is that something you can test for?" Conley asked. "Like, deer guts or whatever?"

"The state crime lab can," he said, his expression grim. "But I'll have to get the car towed over there, which I'd hoped to avoid. That's why I had Poppell just collect the mirror to send over."

"You know, Sheriff, I think it's only fair since I told you about the deer carcass that you tell me what you're looking for on that mirror."

"And I believe I told you I can't comment on an ongoing investigation."

"How about off the record? There's a flock of vultures feasting on that deer carcass right now. If I hadn't seen it and reported it to you, all you'd have to look at is some bleached-out bones."

Instead of responding to her, he picked up the copy of the *Beacon* and studied the front page. "A red substance," he said without looking up. "Something sideswiped that Escalade. Coulda been a car, coulda been that deer." He looked up. "Don't take this the wrong way, but you might ought to air out those clothes you're wearing. Social hour is over now, Miss Hawkins. Thanks for the cake."

47

Winnie was chopping celery and green onions when Conley walked into the kitchen at the Dunes Friday night.

"What's for supper?" Conley asked, helping herself to a boiled shrimp from the blue bowl on the counter.

"Shrimp remoulade," Winnie said. She wrinkled her nose. "Did you step in something nasty today?"

"Sorry," Conley said, taking a step backward. She explained about her trip to visit Margie Barrett earlier in the day and about the old dog rolling around in the remains of a deer carcass.

"You oughta take a shower before dinner," Winnie said. "And put those clothes right in the washing machine. Don't leave 'em laying around and stinking up the whole house."

G'mama walked into the kitchen just then. "What is that ungodly smell?"

Conley recounted the discovery of the deer carcass and its proximity to the crash site where Symmes Robinette had perished.

"Well, I'll be," Winnie said. "You mean to tell me that it was a deer that killed him? Kind of a letdown, if you ask me."

"Winnie!" G'mama chided. "That's not very Christian."

The housekeeper was unrepentant. "I don't have very Christian feelings about that man."

"But the Bible says forgiveness is divine," G'mama reminded her.

"It doesn't say *when* I have to forgive him for letting those railroad bastards kill my sister and poison our whole family," Winnie said. "Seems like I'm not quite ready yet."

She dumped the chopped celery and green onions into the bowl with the shrimp and started on the remoulade sauce as Conley idly watched over her shoulder.

"You're home awful late today," G'mama said.

"That's the life of the modern 'career girl,' as Rowena would say," Conley said. "Guess I'll go upstairs and get cleaned up before dinner."

"Yes, please," G'mama said.

Upstairs, she stood in the doorway of her bedroom to appreciate the pristine beauty of the room. Winnie might have a bad hip and a sassy attitude, but she was relentless in her approach to neatness.

The wooden floors gleamed softly and smelled of lemon wax. The old iron bed was made up with a snowy-white cotton bedspread and freshly ironed pillowcases on plump feather pillows. A box fan whirred in the window. The clothes she'd dumped in the wicker hamper in the bathroom had been laundered and folded and were stacked on top of the old painted dresser waiting for Conley to put them away.

It was a far cry from her haphazard housekeeping in Atlanta, where the apartment she'd shared with Kevin was a perpetual snarl of discarded newspapers and books, dust bunnies, empty takeout containers, and laundry baskets of clothes that never got folded or put away. She'd only been at the Dunes for a week and already she was spoiled.

She went into the bathroom, turned on the hot water to allow it time to heat up, and inhaled the smell of lavender and bleach. Then she stripped, climbed into the cast-iron tub, and pulled down the shower attachment. Like Margie's dog, Sport, she required two rounds of soaping and rinsing to wash away the stench of death.

Her cell phone was ringing as she emerged from the bathroom. She answered and put the call on speakerphone.

"Conley, hello!" Selena Kwan said. "The network loved the stuff you helped with the other night. In fact, we're going to send a camera crew and a reporter for Robinette's funeral. Can you send us your updates?"

"I can," Conley said, donning a clean pair of shorts and pulling a T-shirt over her head. "I did a fairly long piece for the *AJC* skedded to run Sunday, and I'll send you a recap of that. But I think your crew could do a nice human-interest piece—something like the secret family life of a public figure? Highlight the early years, when he was married to his high school sweetheart, poor but proud, raising two young kids, then he goes off to the state legislature, where he's sworn in wearing a suit his first wife sewed for him, then Congress. Fast-forward a few years, and he sheds wife number one, gets a newer model with a new baby, and does a fast fade on family number one. Until he finds out he's dying and suddenly wants to mend fences."

"Love it," Selena said promptly. "What kind of visuals would we do?"

"Toddie—that's wife number one—loaned me some old family photos, and I have a few file photos from the *Beacon* that I can transmit to you. Then your crew could maybe film a stand-up outside the entrance to Oak Springs Farm. I don't know how you could get footage of Robinette's waterfront house, though. It's in a gated community, and the security guards there are hypervigilant."

"We can probably get drone footage of the house if you get us the street address," Selena said. "Now what about the funeral tomorrow?"

"That's at two at the Presbyterian church. They're expecting an overflow crowd, so the reception afterward will be in the gym at the Baptist church. Not sure you want to try to send a crew into the church, but I guess you could ask for permission."

"If not, we'll shoot some footage of mourners going into church, the funeral procession, generic stuff like that," Selena said.

"Tomorrow evening, Vanessa is hosting an invitation-only dinner at her house for what they're calling the *dignitaries*. I think they're expecting a lot of Robinette's political pals—like the governor of Florida, lieutenant governor, and so on."

"Any chance you're going?"

Conley laughed. "Zero chance. But I know somebody who probably is on the list. Our society columnist, Rowena Meigs, has gotten pretty chummy with Vanessa. I'm sure she'd love to give you any deets you need."

"We'll see," Selena said. "Sounds like we'll have plenty to work with. Can I have the crew call you when they hit town tomorrow?"

"Of course."

They ate dinner in the kitchen, on G'mama's gold-rimmed bone china plates with thick damask napkins and the polished "casual" silver. Scoops of chilled shrimp remoulade were placed on green lettuce cups, and there were crisp carrot sticks and tiny, hot cheese biscuits, and sweet iced tea in cut glass tumblers with lemon wedges.

Opie crouched under the table, hoping for an errant crumb to fall, but G'mama was strict about feeding dogs from the table. Just a casual weeknight dinner—and a far cry from the diet of microwave popcorn, delivery pizza, and ramen she'd lived on in Atlanta.

She was really, really going to miss this part of life at the Dunes. After dinner, she cleared the table and hastily washed the few dishes Winnie hadn't already taken care of.

She poured herself a glass of wine and headed toward the porch. "I'm gonna go take a walk on the beach," she called over her shoulder.

She strolled almost all the way to the pier, then turned around and went back, timing it so that she'd be on the swing in time for sunset.

When her phone rang, she answered it out of habit. Five seconds of heavy breathing and then the words that sliced through her brain like a hot knife through butter. "You're dead, bitch." A man's voice, low, disembodied. And then the disconnect. She knew without looking what the caller ID would say. UNKNOWN CALLER.

She felt acid rise in her throat and tried to dispel her own fears. The Robinette story was controversial. The town was divided into two camps, and emotions were running high, so it shouldn't have been unexpected that she'd get death threats. Haters gonna hate, she'd told herself back when it had happened in Atlanta.

Her mind returned to the winter morning more than a year ago when she'd discovered a dead rat, wrapped in the previous day's *AJC* with her story on the front page, on her doorstep. She'd been shaken enough to report the incident to Roger Sistrunk, who'd reported it to the Atlanta police, as well as the newspaper's head of security.

Sistrunk had insisted that the paper put her up in a motel for three or four nights, but when there were no further threats, she'd returned home, right after installing a home security system with a video camera.

But Silver Bay wasn't Atlanta. Her hometown was the kind of place where people rarely locked doors, where you could have a charge account at the grocery store or have your prescriptions delivered by the man who owned the drugstore. *Probably,* she told herself, *this gutless, anonymous caller is just blowing off steam.* But the next time she dropped by the Silver Bay cop shop, she'd mention the call to Claudette. Just in case.

The fierce afternoon sun had cooled enough that the warmth felt good on her shoulders. She leaned her head against the back of the swing and closed her eyes, trying to force herself to release the tension that always came when she was chasing a breaking story. The breeze off the Gulf rippled the sea oats, and she stared out at the waves, trying to find a calm center. She'd never been very good at calm.

"Mind if I join you?"

G'mama walked haltingly down the beach path from the house, stopping at the dune line to deposit her shoes. Conley jumped up, gave her an arm, and guided her over to the swing.

"This is nice," G'mama said with a deep sigh. "Pops and I used to try to make it a point to sit out here and watch the sunset every night we were home. We'd have some good discussions. These days, with all the world's troubles, I forget to enjoy it like I ought to."

"I guess you take it for granted when it's right outside your door," Conley agreed. "But after all that time in Atlanta, I've come to appreciate sunsets again."

G'mama reached over and tucked an errant strand of hair behind her granddaughter's ear. "You could have sunsets like this every night, you know."

Conley rolled her eyes.

"I'm a little bit worried about you, Sarah Conley," G'mama said. "You're working so hard, burning the candle at both ends. Up early, home late. When are you going to stop and smell the roses?"

"I'm working on a hot story. I'll slow down when this Robinette story is over."

"And when will that be?"

Conley gave a noncommittal shrug.

"Grayson tells me you're doing some freelance work for the Atlanta paper and the network. That's wonderful. Pops would be so proud."

Conley smiled and squeezed her grandmother's hand. "You do know this is a onetime gig, right? I still have to find a real job, with real benefits. And we both know that probably isn't going to be in Silver Bay."

G'mama deftly changed the subject. "How's Sean? Have you seen him since the other night?"

"He's fine. I saw him briefly today. I know how much you like Skelly. I like him too, but it's not going to work out the way you want it to."

Lorraine was shameless. "Why not?"

Conley stared out to where the blazing orange sun hung just above the horizon. "We want different things, and we're headed in different directions."

"How do you know what Sean Kelly wants?" G'mama demanded. "Did you ask him?"

"I just know. Okay? It's why his marriage broke up. His first priority is taking care of Miss June and keeping the store running. I admire that, and I admire his loyalty, but it's the total opposite of where I'm going."

"And there's no way you could meet him in the middle?"

"I don't see how," Conley said. "You're gonna tell me I need to compromise, right? Isn't that what my mom did? And look how that worked out."

G'mama's eyes welled with tears, and Conley felt a twinge of guilt at invoking her mother's name.

"Your daddy tried so hard to make Melinda happy. Chet was such a good, good man. Better than she deserved. He never gave up on believing in her. That she would come home and be a wife and mother. He believed it long after I gave up."

"I've never heard you talk about Mom like this before," Conley said.

"Well, it's high time I did," G'mama said briskly. "I had the blinders on where your mother was concerned for too long. I loved my daughter. I still do, but I've done some reading and some studying, and I believe she is what they call a *narcissist,* someone who only lives for themselves. I'm afraid Melinda doesn't really possess the capacity to love someone else, because she never learned to be selfless. I suppose I bear some of the responsibility for that."

"No, G'mama," Conley objected.

"It's all right," Lorraine said. "I've forgiven myself. I tried, but I made mistakes. We wanted a child so badly, we let her do anything she wanted. She was headstrong right from the time she was a toddler, throwing her little sippy cup at me if something made her mad or she didn't get her way. It was easier to just give in and let her do what she wanted. Maybe I wasn't a perfect mother. I should have made her clean up her own messes. But what I did, I did out of love."

"You couldn't have been all that bad," Conley said, sliding an arm around her grandmother's narrow shoulders. "You did a pretty good job raising Grayson and me."

"I hope I learned from my mistakes," G'mama said. "And you know, every night, I pray for Melinda. I pray that she'll find herself, pray that she'll find her place in the world and decide she wants us to be a part of her life."

"You can't do more than that," Conley said. And she leaned her head on her grandmother's shoulder. The two of them watched as the sun slid toward the horizon, and Conley held her breath as it disappeared into the shining dark sea.

48

POLICE BLOTTER WEEK MAY 11

FRIDAY, MAY 8 DOMESTIC DISTURBANCE. Approximately 7:00 a.m. Neighbors on Sycamore Lane reported screaming, cursing, and loud arguments coming from home next door. Officers responding to call were told by male, early forties, answering door that they were not source of noise. Officer observed bright red burn marks on man's face and noticed smoke and smell of fire coming from residence, entered home. Found woman in kitchen, sitting at table drinking Miller Lite beer and holding ice bag to eye. Woman advised boyfriend grew angry after she burned grits for third day in a row. Man claimed woman threw pot of burned grits at his face, then tossed burning pan into trash, catching it on fire, at which point man made obscene remarks about woman's cooking, weight, and mother. Both victims declined medical treatment. Both declined to press assault charges. Officer advised marital counseling and instant grits.

SUNDAY, MAY 10 POSSIBLE BREAKING AND ENTERING. Resident of house on Hibiscus Way reported hearing suspicious noises coming from roof at 2:00 a.m., requested armed patrol response. Upon arrival, officer walked around house with flashlight, noted upstairs bedroom window ajar. Officer entered residence, checked bedroom, found partially undressed sixteen-year-old female entertaining seventeen-year-old male. Advised male to leave house immediately, as female's father was downstairs searching for shotgun. Advised daughter that parents have excellent hearing.

MONDAY, MAY 11 DISTURBING THE PEACE, PUBLIC DRUNKENESS, INDECENT EXPOSURE. Officer dispatched to Jiffy Stop Convenience Store where they encountered boisterous, possibly inebriated sixty-year-old male suspect, loudly cursing store management and throwing discarded beer bottles at side of building. Suspect claimed beer he'd purchased and consumed at store was "poisoned," causing him to become inebriated. Demanded refund, and when management refused, entered store and urinated on beer display. Allegedly poisoned beer impounded for chemical analysis. Suspect transported to Silver Bay jail for observation.

Grayson looked up from the copy she'd just edited and gave her sister a grudging nod. "You're really good at this, you know?"

"What? Picking up police reports?" Conley lounged on the chair in Grayson's office, waiting for the hastily called staff meeting to start.

She'd dressed up in anticipation of a long day, wearing slim-cut black slacks, a pale gray silk short-sleeved silk top, and black ballet flats.

"You know what I mean. The light touch. This is the kind of thing our readers can't get anyplace else. It's hyper-local, it's witty, and they'll eat it up."

"Wow. Thanks, I guess," Conley said, unused to any kind of praise from her big sister. "What's the plan for the funeral today? I should tell you the Atlanta bureau is sending an NBC crew down to cover it, and I've been feeding them color."

"Let's wait for the others," Grayson said, glancing at her watch. It was just after nine.

. . .

Lillian King breezed into the office ten minutes later.

"You're fifteen minutes late," Grayson pointed out.

Lillian plopped a box of doughnuts on top of her desk. "I stopped at Sweet 'n' Tasty and got us breakfast. A dozen doughnuts means I'm only three minutes late, and you know that's five minutes early on LKT. Anyway, it's Saturday, and I hope you know I'm putting in for overtime for all this work I'm doing on my day off."

Conley looked up from the emails she was reading on her phone. "LKT?"

"Lillian King Time," Grayson said.

Michael Torpy walked in and helped himself to a pink-frosted doughnut with sprinkles. With one bite, he demolished half the pastry. "What's up, boss? We talking funeral?"

"We are," Grayson said.

"Good deal," Mike said, spraying sprinkles down the front of his rumpled white dress shirt and skinny black silk tie. He'd slicked down his unruly red hair with gel and worn black jeans for the day's occasion. "Hey, the reason I'm late is I just came by the church. You won't believe it. There are two different TV trucks setting up camp. People are already lining up outside waiting to get in like it's a Taylor Swift concert. You know, if old people went to Taylor Swift concerts."

"This *is* a Taylor Swift concert for these people," Conley said. "Did you shoot some photos?"

Michael held up the Nikon 35mm camera. "I got two old ladies in folding lawn chairs. They're both wearing TEAM VANESSA T-shirts, and then I shot the Boy Scouts practicing their honor guard march over in the courthouse square, and some dudes circling the square in a pickup with a huge spray-painted CHARLIE FOR CONGRESS flag whipping in the wind."

"Sounds good," Grayson said. "Okay, now we're just missing Rowena."

"Noooo," Conley and Michael said.

"I know she's a pain in the ass, but we seriously need her institutional memory today," Grayson said. "She knows everybody who's anybody. I want her up front in the church, right behind the family's pew."

"If I know Rowena, she'll shove her way into the family pew," Conley muttered.

They heard the front door open and then the tapping of their star columnist's cane.

"Yoo-hoo!" a quavery voice called. "Where is everybody?"

Michael went into the outer office and rolled in another chair. "We're back here in Grayson's office, Rowena."

Rowena Meigs was styled for a state funeral. Her hair had been curled and teased and sprayed into a towering blue-white bouffant. Her face was powdered and rouged, and her eyelids were weighted down to half-mast by glued-on false eyelashes. She wore an age-rusted black silk moiré cocktail suit whose rhinestone jacket buttons strained to contain her generous bust. The skirt was so tight they could hear the rustle of the girdle and black pantyhose she wore underneath with each mincing step she took. Even her cane was wrapped in black grosgrain ribbon for the occasion.

"Sit here, Rowena," Michael said, taking her arm.

"Thank you, darlin'," she said, handing him her outsize pocketbook, which was suspiciously squirming.

Tuffy popped his head out and bared his teeth at the hapless young reporter. Tuffy's topknot was fastened with a black grosgrain bow.

"Uh, Rowena, you're not thinking of taking that dog to the funeral, are you?" Grayson asked.

"I certainly am," Rowena said, bristling. "Most people find the presence of a dog very comforting in a time of stress."

The editor shrugged and went back to her battle plan. "Okay," Grayson said. "The team's all here, so let's get started. Rowena, I was just telling the others I want you to sit up front, as close to the family pew as you can get."

"Of course."

"Are you invited to Vanessa's dinner tonight?"

"I certainly am," she said, stroking the thick, triple strand of pearls around her neck.

"We won't have time for you to type up your column in time for the special edition. Do you think you could just call into the office and dictate it to Lillian?"

"Say what?" Lillian said sharply.

"I'm paying you time and a half," Grayson said.

"Double. And I wanna get reimbursed for these doughnuts," Lillian said. "I'm not made of money, you know."

"Mike is going to take the good camera with the zoom lens, and he'll shoot outside the church. And after, at the reception at the Baptist church," Grayson said. "We'll need shots of Vanessa with the governor, that kind of stuff. And of course Charlie. Be great if we could get a shot of Vanessa and Charlie together."

"Not gonna happen," Conley predicted.

"You think Toddie and her kids will show?" Grayson asked.

"If they do, Vanessa's head will explode."

"Then let's hope it happens. Exploding heads make for great front pages," Grayson said. "Either way, I'm thinking we put out another digital special edition. Not tonight, because I think that'd really be pushing it, but in the morning."

"Fuckin' A," Mike said, pumping his fist. He blushed. "Oops. Sorry, Rowena. My bad."

"Conley, you'll be roving," Grayson continued. "We've gotta keep it low-key, but if you see a good photo op, shoot Mike a text. Or if you can be discreet, shoot it with your phone. I want you concentrating on the human-interest angle—family angst, all that. Mike, the political angle is yours. See if you can get the governor to talk about when he'll schedule the special election to fill Symmes's seat in the House. It's a long shot, but maybe he'll weigh in on the Vanessa-Charlie controversy."

"What about me?" Lillian demanded. "What am I gonna do while I sit around here waiting to get dictated to over the phone?"

"I want you to call or email every business that was a new advertiser this week. Tell 'em we're putting out another digital special edition in the morning, and this is their chance to get in with a special rate."

The office manager sighed heavily. "Gonna be a long day."

"Okay, team, that's our game plan," Grayson said. "You guys

already kicked ass once this week, and I know we can do it again. Right?"

"Abso-fuckin'-lutely," Michael said. "Whoops. Sorry again, Rowena."

The elderly columnist was busy feeding a doughnut to Tuffy. "That's all right," she said serenely. She looked over at Conley. "Isn't it nice that the staff meeting is over so early? This way, you'll still have time to go home and get dressed before the funeral."

"I *am* dressed for the funeral, Rowena," Conley said.

"Oh," Rowena said, stroking her pearls again. "Oh my."

49

The midafternoon sun beat down on the mourners gathered outside the white-columned Silver Bay Presbyterian Church. Conley could already feel her silk shirt sticking to her back as people pressed closer and closer to the church entry.

Michael shifted impatiently from foot to foot, tugging at his already loosened tie. "What are we waiting for? Why don't they open the damn doors?"

He obviously hasn't attended many funerals, she thought.

"We're waiting for the funeral procession," Conley informed him. "Long black hearse, pallbearers carrying a long, mahogany coffin. Like that."

"Right. My bad."

They'd managed to spirit Rowena around the crowd fifteen minutes earlier, and she'd worked her dowager queen magic on an usher stationed at a side door, who wordlessly opened the door wide to allow her access.

"Okay," Conley said, pointing toward the street, where a stretch limo was slowly pulling alongside the curb. "That should be Vanessa."

She trailed closely behind him as he moved into position. The limo driver hopped out and came around and opened the door. Vanessa stepped out and, spotting the television crews stationed on the side-walk, straightened her dress and paused for dramatic effect. A dignified older man got out of the other side of the car, came around, and took her arm.

"Who's that?" Mike asked as his shutter clicked away.

"I think that must be George McFall. He owns the funeral home."

Conley reflected that death became Vanessa Robinette. Her red hair was twisted into a chignon. She wore a severely cut black dress with elbow-length sleeves, obviously couture, but Conley, who didn't keep up with such things, couldn't name the designer. A tiny pin twinkled from the scalloped neck of the dress. Symmes's fraternity pin, she remembered. Her eyes were obscured by a veil pinned to a small velvet pillbox hat. It was a very Jackie Kennedy look, Conley had to admit.

A second limo pulled behind the one Vanessa had vacated. The back door opened, and Charlie Robinette emerged, dressed in a charcoal suit, followed by Kennedy McFall. Then Charlie leaned down and lifted a wriggling preschooler out of the back seat, delivering her to her mother's outstretched arms.

Graceanne wore a navy dress with a smocked bodice and puffed sleeves and a ruffled petticoat. As Charlie handed her off, Conley stifled a giggle as the child's bare pink bottom was exposed. She saw, rather than heard, Kennedy gasp, then dart back to the limo to retrieve a pair of lacy white underpants, a pair of black patent Mary Janes, and one sock.

Mike's shutter continued to click as the hearse drew up, followed by another limo. "That's the governor," he said. "Why don't you go inside and grab us some seats. I'll finish up out here."

"I'll be on an aisle, halfway up," she said. She tucked her head down and her elbows out as she moved determinedly through the throng snaking toward the church doors.

She'd grown up going to services in this church. It was an elegant, pre–Civil War building with thickly veined marble floors, mahogany pews, and a soaring ceiling supported by twin rows of fluted columns.

A harpist and string quartet were stationed on the right side of the altar, with the harpist accompanying the church organist, playing something she vaguely recognized as Mendelssohn.

Michael tapped her shoulder, and she scooted in to let him join her in the already packed pew, earning her an angry glare from the middle-aged woman sitting to her right.

"What's it looking like out there?" Conley whispered.

"Total crazy-town. I just saw a sheriff's deputy arrest a lady for parking her handicapped-access van on the sidewalk. Like, seriously on the sidewalk. He told her she'd have to move it, and she took a swing at him with her pocketbook."

"You got that, right?"

He grinned and held up the Nikon. "Shot the shit out of it."

People were still streaming into the church as white-gloved ushers shoehorned them into every available space.

From the pew behind hers, Conley heard a small gasp. Turning, she watched while Hank Robinette, dressed in an ill-fitting sport coat, escorted Toddie and Rebecca Robinette up the aisle toward the front of the church. She recognized both from Toddie's photo.

She glanced at Mike, who had the Nikon in his lap. "That's Toddie," she whispered. "I don't care how you do it, but we need that shot."

He spun around in the pew, clicked off half a dozen frames as Toddie and her children passed, then turned back and put the camera on the pew between them. "Got it."

"Boom," Conley said.

She felt a light tap her on shoulder and looked up to see G'mama walking up the aisle with her hand tucked into Skelly's arm.

Lorraine was dressed in a simple buttercup-yellow linen dress and her favorite turquoise beads. Her grandmother had always had an uncanny sense for wearing classic fashions that never went out of style, and she never wore black because, as she always said, there were so many beautiful colors in nature. Conley realized with a start that it was the same dress G'mama had worn to her father's funeral.

A few minutes later, the large wooden outer doors to the vestibule closed, and the church's massive pipe organ began booming the opening notes to "A Mighty God Is Our God." The church pastor, Dr. Phipps, processed down the main aisle, followed by the black-robed choir, followed by six pallbearers and a rosewood casket containing the earthly remains of C. Symmes Robinette.

Vanessa Robinette came next, on George McFall's arm, followed at a safe distance by Charlie and Kennedy McFall, with a now-docile Graceanne holding their hands.

The service started, but the pastor's voice seemed to Conley to be coming from far away. Despite the air-conditioning in the church, she felt warm, suffocating even. Her palms grew damp, her face flushed, and she felt light-headed.

She didn't realize that she was breathing hard until Michael nudged her. "Are you all right? You look kinda sick."

"I'm okay," she whispered. She closed her eyes and tried to meditate. This church, these funeral rituals, all brought her father's own service rushing back into her memory.

The pastor was a kind-faced, benevolent presence. He yielded the lectern for a brief eulogy from the governor of Florida, who said he'd been a freshman state senator during Symmes Robinette's last term in the Florida Senate and that Robinette had always been a source of strength and inspiration.

The governor yielded to Charlie Robinette, who was already masterful at public speaking—charming, self-deprecating, funny, and touching. If you didn't know him. His voice gave Conley a sour taste in her mouth. He was still the Little Prince. To the manor born.

"I always wanted to be like my dad," he said, placing both hands on the lectern. "But the truth is, nobody could ever fill Symmes Robinette's shoes. And I mean that literally, because my father wore a size 6 shoe. It was a miracle that a man of his height—he was six two in his stocking feet—and weight—which he never divulged to anybody, not even my mother—could stand erect on such tiny, toddler feet."

Gentle laughter rippled through the congregation.

"But as small as his feet were, my father had a heart for everyone. He wasn't a perfect man, and he would be the first to tell you that. Well, actually, my mom would be the first to tell you that, because she is the only person I ever met who could cut Dad down to size with one meaningful glare."

Conley craned her neck and could just see the top of Vanessa's head. She was sitting erect, her shoulders tensed. The widow, she thought, was not amused.

"You know, we all thought Dad would live forever. He thought it too. But last fall, we received the devastating news that he was suffering from cancer. Dad was adamant that he didn't want his condition made public. He said he didn't want to be a poster boy for cancer, and he didn't want anybody feeling sorry for him, because he'd lived a long, productive life. He had work to do in Washington, and he knew that the time he had left was short."

Charlie took a deep breath. "Knowing that, my dad took stock of his life. We had a lot of good talks these last few months. What a tremendous gift that was, for both of us. During one of those late-night talks, Dad divulged to me that he had one big secret, one big regret, something he was deeply ashamed of, and he asked me to help him make things right."

Vanessa's head bowed, and the rest of the congregation sat up, waiting to hear the rest.

"Dad revealed to me that he had what he called a *secret family,* one that I knew nothing about. He told me that he'd been married before he'd met my mother, and he'd had two children with his first wife."

Charlie chuckled ruefully and paused for effect.

"Damn, he's good," Mike whispered, gazing around the church at the rapt faces of all the mourners. "He's got this crowd in the palm of his hand."

"Trust me. It's all an act," Conley whispered back.

"You could have knocked me over with a feather," Charlie said, affecting the folksy accent of a local yokel. "And it turns out that most of my life, that secret family—including my half brother, Hank, and half sister, Rebecca—lived less than an hour away from the spot where I'd spent most of my growing-up years."

Another ripple of murmurs and whispers washed through the room.

"It turns out that in the process of making things right, you sometimes make waves. Sometimes you have to make decisions that will make people you love uncomfortable, even unhappy. I was willing to do that for him. So these last few months, I did what I could to help my dad reconnect with his first family."

Conley scanned the faces around her. Every eye in the cavernous church seemed riveted on Charlie Robinette—except Vanessa's; she seemed to be staring down at her lap.

"It had been more than twenty years since Dad had seen his children. Amazingly, they found it in their hearts to forgive his absence and to accept his apology and his love, however belated it came. Hank and Rebecca and Toddie are here in this church today. I know that they mourn my dad's loss as much as the rest of us do. But I also know that their presence here today would make my dad proud and happy."

Charlie took another deep breath. "I'm not a preacher; I'm just a simple country lawyer."

"Country lawyer, my ass," Conley muttered.

"But I believe there's an object lesson that we can all take in my dad's last months on earth. If there is someone you feel you've wronged or hurt in some way, don't pass up the opportunity to try to make things right. I know I speak for all my family when I say thank y'all for coming today to celebrate the life of my dad."

A bagpiper accompanied the choir and congregation in "Amazing Grace" as the family and pallbearers filed down the center aisle.

"Go!" Conley told Michael, who managed to slither past the other worshippers in their pew to race toward the side exit.

She was almost to the rear door when she spotted a familiar figure, still sitting in the very last pew, dressed in her customary white shirt and black pants. Conley sat down beside her.

"Winnie?"

The housekeeper looked up, grim-faced but resolute. She saw the question in Conley's eyes.

"Had to see it for myself. When she was on her deathbed, I promised Nedra I would see Symmes Robinette dead, and now I have."

"Okay," Conley said. "I gotta get back to work."

By the time she exited the church, there were still knots of people standing around on the church lawn.

Buddy Bright was set up in the shade of a magnolia tree, near a van with the radio station call letters, doing a live remote and interviewing any politicos he managed to buttonhole.

Conley found the NBC camera crew on the opposite side of the church lawn. She introduced herself and pointed out the key players in the day's drama, including Toddie, Hank, and Rebecca. But Tressa, the reporter, had been in church during most of the service and had already zeroed in on both of Symmes Robinette's wives and all his children.

"You know where the Baptist church is, right?" Conley asked, pointing across the street at the imposing redbrick structure. "The reception is there. Maybe you'll get lucky and manage to get all the family in the same frame."

She returned to the front of the church in time to see G'mama emerge, again on Skelly's arm.

"Hey, you two," she said. "G'mama, how did you manage to score such a handsome date?"

Lorraine scowled. "Winnie absolutely refused to drive me here today. Said she had 'other fish to fry.' And of course, as the outgoing president of the altar guild, I couldn't very well not show up. So I called Sean, and he said he was going and he even volunteered to be my chauffeur."

Conley didn't mention seeing Winnie at the back of the church.

"Skelly is our knight in shining armor once again," Conley said. "Are you two going over to the reception?"

"I feel we should at least put in an appearance," G'mama said, giving Skelly a meaningful glance.

"Okay by me," Skelly said. "I've got my high school girl working until four."

"I might see you over there," Conley said. "But I think Rowena's actually going to be working the crowd, taking notes, and misspelling people's names." She touched Skelly's sleeve. "Can I talk to you for a second?"

He shrugged and followed her a few yards away.

"Thanks for being so sweet to G'mama," Conley said. "I know you're mad at me, but I really appreciate that you're not taking it out on her."

"I'm not mad at you," Skelly said, his expression mild. "Maybe it's all for the best that you made it clear you're not interested."

"It's not that I'm not interested," Conley protested. "If we were both in the right place at the right time . . ."

"But we're not," Skelly finished her sentence. "And I've been through this already. Go do your job," he said wearily. "I'll take your grandmama home after the reception. And I'm not doing it as a favor. I'm doing it because that's what neighbors do."

"Okay," she said.

He was standing at the edge of the crowd, hands in his pockets, dressed in a sport coat and tie, trying to blend into the landscape, but the wraparound aviator sunglasses, military bearing, and spit-shined, lace-up shoes gave him away as law enforcement.

"Sheriff," she said, sidling over to him.

"Miss Hawkins."

"I did ask you to call me *Conley*."

"So you did."

"What are you doing here today?" she asked.

"Can't a fella pay respects to his congressman at his homegoing celebration?"

"Of course. But I'm getting a vibe that there's more to your visit than that."

"Who am I to argue with a vibe?" Merle Goggins asked. "Whatever that is."

"I think you owe me, Sheriff. And I think there's something you're not telling me."

"There's a lot I'm not at liberty to tell you, even if I wanted to, this being an ongoing investigation."

"What if you told me off the record?"

His eyes looked straight past her, and she saw that he was watching Vanessa and the rest of the family climb into limos for the short ride to the reception. He seemed to be weighing a decision.

"I had a call from the medical examiner's office late yesterday," he said finally. "We're completely off the record, right?"

"That's right."

"He told me Symmes Robinette was already dead when that deer hit his windshield."

"So I was right! He did hit the deer."

Goggins nod was barely perceptible.

She waited to see if he would explain, but he was still watching the crowd on the church lawn. "How can they tell he was already dead?"

"There wasn't much bleeding from his head injuries. If he'd been alive and his heart had still been pumping, you'd have seen way more blood."

"So what did kill him?" she asked.

The sheriff's smile was enigmatic. "Are we still off the record?"

"Yes, damn it. Quit stalling. Are you going to tell me or not?"

"The medical examiner tells me he had elevated levels of fentanyl in his blood. And a blood alcohol level of .06. Pretty toxic combination."

"I talked to a friend who's an oncology nurse. She said cancer patients using a fentanyl patch can tolerate much higher levels of opioids because they metabolize it at a different rate. Are you saying it was an accidental overdose?"

"I'm not saying anything at all," Goggins said. "Because we didn't have this conversation. Have a nice day, okay?"

50

The Baptist church gym was at or near capacity. Conley edged between clumps of people balancing coffee cups and plates loaded with food, making her way to a row of bleachers on the far side of the room. She climbed halfway up and stood, looking out from her vantage point over the wood-floored room. A buffet had been set up beneath the large electric scoreboard, and a long, white-clothed table held polished silver candelabras and an endless array of silver trays holding dainty tea sandwiches, cookies, and cakes, the tray lineup punctuated by massive arrangements of ferns, palm fronds, white lilies, and white carnations.

Not far from one of the side doors, she spotted Toddie, Rebecca, and Hank sipping coffee and looking ill at ease.

Only a few yards away, Vanessa was stationed in front of a round table holding a silver coffee urn and a cut glass punch bowl, chatting with two white-haired women in dark dresses. If Vanessa saw Toddie and her clan, she made a good show of pretending she hadn't.

While she watched, Charlie walked up to Toddie and her children and began chatting with his half siblings. Kennedy McFall stood a safe distance away in neutral territory, with the dozing Graceanne slung over her shoulder.

As much as she dreaded another confrontation with the Little Prince,

Conley needed an off-the-cuff, unscripted quote from him for her story. She clambered down from the bleachers as quickly as she could, but before she could reach the reunited Robinette siblings, she saw George McFall sidle up and whisper something in Charlie's ear while Toddie and her children drifted away into the crowd, which seemed to swallow them up whole.

As she worked her way through the crowd, keeping an eye on the two men, she saw Charlie shake his head vehemently, brushing off the funeral director with some sort of sharp exchange. McFall turned his back on Charlie, stopped to speak briefly to his daughter, then returned to Vanessa's side.

Conley saw an opening and went for it. "Charlie? Can I have a moment?"

"What the hell do you want?" he snapped.

"That was quite a moment back there in church," she said. "Did your mother know you were going to mention Toddie and the others in your eulogy?"

"She's not currently taking my calls." He started to walk away, but she hurried after him.

"If it's any consolation, she's not taking mine either," Conley said.

He turned around, and the expression on his face said that he wasn't amused. "I read that piece-of-crap story you wrote in the *Beacon*. It's clear you're still nursing some old beef and mounting a personal vendetta against me, so I don't have anything else to say to you."

"No vendetta," Conley said. "This is professional, not personal. I'm a journalist, reporting the news. Like it or not, your father was a public figure. You're running for Congress in this district, and so is your mother, which makes you public figures too. So any comment on what the medical examiner says was your dad's cause of death?"

He blinked. "That hasn't been released yet."

"Not officially, no."

"The sheriff says his car hit a deer," Charlie said. "That's really all we know. Look, I gotta get back to the reception." He turned again to join his waiting fiancée.

"He was already dead when he hit that deer," Conley said.

Charlie whipped around. "You don't know what you're talking about."

"I was there that night. I've been back to the crash site twice. There were no skid marks. Think about that."

"So what's your point? My dad was seventy-seven years old. He was dying. And in case you haven't noticed, Sarah, we're burying him today, so I'd appreciate it if you'd just back the hell away from me and my family."

She was pondering her next move. The gym's air-conditioning wasn't adequate for a crowd this size. It was hot, and the air was thick with the cloying scent of lilies and aftershave. She was trying to spot Toddie in the crowd when George McFall suddenly materialized at her side. "Mrs. Robinette would appreciate it if you would leave now," he murmured, grasping her elbow.

"You're kicking me out of a funeral reception?"

"That story of yours in this week's paper was offensive and libelous," he said, his face stern. "I knew your grandfather, and he never would have printed something like that."

She felt her cheeks burn. With her left hand, she pried his fingers off her arm. "My grandfather was in the news business, and he taught my sister and me that we publish the news—whatever it is, without fear or favor."

"Sarah Conley?" G'mama held out a plate with a slice of cake and an egg salad sandwich. "I thought you might like something to eat." She gave McFall a cool glance. "Is there a problem here?"

"He's kicking me out," Conley said. "Mr. McFall thinks my story was offensive. And libelous."

"George, is that true?" G'mama asked.

"Hello, Lorraine," McFall said, his tone instantly becoming conciliatory. "I pointed out to your granddaughter that it's incredibly poor taste for her to be here after that old stuff she dredged up about Symmes last week. Vanessa objects to her presence."

"Is that so?" Lorraine asked. "Does she object to my presence here

as well? I'm the president of the Presbyterian church altar guild. I
helped organize this function today, you know."

"And I'm sure the family appreciates your efforts," McFall said, furiously backpedaling. "But they don't appreciate that scurrilous garbage
you people printed. Really, Lorraine, Woodrow Conley would never
have published something like that."

G'mama's eyes flickered around the room. "I can assure you that my
husband absolutely would have published that story. As the *Beacon*'s
current publisher, I'm incredibly proud of the work both my grand-
daughters have done this past week. And, George, in case you're not up
on libel law, let me remind you that truth is a defense to libel. Can you
quote me a single sentence in Conley's story that was inaccurate?"

"Not inaccurate," the funeral director sputtered. "Just trashy. And
inflammatory. Symmes Robinette was a war hero. He spent most of his
life as an elected official, serving the people of this community. Good
God, the man is dead. He can't even defend himself."

"Our story made prominent mention of Symmes's achievements,"
Lorraine said. "But we both know he was no saint, and he most certainly wasn't selfless. Conley has researched his financial disclosure
statements, which show that Symmes Robinette managed to line his
own pockets quite nicely while he was in office."

"A funeral reception is not the place to have a discussion like this,"
McFall insisted.

"I agree," Lorraine said, her chin tilted at a dangerous angle. "So
you can tell Vanessa and Charlie that the *Beacon* stands by Conley, and
we stand by her reporting. And we don't intend to back away from this
story."

She tucked her hand under her granddaughter's arm. "It's awfully
close in here, isn't it? Could you walk me outside for some fresh air?"

They found a shaded bench in the church courtyard.

"Thanks for the show of support back there," Conley told her grandmother after they'd seated themselves and she'd eaten the tiny sandwich
in one bite. "You rock, by the way."

"I meant every word I said," G'mama said.

"I'm afraid things are about to get ugly," Conley said apologetically.

"They already have," Lorraine said. "Vivienne Tompkins and Dana Goodman deliberately turned their backs and walked away from me in the church kitchen a little while ago. I've known them both since your mother was in preschool with their daughters."

"They snubbed you? Because of my story? I'm sorry, G'mama."

"Don't be," Lorraine said. "We were never really that close. Forget about them. Have there been any new developments in your story?"

"I saw the sheriff before I walked over here. He confirmed that the wreck happened because Robinette's car struck that deer. But the medical examiner also says Robinette was already dead before he hit it."

"How bizarre."

"He told me—completely off the record, by the way—that Robinette had a toxic combination of fentanyl and alcohol in his system."

"Is that a pain medication he was taking for the cancer?"

"I assume so. Which explains why the sheriff asked Skelly to hand over a list of all Symmes's medications. And Vanessa's."

"Oh my."

"Doesn't necessarily mean there was any foul play," Conley said. She explained what her oncologist nurse friend had told her about the increased levels of fentanyl a long-term cancer patient could tolerate. "So that could explain his cause of death. But it still doesn't really explain what Robinette was doing that far from home that late at night. And what or who he was drinking with."

"With whom he was drinking," G'mama said, automatically correcting her grammar. "I assume you have a theory?" She broke off a morsel of cake and nibbled it.

"I think he must have been visiting Oak Springs Farm. Toddie told me herself that Symmes came out to the farm not long before he died. She said he was trying to make amends for those lost years, which is why he deeded Oak Springs over to her."

They heard footsteps approaching and looked up to see Grayson walking toward them. She'd changed before the funeral and was wearing a belted black silk dress and heels.

"Scoot over," Grayson instructed, seating herself on the other side of their grandmother.

"Did you get kicked out too?" Conley asked.

"Excommunicated is more like it," Grayson said. She sank down onto the bench, slipped her feet out of her high-heeled pumps, and sighed contentedly. "So much for polite society," she said. "I've spent the last thirty minutes getting chewed out by three different little old ladies as well as Kennedy McFall, who's threatening to pull their funeral notices out of the *Beacon* over this brouhaha."

"Yikes," Conley said, grimacing. "That's not good."

"Empty threats," Grayson assured her. "We're the only game in town. And don't forget, they make just as much money charging families for those notices as we do. They're not gonna bite off their own noses to spite their faces."

"I can't understand what a lovely young lady like Kennedy McFall sees in that vile Charlie Robinette," Lorraine said. "She's much too good for the likes of him."

"Agreed," Grayson said. "Conley, maybe you should take Kennedy aside and tell her about the horrible way that gutless weasel treated you back in high school."

Conley did a double take. "How did you know? You were away at college."

"I had my sources," Grayson said. "By the time I heard about those disgusting rumors he was spreading, it was too late to stop them. But I did make sure he knew better than to tangle with the Hawkins girls again."

"Help me up, girls," G'mama said, extending a hand to each of the sisters. "I don't know about you two, but I think I'm ready for a nice, stiff drink at the club. Or two. And I'm buying."

"You can have one drink and one drink only," Grayson said, wagging a finger at Lorraine. "But Conley and I had better stick to seltzer. We've got a paper to put out."

"What about Skelly?" Conley asked, looking around. "We won't have time to take you back out to the beach after this, G'mama."

"Call him up and invite him to join us at the bar," G'mama said. "I really am feeling quite parched."

51

Grayson slowed the BMW at the entryway to the Silver Bay Country Club and waved at the guard standing casually by the open gate.

"When did they put up a gate?" G'mama asked.

"I don't know, maybe two or three months ago?" Grayson said. "I think somebody on the board of directors decided it looked prestigious, but it's really a waste of money. I've never been here when those gates were closed, and the guards always just wave members on through, so it's not like they're keeping out a horde of infidels or something."

"They definitely didn't stop me when I drove through earlier in the week," Conley said thoughtfully. "And I don't even have a membership sticker on my windshield."

"A waste of money," G'mama fussed. "The only criminal activity I've ever heard of over here consists of sandbagging golf scores and a little low-stakes gambling at the poker table."

"Not true, G'mama," Conley said. "Just last week, I included an item in the police blotter about a car that was burglarized here."

"That's right," Grayson said, maneuvering the BMW into a parking spot near the clubhouse. "Seems like whoever broke in stole some pretty valuable stuff. Jewelry or something?"

"Some expensive diamond earrings. And according to the incident

report, the car wasn't even broken into, because it had been left unlocked," Conley said.

The club's bar, formally known as the Tap Room, was decorated to re-
semble a Scottish Highlander tavern plunked down in the Florida Panhandle, with ersatz tartan carpet, dark walnut paneling, and plenty of
vintage fox-hunting and golfing prints.

"Never seen the place so dead," Grayson said as they found a table
in a corner of the mostly empty room. Two golfers sat at the bar, sharing
a pitcher of beer, and a table of women dressed in tennis togs sipped
margaritas.

"All the best people are still at Symmes's funeral," Conley said.

"Be right with you, ladies," the bartender called. A moment later,
he appeared table-side, a supremely tanned septuagenarian in a white
waiter's apron and black bolo tie.

"Well, hey there, Miz Lorraine," he said. "Welcome back. Haven't
seen you around here in a long while." He grinned at Grayson. "Course,
this lady is one of my favorite customers, so I see a good bit of her."

G'mama grasped his hand. "It's good to see you again, Artie. How's
Verna?"

"She's good. Busy with the grandkids and volunteering at church,"
he said. He gestured at Conley. "And who's this young lady? Seems like
I see a family resemblance."

"This is Sarah Conley, my other granddaughter," G'mama said.
"She's working with Grayson at the *Beacon*."

"Temporarily," Conley put in.

"I'm guessing, Miz Lorraine, you want one of your sunsetter
drinks, and Gray, you're Tanqueray and tonic, I know, but what about
you, Miz Sarah Conley?"

"Maybe just a seltzer with a slice of lime, please. I've got a long night
ahead of me," she said. Grayson sighed dramatically. "Make mine weak,
but yes, a Tanqueray and tonic is just what the doctor ordered."

After their drinks arrived, Grayson took a pen from her pocketbook
and began doodling on the cocktail napkin.

G'mama peered at her from across the table. "What's that you're drawing?"

"Hmm? Just starting to think about my story budget for the digital edition. Conley and Mike will share a byline, and then we'll hold a slot for whatever Rowena comes up with for her column."

G'mama stirred her drink, sipped, and nodded her approval. "That was an extraordinary moment at the funeral today, didn't you think? When Charlie acknowledged Toddie and her children?"

"I think he got some kind of sick satisfaction out of rubbing them in Vanessa's face," Grayson said.

"I was watching her at the moment he made that bullshit statement about forgiveness," Conley said. "I couldn't see her face from where I was sitting, because she was staring down at her lap. Charlie definitely didn't help Symmes reunite with the other family out of the goodness of his heart."

"Then what's his agenda?" Grayson asked. "You know he's got one."

"I think it's about power. The Little Prince wants his father's seat in the House. And he'll mow down anybody who gets in his way. Even his own mother," Conley said.

G'mama looked across the room and waved. "Look. Here's Sean."

Skelly's unknotted tie hung loosely around his neck, and he slipped out of his blazer and hung it on the back of the chair. The bartender arrived at their table a moment later with a cold draft beer and a small bowl of mixed nuts.

"Thanks, Artie," Skelly said, taking a long gulp of beer. He wiped his mouth with a napkin. "Man, I needed that," he declared. "Whose idea was it to have that reception at a church that forbids alcohol?"

"The altar guild had no choice. The Baptists have the biggest church downtown," G'mama told him. "And the best parking."

"How come y'all left so early? You missed the fireworks."

"George McFall kicked me out, and Gray got hounded out by a bunch of old biddies," Conley said. "What fireworks? What happened?"

"I'm just messing with you," Skelly said. "I didn't actually see any bad behavior. From what I could tell, Team Charlie and Team Vanessa staked out territory on opposite sides of the gym, with the food tables in the demilitarized zone. It was all very genteel."

"It was weird as hell, if you ask me," Conley said, sipping her seltzer. "I saw poor Toddie and her two kids looking totally adrift."

"I can't imagine why they turned up today," G'mama said. "It must have been terribly awkward for them."

"Toddie and I spoke briefly as she was leaving," Skelly said. He pointed at Conley. "She's pretty upset with you."

"Me? What did I do?"

"She seems to think you sicced the sheriff on her."

"I did no such thing," Conley said indignantly. "I only pointed out to Merle Goggins that Symmes's wreck happened right down the road from Toddie's farm, and I mentioned that she told me, the other day when we met in your store, that Symmes went out there for a visit not long before he died and told her that he was going to deed the property over to her."

"Are you saying Toddie had something to do with the accident?" Skelly asked. "Come on, Conley. I've known her most of my life. I don't think she's capable of anything like that."

"Until the day I tricked you into driving me out to Oak Springs Farm, you hadn't seen her in, what, more than thirty years?" Conley reminded him. "Can you definitely say she had nothing to do with Symmes's death?"

"We don't even know how he died," Skelly said.

Conley let out a long breath. "We do now. He hit a deer."

"A deer? Jesus! That's it? A deer killed him?"

"Not technically. The medical examiner thinks he was dead before he hit the deer. From what I understand, Symmes had toxic levels of fentanyl and alcohol in his system. He was either dead or in a coma when the car struck the deer."

Skelly nodded. "Makes sense, I guess. He had a fentanyl patch, so maybe one or more of his other meds had some kind of interaction."

"So he did have a fentanyl patch," Conley said, seizing on the pharmacist's slipup.

Skelly swore softly under his breath. "You tricked me."

"I didn't," Conley said, glancing from her sister to her grandmother. "Did y'all hear me trick Skelly?"

"Not me," Grayson said, laughing. "You gave up that information on a strictly voluntary basis."

"It's not funny," he said. "You can't quote me as saying anything about Symmes's prescriptions. I could lose my license. I could lose the store."

"I won't," Conley said hastily. "You only confirmed, off the record, what I already knew. I swear, Skelly, I didn't mean to try to trick you."

He downed the last of his beer and reached for his jacket. "Miss Lorraine, can I give you a ride out to the beach? I'm afraid I need to get back to the store now."

"That would be wonderful," G'mama said. "I hate to bother you, but I know the girls are on deadline, and I'm not exactly sure where Winnie's gotten off to today."

"No bother at all," he said, standing to pull out her chair.

"I'll walk you out to the car," Conley said.

"While you do that, I'll just go powder my nose," G'mama said tactfully. "And I'll meet you in the parking lot."

"You have to know I wouldn't do anything to intentionally harm you or your family business," Conley said as Skelly strode away from the bar. "Skelly! Are you listening to me?"

He didn't turn around. "I heard you, all right."

She grabbed at the hem of his jacket. "Hey! Slow down."

He stopped in his tracks. His face was expressionless. "I said, 'I heard you.'"

"But you don't really believe me?"

"I don't know what to believe. You're so damn determined to break the next big story, I'm not sure what you would or wouldn't do to get a scoop."

"I wouldn't betray a confidence. I wouldn't deliberately hurt my oldest friend in the world. Somebody I care deeply about," she said, staring up at him.

They'd reached the club lobby, and suddenly, members were streaming in through the front door, still dressed in their funeral clothes, all marching determinedly toward the bar after three harrowing, booze-free hours in church.

"Okay," he said, shrugging. "I believe you."

Her cell phone rang and when she glanced she saw that her old friend, the unknown caller was back. She let it ring.

"Don't you need to answer that?" Skelly asked, gesturing at her pocketbook.

"Just a crank call," she said.

"All set," G'mama said as she walked up to them.

Skelly half bowed from the waist. "Your carriage awaits."

"Maybe I'll call you when I'm off deadline," Conley said just as Skelly and Lorraine pushed out the doors and into the parking lot.

52

"Where have you two been?" Lillian demanded when Conley and Grayson walked into the *Beacon* office shortly before five o'clock. "People been calling up here all afternoon, wanting to know what time y'all are gonna put out that special edition."

"Really?" Grayson asked. "Did you direct them to the new website and tell them to sign up?"

"I did like you told me to," Lillian said. "But that funeral's been over for a long damn time."

"We were doing research," Grayson said, passing the receptionist's desk on her way to her office.

"Your research smells a lot like gin to me," Lillian said with an indignant sniff.

"Have we heard anything from Rowena yet?" Grayson asked, ignoring the dig.

"Oh yeah. She came sailing in here about an hour ago, all dressed in that black widow Halloween getup of hers. Said she had another 'exclusive' from Vanessa Robinette.

"Did she get anything good from Vanessa?" Conley asked.

"I guess," Lillian said. "It's in the system. I slugged it, 'Vanessa Gonna Sue.'"

"What?" the sisters said in unison.

"Who's she suing?" Conley asked.

The phone rang, and Lillian's hand was poised to answer. "Says she's gonna sue the first wife, her own son, and some other people too."

She picked up the phone. "*Silver Bay Beacon,* shining the light of truth. This is Lillian King speaking."

Conley pulled her cell phone from her purse and glanced at her emails to see if she'd had any messages from Selena Kwan. No new emails, but she saw that she had a voicemail.

She pulled Rowena's column up on her laptop, and absent-mindedly tapped the voicemail arrow. The man's voice was muffled, but the words were clear. "You're dead, bitch."

Conley glanced around the newsroom, shook her head and started to delete the message before thinking better of it. Tomorrow, she told herself, she would report the calls to the cops.

She turned back to the laptop and began to read with growing irritation.

"Hey, Gray," she called to her sister. "Are you looking at this train wreck Rowena calls a column?"

Grayson stood in the doorway of her office. "Yes. And yes, I agree it's unreadable as is. Just fix it, okay? Michael called. He's on the way back with some quotes from the governor and from Vanessa's new campaign chairman. This story is like a damn Hydra. You break off one piece of it and six new pieces grow in its place."

HELLO, SUMMER
By Rowena Meigs

Your correspondent learned in an exclusive interview today with Mrs. Vanessa Robinette (who was tragically widowed after her husband, Congressman Symmes Robinette, was killed in a recent car wreck) that Mrs. Robinette intends to sue Rep. Robinette's first wife, Toddie, because she used "undue influence" to unlawfully persuade Symmes Robinette to deed over title to the family's Oak Springs Farm in Bronson County to Toddie, while Symmes was not entirely in possession of all his faculties due to his terminal cancer.

Oak Springs Farm is a working quail-hunting plantation with eight hundred acres of timberland and is valued at close to $2 million, Vanessa Robinette claims. She said that shortly before his death, while Symmes Robinette was suffering from diminished capacity, his former wife took advantage of him and tricked him into giving the farm to her.

Vanessa said she will sue Toddie Sanderson, as well as her own son, Charlie Robinette, who, she said, duped her husband into believing he should give away the farm, which used to be owned by Toddie's family, out of guilt over their divorce more than thirty years ago.

Conley spent the next thirty minutes rewriting and trying to fact-check Rowena's column. She tried calling and texting first Vanessa Robinette and then Charlie. Finally, in desperation, she called Kennedy McFall, whose tone was noticeably cool when she answered her cell phone.

"Yes?"

"Hi, Kennedy. It's Conley Hawkins over at the *Beacon*."

"What do you want, Conley? Are you writing another story trying to make my fiancé look like a bad guy for following his father's last request?"

"Look, Kennedy," Conley said wearily. "I don't know what Charlie's told you, but I can assure you I do not have some kind of vendetta going against him. I'm a reporter, and I'm covering the news of the day. He might not like it, but that's my job. Just like it was my job to attend your press conference and print the fact that he reported his mother to the state for elder abuse. Right now, I'm fact-checking Rowena Meigs's column."

"That old bat wouldn't know a fact if it bit her on the butt, but do go on," Kennedy said. "I'm listening."

"Rowena's reporting that Vanessa says she's going to sue Toddie— and Charlie—over the Oak Springs Farm title. Do you know anything about that?"

"I know Vanessa texts Charlie several times a day with all kinds of deranged threats," Kennedy said. "Frankly, we've lost track of everything she's pissed off about."

"Do you happen to know who her attorney is?"

"No."

"Would Charlie know?"

"Probably, but he's in a meeting with the governor right now, and I'm not about to disturb him just so you can assassinate his character in print."

Conley was beginning to lose patience. "Tell me one sentence I've written about Charlie Robinette that is inaccurate. Okay? Quote me the place where I've engaged in character assassination. If Charlie and his mom don't like what the *Beacon* has written about this family, maybe they need to look in the mirror. Because I don't make the news, Kennedy. I just report it."

"You report it with your own personal slant," Kennedy retorted. "Because you're still pissed off that Charlie broke it off with you, what? Twenty years ago? That's a long time to nurse a feud, Conley. Maybe you need to grow up and get over yourself."

Kennedy disconnected before Conley could offer her own version of her ugly history with Charlie Robinette.

"Aaaarrrgghhh!" she moaned, burying her head in her hands.

Michael had been working on his own story but turned around and regarded her with sympathy. "Getting stonewalled?"

"At every turn," she said grimly. "Can't get Vanessa on the phone, and I can't get to Charlie. But I really need to get confirmation for Rowena's column."

"Have you tried reaching out to Toddie?" he asked.

"She's my next call, but I'm apparently on her shit list," Conley said with a long sigh.

"It's great, isn't it?" the young reporter enthused. "I'd way rather be hated than ignored."

She laughed despite herself. "You've got a great future in this business, Mike."

She called Toddie's cell phone, and when there was no answer, Conley left a voice mail. A minute later, Robinette's ex-wife returned the call.

"I've got a bone to pick with you," Toddie began.

"Skelly told me you were upset that I sicced the sheriff on you," Conley said quickly. "But I didn't! All I did was point out what you'd told me yourself—that Symmes had visited you on the farm not long before his death. Goggins said he'd been to Oak Springs Farm several times. He knew how close it was to the crash site."

"Of course I know the sheriff. We invite all the fire and sheriff's department folks over every year for a dove shoot," Toddie said. "But I resent the insinuation that I had something to do with Symmes's death. My kids and I gave him the only happiness he'd had in the last few weeks of his life, and now you and that *woman* have managed to make that look like some kind of crime."

Conley had to bite her tongue to keep from repeating the same things she'd been telling people all day. Instead, she pressed on with her questions.

"Vanessa told our columnist today that she intends to sue you and Charlie, claiming you had undue influence on Symmes while he was of diminished capacity."

Toddie laughed hoarsely. "Let her sue. Deeding the farm over to me was entirely Symmes's idea. And don't forget, he was the one who reached out to me, not the other way around. It's not my fault that he had a guilty conscience and wanted to make things right after the way he ripped me off in the divorce settlement."

"Have you heard from her attorney?" Conley asked.

"Not a peep," Toddie said. "This is just a pathetic ploy to get publicity for her campaign. The woman will do anything to get attention. Threatening to sue me? And her only child? On the day she buries her allegedly beloved husband? Not exactly the work of a grieving widow, is it?"

Conley's fingers were flying across the keyboard of her computer. "Did Symmes tell Charlie that he intended to deed the farm over to you?"

Toddie hesitated. "How should I know?"

"Charlie was the one who initially made contact with you, so I thought maybe Symmes shared his intention with his son."

Conley heard a deep, masculine voice. "Mom? Who are you talking to?"

Toddie's voice became muffled, but still audible. "It's that girl who works for the newspaper in Silver Bay. She says Vanessa is going to sue me."

"Hang up, Mom," the man's voice urged. "You don't need to talk to her."

Click.

Conley put her phone down. She'd been kicked out of a funeral, yelled at, ignored, and hung up on. Just another day in the life of a small-town journalist.

53

LONGTIME LAWMAKER LAID TO REST AMID
SWIRLING CONTROVERSY
By Conley Hawkins and Michael Torpy

*Silver Bay, Florida—Veteran local congressman C. Symmes Robi-
nette was laid to rest here Saturday, but peace—among the feuding
family members and constituents left behind—remains an elusive
commodity.*

*Questions linger both about the manner of Robinette's death
and the paradox of his personal life.*

*The seventy-seven-year-old congressman was killed in the
early morning hours of May 11 in a fiery one-car wreck in rural Bronson County, after his 2020 Escalade struck a deer. The
district medical examiner's office has not officially ruled on the
cause of death, but sources have told the* Beacon *that Robinette
was either already dead or unconscious at the time of impact and
that toxic levels of fentanyl, an opioid painkiller commonly prescribed for advanced cancer patients, and alcohol, were found in
his bloodstream.*

Bronson County sheriff Merle Goggins said the congressman's death remains under investigation. He said foul play is not suspected.

Robinette's namesake and heir presumptive to his now vacant seat in the U.S. House, C. Symmes "Charlie" Robinette Jr., startled many in the overflow crowd at Silver Bay Presbyterian Church on Saturday, when, while delivering the eulogy, he acknowledged the presence of his father's "secret family" in the church—including Symmes Robinette's first wife, Emma "Toddie" Sanderson, and her adult children, Hank, fifty, and Rebecca Robinette, forty-eight, who were seated only a few pews away from Vanessa Monck Robinette, fifty-nine, Robinette's widow and the mother of Charlie Robinette, who has also announced her intention to run for her late husband's seat.

During his eulogy, Charlie Robinette said his father only divulged the existence of his first marriage and the children from that marriage recently, following his diagnosis of non-Hodgkin's lymphoma.

The family kept Rep. Robinette's cancer diagnosis a secret from all but his closest friends, Charlie Robinette said, because his father "didn't want to be a poster boy for cancer."

Vanessa Robinette has said she brought her husband back to Silver Bay earlier in the spring because she wanted him to spend his last months in the comfort of his own home.

But the younger Robinette said his mother spirited the ailing congressman away from world-renowned physicians treating him at Walter Reed National Military Medical Center, returning him to Silver Bay, where Vanessa Robinette deliberately cut Symmes Robinette off from all contact with the outside world, keeping him a virtual hostage in the couple's lavish Gulf-front home in Sugar Key. Charlie Robinette said that in the final months of his father's illness, his mother confiscated the congressman's cell phone and instructed Sugar Key security guards to deny Charlie Robinette admittance to the gated community.

A bitter family feud has erupted in the wake of Symmes Robinette's death. Earlier this week, on the same day Symmes Robinette was being memorialized with full honors in the Capitol Rotunda in Washington, D.C., his son skipped that event, instead calling a press conference to announce that he had asked Florida officials to investigate Vanessa Robinette for elder abuse.

Today, Vanessa Robinette told Beacon *columnist Rowena Meigs she intends to sue both Charlie Robinette and Toddie Sanderson over ownership of Oak Springs Farm, the eight-hundred-acre Bronson County quail-hunting plantation that Symmes Robinette deeded to his ex-wife two weeks before his death.*

Vanessa Robinette told the Beacon *that her son and Toddie Sanderson exerted undue influence over her husband while he was suffering from diminished faculties to persuade him to deed over the farm, with an estimated value of $1.8 million, to Toddie Sanderson. Ms. Sanderson, seventy-six, had leased the property from Robinette for decades, following her uncontested divorce from the congressman.*

Reached Saturday night, Toddie Sanderson said it was Symmes Robinette's idea to sell her the farm, which was originally owned by her family, for one dollar "and other considerations" because "he had a guilty conscience and wanted to make things right after the way he ripped me off in the divorce settlement."

"Gray?" Conley swiveled around in her chair to face the open door of the editor's office. "I'm still waiting on callbacks from Charlie and Vanessa Robinette, and then I've got to merge Mike's stuff into my story. Did Rowena call in from the party at Sugar Key?"

Grayson walked out into the newsroom. "About an hour ago. I cut Lillian loose to go home after she typed it into the system."

"Was it as bad as usual?"

"Worse. We got a full description of what the governor's wife was wearing, as well as what the caterers were wearing, what kind of flowers were floating in the swimming pool, and how chic Vanessa looked. There were also some blurry photos of the crab salad on the buffet and of Tuffy peeking out of a potted palm on the veranda. It's gonna take major surgery to make chicken salad out of this batch of chicken shit."

"Sorry, but you're going to have to whip it into shape yourself. I've got at least another hour's worth of work on the main story," Conley said, glancing at the clock on the newsroom wall.

"Me? I'm no writer," Gray protested.

"And I'm no miracle worker. There's no way I can get to Rowena's column and finish the main story. Either fix it yourself or leave it for next week's edition when I can get to it."

"Ugggghhhh," Gray moaned. "This is why I went to law school. So I'd never have to set foot in a newsroom."

"And it's why you make the big bucks," Conley said. "My advice? Hold your nose and get busy."

54

Change was in the wind. He could feel it, had been feeling it since he'd awakened that morning, anxious, moody, tense. Hi-Fi felt it too, had reached out and given him a wicked scratch on the face before retreating under the sofa in the apartment. Buddy Bright didn't believe in astrology or moon phases or any of that woo-woo crap. He believed in his gut. And his gut told him change was on the horizon.

The courthouse square was mostly deserted. It was after eleven, moving toward the midnight hour. If he got up and walked out to the station's tiny reception area, he could see lights burning in the *Beacon* office across the square.

It had been a big news day, for sure, with Symmes Robinette's funeral and all the unfolding drama with his family. Thinking back to their brief, late-night encounters at the Waffle House, Buddy wondered what the congressman would make of it all. He'd wanted to make amends, he said, but all he'd really made was a mess.

The commercial break was winding down. Buddy took one last drag, then stubbed out his cigarette in a foam coffee cup and switched on his mic.

"Welcome back, Silver Bay. This is *Up All Night,* and I'm Buddy Bright. We're gonna be howling at the moon soon, so let's play a little wicked Wilson Pickett, shall we?"

He slotted "In the Midnight Hour" onto the turntable and sat back in his chair. He worked the theme for the next hour or so, following up with Gladys Knight and the Pips' "Midnight Train to Georgia" and the Grass Roots' "Midnight Confessions."

"Gonna open it up to callers now," Buddy drawled. "Let's see who's still up and listening as we approach the midnight hour."

The switchboard lit up, and he picked the first caller.

"Hey, Buddy," the male caller said. "It's me, Pooh Bear. Remember me from the other night?"

"Hiya, Pooh Bear," Buddy said. "You got a midnight confession to share?"

"I don't, but I'm thinking you probably do. See, it was bugging me so bad, I did a little research."

Buddy's hand hovered over the switch. He could cut off the call now, claim operator error, but that would only prolong the inevitable.

"Did you now?" he asked.

"Amazing what you can find on the internet if you know where to look," Pooh Bear said. "And I figured it out. Back in Detroit, in 1992, you were Robert 'Robbie' Breitweis. Isn't that right?"

With shaking hands, Buddy lit another cigarette and inhaled a lungful of smoke.

"Buddy? You still there?"

"I'm here."

"You were a pretty big deal in Detroit, weren't you? Had the morning drive-time slot, were doing television commercials, pulling down the big money."

"If you say so, Pooh Bear."

"Was that where you started the hard partying? I always heard you rock jocks were big partiers back in the day. Drugs, booze, chicks, all of it that you could handle."

The cigarette ash spilled onto Buddy's shirt. He flicked it away. "What's your point here, Pooh Bear?" he said, trying to sound bored. "I got other callers waiting."

"The point is, I found the old newspaper clippings," Pooh Bear said with a mocking laugh. "Online. You killed a chick, right? Drunk driving. Got sent to jail, but then one day, while you were on a high-way work detail, you up and walked away. Disappeared into thin air. But now, here you are, working in Silver Bay, Florida, under a made-up name. That's my point, Buddy—I mean, Robert."

Buddy cut the caller off and cued up the next song on his midnight playlist. He'd met Gregg Allman on tour once. He read somewhere that Allman grew up down in Daytona Beach. He liked this state, liked the weather, the notion that everybody here had escaped from someplace else. Daytona, he decided, would be his next stop.

As Gregg Allman's guttural voice filled the tiny studio, Buddy gath-ered his things, sweeping them into a plastic grocery sack. "I've got to run to keep from hiding," he muttered. The last verse of the song was playing as he turned the lock in the studio door.

"Not gon' let them catch the midnight rider," Buddy whispered.

The Corvette was parked around the back of the studio. He walked around the car, surveying it like always, wiping away a bit of dust with the cuff of his black shirt. The engine rumbled to life, and he steered the sports car slowly around the square. The beacon on the newspaper building's tower cast a yellow light on the darkened street before him. As he passed the building, he spotted the black truck again, parked across the street, and the shadowy figure of a driver behind the steering wheel.

He glanced back at the newspaper and saw, silhouetted in the win-dow, the figures of two women.

Buddy's fingers drummed the steering wheel in a frenzied staccato. He could stop, go inside, warn Conley Hawkins that she was being watched. He could call the newspaper, an anonymous caller like Pooh Bear, and issue some ominous decree.

Or he could keep driving. He made another loop around the square, passing the truck for a second time. It still hadn't moved. The driver was waiting, biding his time. Buddy decided he would do the same.

55

"Okay," Grayson said, emerging barefoot from her office. "I just hit the Send button on issue 2 of *The Silver Bay Beacon* digital edition."

"Yay." Conley was slumped down in her chair. She looked around the office. Michael had clocked out an hour earlier at Grayson's insistence, and Lillian was long gone. Now it was just the Hawkins sisters, in a room littered with grease-stained pizza boxes, empty Diet Coke and Red Bull cans, and trash bins overflowing with multiple discarded drafts of stories prominently featured in the digital edition of *The Silver Bay Beacon*.

Conley felt as grimy as the office. She wanted to go home, take a bath, walk on the beach, drink an entire bottle of wine, and then sleep for a week. But all of that would have to wait. She stood up, yawned, and stretched.

Grayson slung an arm around her sister's shoulder. "We should do a victory dance, don't you think?"

"Too tired," Conley said. "But we did good tonight, right?"

"We did awesome. All of us. Even Rowena, in her own way, bless her heart." Grayson squeezed Conley's shoulder. "I'm so proud of you, Conley. I know I never tell you that, but I really am."

"Thanks," Conley said. "I'm pretty proud of what we achieved together these past few days."

"Okay, then get out of here. Go home and get some sleep."

"And what about you? You can't keep sleeping on that ratty sofa. And you can't keep on living here in the office, Gray. It's not healthy. I'm not driving all the way out to the beach tonight. I'm too tired. I'll stay over at Felicity Street. I can use the Wi-Fi there to finish my freelance piece and sleep in my old room. At least come over there with me tonight. Okay?"

"Maybe I will."

The response surprised Conley. "For real? I was sure you'd tell me to shut up and mind my own business."

"I'll be over after a while. It's only nine out on the coast. I want to call Tony."

"That's great. What will you tell him?"

"That the grass needs cutting. And my back needs scratching. And that I want us to take another shot at making this marriage work and maybe even have a baby."

Conley raised an eyebrow. "All that plus cutting the grass? That's a lot to ask, Gray."

"I know. I miss the guy, And even if you don't stay here at the *Beacon*, I know now that we can make it work, somehow. I got a good piece of advice recently, about asking for help when you need it. And accepting that help, with grace. I'm gonna work on that."

Conley hugged her sister. "That sounds like a great plan. Guess you really are the smarter sister. Okay, I'll head over to G'mama's now. I have absolutely got to have a shower."

Conley called her grandmother from the car and left a message on her voice mail, knowing Lorraine probably would have left her cell phone plugged in on the kitchen counter.

"Hi, G'mama. Sorry to call so late, but we finished putting out the special edition, so I'm going to spend the night at Felicity Street and try to get some work done. I'll see you in the morning."

The air inside the house was stale and overly warm. Conley felt only slightly guilty about turning the thermostat down before trudging upstairs to her old bedroom. After digging around in the closet and dresser, she found a pair of hot-pink gym shorts, an oversize Silver Bay Beach Club T-shirt, and some panties whose elastic had given up the ghost sometime earlier in the decade.

She stayed in the shower until every inch of her flesh was scrubbed and scoured and shriveled and pink, then toweled off and slathered herself with lotion before dressing.

Winnie had done a depressingly thorough job of cleaning out the fridge and pantry before decamping for the beach, but Conley rummaged around the kitchen and the dining room sideboard until she found an overlooked box of saltines and a bottle of Wild Turkey with a Christmas gift tag addressed to her grandfather still attached to a red ribbon around the bottle's neck.

She dropped four ice cubes in one of G'mama's cut glass old-fashioned tumblers and poured two fingers of bourbon over the ice. Sipping her drink, she made her way to the dining room, where she'd dropped her backpack.

Her cell phone rang, and she reached for it but didn't answer when she saw the words unknown caller on the phone screen.

Conley opened the waxed paper sleeve of crackers and dipped one in the bourbon. It tasted surprisingly good, but the trick was to remove the cracker from the liquid before it disintegrated in the bourbon.

She was munching on her second cracker and thinking about how to take the *Beacon* story she'd written earlier and recast it for the *AJC* when her phone rang again. She shook her head and opened her laptop.

The third call from an unknown caller came less than a minute later. It was nearly 1:00 a.m. Annoyed, she stood up and went to the living room window, peering out at the driveway. Where was Grayson? Conley wasn't afraid of being alone in the house, but she was irritated that her sister was apparently choosing to sleep on the sofa in the office for another night, and annoyed at the string of nuisance calls.

Still, she walked around the house, double-checking that all the doors were locked. Then she picked up her phone and dialed the Silver Bay Police Department nonemergency number. Instructed to leave a recorded message to be answered during office hours, she did so.

"Hi. This is Conley Hawkins. I'm staying with my grandmother, Lorraine DuBignon Conley, at 38 Felicity Street, and I want to report that I've been getting harassing and threatening anonymous phone calls. The calls could be coming from a disgruntled reader, since I'm a reporter at *The Silver Bay Beacon*. Just now, there were three from an unknown caller in the space of five minutes. Please have a detective call me at this number as soon as possible."

A vintage white Corvette with working press tags was never meant for covert ops, Buddy realized, as he crept along behind the black pickup. Luckily, the truck's driver seemed oblivious to the fact that he was being tailed. The truck had parked, briefly, on Felicity Street, just down the block from the house where Conley Hawkins had parked her Subaru. Buddy breathed a sigh of relief when, about five minutes later, the truck pulled away from the curb. Just in case, he continued trailing the truck. The driver made two stops, one at a drive-through ATM downtown, and a second at the Toot 'n' Tote convenience store.

Buddy had parked the Vette on the other side of the gas pumps in order to stay out of his quarry's sight. He shifted uncomfortably in the cracked red leather seat. He needed to take a leak, but he didn't want to risk entering the store. In the end, he jumped out, sprinted over to a dumpster, and relieved himself.

He'd just slid back into the seat when the truck's driver emerged from the convenience store. He was drinking a forty-ounce bottle of beer and held a paper sack with his free hand.

The driver was a bulked-up white dude, dressed, like Buddy, in all black—black tactical pants, motorcycle boots, and a black T-shirt whose fabric strained over the guy's outsize biceps. Unlike Buddy's shirt, the front and back of the truck driver's shirt had SWAT printed in bold, four-inch-high yellow letters.

"Shit," Buddy whispered. It was the cop, the same one he'd seen at Waffle House. He wasn't a local cop, because Buddy made it his business to know every cop who worked for either the city or Griffin County.

And now the truck was on the move again. Buddy waited until the cop pulled onto the road and followed, hoping his past-midnight vigil would come to an end soon. He needed to get back to the apartment, pick up Hi-Fi and his stuff, and hit the road. With any luck, he'd be rolling into Daytona Beach by sunrise. He'd find a cheap motel room, get some sleep, and, in the morning, start looking around for a new gig.

Shortly before two, Conley dragged herself—and her laptop—to bed. She'd rewritten her piece for the Atlanta paper, focusing more on the national angle and the bizarre ongoing Robinette family feud, and throwing in, for good measure, some of the backstory on Symmes Robinette's role in defending the railroad against cancer claims in Plattesville.

Once this funeral story died down, she vowed to take a trip over to Plattesville and then to the county courthouse to dig into whatever records she could find about the lawsuits arising from the chemical waste dump there.

She couldn't resist checking the *Beacon*'s Facebook page. Michael had posted links to the digital edition, as well as some of the video footage he'd shot outside the church. It had only been a few hours, but the story had already gotten nearly 800 views, 120 likes, and 40 comments. Tomorrow, she thought, she'd read the comments.

Her eyelids felt like concrete blocks. She set the laptop on the nightstand and turned off the lamp.

Sleep came immediately. When her phone rang sometime later, she fumbled for it in the dark and groggily answered without checking the caller ID.

"Hello?"

No answer. Just heavy breathing. And then that voice again. "You're dead, bitch."

Her scalp prickled, and her pulse quickened. She sat up in bed and looked wildly around the room.

For what? Conley thought. This anonymous caller was obviously trolling her, hoping to get a reaction out of her. And it was working. Because she was scared.

This time, she dialed 911 and got another recording. "You've reached the Silver Bay Sheriff's Office. If this is a nonemergency, please hang up and call back during office hours. If you do have an emergency to report, stay on the line, and a dispatcher will be with you momentarily."

"Shit," Buddy whispered when he realized the cop was headed back toward Felicity Street. This was not good. As the truck approached the house with the Subaru in the driveway, the driver cut the headlights. He drove slowly past the house. The front porch lantern was lit, but no other lights burned from inside the house.

Buddy cut the Vette's headlights and pulled into the driveway of a cottage with a FOR SALE sign in the driveway. Unlike the other homes on the block, this one had no outside lights. The lawn and shrubbery were overgrown, and a handful of yellowing newspapers still encased in plastic bags poked out from a rusted mailbox.

"Now what?" he wondered aloud. The truck hadn't stopped at the reporter's house and hadn't circled back. So where was it? And what should he do now?

"Nine-one-one," the female dispatcher said. "What is the nature of your emergency?"

Conley hesitated. "I'm alone, at my grandmother's house, and I've been receiving harassing, anonymous phone calls all evening. Just now, a man called and said, 'You're dead, bitch.' And then he hung up."

"Address and name?"

"Conley Hawkins, 38 Felicity Street. In Silver Bay. I called earlier and left a message on the nonemergency line, asking that a detective call me, but this feels different."

"Do you feel threatened?"

"I do," Conley said, her voice tightening.

"And you don't know the caller's identity?"

"No."

"Okay, ma'am," the dispatcher said. "I'm going to send a patrol unit over there, just to check things out."

"Thank you," Conley said fervently. "Thanks so much. I feel kind of silly."

"You're not being silly. You're being cautious," the dispatcher said. "What's your name again?"

"Conley Hawkins."

"Well, Conley Hawkins, you sound like you might be the age of my daughter, so I'll tell you what I always tell her. Stay inside. Don't open the door to anybody unless it's an officer. And you call me right back if you need me. Okay?"

"Okay," Conley said meekly, blinking back tears. "I will."

She sat very still, crouched in the dark, in the middle of her childhood bed for a minute or two, feeling vulnerable, even cornered, two emotions she despised with all her heart.

"Fuck this," she said finally. "This asshole doesn't get to do this to me." She shoved her feet into a pair of flip-flops. She glanced out the bedroom window. The street below was deserted. She turned on the overhead light, then went out into the hallway. Moving rapidly, she opened every door on the second floor, flipping on lights as she went.

When she came to the last door, she stopped and leaned her forehead against the white-painted doorjamb. She hadn't been in this room in years. Six years, to be precise.

It had been a warm summer night like this one. G'mama and Winnie were already out at the beach. Grayson and Tony were newly married and living in Tampa. She'd come home to Silver Bay because she was worried about her father. He hadn't been answering her phone calls, and he'd lost a lot of weight, according to her grandmother.

"I don't think things are going well at work. That big bank from Charlotte swallowed them up, and now they keep sending consultants down here, telling Chet how to run a bank he's been running all his grown life," G'mama said. "He hardly eats, and I know he's not sleeping, because I see lights from under his door at all hours of the night."

She'd timed the surprise visit for Father's Day, taking extra care picking out his gifts—a biography of Franklin Roosevelt that he'd mentioned wanting to read, a box of his favorite chocolate-covered cherries, and, as an inside joke, the most hideous necktie she could find, a puke-green satin number with a repeating pattern of purple armadillos.

That Saturday, she'd parked behind her father's Chevy and used her key to unlock the front door. The house was unusually quiet—no radio playing in the kitchen or television playing in the den. She walked through the downstairs rooms, calling for her father.

"Dad? Daddy?" He wasn't in the backyard either. She climbed the stairs, wondering if he was napping, which would have been totally out of character for her father, who claimed he was unable to sleep during daylight hours.

She stood outside his bedroom door. For it was *his* now. Some of Melinda's clothes still hung in the closet, and the room still held the king-size bed they'd shared, but everybody knew Mrs. Chet Hawkins was not coming home again.

"Dad?" she called, tapping on the door. "Are you asleep?" When there was still no answer, she'd turned the knob. He was stretched out on the bed, his face turned away, toward the window, the empty bottle of pills still clutched in his now cold, stiffened fingers.

Conley clenched her teeth together, opened the bedroom door, glanced around, and flipped the light switch. The room was empty except for some boxed-up books and old bank files.

She closed the door again and ran downstairs, moving through the rooms, switching on lights. In the den, she turned the television on, comforted by the high volume. She went into the kitchen and rechecked the back door.

Her phone was tucked into the pocket of her shorts.

It had been ten minutes since she'd called 911. Plenty of time for a police cruiser to be dispatched from anywhere in the city. What was taking so long? She could feel the tension ratcheting up.

This was stupid, she decided. Skelly was two doors away. Yes, it was a ridiculous time to call somebody, but Skelly cared about her. If she called, he would come, and it wouldn't matter what time it was.

She scrolled through her contacts until she came to the *K*s.

When the doorbell rang, it startled her so badly she dropped the phone. She ran toward the door, peeped out the window, and saw the cop. He wore wraparound aviator sunglasses, and a baseball cap shaded his face. He was holding a leather badge holder in front of the window.

Relief swept through her body, and her hands shook as she began to unbolt the door. As soon as the tumblers on the lock clicked, the door slammed violently open. Her mouth opened to scream, but no sound came out.

56

The inside of the Corvette was stifling—like a coffin. Buddy's eyelids drooped, then fluttered. He sat up, shook his head. He had to get out of the car and move around if he was going to stay alert—or else just give up and move on, as the cop driving the pickup had probably done fifteen minutes ago.

He was about to turn the key in the ignition when he saw movement out of the corner of his eye. As he watched, a shadowy figure stepped out of the shrubbery bordering the side of the driveway where Conley Hawkins's Subaru was parked.

The bill of a baseball cap obscured his face, and he now wore dark, wraparound sunglasses, but nothing could disguise his bulked-up physique. He was studying the house, where lights were blinking on, room by room, one after another.

"Shit," Buddy muttered as the cop inched up the driveway. He had to do something. Shit or get off the pot. That girl, Conley, was in trouble. He scrabbled around in the Vette's console, looking for his phone. He heard a dull thud as something bounced on the passenger-side floorboard, and he leaned over to grab for it.

He was still fumbling around in the dark when he heard the crack of wood, and when he sat up, he saw that the door of the house had been kicked in and the cop was inside.

"Shit, shit, shit!" He was frantic. The phone must have slid beneath the seat. He got out of the car and sped around to the passenger side, opening the door and kneeling on the cracked asphalt, groping around, trying to find the phone.

Finally, his fingers closed on it. He dialed 911 and waited.

"Come on, come on." He was staring at the door waiting to see what happened next.

"Nine-one-one," a male dispatcher said.

"I want to report a break-in at a house over here on Felicity Street," Buddy said.

"What's that street number?"

"Uh, I don't know. It's uh, between Liberty and, well, I can't see the sign."

"Can you describe the situation?"

"Hell yes," Buddy said. "There's a woman in that house, and a cop just kicked in the door."

"Sir? That's one of our officers. He was dispatched to that address after the resident called for assistance."

"No," Buddy insisted. "This guy, he's been stalking this woman. I watched him—he's been following her for the past week."

"Okay," the dispatcher said, sounding unconvinced. "I'll let the officer on the way to the scene know about your concern."

"So do you have a cop on the way?" Buddy asked. He sounded hysterical, he knew.

"Yes, sir."

"Well, where the hell is he? This guy just kicked in the door."

"He's en route," the dispatcher said.

Conley stared up at the black-garbed figure who'd just forced his way into the house. She'd been knocked to the floor when the door flew open.

The cop. She knew him. Popps. He was Skelly's friend, the deputy who'd been at the crash the night Symmes Robinette was killed.

He grabbed her by the forearm and jerked her upright, and she yelped. "What are you doing?"

He smiled, his perfect white teeth gleaming in contrast to his deeply tanned face.

"Hey. You wanna hang out now?"

It was the voice. The same voice on the phone.

"Why?" she managed, still in shock. "Why are you doing this?"

He squeezed her arm, and she yelped again in pain. "I asked you out. I asked nicely. You think you're too good to date a cop?"

"No. Why are you doing this? I don't even know you." She looked around, wondering what had happened to her phone. She'd been about to tap Skelly's number. Had the call gone through?

"What are you looking at?" He saw the phone on the floor and brought his boot down on it with full force. "Sorry, no phone-a-friend for you." He laughed. "Why am I doing this?" he asked in a singsongy voice. "You got me fired, bitch."

"I didn't," she protested.

He grabbed a handful of her hair and twisted it so hard she screamed in pain.

"You told Goggins I screwed up the Robinette investigation."

"No," she said.

"Not even a suspension. The sumbitch fired me. You know what that does to my career? I'm in the shitter. All because of you."

"I didn't get you fired," she repeated.

"So maybe you do like me. Cool. Let's hang out. Like at my place." His eyes skimmed meaningfully down her body. "Or we could just stay right here. Bedroom's upstairs, right?"

"I called 911," Conley said, willing herself to stay calm. "Right after you called. There's a patrol car on the way."

He shrugged. "So we'll go to my place."

"No!" she yelled. "I'm not going anyplace."

He looked around the living room with its polished antiques, thick carpets, and gilt-framed family portraits. "Nice house. You got a nice house out at the beach too. Is that where your grandma's at?"

Conley felt a ripple of terror shoot up her spine. He'd been watching her. That night when she and Skelly were on the beach. Skelly had joked about G'mama peeking out the windows, but it was him. Walter Poppell.

"Come on," he said, pulling her toward the door. "Let's go for a ride. Maybe we'll take a moonlight walk on the beach. Hey, why don't we do it in the dunes?"

She knew with an absolute certainty if he got her out of the house, she was dead. She had to stall him, no matter what it took.

"Get out!" she screamed. "Get out and leave me alone!"

He slapped her with such force she was knocked off balance. Her ears were ringing, and she felt a warm trickle of blood slide down her cheek.

"Leave me alone," she sobbed, kicking out at him.

Poppell yanked her to her feet. She screamed again, and he clamped a hand over her mouth and began dragging her toward the door.

Conley closed her eyes and opened her jaws and bit down on his hand, feeling his flesh tear, tasting the hot salt of his blood.

"Bitch!" He howled and slapped her, but she hung on, attacking him with the only weapon she had like a crazed, rabid dog.

Suddenly, she felt cold metal pressing against her temple. She opened her eyes. He had a gun to her head. She heard the click as the hammer was drawn back.

"I'll fucking shoot you," he said, his voice hoarse. "I'll splatter your brains all over your grandma's pretty house."

With the gun to her head, he dragged her out the door and onto the porch.

"Oh shit," Buddy muttered, seeing the cop emerge from the house. He saw the glint of metal. "Oh shit. Dude's got a gun."

He glanced wildly up and down the street. Quiet as a graveyard. Not a soul around. No flashing blue lights. It was the oldest joke in the world, and it was suddenly the unfunniest oldest joke in the world. Where were the cops when you needed them?

The girl was kicking and dragging her feet, but the cop seemed unfazed by her struggling. Where was he taking her? He must have parked his truck on the block behind the house and cut through the backyard. If he got her in his vehicle, no telling where he'd go or what he'd do to her.

Buddy didn't stop to think. He gunned the motor and threw the Vette into reverse, backing out of the driveway with screeching tires. The cop looked up, surprised and maybe confused.

Suddenly, Gregg Allman's ghostly verses popped into his head again. *Screw Daytona. Not gon' let 'em catch the midnight rider,* he vowed.

Buddy stomped on the accelerator, and the Corvette flew down the street. He flipped on his brights and steered the car toward the house, hurtling over the curb, plowing through the thick grass, aiming straight at the cop, who, in his surprise, had relinquished his hold on the girl.

On her hands and knees, the girl was frantically scrabbling backward. *Good. Get away,* Buddy thought grimly. *Get. The. Fuck. Away.*

The cop planted his feet apart, knees bent, both hands clutching the gun, which was aimed straight at the car.

"Shit, shit, shit," Buddy muttered. He kept his foot on the accelerator, even as he heard the crack of the shot, saw the bright flash from the gun's barrel, and—the very last thing he saw—the Vette's windshield spiderwebbing.

The white Corvette kept moving straight at them. In desperation, Conley crawled as fast as she could away from the oncoming car.

Poppell saw it coming, but instead of running, he assumed the stance, holding the gun, straight-armed, in front of him.

She screamed. She screamed until she felt her throat was being ripped in two. She heard the gunshot and quickly looked away, curling herself into a tight ball, head tucked under her arms like a defenseless toddler.

At some point, she realized Poppell's scream merged briefly with hers. And then it stopped. She heard the impact of the Corvette, slamming into the front porch of G'mama's house, and the sharp crack of wood.

When she finally looked up, she saw that the thick plaster columns were split in half where the Corvette came to rest between them. A moment later, the porch roof began to sag and slowly tear loose from the old wood-frame house. As if in slow motion, it crumpled onto the top of the white Corvette, raining timber, shingles, and pieces of framing all around the car.

She was still numb, but she somehow managed to stagger to her feet and wobble over toward the house. When she saw the front of the Corvette, with the working press license tag and the shattered windshield, she gasped.

Averting her eyes past the broken body sprawled on the lawn, she made her way through the debris toward the porch, where she clambered over the bits of boards and plaster.

The driver was slumped sideways, his head covered in blood. She hesitated, then remembered that the driver had not hesitated but had sped up and barreled straight ahead into Walter Poppell and his bullet. She reached in through the open window and gingerly touched a finger to the driver's neck. There was no pulse.

Conley heard the scream of police sirens approaching, and looking toward the street, saw three cruisers streaming toward the house.

"Conley!" The lights on the front of the house were so bright she had to squint, but she knew that voice and ran straight toward it now, throwing herself into Sean Kelly's open arms.

He held her tightly against his chest, stroking her hair, whispering in her ear, "It's over. You're okay. It's over, Conley."

Her voice was muffled by his shirt. She looked up at him. "He's dead, Skelly."

"Poppell? Yeah, I saw."

"Not him. Buddy Bright. He's dead. He saved my life." She shuddered violently. "Poppell would have killed me. He said he was going to. He was watching me, Skelly. I don't know how Buddy knew, but he did. Poppell was dragging me out of the house. He said he'd take me out to the beach and—"

"Never mind," Skelly said quickly. He touched the side of her face. "Your face is bleeding, and it's starting to swell and bruise. I think we need to get you to the hospital."

"No!" She shook her head. "I'm okay. Really. Poppell slapped me is all. I'm fine."

"Ma'am?" A man's voice cut through the far-off sound of more sirens. Two uniformed Silver Bay police officers approached. "Are you the person who called to report an intruder? We need to talk to you, ma'am."

Skelly wrapped a protective arm around her waist.

"I know." Her voice was shaky. "I'll tell you everything. Can we . . . go someplace else to talk? This is my grandmother's house. Maybe we could go around back and go in the kitchen?"

"Do you know who those men are?" the other officer asked, pointing toward the bodies.

"Yeah," she said. "The driver of the Corvette's name is Buddy Bright, and the one on the grass is a Bronson County sheriff's deputy."

"His name is Walter Poppell," Skelly said.

Conley looked up at him again. "I've got to give these guys a statement. But could you do me a favor? Call Grayson. She must have slept at the paper tonight. Tell her what happened here and ask her to send Michael Torpy over. And tell her to tell him to bring the good camera."

57

The kitchen door banged open. "Conley?"

Grayson rushed into the kitchen, nearly knocking aside the Silver Bay Police detective who'd been interviewing Conley. "Oh my God! Are you okay? Wait. You're bleeding. What happened?"

"Sit down," Conley said wearily, gesturing toward the only empty chair at the kitchen table. "It's a long story."

"I'm getting you an ice pack for that bruise on your face," Grayson said. She opened a drawer, got out a plastic bag, filled it with ice cubes, and handed it to Conley. "Put that on your face. I feel horrible. Tony and I talked for over an hour, and then I guess I fell asleep on the sofa. Maybe if I'd been here, none of this would have happened."

"It's not anybody's fault," Conley said. "If you'd been here, he would have waited for another time. Poppell was determined to hurt me. I'm glad you weren't here."

"Who's this?" the detective asked, looking annoyed. He addressed himself to Grayson. "We're working on a homicide investigation here, ma'am, so maybe you could come back later?"

Grayson pulled herself up to her full five-foot-four height. "I'm not going anywhere. I happen to be her attorney." She looked over at her bruised and battered sibling and her expression softened. "And her big sister."

"And my boss," Conley added. "Detective Jefferson, meet Grayson Hawkins, managing editor of *The Silver Bay Beacon*."

"Anything you hear in here is off the record," Jefferson said. "And if you're not okay with that, we can continue this interview at the police station."

Three hours later, Jefferson finally declared himself done with the formal interview. "For now," he cautioned as he stood by the kitchen door. "We'll have more questions after we talk to the sheriff over in Bronson County."

"Where's Michael?" Conley asked as soon as the detective was out of earshot. "Did he get photos of everything? And have you called G'mama yet? I don't want her hearing about this from anybody but us."

"I called G'mama on the way over here from the office," Grayson said. "She's worried, but I assured her that you're okay."

"Can't say the same about the front of this house," Conley said sadly. "You still haven't answered my questions about Michael. Is he outside, shooting?"

"The cops have the whole front yard taped off, but he got some good stuff with the zoom lens. And," she added, pulling out her cell phone, "I got a great shot of Detective Jefferson interviewing you, from right outside the kitchen door."

"That's good. Now Mike needs to start doing some background work on that freak Poppell. He needs to get the sheriff in Bronson County to talk about why he fired Poppell, and then we need his background. I know he went to high school and played jayvee football with Skelly. Find out if he has family here, all of it."

"Hold up!" Grayson said. "Michael is working as hard and as fast as he can. But you need to back off and slow down. When was the last time you slept?"

"Maybe a few hours Friday night?"

Grayson leaned over and placed a hand on each of Conley's shoulders. "I need you to go upstairs and try to get some sleep. The story will still be here after you've rested."

"I'm fine," Conley protested.

"You're not fine. Look at you! You've got cuts and scrapes and bruises on your legs and hands and arms. Your face is swollen. In fact, maybe we should take you to the hospital to get you checked out."

"No way!" Conley said. "I've got a story to write." She flexed her arms and legs. "See? No broken bones. I'm just a little banged up. After a shower and some clean clothes, I'll be good as new."

The kitchen door opened, and Skelly walked in. "Thank God," Grayson said. "Sean, can you talk some sense into my little sister? She barely survived being abducted by a homicidal maniac who was then mowed down by an avenging angel, but she still thinks she's on deadline."

"Conley?" he asked. "Would you listen to me if I tried to tell you to slow down and take it easy? As your sister pointed out, you've had quite a morning already."

"No," Conley admitted. "I promise I'll slow down. Later. Right now, I need two things. A phone and a car. Your pal Poppell smashed my phone, and I'm guessing the cops still have the driveway blocked."

"Where do you think you're going?" Grayson asked.

"Buddy Bright saved my life. He literally took a bullet for me. I think I owe it to him to find out what his story was and report it."

"I'll take you wherever you need to go," Skelly said. "One of Mama's old friends takes her to church on Sundays, then over to the country club for brunch. You can use my phone 'til you get a new one tomorrow."

Grayson shrugged. "I guess I've been overruled."

By the time Conley showered and changed into a threadbare pair of jeans and a T-shirt, Skelly had managed to perform a miracle in the kitchen.

"First we eat," he said, motioning for her to sit at the table. He opened the oven and brought out a cast-iron skillet. The smell of onions and bacon filled the room.

"First, how did you know I was starved?" Conley asked. "Second, where did that food come from? And what is this magical dish?"

"You're always starved," he said, bringing two plates loaded with food to the table. "This is just a simple Spanish tortilla I made with some leftovers from my house. Eggs, bacon, sliced potatoes, some onion, and red pepper."

She took a bite, chewed, and rolled her eyes in ecstasy. "You never fail to amaze me, Skelly. Where'd you learn to make something like this?"

"Pharmacy school," he said, pouring her a cup of coffee. "Like I said, we'd have these study sessions, and everybody would bring potluck. One of the women had spent a year studying abroad in Spain, and she'd always bring this dish. I like it because you can use whatever you've got hanging around in the fridge, and it can be breakfast or lunch or dinner."

"Or brunch *après* a postapocalyptic night from hell," she added. "Who are you really, Sean Kelly?"

"Just a guy, trying to impress a girl he's kinda got a crush on."

"A crush?"

"Yeah. Pretty goofy, huh?"

She leaned across the kitchen table and kissed him on the lips. "I heart goofy."

He caught her face gently between his hands and gave her a lingering kiss before finally releasing her.

She resumed devouring the tortilla, but he put his fork down.

"Can I tell you something? Seriously?" he said.

"Of course."

"Last night, when I saw that car barreling at you, that was the worst moment of my life. Worse than when my dad died. Worse than when the doctors finally diagnosed my mom. I thought I'd lost you, Conley." He exhaled slowly. "I thought I'd lost you, but then, I realized I never really had you. Did I?"

"Don't talk about it like that," she said, shaking her head. "But I still don't get how you even saw what was going on."

"Mom was having a bad night. I finally managed to get her to bed around one, but then I couldn't get to sleep, so I went out, and I was sitting on the porch, just kind of enjoying the peace and quiet. I guess I was looking down the block toward your house, and then I saw the Corvette, parked in the driveway of the Bennetts' old house. Suddenly, the driver revved the engine and shot backward out of there like a rocket. Then he screeched off, and the next thing I knew . . ." He took a sip of coffee. "I've never been so scared in my life."

"Me either," she admitted. "While it was happening, it felt so surreal. I called 911 to report the phone calls, and they said they'd send an officer to check it out, and the next thing I know, somebody's right there, holding up a badge. I was so relieved! I was unlocking the door, but then he kicked it in. Like it was nothing."

"What phone calls?" Skelly said, frowning.

"The calls only started recently. At first I just assumed it was a disgruntled reader. Like, harmless crank calls. It would be a man's voice, and he'd say, 'You're dead, bitch,' and then he'd hang up."

"I should have warned you about Poppell after that night at the wreck," Skelly said. "I saw the way he was checking you out. He was hitting on you, but I thought that was just Popps being Popps. Same old weirdo. Nobody ever took him seriously, back in the day, when he'd say crude stuff to girls."

"He was always like that?"

"Yeah. He kind of had a reputation as a perv even back then."

"Did he ever get into serious trouble?" Conley asked.

"You know," Skelly said slowly, "he did get kicked off the football team, which was weird, because you saw him—he was a beast. I don't remember what the reason was."

"I ran into Poppell a couple of more times when I was at the sheriff's office, working on the Robinette story," Conley said. "He asked me out, and I didn't really think anything of it. I told him I was busy, which I guess made him angry. And then, when Sheriff Goggins fired him, Poppell blamed me."

She took a last bite of tortilla and pushed her plate away. "He'd been stalking me, Skelly. He told me so. He even followed me out to the Dunes. He said he saw us that night. On the beach."

"Jesus! I should have known! I should have warned you about him," Skelly said.

"Stop," Conley said calmly. "It's not Grayson's fault, and it's not your fault. It's not anybody's fault. Clearly, Poppell had some kind of mental issues."

"How does a guy like that get a job with a gun and a badge?" Skelly wondered aloud.

"That's what I want Michael to find out."

"While you figure out Buddy Bright?" Skelly asked.

"With your help."

"What's our first stop?" he asked.

"The radio station. They knew the guy, worked with him, right?"

Neal Evancho sat slumped at the desk in the reception area. "I already told all this to the cops," he said, running a hand through his thinning hair. "He came in here, according to my records, six years ago. Had a good voice, said he'd been in radio a long time, and after I tried him out, I knew he was the goods, so I hired him."

Conley considered this. "Don't deejays usually have tapes from previous jobs? Résumés, references that you check?"

"I was shorthanded," Evancho said. "My night guy just didn't show up one day. I was filling in his slot myself, and I'm getting too old for this shit. Buddy showed up out of nowhere, and I figured, what the hell? He was a godsend. Listeners loved him."

"Let me guess," Conley said. "He worked for cheap?"

"I prefer to say his wage was reasonable. I guess, though, since he's dead, I could tell you that he was a bargain. Never asked for much. Worked whatever shifts I needed, including double shifts. But the deal was, he had to be paid in cash."

"That didn't seem odd to you?" she asked.

"Everything about Buddy was odd," Evancho said. "That dyed-black hair and him never wearing anything except black? The car with the homemade license plate. working press? The guy never slept. He'd get off the late-night shift, drive around all over the place. He was always calling in from some wreck somewhere. I guess he was an old newshound. The station's got a website, you know? We put all the deejays' photos on there, and their bios, but Buddy flat refused. He had some excuse about an ex-wife trying to nail him for alimony."

"What did you do about his paperwork, social security, all that?"

Evancho shifted uncomfortably in his chair. "I can't get into that."

"You paid him under the table, in cash, and there was no paper-work, right?"

"I didn't say that."

"You don't even know if that was his real name, do you?"

"Nobody's real name is Buddy Bright," Evancho protested. "Lots of folks in this business have radio names."

"But don't most station managers and owners actually know their employees' real names?" Conley asked.

Evancho fiddled with a paper clip, bending and twisting it. "You didn't happen to be listening to *Up All Night* last night, did you?"

"No," she said. "I was on deadline at the *Beacon*."

"Right," he said slowly. "The competition. Anyway, I'm not normally up that late, but my lady friend fixed enchiladas for supper, and I had some awful acid reflux. I did happen to be listening. Buddy had a caller—guy called himself Pooh Bear—and he said he recognized Buddy's voice from when he lived in Detroit. Buddy was playing it cool, but then the guy said he knew Buddy wasn't even his name, that it was really Robert Breitweis, that he had killed some girl and then walked away from jail and was a wanted man."

"What?"

"I can tell you *that* got my attention," Evancho said. "Buddy cut the guy off, and then he cut his shift short. Put on one of his old 'Best of Buddy' tapes, and that was it. Didn't even sign off. When my morning girl got here today, the station was locked up tight, and Buddy was gone."

Conley was taking notes as fast as she could. She looked up at Evancho. "Did you tell that to the cops?"

The station owner nodded and sighed heavily. "That detective? I forget his name. He looked the name up on some database he had on his phone and got all excited. Said it was true about Buddy being a fugitive.

Can't hardly believe it. I hate like hell this happened to Buddy. He was born for radio. Not many like that these days. Folks really liked him. We're gonna miss him."

Winnie, Conley thought, would be brokenhearted. Like a lot of other people.

"Did he ever talk about his personal life? Family? Friends?"

"Not really. He knew a lot about music. Could tell you anything about sixties and seventies rock. That's mostly what he talked about. Music. And his car." Evancho gave Conley an appraising look. "That cop told me Buddy saved your life by running over that dude, then ramming it into your house. Buddy must've thought an awful lot of you to do something like that."

"Yeah," Conley said. "Guess so. Do you know where Buddy lived?"

Evancho scribbled an address on a piece of paper. "I had to drop off his pay one time, when he was off work sick. It's just a bitty little apartment, round back of the house."

58

Skelly was in the car, waiting in the parking lot. "Did you get what you needed?"

"Sort of." She gave him a quick recap of what Neal Evancho had revealed about the late Buddy Bright.

"That's pretty damn odd," Skelly said. "What's our next move?"

She showed him the slip of paper from Evancho. "We're going to 505 Oleander Trail."

"That's not too far away. What's there?"

"It's Buddy's place."

The house was a modest, pale-yellow, concrete-block bungalow on a block of modest pastel houses of the same fifties vintage, with jalousie windows and a row of citrus trees in the front yard and an unpaved crushed-shell driveway.

"The guy at the radio station said it's around back," she told Skelly.

They heard the cat's plaintive yowling as they walked down the vacant driveway.

"Sounds like kitty's missing Buddy," Conley said.

The apartment had once been a garage. Conley turned the door handle. It was locked.

"No dice," Skelly said, turning to go.

Conley caught him by the arm. "Not so fast. Let's check around back."

He gave a martyred sigh. "You're going to make me do something illegal, aren't you?"

"You could just stay right here and be the lookout," she said.

"If we get caught breaking and entering, that's called *aiding and abetting.*"

"You don't remember our motto from when we were kids?" she asked.

"'Drink all the beer, smoke all the cigs'?"

"That, plus 'Don't get caught.'"

The cat was barely more than a kitten, black with a white-tipped nose and handsome tuxedo markings. It was waiting for them at the screen door, rubbing its face against the screen. They could see the hook-and-eye latch.

"Hey, kitty," Conley said. "I bet you're missing your Buddy."

"I bet she's missing her dinner," Skelly said, taking a step backward.

"Give me your credit card," Conley said, holding out her hand.

"I've never handed over a credit card to a woman I wasn't engaged to," Skelly said.

She snapped her fingers impatiently. "Cut the comedy. The cops will be here soon."

Conley slid the Visa card through the gap in the doorjamb and easily nudged the hook upward. They stepped inside the apartment, and the cat started yowling even louder, rubbing up against Conley's legs.

They were standing in one main room, probably less than five hundred square feet, that had been divided up into areas for kitchen, living, and sleeping. The kitchen consisted of a tiny, two-burner stove and dorm-size refrigerator. There was a microwave and a sink. Everything was scrupulously clean.

The living room consisted of a sofa that looked like a curb rescue, and a small flat-screen television balanced on top of a plastic milk crate. There was a bed, which had been made, and a minuscule bathroom.

Three more milk crates and a medium-size suitcase were stacked in the middle of the room, along with a cat carrier. Two of the crates held record albums, the third held some books and papers.

She riffled through the albums. Santana, Allman Brothers, Linda Ronstadt, James Taylor. More albums from eighties and nineties. "Guess he didn't think much of contemporary music," she said. "The time machine stopped in 1998 for Buddy Bright."

Conley knelt and unzipped the suitcase. All the clothes inside were black. "He was getting ready to run again," she said with a stricken expression on her face. "But he didn't get the chance." The cat came back, mewing and rubbing against her legs.

She went into the kitchen and opened one of the cabinets.

"You can't just ransack a man's house, even if he's dead," Skelly protested. "Even if he's a fugitive from the law."

"This isn't ransacking. I'm looking for the cat food," she explained. The cupboards held little other than some canned soup, Kraft mac 'n' cheese, and a package of ramen noodles. She opened the cupboard under the sink and found a bag of Friskies.

The cat's bowl was beside the fridge. She poured in the food, and the cat pounced on it.

"Poor thing," she said.

"Okay, you fed the cat—now can we leave?" Skelly asked.

She sat down on the floor near the milk crates and began removing a handful of file folders. "*Now* I'm ransacking," she told her unwilling accomplice.

"I don't like this," Skelly said. He went to the window and looked out, expecting a caravan of armed police to come blazing up at any moment.

"Okay," Conley said. "Go sit in the car. I'll be out in, like, five minutes."

"My mother warned me about girls like you," he said.

She was riffling through a file of old black-and-white headshots. They were all of a younger Buddy, or Robert, or whatever his real name was, and they were a time capsule of the last half of the twentieth century, with a baby-faced Buddy sporting a Beatles bowl cut, to a seventies pony-tail and sideburns, to an eighties mullet and porn-star 'stache.

"Hmm?" she said.

"She warned me about messing around with girls with questionable morals," he added.

"My morals aren't questionable," she said. "They're absolute. I don't sleep with married men, or steal, or cheat. I only lie if it's absolutely necessary." She held up the photos. "These are all from different radio stations. He called himself Robby Breitweis or variations of that every-where he went. The last headshot is from a radio station in Detroit."

"Now we know his real name. Can we go?"

"Soon," she promised.

"Can I ask what you're looking for?"

"Answers."

A minute later, she stood up, dusted off her pants, and grabbed the cat carrier. "Got it," she said.

"What?"

She showed him a yellowing newspaper clipping from the *Detroit News,* dated 1998, which she carefully folded and placed in her pocket. "Grab the cat, and let's get out of here," she said.

"The cat?" Skelly looked officially appalled. "We're not stealing the poor guy's cat."

"He's dead. The cat's hungry. It's the least we can do."

"Can't you grab the cat?" he asked.

"I can, but what's the problem?"

"I'm kind of cat-phobic," he said. "It's a Kelly thing. Going back gen-erations, all the way back to County Armagh. We are not cat people."

"For God's sake," she groused. "Get the bag of cat food, okay?"

Having finished its meal, the cat was curled up in the middle of the bed. She picked it up and placed it gently in the cat carrier.

"Now we go," she told Skelly, walking out the back door with the carrier tucked under her arm.

She turned and taunted him over her shoulder. "Fraidycat."

"Burglar."

"Despoiler of young girls," she countered.

The insults carried them all the way back to Skelly's car.

"Seducer of middle-aged men," he said, taking the carrier and placing it in the back seat.

"You can't be middle-aged," she told him.

"Why not?"

"Because that makes me middle-aged, and I'm not ready for that yet."

"Fair enough. Strike that. You're a cat burglar."

"I'm good with that."

"What's our next stop?" he asked as they drove away from Oleander Trail.

"I think you'd better take me back to G'mama's house. I can get my car and my laptop and go over to the office to start making some phone calls."

"You promised your sister you were going to get some rest," Skelly reminded her.

"And I will. Just as soon as I make some phone calls. I want to try to track down somebody in Detroit who knew Buddy, or Robert, when he worked there."

"And then you'll go back to Felicity Street and sleep. Promise?"

She shuddered. "Not Felicity Street."

"Can I ask why? Is it Poppell?"

Conley closed her eyes. "Yeah. Well, partly."

"What else?" he asked. "Something's bugging you. I can tell."

"It's not really Poppell," she admitted. "Last night, after he called the last time and told me I was going to die, after I called the cops, I went into every room, flipping on the lights. I figured if somebody was out there, they'd think I wasn't alone. And when I got to my dad's old bedroom, I just . . . froze."

"It's hard," Skelly said. "Mama won't go in Dad's office, still."

"I found him," Conley said. "That day. I'm the one who found the body. Nobody else was home. It was supposed to be a surprise. I walked all around the house, calling his name, and then I went upstairs, thinking, well, maybe he was sleeping."

Tears welled up in her eyes, and the next minute she was sobbing. "He was dead! He wasn't supposed to be the one to die. She should have died! She was so selfish, and he loved her so much, and she killed him. She did. When she left the last time, she took everything with her."

Skelly pulled the car over to the curb, put his arms around her, and let her cry. After five minutes, he handed her a tissue and she blew her nose. "I'm horrible, I know. But I'll never forgive my mother for what she did to him. Grayson and I, we had G'mama and Pops, and Daddy, of course, but he was so damn lonesome without her. G'mama said he grieved to death."

"Your dad was a great guy," Skelly said.

She nodded and took a deep breath. "He didn't really die of a heart attack, you know."

"I know."

"How?" She clutched his wrist. "I never told anybody. G'mama knew, of course, but we never talked about it, and we never told Grayson the truth."

"I filled his prescriptions," Skelly said. "He'd been seeing a new doctor after my dad retired. He was on some pretty heavy-duty anti-depressants, which he didn't like. Said they made him feel like a zombie. And he was taking sleeping pills too. I warned him, the last time he got a refill, about mixing the meds. He made some joke about 'the big sleep,' but I didn't think anything of it."

"You've known the truth all this time?" she asked, her voice quavering. "And you never said a word."

"It wasn't my truth to tell," Skelly said, touching her face lightly. "But that's an awful secret for you to carry around all this time, isn't it?"

"I guess." She sniffed and wiped at her face. "Grayson keeps guilt-tripping me about never coming home. I couldn't tell her about Dad. I couldn't tell her how the dread just washes over me every time I think about that night. And then I was in the funeral home, and yesterday, during Robinette's funeral—in the church where Dad was buried from? I think I was having a panic attack. Being in his old room last night?" She shuddered. "I'm not going back to Felicity Street, Skelly. Not after last night."

The cat meowed softly from the back seat.

Conley turned around. "It's okay, kitty. You're not going to Felicity Street either."

"Is it okay for your oldest friend to have an opinion on this stuff?" Skelly asked.

"I guess." She sniffed loudly.

"Maybe you should talk to your sister. Like you just did to me. Get this big, dark secret out in the open, and it won't be so awful."

"I can't," she said, tearing up again.

"You told me," he pointed out.

"You're different. You're Skelly. I can tell you anything."

He kissed her forehead and sighed. "Anything except the one thing I want to hear."

Skelly put the car in gear and drove back to Felicity Street. The police cars were gone, but the front yard was ruined. The lawn was crisscrossed with deep tire ruts, shrubs had been knocked over, and a wrecker was in the process of winching the ruined Corvette off Lorraine's front porch.

Conley's stomach churned. "I think I'm gonna hurl." She threw the car door open, bent double at the waist, and vomited in the street.

"I'll go inside and get your stuff," Skelly said. "I'll put it in your car and back it out of the drive. Will you be okay out here?"

"Yeah," she said, panting. "My keys and stuff are in the backpack, upstairs in my room. Can you please find what's left of my phone? I need the SIM card."

"It's taken care of," he said.

59

Michael was on the phone and typing a mile a minute when she walked into the newsroom. His eyes widened at the sight of her. "Are you okay?" he mouthed.

"Fine," she mouthed back.

She sat at her desk and unloaded her backpack, setting up her laptop, taking out her notebooks and pen, and retrieving the newspaper clipping from her pocket.

LOCAL ROCK JOCK ARRESTED IN DUI DEATH was the headline in the *Detroit News*.

It had been a big story. Robert "Robbie" Breitweis was the morning-drive-time deejay, back in the day when big-market deejays were a big deal in a town like Detroit. According to the newspaper, he'd had the highest ratings in town. Never married but always a fixture at the hippest new bars and clubs in town.

His fall had been fast and hard. She opened the browser on her laptop and began searching for more of the original news coverage. After forty minutes, she had the hard facts. The victim, a pretty teenager, the name of the car dealership where he'd been doing the remote broadcast, quotes from witnesses who said he'd been covertly drinking all afternoon.

They gave Conley a snapshot of the crime and the sentence, but she still didn't know much about the Buddy Bright who'd ended up in Silver Bay, Florida.

She found the name of another deejay, a woman named Kady O'Keefe, who'd worked with him at his next-to-last job at a station in Madison, Wisconsin. After another ten minutes of searching, she found a reference to a Kady O'Keefe who worked at an NPR affiliate in Columbus, Ohio.

"No chance in hell she's working Sunday," Conley muttered, but she made the call anyway, grateful for once for the *Beacon*'s landlines.

She got the expected recorded message, with the instructions that she could leave a message for a station employee by typing in the employee's name on a touch-tone dial.

"Hi," she said. "My name is Conley Hawkins. I'm a reporter for a newspaper in Florida, and I'm calling Kady O'Keefe to ask her about a former coworker named Robert Breitweis. It's kind of urgent, so I'd really appreciate a callback." She left the paper's number and went back to work hunting for clues.

Her phone rang less than five minutes later. She snatched it up. "*Silver Bay Beacon*. This is Conley Hawkins."

"I'm calling for um, Connie, something." The woman's voice was deep and throaty and reminded her of Stevie Nicks.

"This is Conley. Are you Kady?"

"Yes. What's this about Robbie? Has he finally turned up somewhere? I always figured he was long dead by now."

"Were you a close friend?" Conley asked.

"We were an item for a few months, but Robbie was an item with every woman he met back then," she said, laughing. "He screwed anything that moved. Come to think of it, I guess you could say the same thing about me. Not anymore, of course," she said hastily. "I've got grandkids, if you can believe it, so don't quote me on the sex stuff."

"I won't," Conley promised. "But you hadn't been in touch with him in recent years?"

"Nobody that I know of has been in touch with him since he went to prison," Kady said. "Why don't you just come out and tell me what this is all about?"

"I'm afraid he is dead, but it only happened this morning," Conley said.

"You're shitting me! Where was this? Someplace in Florida? How the hell did he end up all the way down there?"

"That's what I'm hoping to find out," Conley said. "He was working at a small local radio station here, using the name Buddy Bright. The station owner said he just showed up a few years ago, and he hired him on the spot."

"And he didn't think to check to see if he had a record? I mean, I think it was a big deal when he walked away from that prison detail. There were billboards with his picture on the interstate."

"As I said, it's a small station in a small town, and we're a long way from Detroit. We're, I guess you'd say, quirky."

"You mind telling me how he died?"

Conley gave her an abbreviated account of the early-morning events.

"Wow," Kady said. "That's, like, mind-blowing. So are you saying he died a hero?"

"I guess I am," Conley said. "I'm trying to put together a story on him. I know the stuff about the hit-and-run, but I'd really like to get some understanding of who he was before the accident."

"He was your typical rock jock," Kady said. "This was before political correctness. Cocky, sexy, full of himself. He could be a lot of fun, but he could be mean too. You never knew which Robbie you were gonna get. Although I will say he had a certain sweetness if you stayed around long enough. Hey, did he still drive a white Corvette?"

"Yeah," Conley said. "The station owner said he treated it like it was his baby."

"That was Robbie. I think he was driving a Vette when he hit that girl. Not the same one, obviously. And did he still dress in all black? I never said anything, but come on, calling yourself the *Man in Black*? How hokey was that?"

"Still dressed in black," Conley said. "I guess that was his trademark. That and the Vette."

"You can't say the guy wasn't predictable." Kady chuckled. "But then, what man isn't totally predictable?"

Conley thought about Skelly and how he managed to surprise her almost every time they were together. "Right," she said for the sake of agreement. "Is there anything else you can think of to tell me about him? Like, did he have family?"

"None that he ever talked about. I think he thought his listeners were his family. That wasn't just bullshit either. He really thought like that."

"Well, thanks so much for talking to me about him," Conley said. "You've been a big help."

Michael had turned around in his desk and was wildly waving to get her attention.

"Can you hang on for a sec, Kady?"

"Okay."

She put her hand over the receiver. "What's up, Mike?"

He held up the receiver of the phone on his own desk. "This is a producer from NBC. She says she's been trying to reach you all morning."

"Selena Kwan?"

"Yeah. What should I tell her?"

"Tell her to hold. I'm almost done with this call." She continued, "Hi, Kady. Anyway, I really appreciate your talking to me. If you think of anybody else who might remember Robbie, can you give them my number?"

"What about the cat?" Kady said abruptly.

"Cat?"

"Robbie loved cats. He always had one. Whatever market he'd get a job in, first thing he'd do, he told me, was go to a shelter and adopt a stray. But they always had to be black. You know, 'cuz he was the Man in Black."

"He did have a cat," Conley said. "In fact, don't tell anybody, but when my friend and I went to his apartment, we found the cat, and we kind of kidnapped it because I didn't want it to end up in a shelter. I don't know what we'll do with her. My family has a dog, and my friend claims he's cat-phobic. We don't even know the cat's name."

"It's Hi-Fi," Kady said. "He told me that one time. Every cat he ever got, it was black, and he named it Hi-Fi. Predictable, right?"

"Can you transfer that call?" Conley asked Michael.

"Sure. But, uh, I gotta give you the heads-up—I went ahead and filed a story about the shooting and everything. Because it's such a huge story. Your name's in it, because, like, you were there. The guy was trying to kidnap you. Grayson gave me the okay. She said you wouldn't mind."

"Oh." She didn't know what to say. She'd interviewed dozens of crime victims over the years, but this was the first time she'd ended up in another reporter's notebook. Of course, it had been her idea to call in Michael, so she could hardly complain that he'd done his job.

"I'll transfer her over."

The phone buzzed, and she picked up the receiver. "Hi, Selena."

"Conley! We just got a Google Alert from Silver Bay about the kidnapping and the shooting and the other thing. I've been trying to call your cell all day. Are you all right?"

"Just a little shaken up," Conley said. "My phone's temporarily out of commission."

"Your colleague Michael? He filed some amazing photos. That one of the car with the porch roof falling down on it? And the body bag in the yard? Unbelievable."

"That's my grandmother's front porch," she said quietly. "And her front yard."

"Oh my God. That makes it worse."

"It doesn't get much worse than what happened this morning," Conley agreed.

"I hate to ask, but are you too shaken up to work? Because I've got a crew on the way down there. We want to do an on-camera interview with you, of course, but from that brief Michael filed earlier, I can tell there's a lot more to this story. I mean, what? A rogue cop? And I understand he was stalking you?"

Conley felt her face flush. "Yes."

"And the deejay, the one who got shot, trying to save your life, he was a fugitive?"

"It seems so."

"I know I keep repeating myself, but this whole thing is so unbelievable. And coming so close on the heels of this whole Robinette story. It's like the Bermuda Triangle of bad news down there."

"Yeah," Conley agreed, remembering her complaint that nothing ever happened in Silver Bay.

"It's too late to get anything out of Atlanta now, but tomorrow I'm gonna fly into . . . Where's the nearest airport?"

"Probably Pensacola," Conley said.

"I'll text you when I land, okay? Wait, you said your phone's broken?"

"Call the office like you just did," Conley said. "I'll be here."

"Unbelievable," Selena said. "You're like my shero. Can't wait to see you again tomorrow."

She hung up the phone.

"Well?" Michael had been unashamedly eavesdropping, but that was typical of every newsroom in which she'd ever worked.

"She's coming down tomorrow, and they're bringing a camera crew," Conley said slowly.

He pounded his desktop. "I knew it. This story is your ticket out of here."

"What?"

"You know, your ticket out. To the bigs. First, the Robinette thing, and now this? You said you were just here temporarily, right?"

"Right. But that doesn't mean I'm going to work for the network. That's a big leap, you know."

"Not for you," he said, ever loyal.

"So. What have you found out about Walter Poppell?" she asked, changing the subject.

"Oh, man. So much. For one thing, he had a juvie record."

"Huh. My friend Skelly played football with him back in high school. He mentioned that Poppell got kicked off the team, but he said nobody ever knew why. It was hushed up. What did he do?"

"Beat up a girl and sexually assaulted her."

"Oh my God," Conley whispered. Her stomach lurched, and she was afraid she'd vomit again. She swallowed hard. "How does something like that get hushed up? How did he get hired as a cop?"

"The girl's mother reported it, and then the girl recanted," Michael said. "He was sentenced to some kind of intervention program for a lesser charge, did some volunteer work, and his record was expunged. Juvie records are sealed in Florida anyway."

"Then how'd you hear about the rape allegation?"

Michael grinned. "I have my sources. People in this town really didn't like the guy. Guess that's why he had to go to Bronson County to get a job."

"Did you talk to Merle Goggins over there?"

"I called, then I drove over there to see him. Goggins wasn't happy to see me, but after I pointed out that it was one of our reporters who'd been assaulted, he relented and gave me a quote."

"What'd he say?"

Michael flipped through the pages of his notebook. "Shocked and disgusted that a former employee had betrayed the public trust. Recently discharged for dereliction of duty. Since juvenile records are sealed, he had no way of knowing about Poppell's past. Like that."

"It's better than nothing," Conley pointed out, turning back to her own story.

"Hey," Michael said. "He said for me to tell you that he's sorry. And I believe him. The dude's not a friendly type, but he asked me to let him know if you need anything. At all. And that's a direct quote. 'Tell her anything she needs, at all, I'm here.'"

60

A VOICE IN THE NIGHT,
LOCAL DEEJAY WAS AN ENIGMA
By Conley Hawkins

For fans like Winnie Churchwell, Silver Bay disc jockey Buddy
Bright was a welcome guest in the kitchen, relaying the local news
and weather reports and playing favorite rock music from the '60s
and '70s during his popular Up All Night with Buddy Bright late-
night shift. In high school football and baseball press boxes, he was
the Man in Black, the familiar voice providing play-by-play com-
mentary for the past six seasons.

Melissa Padgett-Holland, a night-shift waitress at the Waffle
House on State Route 28, knew him only as a regular customer.
As soon as she saw his vintage white Corvette with the distinctive
WORKING PRESS license plate pull up to the front of the restaurant
in the early-morning hours, she'd put in his order for eggs over easy,
crisp bacon, and grits. "Nice guy," Joyner said. "Real easy to talk to;
although he never said much about himself, he'd always ask about
my kids. He'd talk to some of the other regulars here too. And he never
left less than a ten-dollar tip."

Neal Evancho, station manager/owner of WSVR, said Bright showed up "outta nowhere" six years ago, asking for a job at the exact moment Evancho's previous nighttime deejay departed without notice. Bright had no audition tapes or résumé, but Evancho said his new employee was obviously a seasoned pro. "I hired him on the spot."

Like most of Silver Bay, Evancho was shocked to learn of Bright's murder on a quiet, leafy block of Felicity Street on Sunday morning.

That shock was compounded when he learned that the amiable Buddy Bright was really a fugitive named Robert Breitweis, a disgraced Detroit deejay convicted of killing a Michigan teenager in an alcohol-fueled hit-and-run accident. Authorities there say Breitweis was working on a prisoner highway detail in 2008 when he simply walked away into obscurity.

Over his years on the run, Breitweis bounced around small-market radio stations in the Midwest and the South, working under several assumed names, including Buddy Bright.

The sixty-eight-year-old disc jockey was killed by a single gunshot fired by a disgruntled former Bronson County sheriff's deputy as he rescued a local woman the deputy was attempting to abduct.

I am that local woman. My name is Sarah Conley Hawkins. I was born and raised in Silver Bay, and I grew up in that house on Felicity Street. My great-grandfather founded The Silver Bay Beacon, *and I am the fourth generation of my family to work in our family enterprise.*

Until Sunday morning, in the moment before he saved my life, I had never come face-to-face with the man we thought we knew as Buddy Bright.

Brittany Michelle Pakowsky only met the man she knew as Robbie Breitweis once. At seventeen, the suburban Detroit teenager and some friends snuck into a hotel bar in Bloomfield Hills, where they encountered Breitweis, who'd earlier worked a live remote broadcast from a nearby auto dealership. It was December 1998, the week before Christmas.

According to witnesses, Breitweis, who'd been drinking steadily most of the day, plied the girls with frozen daiquiris and invited them to accompany him to a private party. The teens declined his offer and were walking to their car when Breitweis, driving a white Corvette at a high rate of speed, struck Brittany Pakowsky in the hotel parking lot before driving away. The teenager died two days later.

Marlene Pakowsky, Brittany's mother, said she will never stop grieving the loss of her youngest daughter. She still lives in the home where Brittany grew up and keeps a small artificial Christmas tree in Brittany's room, which she lights up every night, year-round.

"I'm not glad he's dead, because he got it easy," Mrs. Pakowsky told me. "I prayed for years that he'd get caught so he'd have to rot in jail. You tell me he's been out there, living, enjoying life, while my baby is cold in the grave all this time? I don't know what to say."

Conley wrote the story in an adrenaline-fueled burst of creative energy, melding her harrowing first-person experience with facts and quotes and observations of an experience she couldn't afford to forget.

At four, she typed the last paragraph, and as she sat back in her chair, overcome with mental and physical exhaustion, she heard a faint mewling coming from the vicinity of her backpack.

Michael whirled around on his chair. "What was that?"

"Oh Lord, I completely forgot she was in there," Conley said guiltily. "She's been traumatized. I couldn't leave her alone in that cat-carrier." She picked up the backpack and brought out the squirming cat. "This is Hi-Fi."

Michael's freckled face lit up as he reached for her. "A stowaway!"

"She's, uh, a rescue," Conley said. "And I guess you could say she's an orphan now."

She confessed the breaking-and-entering episode at Buddy Bright's apartment and repeated her concern that the police, when they finally searched the apartment, would turn the cat over to an animal shelter.

"What will you do with her?" Michael asked.

"I'm not sure. I can't take her home because of Opie, my grand-mother's dog. And my boyfriend claims to be cat phobic."

"You've got a boyfriend? Cool."

Conley felt herself blush as she realized she'd just referred to Skelly, out loud, as something other than a platonic friend.

Michael placed the cat on his desktop, and she promptly curled up in a ball and fell back asleep. "Can I have her?"

"You like cats?" She didn't know a lot of millennial guys who were cat fanciers, but Michael continued to challenge her opinions about that generation.

"Love 'em. We always had cats growing up. The place where I live now doesn't allow pets, but I'm moving in with my girlfriend next week-end, and we've been talking about adopting a cat, so this would be per-fect. I even like her name. Hi-Fi. Kind of retro, right?"

"Very retro," she assured him. "I'm glad you like the name, because if you didn't, I'm afraid that would be a deal-breaker."

He picked the cat up and nuzzled her under his chin. "Awesome!"

"Well, look what the cat dragged in," Winnie said when Conley finally made it back to the Dunes. "Glad you made it before the storm came through."

The housekeeper and G'mama were sitting on the screened porch, looking out at the Gulf, where dark clouds hovered just at eye level.

"You don't know how true that is," Conley said.

"We saved you some supper," G'mama said. "There's fried chicken and butter beans on a plate on the stove, and Winnie's potato salad in the icebox."

Conley shook her head. "Thanks, but I'm really not hungry." She sat down on a wicker armchair beside her grandmother. "I'm sorry," she started, but Lorraine shook her head.

"Enough of that," she said briskly. "Your sister sent me pictures. It's an awful-looking mess, isn't it?"

"Yeah."

"I called my insurance agent, and he's already sent an adjuster over there to take a look," Lorraine said. "Tomorrow, we'll get a contractor to give us some estimates for repairs."

"The whole front porch roof collapsed," Conley said. "That car was going full speed when it hit. I'm afraid it probably damaged the foundation too."

G'mama waved away her concerns. "The only thing of real value in that house is standing right here in front of me. A little worse for wear, but alive. I don't care about anything else, Sarah Conley. It's just things. And things can be replaced."

She pointed out toward the horizon at the breeze blowing the sea oats. "We're lucky to have a roof over our heads and beds to sleep in. And speaking of that," she said, giving her granddaughter an appraising look, "your sister said that as soon as you got home, I should feed you and send you to bed."

"Who died and left her boss?" Conley joked. "Are you putting me in time-out for wrecking your house and beautiful yard?"

"I'm putting you in time-out for working too hard. I'll bet you haven't even eaten today."

"Not true. Skelly fixed me this huge breakfast tortilla with eggs and bacon and potatoes. And he forced me to eat almost all of it."

"I tell you, Sarah, if you don't snap that man up soon, I'm gonna steal him right out from under you," Lorraine said.

61

It felt weirdly liberating and yet terrifying to be untethered to a cell phone as she drove to Bronson County on Monday morning. Conley kept glancing anxiously at the dashboard-mounted clip where her phone was usually anchored.

When she walked into the sheriff's office, she politely insisted that Merle Goggins would want to see her, in fact had requested her presence. The deputy working the desk looked unconvinced, but after a quick phone call, she was ushered into Goggins's office.

"Oh, uh, hi," Goggins said. He pointed at her cheek, where an ugly palm-shaped bruise bloomed overnight. "That happen yesterday?"

"Yes," she said, sitting down.

He winced.

"You owe me," she told the sheriff.

"How do you figure?"

"You hired a psychopath as a law enforcement officer. A mentally unbalanced bully who stalked and harassed and ultimately attempted to kill me."

"First off, I didn't hire Poppell. I inherited him from my predecessor. I was in the process of trying to fire him the first time you encountered him," Goggins said.

"Did you know he had a juvenile record? Of violent sexual assault?"

Goggins rubbed his chin nervously. "You know juvenile records are sealed in this state. The first I heard of this was when I read that story in the *Beacon*'s digital edition this morning."

"Poppell blamed me for getting fired," Conley said. "What was the cause?"

"Dereliction of duty was the official cause. Unofficially, it was chronic laziness and general dumb-assery."

"My sister, who is a lawyer, says we should sue you, individually, and the county," Conley said, crossing and uncrossing her legs.

"Christ," Goggins muttered. "The county attorney would have my ass if he knew I was talking to you right now." He got up and paced around the small office, stopping to wipe an invisible speck of dust from one of the picture frames. "I told that kid reporter, Torpy, I told him to tell you I feel terrible about Poppell. What he did to you. I've got a daughter. She's only fifteen, but if something like that happened to her?" He shook his head. "But that's all I can say about this mess. You understand? If the lawyers get involved, it'll be real bad."

"I don't want to sue you," Conley said.

"No? You don't want your pound of flesh?"

"I don't want to spend years hashing it over, talking about it and reliving the worst night of my life," Conley said. "Poppell's dead. And I guess I believe you when you say you didn't know about his history."

Goggins raised his right hand, palm out. "Swear to God, I'd have fired him my first day in office if I'd known what a sick bastard he was. So if you don't want to sue, why are you here?"

"Just doing my job," Conley said lightly. "I need to know where you are with the Robinette investigation. You said at the funeral that the medical examiner found a toxic combination of fentanyl and alcohol in his system. Does that mean you suspect foul play?"

"You think you're gonna bargain information in return for a promise not to sue me?" Goggins asked, chuckling. "Like this is some kind of bartering situation?"

"Not at all. I'm a journalist. You're in law enforcement. Congressman Robinette's death is a matter of public interest. Now what's the story?"

"Off the record?"

"I'd prefer to be on the record."

He shrugged. "Then it's still under investigation."

"Okay, tell me what's not under investigation."

"He had a shitload of fentanyl in his system. But he was being treated for terminal cancer, and he had a transdermal pain patch, which was prescribed by his doctor."

"Not news," Conley said. "You already told me he was dead when he hit the deer. And that he had a blood alcohol level of .06."

"It's in the medical examiner's report, but that still hasn't been released yet, so you can't say I was the source," Goggins cautioned.

"Where'd he get the booze at that hour of the night?" Conley asked. "I thought Vanessa was keeping him on a pretty tight rein. His neighbor said Symmes had to sneak over to his house just to have a beer."

"Vanessa Robinette was adamant that she'd gotten rid of all the booze in the house. She said Symmes was pretty mad about it, but his doctors told her he couldn't drink. Not while he was wearing that patch," Goggins said.

"I bet the first Mrs. Robinette was more than happy to play bartender to the old man," Conley said. "Toddie never would tell me if he was at the farm that night."

"She didn't want to tell us, either," Goggins said. "But we've got proof that he was there."

"What kind of proof?"

"We tracked his cell phone."

"Charlie said Vanessa took his phone away."

"Somebody gave him a new phone that the wife didn't know about," Goggins said. "I tell you what, this family? Rich folks? These people will turn on their own kin in a heartbeat."

"I'm guessing Charlie gave him a phone," Conley said. "Just to piss off his mother. But how did he get it to Symmes? Vanessa had him locked out of Sugar Key, although he hinted that he'd come up with some kind of workaround, which was how he'd managed the Symmes-and-Toddie reunion in the first place."

"Charlie Robinette hasn't been 'available' for follow-up interviews, but we looked at the video footage from the Sugar Key security gates," Goggins said. "He came and went half a dozen times in the month before his father died. He sailed right through the gates for residents."

Conley looked up from her notebook. "Because he had a transponder. And I bet I know where he got it."

"How's that?" Goggins asked.

"Just a hunch," she said, being deliberately vague. "I'll let you know if it pans out. Tell me more about the alcohol. Did you get Toddie to admit Symmes was drinking that night?"

"Once we told her we had the cell phone records, she became a little more cooperative. She confirmed that Symmes called shortly before midnight. Said he was upset and wanted to talk. She urged him to wait until morning, but he knew Vanessa was watching him like a hawk. According to Toddie, Symmes told her Vanessa took a sleeping pill and went to bed around eleven that night."

"So he took a midnight ramble," Conley said. "I wonder what upset him?"

"Toddie wouldn't say," Goggins said. "Her story is that he got there, they talked, and he wanted a drink. She tried to talk him out of it, because he had to drive back to Sugar Key, and it was late, but he insisted. So she let him fix himself a dirty martini."

Conley laughed. "That's appropriate."

"Toddie Sanderson isn't the most reliable witness," Goggins commented. "First, she said it was just the one drink. Later, when we told her about her ex's blood alcohol level, she allowed that maybe it was two martinis. Okay three, but no more than that."

"Three martinis?" Conley exclaimed. "How was he even standing upright at that point? And she was okay with letting him drive forty-five miles home in the middle of the night? It's a freakin' miracle he didn't hit and kill something much worse than a deer that night. Can you say 'death wish'?"

"Bad decisions don't equal foul play, though," Goggins pointed out. "Seems to me every member of that screwed-up family had a part to play in Symmes Robinette's death. The son was playing mind games with his mama, the wife locked up the husband out of spite, and the ex-wife fed him enough booze to put down an elephant, then let him loose on a dark country road. I can't prove any of this, of course, but I guarantee, it all boils down to money."

"Symmes Robinette had a lot of it too," Conley said. "He was a millionaire many times over. It'll be interesting to see how all of this shakes out when his will is probated."

"Blood money," Goggins said, his expression serious. "They might get their hands on his money, but those same hands will have his blood all over them."

"Guess I'd better get back to work," Conley said. "Deadlines, you know."

"You going to be writing about any of what I just told you?" he asked. "Remember, all of that was off the record."

"Deep background," Conley said. She held out her hand, which was still scratched and bruised, and the sheriff, though looking surprised, clasped it.

"I'd tell you to take care of yourself," he said, "but I guess you already proved you can."

She had one more stop to make before she headed into the *Beacon* office, where she was sure Grayson would be frantic, wondering about her whereabouts.

There was only one car in the parking lot at the funeral home. Mondays, she guessed, were slow days for dead people.

Conley heard Graceanne's giggle echoing in the high-ceilinged hallway and followed it until she reached the marketing director's office.

The little girl was sitting on the floor, playing with a pair of stuffed unicorns. Kennedy McFall was staring intently at a computer terminal, chewing on a pencil. She looked up at the sound of footsteps and frowned when Conley appeared in her doorway.

"I don't want to be rude," she started to say.

"Then don't." Conley sat without being invited. Her grandmother would not have approved. "Are you in the habit of breaking into people's cars and stealing jewelry?" she asked, her face and voice pleasantly bland.

"I have no idea what you're talking about," Kennedy said. She was a terrible liar, which didn't bode well for her future as a political wife, Conley thought. But then, maybe Vanessa could give her lessons.

"Sure you do. You were at the country club one day, and your fiancé was venting about how pissed he was that his mommy was denying him access to his daddy. I guess you parked next to a car with one of those Sugar Key decals on the windshield, looked in, and saw a transponder sitting there in the cup holder. It must have seemed like the perfect crime of opportunity. The car was unlocked. You were right there, nobody was around . . ."

"That's insane. Are you accusing me of being a petty thief?"

"Technically, it's not petty theft. Those diamond earrings you took were worth more than $25,000. So that's a felony. I don't know about the cost of a Yeti cup and a transponder, but I think the police could look that up."

Kennedy glanced down at her daughter. "Look," she said, her voice low. "I don't know what you've got against Charlie, but you're dead wrong about him. And me. I never took any earrings. There weren't any earrings in that car."

"The owner filed a police report that said the earrings were there."

"The owner's a friggin' liar," Kennedy said. "I'm telling you I didn't take any earrings."

Graceanne looked up, interested. "Mommy. I want my earrings. I want to play dress-up."

"Not now, honey," Kennedy said. "Why don't you go in Granddaddy's office and get some paper from the printer. Then you can color him a pretty picture."

"A picture of earrings," Graceanne said. "Purple earrings."

"Whatever," Kennedy said, making a shooing motion. "Okay, what's your point?" she asked when the child was out of earshot. "What's the big deal? Yes, I borrowed the transponder. Vanessa was being such a bitch. Charlie knew she was cooking up some plot against him, poisoning his dad's opinion of him. He just wanted to see his dad. Talk to him before he was gone. Is that so wrong?"

"You mean, talk to Symmes and tell him he'd found his long-lost ex-wife and kids? Maybe stir up a little trouble in paradise?" Conley asked.

"Symmes was thrilled to get a chance to reconnect with his family. It had been eating at him for years, the way Vanessa forced him to abandon them. We knew he only had weeks to live. It was an act of mercy."

"Do you really believe that bullshit?" Conley asked. "C'mon, Kennedy. You're a smart girl. When was the last time you saw Charlie do something—spontaneously—out of the kindness of his heart?"

"He's wonderful with Graceanne," Kennedy said. "And she adores him."

"You haven't answered my question. So I'll answer yours, the one you asked me earlier. You want to know what I have against C. Symmes Robinette Jr.? He's a fraud. A charming, entitled, vicious fraud."

"No. He was just a kid when the two of you had your silly little breakup. He told me about it. He's changed in ways you can never appreciate."

"Skunks don't change their stripes, Kennedy. I'll tell you what really happened, if you're interested. I came home from boarding school the summer before my freshman year of college. Symmes and Vanessa had shipped Charlie off to military school for reasons nobody ever disclosed, but I guarantee it wasn't because he was interested in marching and drilling. I didn't really know him, but I was hanging around the pool at the club, and I thought he was cute, and the other girls thought he was quite the catch. He asked me out a couple of times, and I went, but then on our second date, when he tried to get in my pants, I told him no. He was furious but polite. Took me home at nine o'clock. The next thing I know, he's texting all his guy friends, telling them about how I pulled a 'train'—you know what that is, right?"

Kennedy's face paled a little. "Group sex. Charlie wouldn't do that. He probably thought it was a joke."

"It wasn't a joke," Conley said, looking her straight in the eye. "Guys were calling me up, saying the vilest, most obscene things you can imagine. They drove past my house at night and tossed packages of condoms in the yard. In my grandmother's yard, Kennedy! Somebody keyed the side of my car—they wrote WHORE in foot-high letters. I didn't have a lot of girlfriends in town before that, because I'd been away at school, and people thought I was some kind of snob. After Charlie started that rumor? They thought I was a slut and a snob. Everybody believed that shit. He made my life a living hell because he could. That's the kind of man you're engaged to."

"I don't believe you," Kennedy said, her lips quivering. She blinked back tears.

Graceanne was back now with a sheaf of printer paper in her chubby hands. She plopped down onto the floor, found a basket of crayons, and began scribbling away.

"That's your choice," Conley said, speaking in a low voice. "But ask yourself why I'd lie about something like this. Ask yourself about this clan of vipers you're about to marry into. Take a good, long look at that family tree. Symmes Robinette walked away from his wife and kids after he got Vanessa pregnant. He might have been feeling pangs of regret three decades later when he was facing his own mortality, but he was perfectly content to leave Toddie for the next shiny thing that came along. And then there's Charlie's mama, Vanessa. You've seen firsthand the kind of evil she's capable of."

"You have no idea what it's like to be a single mother in this town," Kennedy said, twisting the diamond solitaire engagement ring around and around on her finger.

"And the Robinettes are rich, right? Well, financially rich but morally bankrupt," Conley said. "I've seen Symmes's recent financial disclosure statements. *Filthy rich* is the applicable term here. The old man made his first millions defending his pal Miles Schoendienst's railroad after they poisoned dozens of people with toxic chemicals stored at a switchyard they abandoned in Plattesville."

She looked up sharply. "What about Plattesville? My aunt and uncle lived there."

"Did they die of cancer?" Conley asked.

"My uncle did, but he was a heavy smoker, and this has got nothing to do with Charlie and me."

"Okay," Conley said wearily. "I've got to get to work. I only stopped to see you as a courtesy call today. That first time we met, right here in this office, I thought, 'She seems pretty nice. Smart, funny, somebody I'd want to be in a book club with.' Believe me, Kennedy, you are better off single than with a man like Charlie Robinette. You deserve better. And so does your daughter."

She stood up to go.

"Bye-bye," Graceanne said, smiling and waving a purple crayon.

Kennedy followed her to the front door. "You're not going to tell anybody about the transponder, are you? It could be bad for Charlie's campaign."

"You ever steal anything before? I mean, as an adult?"

"God, no!"

Conley gave her a pitying smile. "That's the thing, Kennedy. You stay around slime long enough, it doesn't wash off. Pretty soon, you're doing slimy stuff too. Have a nice life, okay?"

62

"Where have you been?" Lillian demanded when Conley walked into the *Beacon* office. She snatched up a handful of pink message slips. "People have been calling you all morning long. You can't answer your own damn phone? You think I'm your secretary or something?"

Conley took the message slips. "I've been working. Following leads. Doing interviews. I couldn't answer my phone because it got smashed yesterday."

"Nobody ever tells me anything," Lillian grumbled. "How's your face?"

"Beat to hell," Conley said. "Thanks for asking."

"Go buy yourself a new phone, okay?" Lillian said. "And your sister wants to see you in her office."

"Is this like a trip to the woodshed?" she asked, slumping into the chair in Grayson's office.

"Why do you always assume the worst with me?" Grayson asked.

"Maybe because we don't have a long history of pleasant interactions in this office?"

Conley was leafing through the message slips and stopped when she saw one from Roger Sistrunk, her old boss at the *AJC*. Lillian had misspelled his name as *SISSTUNK* and written in all caps: "WILL YOU PLEASE CALL THIS ASSHOLE? HE'S CALLED HERE FOUR TIMES LOOKING FOR YOU."

"Not today," Grayson assured her. "I read your piece about Buddy Bright this morning, and I honest to God cried."

"You cried?"

Grayson was a notorious non-crier. When she was ten, she'd accidentally gotten her finger slammed in a car door and had been so stoic about the pain that it wasn't until her fifth-grade teacher sent a note home from school that the family discovered she had a broken finger.

"I did. It was poignant and sad and surprising. And I usually hate first-person in a newspaper story because I find it treacly and self-indulgent. But not this time. Conley, it was just so . . ."

"Non-sucky?"

"Definitely non-sucky. I had Michael upload it to the website this morning. We've had over six thousand likes already."

"How? We don't have anywhere near that many followers."

"I know. But Michael, our boy genius, has been working his magic on social media, tagging *The Detroit News* and everybody else he can think of. The story's gotten picked up by a ton of newspapers around the country."

"Maybe that accounts for all the phone messages Lillian just handed me," Conley said.

"I know your hotshot NBC producer called and left word that her flight landed and she and her camera crew would be here after lunch," Grayson said.

"Do you have a problem with that?"

"No. Why do you always assume I'm going to yell at you?"

"Because you usually do?"

"Not this time. As awful and traumatic as yesterday was for you, it's great publicity for the *Beacon*. It turns out that Buddy Bright had a huge, loyal local following. People are really responding to your story. Lillian signed up a couple of dozen new subscribers this morning."

"Then it's all good," Conley said, turning to leave.

Grayson put a restraining hand on her arm. "Not all of it. G'mama's insurance agent called me a little while ago because we're in Rotary together."

"I was surprised G'mama wasn't more upset last night, but she said the house is insured so she wasn't too worried about it," Conley said.

Grayson's face had a pained expression. "We heard from a contractor this morning. When the porch ceiling collapsed, it pulled away part of the siding on the front of the house. Conley, he says the house is absolutely ridden with termites."

"But they can, like, spray or tent it or something, right?" Conley asked.

"It's too late to spray. We've got three different kinds of infestation—subterranean, flying, and Formosan termites. He went all around the house. He says the foundation is like swiss cheese, the rafters up in the attic are crumbling, the window frames, everything."

Conley collapsed back onto her chair. "Does G'mama know? What are we gonna do?"

"She knows," Grayson said. "I had to be straight with her. And I don't know what we'll do. This contractor said it'd be cheaper to pull the whole house down and start from scratch."

"Can we get another opinion?"

"We can, but I met the contractor over there after he called. You can take a stick and poke it right into the foundation beams. Same with the windowsills. I think it's true. It's just a matter of time before the whole damn house crumbles."

"Will the insurance cover that?"

"I doubt it. G'mama says she used to have a termite bond, but she let it lapse after Pops died because she thought it was just another unnecessary expense."

"Is she devastated?" Conley asked. "I mean, her grandfather built that house. She's lived there her whole life. Our whole lives."

"I was more upset than she was," Grayson said. "G'mama seems to roll with the punches."

"I guess if the house can't be saved, she'll rebuild?"

"She says not," Grayson reported. "She says she's been thinking for a while now that having two houses doesn't make sense at her age. She loved Felicity Street, but the stairs were getting harder and harder for her and Winnie to manage, especially with the laundry room down in the basement. At least at the Dunes she has the elevator, and the laundry room is on the same floor as the bunk rooms."

"You said the Dunes was a firetrap," Conley pointed out. "The wiring, the roof . . ."

"I know. But if she sells Felicity Street, that's a double lot on the best street in town. The contractor this morning told me flat out he'd buy it to build a spec mansion."

"Conley!" Lillian poked her head in the doorway. "There's a whole TV crew out front looking for you. If you and your sister aren't too busy jib-jabbing in here maybe you could come out and talk to them."

"Coming," Conley said.

Selena explained her idea in the car on the way to Felicity Street. "I basically want you to humanize your newspaper story. I mean, it was great, but you distanced yourself from the subject matter. In your story, you were an observer, not a participant. I want you to stand in the living room and talk about how it felt, the moment the deputy kicked in the door—that's okay, right? I mean, it's your family house, right?"

"Whoa," Conley said. "I don't know that my grandmother wants to invite the whole world into her living room. That seems icky. And invasive."

"But it puts the viewer right there, with you, in the moment," Selena said. "I get chills thinking about it."

"Maybe so, but my grandmother is a proper Southern lady, so no."

Selena brushed back her fringe of dark shining bangs in frustration. "Well, that puts a crimp in my plans."

"You're welcome to shoot outside the house," Conley said. "After all, I'm sure most of Silver Bay has driven past it today to take a look for themselves."

She pulled the Subaru to the curb, and the network van pulled up behind them, outside G'mama's house. The carnage looked even worse a day later. The velvety green expanse of lawn looked like a stock car dirt track with countless crisscross tire marks. The carefully tended borders of azaleas, camellias, and boxwoods had been knocked down by all the police cars and rescue vehicles. Worst of all, Conley thought, was the pair of deep trenches that ended in the collapsed front porch.

Selena clapped her hands in excitement. "You're right. This is way better. My God, it looks like a tornado hit."

They got out of the car.

"When were you thinking of doing your hair and makeup?" Selena asked.

"It's done," Conley said. "I've showered. My hair is clean, I'm wearing eyebrow pencil and lipstick, and my clothes all match. I'd call myself a fashion triumph."

"Hang on a sec." Selena went back to the van, where the camera operator was unloading his equipment, and came back with what looked like an airline-approved carry-on suitcase on wheels.

"Let's go inside the house and, uh, freshen you up a little," she said.

Conley took a final look at herself in the bedroom mirror. Her hair had been hot-rollered, back-combed, and sprayed. Selena had used an actual airbrush to apply a thick coating of foundation to her face, followed by face powder, blush, bronzer, and contouring. She was wearing four shades of eye shadow, eyeliner, eye pencil, lip liner, lipstick, and multiple coats of mascara.

"I didn't wear this much makeup when I was my sister's maid of honor," she told the producer. "But I notice you didn't cover up the bruises on my cheek."

"We want viewers to really see your injuries," Selena explained. "But I only brought the basics because I know you print gals are into minimalism. You'll have to get used to it if you're going to do this for a living."

"Who said I'm doing this for a living?" Conley asked.

"Let's talk after we've finished the shoot," Selena said.

They positioned her in front of the collapsed porch, and Selena ran through her directions.

"Just relax and look directly into the camera. Give us a summary of what happened and how you felt. I'll ask you a few questions, but the camera will be focused on you."

Conley had done a few television interviews over the years, so she wasn't unused to the glare of a camera, but being interviewed as a victim was a new and unwelcome experience.

"Tell us how you felt when you realized that the man who'd stalked and terrorized you after you'd spurned his advances was dead," Selena prompted.

"I wasn't happy. It was a horrible experience, but I never wanted him dead. I just wanted him to leave me alone. I guess I was mostly relieved."

"Now, your newspaper has reported that the man who attacked you, Deputy Walter Poppell, had a juvenile record for sexual assault, is that correct?"

"Yes," Conley said. "My colleague Michael Torpy talked to a law enforcement source who confirmed that after being charged with beating and assaulting a girl as a young teen, Poppell was sentenced to some kind of public service in a juvenile intervention center, and afterward, his record was expunged."

"And yet he was hired by the Bronson County Sheriff's Office as a deputy. Do you think the sheriff's office should be held accountable for the actions of Deputy Poppell?"

It was a question Selena hadn't asked her during her brief run-through.

Conley thought back to Merle Goggins's concern for her well-being and his final words to her earlier that morning, when he'd clasped her hand and told her to take care of herself.

"No," she said slowly. "Juvenile records are sealed in this state, and the sheriff assured me he had no knowledge of Poppell's history. But I do think every person who ever looked the other way when a 'boy' like Poppell made a lewd comment or sexted pictures of a classmate should be accountable. Every coach who let an athlete play despite knowing he was a violent bully is accountable. And every parent who refused to acknowledge or discipline a child for those kinds of behaviors is accountable. I don't think men like Walter Poppell are born like that. I think they mutate."

Selena Kwan was hopping up and down in her excitement. "That was perfect! I knew it! I knew you'd be a natural in front of the camera."

Conley thought she'd never felt as unnatural in her entire life. She'd been nervous and sweaty and felt like a stranger in her own skin.

"Thanks, I guess."

"Believe me. That was great. Part of the reason I came down here today was to see for myself, but now I have. Here's the situation. One of my reporters is going out on maternity leave. The slot is yours if you want it. Great timing, right? And you'd be back in Atlanta."

"I don't know. Can I think about it?"

"What's to think about?" Selena asked. "I have half a dozen other candidates right now—seasoned, on-camera talent who'd give their left boob for this slot. We'd give you a three-month trial, reporting, producing, lots of enterprise stuff, which I can see is right in your wheelhouse."

"I'm flattered, really," Conley said, "but I've got a lot going on in my life right now."

"Somebody else made you an offer already?" Selena asked. "I can pretty much guarantee that our offer will be much more than you'd ever make at any print outlet in the country."

"I did get a lot of phone messages this morning, after the story was picked up," Conley said, "but it's not really about the money."

The producer shook her head. "People always say it's not about the money, but it actually is about the money. Every time."

"Maybe I'm the exception," Conley said.

The camera operator was waiting in the van.

"Well, give it some thought, then," Selena said. "But I'll need to know in the next week or so."

63

Conley walked back inside the silent house. Already, she thought, the scent of disuse and decay had begun to settle like a thin layer of dust. Or maybe that was her. She walked around the kitchen and living and dining rooms, letting her fingers trail across the lemon-scented mahogany, the polished silver candlesticks, and the gilt-framed family portraits.

Upstairs, she sat on the bed in her old room, looking out the window at the treetops. She went to the bookcase in the corner of the room and picked out her childhood favorites—*Little Women,* because, like Jo, she intended to be a writer one day; her favorite Maud Hart Lovelace Betsy-Tacy books, because Betsy wanted to be a writer too; and *Anne of Green Gables,* because she'd always loved Anne Shirley's fierceness and ambition.

There was nothing else she needed from this room now, Conley thought. G'mama had told her that the contents of this beloved family home had just been things—things that could easily be replaced. But these books had been what Anne Shirley would call her "boon companions."

She tucked the books in an old canvas tote bag and walked down the hall to her father's room again. This time, after switching on the light, she went inside and sat down on a heavy wooden packing crate. She waited for the familiar tightness in her chest. But it never came. This was just a room now. She felt lighter. Skelly had been right. He'd been right about a lot of things.

Conley called Roger Sistrunk from the phone on her desk.

"About damn time," he said as soon as he picked up. "You playing hard to get all of a sudden? We've all been trying to reach you. Me, Tia, even Kevin. Calling, texting, emailing, but nothing."

"Sorry. My phone was destroyed in the, uh, incident yesterday. What's up?"

"Wanted to make sure you're really okay," he said, his tone gruff. "That was a hell of a story you filed last night. Really powerful stuff."

"Thanks. Not an experience I ever want to repeat."

"Hey," he said abruptly. "The thing is, we've got an opening on the national desk, and before we post it officially, I thought I'd give you first shot."

"On the national desk? I've only ever worked city-side."

Michael Torpy spun around on his desk chair. The kid had no shame about eavesdropping.

"We know that, but these stories you've been writing in that little one-stoplight town, you've shown me you're more than ready."

She stared pointedly at Michael until he finally turned back around.

"I'll have you know Silver Bay has three stoplights. When would you want me to start?" she asked.

"Right away. You can pack up today and be back at your old desk here in Atlanta tomorrow."

"And the pay?"

"Awww," Roger protested. "Are you gonna try to jack me up for a raise after all we've been through together?"

"As a matter of fact . . ." Conley started to say. Her gaze traveled past Michael and landed on Grayson's office. The door was open, and she glimpsed her sister, gesturing dramatically. She was talking to someone. Conley half stood and saw that Rowena Meigs was seated on the chair opposite Grayson, with Tuffy perched in her lap.

From her standing position, she saw that Michael was working on the *Beacon*'s website, adding photos he'd shot earlier in the day of a beauty pageant at the local nursing home and a Little League baseball game.

"Conley!" Lillian yelled from across the other side of the newsroom. "Damn it, Conley, I got two more calls waiting on you. Get yourself a phone, you hear? I don't have time to be messing with your personal business."

"Hawkins?" Sistrunk was still talking. "You there?"

"I'm still here, Roger. But on second thought, never mind."

"Never mind the raise? Okay, if you're gonna be a prima donna, maybe I can squeeze another fifty bucks a week out of the budget."

"Never mind the job, Roger," she said. "I love you for offering it, and I will always appreciate everything you taught me, but I think, for now, I could do more good someplace else."

"Damn it! You're taking a job with the network, aren't you? I knew it. Listen to me, Hawkins. You'd hate TV . . ."

She walked over to Lillian's desk and picked up her messages. "A messenger came by while you were on the phone and left a package for you," Lillian said.

"Where is it?"

"It's outside. You been pissing off a lot of people in this town lately. I'm not fixing to get blown up by one of them pipe bombs," Lillian said.

Conley found a manila envelope leaning against the brick planter box by the front door. It felt too light to be a pipe bomb, so she slit the flap open with her thumbnail and shook the contents out. It was a plastic transponder. There was no note, but she didn't need one.

Rowena sailed past Conley's desk, slowing only to glare at her before exiting the building.

"What's up with Rowena?" Conley asked, sitting in the doorway of Grayson's office. "She shot me some major stink eye out there."

"She came in mad at me because she finally figured out you've been rewriting her column so that it's actually lucid, and then I went and pissed her off even more when I told her no more dictating to Lillian or handing in typewritten columns. I told her she either learns how to use a computer or she hits the bricks."

"Dayyyyumm, Gray. All of a sudden, you're a hard-core badass."

"Not badass. Just fed up. How did the television shoot go?"

Conley sat on the chair across from the desk. "Okay. But it was weird to be talking about myself on camera."

"I guess you'd better get used to it," Grayson said gloomily. "Michael says he's sure they offered you a job."

"Michael needs to learn to be a little more discreet with his eavesdropping," Conley said.

"They did offer you a job, didn't they?"

"Yeah."

Grayson shrugged. "Congratulations, I guess."

"I told her I'd think about it," Conley said.

"And?"

"After they finished the shoot out front, I walked all over the house. I sat in my old bedroom and picked out a few of my favorite books. And then I walked down the hall to Dad's room and went inside."

Grayson looked puzzled. "There's no furniture or books in there. G'mama cleared it out years ago."

"I know. There are some old files from the bank, and I guess some of Pops's files."

"Are you upset? That we're probably going to have to demolish the house?"

Conley shook her head. "No. I hadn't been in Dad's room since the night he died."

"Ohhhh." Gray sighed the word. "I forgot. You found him, right?"

"Yeah." She looked down at her hands and then back up at her sister. "The thing is, Gray, I never told you. G'mama knew, of course, but I never told anybody, until Skelly. And I didn't really tell him. He mostly guessed."

"Told me what?"

"It wasn't a heart attack, Gray. Dad . . . killed himself. He took an overdose of pills."

Grayson nodded. "That makes sense."

"That's it?" Conley exclaimed. "You're not shocked or appalled or, I don't know, horrified?"

"No. Maybe I should be, but I'm not. It was selfish of me, but at the time, I was maybe a little relieved."

"Jesus, Gray!"

"He'd been so sad, so lonely, for so long. You were closer to Dad than I was. You were always his baby. By the time he died, Tony and I were just starting our life together, and you were at a new job. I secretly always wondered if maybe he'd finally given up on waiting for Mom to come home, but I guess I really didn't want to know the truth."

"And I wished I didn't know it," Conley admitted.

"That's why you hardly ever came home, right?" Gray asked.

Conley nodded. "I've dreaded it," she whispered. "Being in that house, just down the hall from where I found him. And then this stuff with Symmes Robinette happened. I had to go back to that same damn funeral home and even the same church. I swear, Gray, sitting in that pew Saturday, I thought I was going to hyperventilate. Even Michael noticed I was acting weird."

Grayson walked over and knelt on the floor by her. "Honey, why didn't you say something? Why didn't you tell me about Dad? I'm your sister. You should have told me."

"I thought it was my fault. I knew how depressed he was, but I went off and took a job out of town and told myself it would be all right. I've felt so guilty. Maybe if I'd been around more, I could have done something, been there for him."

"No." Grayson was emphatic. "You couldn't. No matter how much we loved Dad, we couldn't save him. Nobody could."

"How can you know that?"

"How can you not and stay sane? Here's the truth, Conley. Dad's gone. It's okay to grieve for him, but you and I have got to move on. I don't want to be like G'mama, hanging on to a landline, hoping that someday my daughter will magically call home and ask for forgiveness."

"How do you do that?" Conley asked. "How am I supposed to move on when I still wake up in the middle of the night, hearing his voice?"

"You don't do it by running away," Grayson said.

"I'm not."

Grayson looked dubious.

"I don't want to work for the network. At least not full-time. And I don't want to go back to work for the Atlanta paper either. I've done that already."

"Soooo?"

"I was thinking," Conley said slowly. "What if we can find a way to make the *Beacon* solvent again?"

"How would *we* accomplish that? The last week has been an amazing morale booster for all of us, but less than a hundred new subscribers and a handful of new advertisers aren't gonna cut it."

"We've gotta look for new ways to do community journalism," Conley said. "Maybe we look for investors—not to buy us out but to partner with us. There are grants too. I've read about several foundations that are funding small-scale investigative journalism projects. And if we can hang on to our boy genius out there, maybe he can help us figure out how to monetize our social media."

"That all sounds really promising," Grayson said, "but I don't want you thinking you have to give up your career to save the *Beacon* out of some misguided sense of guilt. There's been enough of that in this family."

"What about you? You gave up a law career to come home and run this paper, and you've sacrificed everything to try to save it. Why are you sticking around?"

"Because I believe in what we're trying to do? Because this is my home, and I want to make this a better place to someday raise my own family?"

"Does that mean you and Tony are on again?"

Gray looked at her watch. "His plane got in a little while ago. I promised him I'd make sure there was gas for the lawnmower and that I'd be home for dinner tonight—deadline or no deadline."

"Sounds like a sensible plan," Conley said. "Speaking of deadlines, guess I'd better get over to the cop shop and pick up the incident reports for this week's police blotter, huh?"

"It's already done," Gray said.

"By whom?"

"Our new police reporter, Lillian King. She's got a lot more free time now that she doesn't have to retype Rowena's column. Why don't you go on out to the Dunes? I think we can cut you a little slack this once, considering what you went through this weekend. In fact, that's an order. Go home."

"Thanks. I've got one last loose end to tie up, and then I will."

She called Skelly from her desk phone.

"Hi." He sounded surprised to hear from her.

"Hi yourself. I realize this is short notice, but I was wondering if you'd care to have a late dinner with me tonight?"

"I'd love to if I can get my mom's caregiver to stay late. But that shouldn't be a problem. What time and where?"

"The Dunes. Can you make it by seven?"

"What can I bring?"

"Anything at all, as long as you're there by seven."

64

The bird dogs announced her presence at Oak Springs Farm before she'd even climbed out of the Subaru.

Toddie was seated on a rocking chair in the shade of the porch, sipping from an ice-frosted glass. "Hush!" she hollered. The three dogs ceased their barking and settled themselves in a semicircle around their mistress.

"Hi there," she called as Conley climbed the steps. "What brings you all the way out here to the country? Heard you had some excitement in town last night."

"*Excitement* is one word for it," Conley said. She pointed at the chair next to Toddie, who had not invited her to sit. "I've got something on my mind, and I wanted to run it by you," Conley said.

"Go ahead."

Conley sat down anyway. "I spoke to the sheriff this morning about how Symmes was killed."

"Damn deer."

"Well, that and the fentanyl. Mixed with a pretty substantial amount of alcohol in his bloodstream," Conley said.

Toddie rocked backward in her chair and crossed a slender leg. She was still dressed for work, in blue jeans and a polo shirt with OAK SPRINGS

FARM embroidered above her breast. With her deeply tanned complexion and snow-white hair held back with a knotted bandanna headband, she looked like something from a *Garden and Gun* ad.

"Did you come all the way out here to tell me how my ex-husband died? I could have saved you the trip, because I talked to the sheriff myself today."

"No, I came out here because I have a theory—not about how he died but why."

"Symmes died because he had end-stage non-Hodgkin's lymphoma. He was an old man, and his body was worn out from all the meds," Toddie said. She reached out a hand and scratched the nearest dog's ear.

"I think there was more to it than that," Conley said.

"Do tell."

"A man I know in Silver Bay—a man who blamed his mom's death on Symmes Robinette—told me he spotted Symmes a while back, sitting in a Waffle House just down the road here, holding hands with a pretty, much younger woman. This man—who has a good reason for hating your ex—snapped a picture of the couple with his smartphone. And then, because he assumed the young woman was Symmes's new girlfriend, he emailed the photo, out of spite, to Vanessa."

"I'll bet that frosted her fanny," Toddie said, chuckling.

"I'm sure it did, but only because she recognized the younger woman as your daughter Rebecca, whom Symmes had been seeing on the sly," Conley said. "Vanessa is nothing if not intuitive, and I think she figured out pretty fast that the old fox had outfoxed her."

"Vanessa told you all this?"

"No, but I'm pretty good at putting stuff together."

"You seem good at spinning an entertaining yarn, I'll give you that."

"It gets better," Conley promised. "Vanessa had already tightened the screws and cut him off from Charlie, but she didn't count on Symmes and his midnight rambles. I think after she saw that photo, she confronted him about seeing you and the kids."

"This story is getting pretty wild," Toddie said. "Sounds like a novel. Not that I have time to read a lot of fiction. Because unlike the lovely Vanessa, I have to work for a living."

"It would make a good novel, wouldn't it? Anyway, here's how I think it played out. I think Vanessa somehow found out Symmes deeded the farm over to you. Now, I admit, I'm not sure *how* she found out. I wouldn't put it past the Little Prince telling her, just to rub her nose in it."

"The Little Prince?"

"Charlie."

"Hahaha," Toddie laughed hoarsely. "That fits."

"Glad you agree. Of course, it could be that Symmes confessed it himself. I hear he was looking for redemption in those last days. However it happened, here's what I think went down that night. I think Vanessa flipped all the way out when Symmes admitted he'd literally signed away the farm to you. As you say, he was sick and weak. Maybe she begged, maybe she threatened, but I'm wondering if Vanessa didn't wear Symmes down to the point that he changed his mind about giving away a piece of real estate worth close to two million."

Toddie kept rocking and sipping her drink. "Does this story of yours have an ending? 'Cause I'm getting pretty bored with all these theories of yours."

"Obviously, it ends with Symmes dying from a fatal mixture of fentanyl and dirty martinis. After which, he hits a deer, his car bursts into flames, and suddenly, there's a House seat up for grabs," Conley said. "And his ex-wife falls into a very valuable piece of property."

"Which was rightfully hers anyway," Toddie said.

"But let's not forget the penultimate part of the story. We know for a fact that Symmes waited until Vanessa was asleep that night, and then he took one of his midnight rides. He came to see you, didn't he?"

"I already told the sheriff he did."

"Only after the sheriff told you they'd tracked Symmes's movements that night through his cell phone. And when the sheriff told you Symmes had alcohol in his bloodstream, you eventually admitted you'd played bartender for him."

"Vanessa didn't just cut him off from his friends and his son, she wouldn't even let him have a damn drink. It was pure meanness. I mean, he was dying. What difference was a martini going to make?"

"Not just one martini. Two, possibly three," Conley said. "And I think you knew what difference it would make, since you knew he was wearing a fentanyl patch."

"How would I know something like that?" Toddie asked. "I'm not a doctor." She shot out of the rocking chair with surprising speed for a woman of her age, her formerly placid face flushed with anger. The dogs sat up on their haunches, attentive to the sudden change in mood.

"I've been real patient with you today, out of respect for who your family is, but now I'm going to ask you to get off my property before I lose my temper."

"I bet you lost your temper that night, after Symmes told you he wanted to back out of giving you Oak Springs Farm," Conley said.

"Off my porch!" Toddie said, her mouth twisting into a snarl. One of the dogs let out a low growl and crept closer, until it was almost on top of her moccasins.

Conley stood up, her face inches away from Toddie's. "It was easy to give him one martini, then two, maybe three. And then send him on his way, zonked out of his head on fentanyl and gin. I guess it's lucky for all of us that the only other living thing that died that night—other than Symmes Robinette—was a deer."

"We'll never know about that, will we?" Toddie said. Her demeanor was shockingly calm again. Lethally pleasant. "Because there were only two people in the room that night. And one of them is dead. Vanessa can fuss and cuss and threaten to sue all she wants. I let her win, years ago, because I didn't have any choice. I had young kids to raise and no money of my own back then. It's different now."

"Charlie and Vanessa don't want a court battle with you, do they?" Conley asked. "Not with their political ambitions."

"I'm the wronged party," Toddie agreed. "How would it look if they took me to court? Me, a kindly, white-haired grandma who just wants to live out her life on her farm, with her dogs and her family? Totally harmless. Sometimes, you know, age has its privilege. People almost always underestimate you."

"At their own peril," Conley said.

"You'd best be going now," Toddie said. "Before I forget my good manners."

The dogs followed her to the edge of the porch. "Stay," Toddie said. They all did, wagging their tails in unison as Conley walked out to her car and drove away.

65

Winnie and G'mama had a new jigsaw puzzle spread out on the dining room table. It featured snow-covered mountains, delicately frosted trees, and a variety of snow-loving birds and other wildlife.

Conley peered down at it. "What's that supposed to be?"

"It's either the Alps or Maine," Winnie said, slotting together two corner pieces. "I get all those cold places mixed up."

G'mama picked up the box top and waved it in her friend's face. "It's Alaska, you old fool. Pay attention."

"We saw you on television tonight," Winnie said excitedly. "You looked real cute, once I got over how awful the yard looks at the house."

"Gray said the contractor doesn't think the house can be saved because of all the termite damage," Conley said. She glanced over at her grandmother, who was sipping her drink and studying the puzzle.

"I gave myself exactly an hour to feel sad about it, and then I made up my mind that I won't be sad anymore," Lorraine said. "Termites didn't take the things I care most about. So we'll sell the lot and use the money to put some air-conditioning in this house."

"And a dishwasher, praise baby Jesus," Winnie added.

"You did look cute on TV," G'mama said. "Should wear your hair like that all the time."

She paused, then continued. "By the way, I talked to your sister before you got home. She tells me you've got something important to tell me."

"She's such a tattletale," Conley said. "I guess she also told you I'm planning on staying on to work at the paper."

"She did mention something like that," Lorraine admitted. She snaked an arm around her granddaughter's waist. "That's the best news I've had all year."

"You might not be happy with some of the stories I want to write," she warned her grandmother. "I'll probably be rocking some boats and pissing off a lot more people."

"Good," Winnie said approvingly. "This town needs shaking up."

"I might need your help, though, Winnie. I want to write a big piece about that cancer cluster in Plattesville and the railroad's history of denying responsibility. I'd like to find more families, besides yours, that were affected."

"I'll put you in touch with Randee, that lawyer lady," Winnie said. "She's got everybody's names and all their medical records. I hear from her every year, on the anniversary of the day Nedra died."

"Okay. That'll be my first project, now that I've got a little job security. On a lighter note, what do we have in the refrigerator that I could cook for dinner tonight?" Conley asked. "Preferably something simple."

"Your grandmama and I had a late, big lunch, so I didn't fix us anything for dinner tonight," Winnie said. "You might could find some leftovers in there if you look around."

"Have you got company coming?" Lorraine asked, playing coy. She picked up a puzzle piece and twisted and turned it, trying to fit it in a slot where it obviously didn't belong.

"I invited Skelly to come out and watch the sunset and have dinner."

She could almost see her grandmother's matchmaking antennae quiver. "Any special occasion?"

"Every sunset is special, especially the night after you thought you might not get to see another one," Conley said.

Winnie put together another corner of the puzzle. "I picked the last of the baby lettuce from the garden this morning and some sweet little cherry tomatoes. And there are a couple of fillets in the fridge. All you need to do is sauté some shallots in some butter, add in some of the mushrooms from the crisper drawer, then drop in a good-size knob of blue cheese. Deglaze the pan with some white wine, and that'll make a pretty fancy steak sauce for a Monday night dinner."

"Perfect!" Conley said.

Lorraine picked up the cut glass tumbler with the dregs of her sun-setter and pounded it on the uncooperative puzzle piece. "You know, sometime soon, you're going to have to learn how to cook a proper meal if you're ever going to find a man to settle down with."

"You never learned how to cook, and I seem to recall you did just fine in the husband department," Winnie pointed out. She snatched away the offending puzzle piece, which showed a portion of a mountain goat's head, and put it in its rightful place, on the other side of the puzzle, atop a mountain goat's body.

G'mama glared at her. "Times are different now. That's all I'm saying."

Conley picked up a rounded corner piece and offered it to her grandmother. "What if I told you I think I already found a man to settle down with? And he happens to be a way better cook than I'll ever be?"

Lorraine held up her empty glass and jiggled what was left of the ice cubes. "I'd say this calls for a toast."

He arrived early, with a slightly wilted bouquet of zinnias in a fruit jar and a large brown paper bag, and Conley couldn't decide if she loved him more for the early arrival or for the gift of groceries.

G'mama eyed the zinnias with suspicion. "Are those flowers from my garden in town?"

"Yes, ma'am," Skelly admitted. "Mama wanted to walk down and see your house, and before I could stop her, she'd picked every single flower in your garden."

"Well, it would have been a shame to let a bulldozer knock 'em down," Lorraine said. "What's in the sack?"

He handed it over. She reached inside and pulled out an ear of corn.

G'mama sniffed it appreciatively. "Mmm. Fresh Silver Queen. I know that didn't come out of my garden."

"No, ma'am. I stopped at the farm stand on the way out here," he said.

"Save me an ear, and I'll have it for breakfast," G'mama said, standing up and giving him a peck on the cheek.

"You're not having dinner with us?" he asked.

"I wasn't invited," G'mama said. "Winnie and I are going to sit on the porch and watch the sunset before our programs come on. You're welcome to join us."

"No, thanks," Conley said, taking his arm. "We'll be on the beach if you need us."

They left their shoes at the base of the stairway and walked barefoot down the path through the dunes to the little cove.

Conley plopped down onto the swing and patted the seat beside her as an invitation.

Skelly crossed his arms over his chest and cocked his head, trying to read her expression. "No sunset beach walk before dinner?"

"Not enough time," she said, pointing toward the horizon, where the sky was streaked with vivid violet and orange and periwinkle and half a dozen other colors whose names she couldn't currently remember.

"Just look at that," she said softly. The Gulf had turned from green to deep blue, but it was lavender now, barely rippled, and the fading sun cast a reflected orange stripe on the surface of the water.

Skelly sat down and stretched his arm around her shoulders. "I know how you love your sunsets. But is there something special about this one tonight?"

"I hope so," she said. She lifted his hand from her shoulder and kissed the palm of it.

He looked startled for a moment. "Seems like you have something important on your mind."

"Very important," she agreed, laying her head on his shoulder and snuggling close beside him.

She stayed like that, listening to the rise and fall of his breathing, studying the curve of his jaw, his profile, the barely gray stubble of his beard. She reached up and removed the sunglasses perched on his nose.

"Why'd you do that?"

"Because I want to see your eyes," she said.

He blinked rapidly. "They're the same eyes you've been looking at your whole life."

Skelly's eyes were brownish-greenish with flecks of black and luxurious lashes that she'd never appreciated until lately.

"You're right," Conley said. "Maybe it's my eyes that have changed. Maybe I'm finally seeing you the way I should have seen you all along."

He kissed her. "About time. Now what's all this about my eyes?"

"I want to be looking right at them when I tell you I love you, that's all."

He grasped her shoulders with both hands. "You love me?"

She nodded. "Yeah. Maybe I did all along. Maybe I was waiting all this time, to come back home and finally discover the man of my dreams was actually the boy next door."

Skelly pulled her closer and was about to kiss her again, when she put a finger to his lips.

"Hold on," she said. "Isn't there something you want to tell me?"

"Oh." He gave it a moment's thought. "Is this the part where I tell you that I've been here all along, trying to convince myself I could somehow be happy with somebody else but at the same time patiently waiting for you to finally come home and fall in love with the skinny guy down the block who broke your heart a million years ago but who was secretly in love with you all along?"

She smiled. "Yes."

She wrapped her arms around him and fell into him, and they kissed. When she looked up, fifteen minutes later, the sun had set, and a million tiny stars spattered the dark velvet sky.

"We missed the sunset," Skelly pointed out. They were reclined on the sand now, and his arm cushioned the back of her head.

"I know, but there'll be others," she said.

"Does this mean you'll marry me?" he asked.

"I think I have to," Conley said, kissing him again. "Because if I don't, G'mama will."

Epilogue

HELLO, SUMMER
By Rowena Meigs

FEBRUARY 19, 2020

My goodness, but February has already been a month of happiness, heartbreak, housewarmings, and all-around change in our charming little village of Silver Bay.

Cupid's arrows were zinging right and left this past year, resulting in a slew of engagements and nuptials.

Most recently the Beacon's *own star reporter and Silver Bay native Miss Sarah Conley Hawkins, daughter of the late Mr. Chester W. Hawkins and Melinda Conley Hawkins, and the granddaughter of Mrs. Lorraine DuBignon Conley and the late Woodrow Conley, exchanged wedding vows with Mr. Sean Patrick Kelly, son of the late Dr. Patrick Kelly and June Sewell Kelly.*

Sean, of course, is also a Silver Bay native and the owner-manager of Kelly's Drugs, a Silver Bay institution, who grew up two doors down from his blushing bride, who now prefers to be called Conley. Like many modern career gals, Conley says she will keep her maiden name as a tribute to her late father Chet, who was the longtime president of the now-defunct Silver Bay Savings and Loan.

The nuptials took place on Valentine's Day, at sunset on the beach behind the bride's grandparents' home, The Dunes. Officiating at the service was the bride's close friend, Branson "Butch" Culpepper, of Atlanta, who became a minister for the event. The blushing bride was breathtaking in a tea-length silk organza gown with exquisite hand-beaded pearls over imported French lace, which was handed down to her by her maternal grandmother, who wore it at her debutante ball. The bride's bouquet consisted of a rosette of miniature palm fronds, white roses, and gardenias from the family garden. The groom wore a blue suit accented with a red bow tie which was his late father's favorite. Neither wore shoes.

The bride's sole attendant was her older sister, Grayson Hawkins Willingham, who wore a floral silk tea-length dress accented with a bouquet of miniature palm fronds and pink, yellow, and orange roses.

Following the ceremony, guests gathered under a festive tent and enjoyed an unusual repast of barbecued pork, coleslaw, chili dogs, and miniature ice cream sandwiches, all prepared for the reception by cooks from Kelly's Drugs' luncheonette. Dance music was provided by Mickey Mannington and the Mellowtones.

After the newlyweds return from their honeymoon they will be "at home" at the groom's childhood residence on Felicity Street. A sad note to this happy occasion is that the wedding was preceded, by only a month, by the death of the groom's mother, June Sewell Kelly, a beloved lifelong resident of this community, who passed, peacefully, in her sleep, at home. She was sixty-six.

In other Hawkins family news of note, our own Silver Bay Beacon *managing editor and publisher Grayson Hawkins Willingham and her husband Tony recently completed construction of their new home on the site of her grandparents' former family home on Felicity Street, just in time to welcome the arrival of twins Lorraine, called Lolo by her adoring family, and her brother Chester called*

Chet. With Grayson's little sister Conley living just two doors down, and great-grandmother Lorraine a frequent guest, these twins will have plenty of family to cuddle and babysit them.

Although the Hawkins-Kelly nuptials have been in the works for some time now, your columnist admits she was caught off-guard by the whirlwind romance and subsequent marriage of Kennedy Marie McFall to Davis Whelan, of Panama City, the son of Mr. and Mrs. Thomas Whelan. The marriage represents a business as well as romantic union, as the groom's family, who owns a chain of funeral homes in Northwest Florida, have acquired McFall-Peeples Funeral Home. The bride will assume the role of marketing manager for the newly formed partnership. Some may recall that Kennedy, the daughter of Mr. and Mrs. George McFall, was briefly engaged last year to our town's most eligible bachelor, Charlie Robinette.

And speaking of whirlwind, Vanessa Robinette stunned many here when she eloped recently with retired entrepreneur Osbert Tracy, less than a year after the death of her first husband, U.S. Rep. Symmes Robinette. Mr. Tracy, 80, is the billionaire founder of PayDay Pawn. A little bird tells us that the two lovebirds met through the online dating site Silver Singles, following Vanessa's unsuccessful bid for her late husband's seat in Congress. The new Mrs. Tracy has sold her oceanfront mansion on Sugar Key, and the couple will reside in the groom's home in Palm Beach.

Vanessa's estranged son Charlie Robinette has also quietly pulled up stakes and put his home here on the market, following his upset defeat in the general election by the Democratic candidate, popular Bronson County Sheriff Merle Goggins. Charlie has reportedly accepted a position with a Washington, D.C., firm of lobbyists.

Also saying a temporary farewell to our fair community is former railroad titan and would-be political king-maker Miles Schoendienst, who is due to report to federal prison following his conviction for mail and insurance fraud. The charges stemmed from Schoendienst's filing of a spurious insurance claim last May, following *a theft from Miles's Mercedes while it was parked at the Silver Bay Country Club. Among the items he claimed stolen from the unlocked car was a pair of $36,000 diamond and sapphire earrings belonging to his wife. The insurance company filed charges against Miles after receiving a photograph of Candace Schoendienst, Miles's vivacious wife, wearing the "stolen" earrings at a campaign fund-raiser for Charlie Robinette, sent by an anonymous source.*

And now, dear readers, for a farewell of my own. Your longtime correspondent has decided to hand over the reins of Hello, Summer to her respected Beacon colleague Lillian King. But not to worry, Tuffy and I will still be keeping you filled in on all the local Silver Bay social notes as we start an exciting new chapter in our lives. I am pleased to report that we'll be live and local on radio station WSVR with our brand-new Sunday night broadcast Talk of the Town with Rowena and Tuffy! So, #TTFN. (That's ta-ta for now!)

Acknowledgments

Although this is a work of fiction, as always, I am indebted to many who were so generous and cooperative in sharing their knowledge and expertise while I conducted the research needed to build the universe of *Hello, Summer.*

Of course, Silver Bay is a speck on the map of the Florida Panhandle and exists only in my imagination. *The Silver Bay Beacon* is also a product of my imagination and was brought to life with the help of my old newspaper friends. Mega thanks to Andrew Meacham whose fascinating obituaries got me thinking. Dianne and Patrick Yost of the Georgia *Morgan County Citizen,* Bo Emerson of *The Atlanta Journal-Constitution,* and Bert Roughton AJC emeritus, all of whom provided invaluable insight into the world of modern-day print journalism.

Many thanks also go to Albert Oetgen for his knowledge of network newsgathering, and Mara Davis for her insight into the world of radio deejays.

Huge thanks go out to Gwinnett County Medical Examiner Carol A. Terry, MD, and her staff who helped with the technical medical stuff, and also Carol Knox Lavender, RN.

Additional thanks go to Fire Chief Toni Washington and Assistant

Fire Chief Ninetta Violante of Decatur Fire & Rescue for their firefighting expertise.

Leslie Anne Tarabella was my spirit guide in Fairhope, Alabama, while I researched small-town Gulf-coast life, who introduced me to former reporter Cliff McCollum, and Lori DuBose of WABF radio.

It's been nearly three decades since I left newspaper journalism, but the friendships I formed, and the skills I acquired—reading upside down! Writing on deadline! Knowing the difference between robbery and burglary!—are ones I'll always treasure. Writing *Hello, Summer* reinforced in me the absolute vital importance of a vigorous and independent press.

Speaking of treasures, my publishing team: literary agent Stuart Krichevsky at SKLA, marketing guru Meghan Walker of Tandem Literary, publicist extraordinaire Kathleen Carter, and all the folks at St. Martin's Press, including but not limited to my publishers Sally Richardson and the essential Jennifer Enderlin. Thank you to Jessica Zimmerman, Tracey Guest, Erica Martirano, Brant Janeway, and as always, huge thanks to Michael Storrings, for another evocative cover.

My greatest blessing in life is and always has been my amazingly supportive family led by my husband, Tom; daughter, Katie; son-in-law Mark; son, Andrew; and the light of our lives, grandchildren Molly and Griffin.

A Letter from

MARY KAY ANDREWS

Dear Target Guest:

Sarah Conley Hawkins is an award-winning investigative newspaper reporter about to embark on the next chapter of her career—working for an acclaimed digital newsgathering organization in Washington, DC— when she gets a devastating text from her older sister, informing her that her new job, and her new employer, are no more.

The timing couldn't be worse for Conley. At the moment she gets the bad news she's about to cut the cake at her going-away party in the newsroom of *The Atlanta Journal-Constitution*. Her desk is packed, she's broken up with her boyfriend—who's standing just a few feet away in that same newsroom—and she's given up her apartment.

That's the premise, or setup for my newest novel, *Hello, Summer*. But it's also the reality for journalists all over the country, who are encountering seismic changes in the newspaper business, with papers everywhere facing shrinking ad revenue, rising production costs, and a generation of readers accustomed to getting their news for free online.

As a former career newspaper reporter, who had her own going-away party in The *Atlanta Journal-Constitution* newsroom decades ago, I've always gotten ideas for plots for my fiction from headlines. But this time, with *Hello, Summer*, I decided to give readers a peek behind the headlines.

When Conley's job prospects are snuffed out, her only recourse is to head to her hometown—tiny Silver Bay, in the Florida Panhandle, where her family owns the struggling weekly paper, *The Silver Bay Beacon*, now run by her older sister, Grayson.

Her plan is to hang out at her grandmother's beach house, send out some résumés, and wait for a job offer, but as soon as she arrives home, her grandmother, the family matriarch and publisher of the newspaper, insists she should go to work at the *Beacon*, a move opposed by both Conley and Grayson.

As is always the case, my research for this novel put me back into newsgathering mode. The research is always my favorite part of story-telling. This time, I interviewed the publishers of a small weekly news-paper in Madison, Georgia, turned up in the newsroom of the *AJC* after a nearly thirty-year absence, and talked to former and current newspaper, television, and radio journalists about the state of the business these days.

For inspiration for the book's plot, I returned to a memorable story written years earlier by my oldest friend at my hometown newspaper, *The Tampa Bay Times,* a reporter who'd made a career of writing richly detailed obituaries. For this particular story, my friend wrote about a revered local politician, whose not-so-newsworthy death from cancer made national headlines when it was revealed that this man, a rock-ribbed family-values conservative, had, years earlier, walked away from his "secret first family," including his high school sweetheart wife and children, after fathering an out-of-wedlock child with a decades-younger staffer in his office, whom he subsequently married.

I gave my fictional congressman, C. Symmes Robinette, a similarly complicated marital history, but instead of dying in a hospital bed, Robinette perishes mysteriously in a fiery one-car crash at three in the morning, on a remote country road miles from home. And the only wit-nesses are Conley and her childhood friend Sean, who happen on the wreck after a night of drinking at the local American Legion bar.

Not everybody in Silver Bay is in mourning for the late congress-man. There's Conley's grandmother's longtime housekeeper, Winnie, who blames Robinette for the death of her older sister, Nedra. The two sisters grew up poor in Plattesville, a nearby working-class neighbor-hood, whose soil and water were tainted by toxic runoff from a nearby railroad switching yard. After dozens of current and former residents of the neighborhood sicken and die from the effects of the chemicals, they unsuccessfully attempt to sue the railroad for damages. The railroad's attorney is none other than Symmes Robinette, who deliberately drags out the court case until after most of the cancer cluster victims are dead or too sick to keep fighting.

The toxic waste plot was another thread inspired by a story about an ongoing cancer cluster in a small south Georgia community, and another in a poor neighborhood in Birmingham, Alabama.

My research for *Hello, Summer* included visiting and spending time with the medical examiner who runs one of Georgia's largest county morgues. While grateful for her advice and expertise on determining the cause of death in an accident involving fire, I'll admit I gave a hard pass to witnessing an autopsy. I also interviewed firefighters about protocol involved in fighting passenger-involved car fires, and an oncology nurse about dosages for terminal cancer patients.

Probably my favorite part of the research for this book was creating fictional characters inspired by the quirky and unforgettable personalities encountered years ago in Savannah and Atlanta newsrooms. The *Beacon*'s aging Southern belle society columnist, Rowena Meigs (and her dog Tuffy) were inspired by the late Yolande Gwin, who, according to local legend, once avoided being fired from the *AJC* by enlisting the help of her wealthy friends. They supposedly called the owner of Atlanta's largest department store, Rich's, and threatened to cut up their Rich's charge cards unless Yolande's firing was retracted. Since Rich's was the Atlanta paper's largest advertiser, and the indomitable Yolande was still writing her column well into the 1980s, I can only assume the tactic worked.

I first met Yolie, as we all called her, after I was assigned the desk next to hers when I joined the *AJC*'s features staff in 1982. She was in her late seventies by then, but still regarded as the grande dame of Atlanta society, who'd covered the 1939 Atlanta premiere party for *Gone With the Wind*. She loved to tell of being in the ladies lounge at the very elite Piedmont Driving Club when a snippy young thing asked to borrow her lipstick. "Of course I said no," Yolie told me. "A lady doesn't loan out her lipstick." She was chagrined to learn, later, that the would-be borrower was Vivien Leigh, who played Scarlett O'Hara in the movie.

As for Buddy Bright, the fictional night-loving deejay in *Hello, Summer*, I'll again plead guilty to theft, this time using Buddy as a fictional stand-in for a long-ago photographer I met at my first newspaper job at the *Savannah Morning News*. The late Bob Morris was a chain smoker who never dressed in anything but black and drove a vintage Corvette with a homemade working press license plate. Like his fictional counterpart, he roamed the streets of his town, long after quitting time, always in search of that next elusive breaking news story.

All my novels bear some of my DNA, but *Hello, Summer*, for me, is a valentine of sorts, to the world of newspapers and newspaper reporters everywhere. Writing this book reminded me that like Conley, even after all these years, I still have printer's ink in my blood.

An Exclusive to Target
deleted scene from

Hello, Summer

July 1956

"Lookit here," the older girl whispered, extending her hand. Winnie bent over, breathless, waiting for her big sister to reveal her prize. Nedra slowly uncurled chubby fingers, the ragged nails caked with grime. Nested in the palm of her hand was a cigarette lighter, its brass case illustrated with the silhouette of a beautiful naked lady, her legs folded beneath her and a sailor's cap perched on long red hair.

"Whoa," Winnie gasped. "Where'd you get that?"

"Found it," Nedra said, a little too casually.

They were standing in their clubhouse, a long-abandoned toolshed at the edge of the rail yard that ran smack through the middle of their neighborhood. Just a week earlier Winnie had been the one to spot the place where the railroad's fencing had rotted out. They'd been picking blackberries along the fence-line, stabbing at the prickly vines with stout sticks to scare off rattlesnakes, and Winnie's stick went clean through the board. But Nedra, older, braver, bolder, had been the first to kick a hole in the boards and clamber through.

She stuck her head out the jagged hole. "Come on."

Winnie pointed at the orange lettered sign bolted to the fence not three feet away. POSTED: NO TRESPASSING. VIOLATORS WILL BE PROSECUTED.

"It's private property."

"Who cares?" Nedra's head disappeared and Winnie had no choice but to follow.

The toolshed, just a few yards from the fence, was barely visible beneath the tangle of kudzu and blackberry brambles, but the two girls had spied it, and Nedra used her stick to whack at the rusted-out hasp of the lock until it and the padlock fell away from the door. She'd declared it their clubhouse, and they'd immediately busied themselves sweeping out the cobwebs, leaves, and rat turds and ferrying in supplies; a six-pack of grape Nehi soda, a wobbly three-legged wooden stool they'd rescued from a ditch, along with a rust-speckled cast iron skillet, and three dented cans of Spam and a bulging can of peaches—all from the trash pile back behind the Silver Bay IGA. These had been augmented with the items the sisters liberated from home—a couple of cracked china plates with smudgy painted rosebuds, a can opener, and Winnie's most treasured possession in the world, a turquoise transistor radio, purchased with ten books of S&H Green Stamps as a birthday gift from her Mamaw.

The shed itself had yielded up a few useful things: a kerosene lantern, a half-full red tin of Prince Albert chewing tobacco, a five-gallon galvanized bucket that when overturned made a perfect table, and a wooden peach crate that served as storage.

"Nedra?" Winnie searched her sister's face. "Found it where?"

"None of your beeswax." The older girl reached up and turned on the radio, which they'd hung from a nail on the wall by the door. Tinny music flooded the shack. "'Hound Dog'!" Nedra yelled, singing along and breaking into an impromptu jig. "Elvis forever!"

"He is the coolest," Winnie said dreamily.

The song ended, and a commercial for Family Tire came on. "Come on," Nedra said. "Let's fix lunch." She grabbed the skillet from the nail beside the radio and took the can of Spam from the makeshift cupboard, loading everything into the big bucket. "Bring the can opener. And the plates," she called to her sister, as she hurried out the door.

Winnie caught up with Nedra by the lake. Winnie knew it wasn't a real lake. Just a drainage pond that had always been there, dug by railroad workers a long, long time ago. The Gulf Coast of Florida was a green, leafy place, but nothing flourished in this spot. Tall, long-leaf pines that ringed the pond's circumference were dead and blackened, and even the kudzu vines were brown and sickly. Ditches leached out from the pond and wound their way throughout their neighborhood, Plattesville—or

Flattsville, as locals from the richer part of town called it. The pond water was the color of murky coffee, with an evil smell that reminded her of rotten eggs. Nedra and some of the older kids would swim in the ditches when rainwater spilled over the grassy banks, but not Winnie.

"Go get some more sticks," Nedra ordered. She'd already begun scraping out a hole in the gravel and cinders strewn atop the hard-packed dirt embankment, and was busily filling it with bits of dried weeds and scrap wood.

"What for?"

"So we can cook the damn Spam, dummy," her sister retorted.

"Like, on a fire? You know what Mama said, Nedra. If she finds out you've been messin' with fire again . . ."

"It's not messing. It's cooking. And Mama's not gonna find out, unless you tattle, ya little chickenshit." Nedra squatted by the pit she'd made.

Winnie knew better than to argue. Anyway, breakfast had been a long time ago and she was getting hungry. She gathered an armload of pine cones and dried-out branches and dumped them on the ground beside the pit.

In the meantime, Nedra had opened the can of Spam, cut it into thick slices with the pocket knife she always carried, and laid them in the bottom of the skillet, which she set atop the upended bucket. She held the lighter up against a bundle of dried weeds and clicked. An orange flame licked at the weeds and a thin plume of white smoke hung in the still air for only a matter of seconds before flickering out.

"Huh." Nedra grabbed a handful of pinecones and dumped them into the fire pit, then added a layer of dried weeds. Squatting on her haunches, she held the lighter up to a strand of dried grass, which caught, then went out.

The older girl swore under her breath. Winnie swatted at a mosquito that landed on her forearm. Sweat was dripping down the side of her face, and her ankles were scratched and bleeding from the blackberry brambles.

"Be careful," she begged.

"'Be careful,'" Nedra said in a hateful, mocking sneer.

Winnie ignored the taunt. She moved the skillet, then took the bucket and dipped it into the pond until it was nearly full, then dragged it back to the fire pit, setting it a few feet away.

"What's that supposed to be?"

"Fire safety. We learned it in Girl Scouts."

"Girl Scouts! Bunch of sissies. If you wanna help, go fetch me that lantern from the clubhouse," Nedra said.

Winnie knew better than to ask why. A moment later she trotted back with the lantern.

Nedra used the hem of her T-shirt, working at the rusted-out cap on the base of the lantern until she managed to unscrew it. She upended the lantern and fuel spilled out and onto the kindling.

"Cool." Nedra was grinning up at her sister when an orange flame shot three feet into the air, startling her so badly that she sprawled backwards, onto her butt.

Winnie stared at her sister in horror. Her pale blond bangs and eyelashes were singed. A patch of her cheek was already bright red.

"Nedra," she screamed. Her sister's eyes widened in shock, but she didn't move. The flames leapt out of the fire pit, engulfing the stack of pinecones and dried kindling inches from her sister's faded red Keds.

"Come on," Winnie urged, grabbing her sister's hand, jerking her to her feet. The two stumbled backwards, away from the fire.

Nedra seemed transfixed by the flames. "Shitfire and save matches. Let's get out of here, before somebody from the railroad catches us." But she was rooted to the spot where she stood.

"We need to try to put it out," Winnie said. Nedra shrugged, still didn't move.

Winnie hesitated, then darted forward. She grabbed the bucket and lifted. Pond water slopped over the side, onto her shoes. She could only lift it knee-high, and her hands were shaking with fear, but somehow, she swung the bucket forward, sending a stream of water onto the fire.

A column of flame erupted with a monstrous roar. Oily black smoke filled the air.

Winnie screamed, and she heard her sister's scream join hers. The force of the explosion knocked her off her feet, and for a moment she blacked out.

When she regained consciousness, Nedra was grasping her by her forearms, dragging her in the direction of the shed. "Stand up," Nedra begged, bending down to face her. Tears streamed down her soot-blackened cheeks. "Come on, baby. You gotta stand up. I can't carry you."

Winnie nodded dumbly. "What happened?"

Nedra pointed toward the embankment, where orange and crimson flames flared skyward. "It's real bad. We set the lake on fire." She yanked her sister forcibly upward, until she was standing on her feet. "Come on, now. We gotta get out of here." She ran toward the fence, not stopping until she'd slung one leg through the jagged hole in the boards. Then she looked back and realized she was alone. "Winnie," she hollered. "Come on. Or I will by God leave you right here."

A minute passed. Nedra covered her nose and mouth with her hand as the acrid black smoke filled the air. She coughed and spat. "Winifred Lee! I swear to God, I don't care if you get burned to a cinder. I'm going."

Winnie stumbled away from the clubhouse and toward the fence. "Wait for me!" Her hair and eyelashes were singed too, her pink blouse and green cotton pedal pushers smeared with blood and soot. Her sneakers were gone and she was barefoot. She clutched something tightly in her right hand as she crawled through the rotted fence. As she emerged on the other side, into the blackberry brambles, she held it up for her sister to see. It was the turquoise transistor radio.

Nedra rolled her eyes. "All right then. Let's go. But you better not say a word about this to anybody. You hear me?"

"We oughta tell somebody," Winnie protested. "Like the sheriff. Or the fire department. What if that fire keeps coming? What if somebody's house gets burned?"

Her sister grabbed a handful of Winnie's shirt. "Are you crazy? The sheriff? You wanna get put in the jailhouse for being a firebug?"

Winnie shook her head slowly. "Nnnno."

"Okay then. You just keep your trap shut. You don't know nothing about a fire."